THE ARCHITECT OF REVENGE

A September 11th Novel

T. W. AINSWORTH
2014

ISBN: 1449930077
ISBN-13: 9781449930073
Library of Congress Control Number: 2013923840
CreateSpace Independent Publishing Platform
North Charleston, South Carolina

DISCLAIMER

This book is a work of fiction. Names, characters, places, and incidents are products of the author's imagination or are used fictitiously. Any resemblance to actual events or persons, living or dead, is entirely coincidental. Any references to actual persons, organizations, or locales are used fictitiously, without any intent to describe either the actual conduct or character of such persons or organizations or any actual incidents that occurred at such locales.

PREFACE

This story is dedicated to the victims of September 11, 2001; their spouses, lovers, children, families, and friends; and to those heroes who arose to sanctify that day and finally brought justice on May 2, 2011.

For all of them…

<u>ONE</u>

New York City September 11, 2001

The inbound rush-hour traffic continued to thicken, forcing the taxi to lurch to another stop. The yellow lights lining the concrete walls of the Holland Tunnel were a poor substitute for the daylight up ahead that remained seemingly unreachable.

Wesley Morgan grimaced at his wristwatch. He had missed the breakfast. His fingers tensed. Slapping a thigh he looked at the other vehicles creeping along.

"Damn it."

He still hoped to get there before Caroline received her award. It was going to be close.

The cab reached the exit ramp but paused again.

"Driver, do you know a faster way to get there?"

"Morning," the man grunted through the Plexiglas divider. "See cars?"

Without pity the meter added another dollar.

Morgan now knew he was going to be late. He called Caroline on his cell phone.

"All circuits are busy. Please try again later."

With a sigh he slid the phone into the pocket of his tropical wool suit coat. Through his shirt he felt the phone nudge the little box. His long fingers wrapped reassuringly around it. At least he had tried. When Cay got the ring today she would be surprised—and happy—

but, as usual, his plans were thwarted. His little patients ruled his life, and yesterday their problems had cascaded, consuming every second he didn't have. The department secretary was forced to rebook his flight out of Chicago three times.

The taxi ascended to street level. Under the blue sky, the yard-by-yard slog continued.

"Su-moke," the cabbie said, thumping the glass with his knuckles.

Morgan heard the guttural blast of a horn followed by sirens. The cabbie pulled the wheel hard right and punched the gas to get out of the way. A fire truck barreled past, an ambulance riding its exhaust. The surgeon moved to the other side of the backseat to look.

"I'll say...Lots of smoke," Morgan said. Looking at the World Trade Center's North Tower, his panic escalated.

With more emergency vehicles forcing their way, traffic completely froze. People got out of their cars and looked southward.

"What the hell?" Morgan spat out, tossing some folded bills for the fare in the tray. "Keep it! I'll walk!"

Hearing the lock release, his free hand fumbled for his phone. He read the display—NO SIGNAL.

"Shit!"

Morgan sprinted two blocks. Unable to see above the wall of brick and masonry buildings, he watched as more emergency vehicles passed him screaming around the corner. He chased their echoing reports as sweat built up in his armpits and on his chest. Several blocks later he saw the smoke again. The billowing cloud was larger. The South Tower was consumed in fire too.

His phone vibrated. It was a voice message. He stopped to listen.

"*Wes...call me! Something hit the building!*" The alarm in Caroline's voice chilled him.

He punched in her number and began running again, oblivious to the people getting out of his way.

She answered, terror reverberating in her voice. "Wes! There's smoke everywhere!"

"Cay! I'm in New York! I'm coming!"

The connection went dead.

"Goddamn it!" he yelled.

He raced ahead until a police officer's outstretched arms barricaded him to allow a fire truck to pass. Morgan charged around the officer, pressing ahead through the diesel fumes and reek of hot tires, a cascade of white paper tumbling into his face. He slammed into a man who recoiled away, but the wall of invisibly tethered people was becoming dense. His struggle south became slower, finally impossible.

Wesley Morgan halted. His eyes traced the steel seams upward. The beveled corners seemed close enough to touch. His brown eyes tightened as they met the bright sky.

He stared at the top of the North Tower.

"Oh my God..."

She was up there.

From gaping holes, angry flames wrestled with twisting arms of smoke.

He squinted.

A large cloth flapped back and forth like a flag.

"Are those people?" a woman cried.

Heads projected out mangled windows. Human forms clung to ledges. Morgan watched a pair of shadows tumble down the building's skin. They were holding hands.

"Why are they jumping?" a man shouted.

Morgan's phone rang.

Plugging his other ear, he heard Caroline wheezing. "Wes..." she whispered hoarsely.

Her anguish overcame him, but he had to reassure her.

"Cay! Darling! I'm here! Hang on! You'll be okay!"

"Can't breathe...smoke."

"The firemen, they're coming!"

"No...they...can't." She struggled for air with every word. "Fire... smoke...the stairwells..."

More people fell.

"Caroline!" he cried. "I love you. Oh baby...I love—"

"I love you…Wesley Morgan." A powerful inhale followed. "From the moment…we met." Then he heard her say softly, "Darling…I will… forever."

The line went dead.

"No!" he yelled into the phone, his eyes riveted on the building.

He called her back, his whole being in agony.

She didn't answer.

"Please call me," he begged.

Another person dropped, then another and another.

"No…"

His lips trembled.

*God…please no…*he prayed.

The fragile seconds became minutes—eternity first counted by each gritty tear, until he was forced to run from the gale of ash.

TWO

Chicago October 2000 Eleven months earlier

"**R**oss, why are *you* scrubbing?" Baffled, Morgan glanced over his magnifying glasses to see drops of water fall from the elbows of the Chief of Pediatric Cardiothoracic Surgery, while a sterile towel rubbed his hands dry. "I'm ready to close."

Morgan was hovering over a sleeping baby the size of a football. Her little heart repaired and beating perfectly, she had been separated for several minutes from the bypass machine without a problem. He hadn't asked for help and rarely needed it anyway, especially at this point in the operation.

"Here to save your day, brother," Ross Merrimac answered with his usual cheer while eyeballing the wall of monitors displaying the baby's vital signs. "And to get your butt to that noon walkthrough of the new hospital operating rooms."

Morgan knew the man was grinning, even though his face was hidden behind a mask. The chief seemed forever grinning, at least when he was talking to Morgan. They were friends, and with that relationship came the occasional good-humored public taunt. Morgan's entire operating team expected as much.

Passing off the faded blue towel to the nearest person, the former Penn State linebacker raised his arms forward, waiting for the chief scrub nurse to gown him.

"Thank you, Abby," he said, again looking at Morgan. "You forgot, my man." His gray sideburns wiggled with each word.

"You scrubbed in for *that* reason?" Morgan asked through his mask. He had seen the plans months before but couldn't understand a blueprint if he tried. "I signed off on them, for crying out loud."

"They want to show you *your* recommendations, friend," Ross replied. "If my old brain remembers correctly, I hired you to put a transplant program together here at Potts Children's Hospital… and *this* stuff was in the fine print—at least the contract I saw." He laughed. "You know going back and fixing things later's expensive. Those people managing the money don't like that." Another laugh erupted, this one more mirthful than his last.

"Come on! Let me operate!" Morgan's gloved hand opened. "Suture," he said.

By the middle of the word, Abby had slapped a sleek steel instrument gripping a microscopic crescent needle with long hair-like suture in his palm.

"Ross, you know I've got another case. I'll be operating into the evening. Next kid needs a complex reconstruction, going to take five hours." Morgan looked to Abby for support. "Please. Explain to Ross I can't go. I need to keep working…" He winked. "Or I'll have to cancel my plans for tonight."

He knew the bespectacled grandmother was unlikely to offer sympathy. When he was a resident and they first worked together, being around the brash resident challenged her dignified civility. After years of sleepless nights and everlasting days as Morgan evolved into a confident surgeon, her respect for him grew—and so did their relationship. His ability to quickly identify a problem with a patient and decide on the correct treatment impressed her, but equally so did Morgan's gentle assurance to every terrified parent. In his hands they trusted that their child would be okay.

By the time Morgan took charge of the nascent transplant program, Abby held him in such esteem that she used her seniority and assigned herself to work with him. However, two subjects remained forbidden: profanity and any sordid details of his social life. He made each mistake early in his training and only once. While he may have been the surgeon, her tenure made it *her* operating room, and she made the rules.

"Dr. Morgan," she replied quietly, "what Dr. Merrimac says is right."

"Somehow I thought you'd say that, Miss Abby," he sighed. The entire time, Morgan's fingers never stopped suturing and tying knots.

"See, Morgan…maturity speaks," continued Merrimac. His curled crow's-feet suggested a prolonged smirk. "Seriously. You've done your magic for this kid. I'll finish up."

"Architects: hopeless dreamers." Morgan knew he'd lost and stepped away from the operating table. "Fine. I'll go approve the fountain for the lobby."

Morgan broke scrub and headed to the locker room. Damp fingers reorganized his matted black hair mushed for hours under an impermeable surgical cap. His triangular face already had stubble on his sharp jaw and carved chin. Dressing quickly, he did a final check in the mirror, pausing to seal his neck behind the perfect dimple of the silk tie. He grabbed his white coat, buttoning it as he left.

A corridor guided him to a temporary wooden door framed in a wall adorned with warning signs about the danger beyond. As he listened to the construction sounds, his impatience grew. How he wished he would be paged to an emergency. Joined soon by two hospital administrators and the nursing director, it dawned on him they were wearing overcoats and he wasn't.

He jumped to one side as the door bumped him. A woman stepped backward through the opening.

Morgan heard: "I'll let y'all know by tomorrow. Got folks waiting for me."

Her soft refined drawl carried oddly above the bedlam of riveting tools, air hammers, and cursing. He saw a rich mahogany-colored ponytail mashed under a hardhat. She turned around.

Wow!

"Hi, y'all!" she said with a wave. "I'm Caroline Pruitt…for those I haven't met." Dust from her jeans trailed delightfully behind as she stepped over the threshold toward him. "I'm guessing by the white coat"—she stooped to read the name—"that you're...Dr. Morgan. Pleased to meet you, sir."

Through the din, her caramel soprano voice serenaded his ears while their hands briefly joined. "Sorry...didn't have time to wash up." She flashed a smile.

"Um...that's...okay." He never stammered. "Please...call me *Wes*."

He became lost in the translucent blueness of her eyes. He blinked hard, holding his gaze on her face; terrified his eyes would descend to survey her body. Shivering, he exhaled in the cold air that came through the open door.

"Chicago's a bit chilly this time of year, I've learned," she said, observing the foggy cloud that accompanied his introduction to the building under construction. "I'm from Virginia; took me the longest time to get Yankee blood." She laughed.

Her voice was just musical.

"I'm kidding! Anyway"—she turned her attention to the group— "glad y'all wore coats. Even though our adventure takes us to the new operating rooms, there's not much heat in there." Waving her hardhat, her auburn highlights glimmered. "And everybody gets one of these bonnets. Bit of a dangerous place in there."

She reached in a trunk and handed Morgan one of the helmets.

"I'm better in yellow," he said, still mesmerized.

"Visitors wear red," said Pruitt. Each word was irresistible. "Now... y'all please come along with me."

Morgan struggled to conceal his unrelenting stare. Despite her work boots, she walked like a runway model, her bulky sweatshirt adding to the natural charm.

Pruitt continued talking. "I design large-building environmental systems in urban environments...so I'm at home in all of this." They went deeper into the huge exoskeleton. "Let me orient you to my world."

Facing the chaos, her polished fingernails floated up to various points of the frame. "Many of these conduits and pipes deliver things like water and oxygen."

Try as he might, all Morgan saw were the empty spaces between the floors so his attention returned to her balletic fingers and focused specifically on the fourth finger of her left hand. There was no ring.

"True to form," she said, "architects mold the specifics of the project with the desired aesthetics…be it a skyscraper or hospital." She spoke about building design for more than five minutes. "So… if there are questions along the way, please ask. And…Dr. Morgan… *Please* stop me if you have comments or suggestions. I can provide as much detail as you'd like."

He gave a blank nod. That voice! *My god! Does she realize she sounds like music?*

"Now we're going up," Pruitt said, pointing to a construction elevator.

"Up?" Morgan's trance transformed instantly to nausea.

"Yes, Dr. Morgan. Your ORs are on the fourth floor."

The cage overshot the floor by a foot. Opening the gate, Pruitt hopped down and held out her hand to each rider. Morgan remained in the center.

"Coming?" she asked.

"No," he mumbled, her confidence making the normally unflappable surgeon feel awkward. "I don't do well with heights."

"Take my hand, Wes," she said. "Trust me."

———

Surrounded by medieval armor and weapons in the great hallway of Chicago's famed Art Institute, Morgan felt trapped. Standing in the same place for countless minutes, there was little he could do but listen and answer. In an endless stream, patrons of the fundraiser kept coming to him asking about babies and heart transplants. Detailed descriptions were likely to ruin the appetite of the unaccustomed tourist in his world, so Morgan drew from his well-used stockpile of responses.

"Being a surgeon is my calling."

"There aren't enough hours in the day."

"The transplant program will provide a great service to our community."

Each listener would give an enlightened nod, shake his hand, and move away. The litany would immediately begin again as the next cluster of people crowded closer. Over the months, he learned to accept the duty and smile. Millions of dollars were needed to help Morgan fulfill his passion of performing heart transplants in children.

Finally he saw his chance to escape and headed to the washroom for a needed break. He could barely get his pants unzipped in time.

Ross, I did as you asked and came alone, he thought, finishing his business. The only other man at the urinals had left, allowing Morgan a moment to reflect.

Merrimac had made it clear days earlier: *"This fundraiser is too important. Don't bring one of your women with all that cleavage pointing everywhere. There'll be photographers. You're onstage, brother. Persuade those rich folks to open their wallets. You like fixing baby hearts, tell them why."*

Thirsty as hell, Morgan went back to the fray.

After stopping a waiter with champagne, he surveyed the room teeming with people. In the distance he recognized an older woman with abundant buttocks and vast blond hair whose voice poured words out of a bottomless pitcher.

Oh bother…Janie's here.

His former interior decorator was chair of the hospital foundation board. The planning committee, with her at the helm, had organized the evening's event.

Planning a party was never a problem for Janie. The issue was her guest list when it was *not* a public affair. Since befriending Morgan three years ago she'd had a misguided penchant for setting him up on blind dates, believing that his long hours in the OR made it impossible for him to meet women. Every time he attended one of her private parties of close friends (but mostly clients), he was introduced to at least one affluent woman aspiring to augment her prestige. The desirous face above persuasive slalom curves invariably enticed him into a one- or two-nighter at his townhouse. Janie had a good heart though, and for a while he really didn't mind that she obviously had no idea what he was looking for in a woman, so he tolerated her efforts. That was, until the last woman Morgan brought back removed her skirt on his front steps. The indiscretion didn't go unnoticed apparently. A week later returning from a jog, Morgan was stopped and berated by an elderly neighbor and her sheltie. After that, despite Janie's good intentions, he told her no more blind dates and asked out only women of his own choosing. For the most part he remained alone and lonely, absorbing himself in his work.

That night Morgan knew he'd run into Janie and hoped to avoid her as long as he could. But when he saw her talking to a brunette in a sculpted evening dress, he realized it was Caroline Pruitt and immediately changed his mind. He went over to say hello.

"Janie Bonwitt...Hi!"

"Ooo! Wes Morgan! Look at you in your tuxedo! I hoped I'd see you!" she beamed. "Give me a kiss!"

He pecked a cheek. As he tasted her makeup, perfume engulfed him. Her usual fawning began instantly.

"How are you? You look wonderful! Staying so trim! I don't know how he does it..." Bonwitt said to Pruitt without introducing her. "He works all the time, and still finds time to run." Janie tugged Morgan's jacket sleeve. "You did the Chicago marathon last month, if I remember. Ooo...tied up the streets..."

"Janie, I didn't run the—"

"Ooo! You know Cay! I know you've met!"

Caroline Pruitt gave Bonwitt a disapproving wince. When Morgan saw her blue eyes, an electric sensation sped through him.

"Sorry—*Caroline*," Janie corrected herself while placing Pruitt's hand in his. "Must be formal at parties! I'm so glad..."

"Good to see you again, Dr. Morgan." A waft of spicy jasmine arrived.

"Please. Call me *Wes*."

He could only hope.

"Caroline's from Virginia!" said Janie.

"Originally." As Caroline began to speak the delicate chain of diamonds around her neck caught the light and flashed like fireflies. "But I've been—"

"Ooo! Caroline lived in New York and then…moved here! Last January!" Bonwitt's flowing gab grew more excited. "Survived her first winter! So now she's truly a native!"

"How did *you* meet?" Speaking directly at Caroline, Morgan forced the question into Janie's river of words.

"Oh, what a great story!" Bonwitt began. "First, at a project on the North Side! Her firm did the outside, and mine…the inside! Then, can you believe it…we met again because of *your* hospital! Girlfriends ever since! Teaching me Southern charm!"

Pruitt's smile never changed. Morgan watched as she finished her final drops of champagne and studied the bottom of the flute with a hopeful look that suggested a desire for a refill. All the while Janie kept talking, touching their arms over and over to make certain they were listening, and looking at each other.

"Cay, dearie…maybe if I learn to say *y'all* I'll snag another husband who—"

"Janie, honey…" Caroline gently waved her empty glass so she could see it. "I've got a hospital design question for Wes. Would you be sweet and get us both more champagne?"

Bonwitt grinned. "Oh, I'd love to! Be right back…don't go anywhere." Stepping away, she was instantly sidetracked into another conversation.

"I'm exhausted," Caroline sighed. Whenever she spoke, her voice was lyrical. "Janie's a dear but chatters a blue streak after only one glass. She gets worse with more."

"Believe me, I know," he said. "I've been out to dinner with her and her friends more than once."

Caroline looked around then smiled. "I doubt she's coming back."

"Like another glass?" he asked hopefully.

"Love one."

He waved a waiter over who was carrying a fresh tray of champagne. Morgan removed two flutes.

"Thank you," Caroline said, taking a generous swallow.

As her head tipped back slightly, Morgan caught a glance of her hair swept high above her neck. Their eyes aligned for only a moment before Caroline subtly launched a stern *No Trespassing* warning to an approaching man off to Morgan's side. Out of the corner of his eye, he watched the man turn away.

"So...how did Janie find you?" she asked unaffected.

He casually altered his stance so as not to call attention to the interaction he had just witnessed. Morgan had a strong suspicion there was more than just a sociable connection between Caroline and the man.

"For years," he replied, "she's chaired the board that puts this thing on." Caroline's eyes didn't waver from his face. "So she gets a list of all the new staff doctors...then hits them up for money." He laughed. "Usually they could use better furniture too. One visit is all she needs."

"She's very good at that," Caroline nodded with a warm smile. Even her most subtle movements distracted him. "And you fell prey?"

"Yes...The same way." He was really struggling to continue the story. "When I finished my fellowship, I bought a townhouse in Lincoln Park. The day I moved in, Janie double-parked her Mercedes behind my U-Haul, presented herself at the door...said we'd already met. Before I said *I don't think so,* she started doing inventory. Of course, none of it's suitable for the address...and..."

Amused, Caroline turned slightly to one side. Morgan again restrained his desire to look down at her figure.

"Sorry...what was I saying?" he asked.

"You were a victim," she helped.

"Forty-five thousand bucks later..."

"That sounds about right." Caroline nodded. "She did my place too."

He grinned, his mind in a frenzy searching for a way to get her to linger, hoping the man she had made eye contact with wasn't circling behind him. Morgan thought it unlikely Janie was her date for the night.

"You know," he said as the fresh champagne swam in his head, "until your tour, the only thing I knew about architecture was how to build an outhouse. When I was a kid I helped a friend make one for his grandfather's farm."

"How lovely…" Pruitt elevated the glass to her lips.

"I cut a crescent moon in the door." When he saw her lips glisten with a twitch, he realized his banal remark had probably guillotined the rest of their conversation.

She sipped again. "Was it for one or two users?"

"Are you kidding?"

"With your familiarity of the subject, I'm curious." Her expression became devious. "My firm's working on a privy design with air-conditioning, a sink, and TV. So with your experience…I'm just wondering…should we add in that option?"

"Really?" Morgan's forehead grew warm. "Two seats?"

"No." The champagne glass hid a smirk. "You were so serious though…"

He felt his cheeks blossom red. "Just getting my general ignorance out of the way," he admitted sheepishly.

"Good idea," was her deadpan reply.

He drew a long breath to recompose before opening his mouth again.

"So…at the risk of treading deeper into your waters," he said, pointing to the model of the hospital nearby, "want to tell me more… about this?"

White-gloved ushers tapped dinner chimes.

Rattled, he said, "Later…maybe?"

"Maybe…" she replied.

"Do you mind if I walk you in?" he asked, almost frantic.

"I'd like that." She took his arm. "Table three please, sir."

"No kidding! Me too!" He had to ask: "Is anyone joining you?"

"I believe…" Caroline's clasp grew firm. "A Dr. Wesley Morgan."

"Fantastic!" he said, amazed and pleased by the splendid coincidence. He'd do whatever he could to keep from screwing up the rest of the evening, and agonize over outhouses later. Walking arm-in-arm, Morgan paused at the silent auction tables.

"I think it's around here…" he said, his eyes searching until he found what he was looking for. "Give me a second." He slipped from her grasp, writing his name and phone number on the card for one of the items.

Saying nothing, Caroline watched.

"Bears tickets," he said with a shrug, knowing his intent was obvious. "Excuse to get me out of the hospital. You like football?"

"Why would you presume that?" she asked.

"Being from the South and all, I thought…"

She produced an enthralling smile. "Football *is* sacred. Yes, I like it."

"Remind me to keep bidding," he said with a grin.

The couple continued toward the stock exchange ballroom, deflecting ubiquitous stares.

"Doctor!"

Morgan turned.

"A picture of you both!"

A flash.

"Cheese! Again!"

The photographer clicked the shutter long after the usual two photos.

"You're a fabulous-looking pair! Your wife is beautiful."

Morgan laughed awkwardly.

"Thank you," they said together.

"Onward." Caroline squeezed his arm. "Time to schmooze the high rollers. We've got a hospital to build."

Seated for only moments, Morgan heard his name and was back up, being recognized from the dais. When the architects were introduced, Caroline rose with her colleagues. Every eye in the room came to her.

Finally, they sat down.

Waiters poured wine while others dressed the salads. A plate of rolls circled the table.

"To dinner with eight strangers," he toasted, pleased they were together.

"Not us," she countered.

Her words tantalized him.

His fork went up and down only once. The salad would have to wait. Ross Merrimac and his wife, Shandra, were on their way to say hello.

As Morgan rose to greet the couple, Shandra's necklace caught his attention. The elegant but simple liquid gold strands always adorned her long neck, even when Morgan dined at their home. Once, he asked Ross the significance. *"A present for my queen..."* Merrimac hugged his wife. *"For the gift of a son..."*

"So, Wes," said Ross, "I see you and Ms. Pruitt have become better acquainted."

Morgan swore his boss winked at her.

For days following the hospital tour, Merrimac had heard little from his star surgeon about the building's design but everything about the woman he had met. There was little Ross could do but nod and listen. Jane Bonwitt had already called, assigning him the sole mission of getting Morgan to the Art Institute without a date. She would arrange the rest.

"Dr. Merrimac," Caroline began, "how's the transplant program coming together?"

"Well," he replied, "I think we're ready to go. Your building will just give it a permanent home."

Caroline gave a gracious smile. "What an accomplishment for your department!"

"Kind words, Ms. Pruitt," said Shandra. "However, Ross tells me all the real work's been done by Wes."

Morgan was blindsided by the compliment.

"Ross is eternally glad he came aboard." She leaned toward Caroline and said, "Says Wes is the best there is."

"So I've been told." Caroline gently touched his arm.

Morgan was taken aback by her apparent interest in his work—and him.

Ross winked again at them. "Got to press more flesh. Enjoy the night. Party on!"

The Merrimacs headed away.

"Caroline..." He still wasn't blinking. "Thank you."

"Word gets around."

"At this point that may not be good."

Morgan's professional reputation was stellar, his personal one perhaps not so much. He wasn't confident what Caroline might have heard, but if she knew Janie, no secret was safe. With Caroline's fortuitous companionship, his past was abruptly haunting him. All he could hope for was that she enjoyed his company enough to see him again—that her present behavior wasn't just Southern politeness.

After suffering several more interruptions at their table and speeches from the podium, the guests in the room settled down to enjoy the meal.

Once the rhythm of the conversations blended, Morgan asked Caroline, "Do you miss New York?"

"I lived there about four years." A slight shake of her head suggested she was editing the answer. "No, I don't...though I have to keep going back."

"Work?" Morgan hoped he was right.

"My firm's developing a full-service clinic in the city. Call it community outreach." She smiled directly at him. "For Downs kids. I'm in charge of the project."

"That's incredible!"

He sat back in disbelief, elated that they shared that common interest. Many of his little patients were Downs; one unfortunate consequence of the syndrome was that they were often born with heart defects.

"The original children's hospital here was named in honor of Willis Potts," Morgan began, "because he was one of the first surgeons who figured out an operation to keep those kids alive." A knowledgeable smile followed a quick grimace. "It was a major thing back then, but like everything else in surgery, it's all changed—the techniques, anesthesia, the bypass pump."

He paused, assessing Caroline's face for cues of boredom. Relieved when the slight forward motion of her head toward him suggested she was waiting for more, he said, "Today, we operate on all sorts of problems—and they're routine...I suppose. After years of training, it becomes intuitive. In the OR I guess I get in a zone, and my fingers know what to do. Does that sound odd?"

"Not at all," Caroline said, slowly gliding her palm down the length of her arm to her wrist.

As he watched, Morgan felt his own arm tingling. There were so many things other than surgery he wanted to talk about with her.

"How did you get interested in Downs?" he asked. His heart was pounding.

"A really dear friend has a little boy...just a sweetie...wants to grow up and get a job chasing butterflies." Her napkin wiped a tear. "So I jumped at the opportunity...What a blessing!"

"I understand completely," he said, realizing he'd been listening intently—that appreciating her for just her looks was long departed.

"Wes...Can I ask you something?"

"I hope so."

Caroline put down her fork.

"I guess it's just natural to love babies..." Her eyes became shiny again. "How do you deal with it when they're that innocent?"

"That's...a tough question." His lips curled up as he released a muted whistle. "They're angels...dealt a bad hand. Guess I want to help them."

"Does it scare you?"

"You mean operating on them?" he asked. "Surgeons never think about that." He smiled. "We're trained to make decisions...Rules our persona. I'll tell you, though...The kids are braver than I am."

He never confided this way to anyone—but Caroline was drawing it out. He wanted to tell her.

"Most of the time, whatever you throw at them, they get better."

Caroline's eyes remained focused on his face.

"It's tough when they don't do well...and very humbling." He confessed more. "I'd go to the ends of the earth for them. Stay up all night...Whatever it takes. They make me understand what caring truly means." He laughed self-consciously. "Did you really want to hear all this introspection?"

Caroline's hand had been resting on his the entire time. She nodded gently. "Thanks for telling me."

"You're welcome." Morgan smiled. "That wasn't easy. How'd you get that out of me?" he said, staring at her beautiful face. "Surgeons are supposed to swagger. Please don't let anyone know."

A manicured finger came to rest on her puckered lips. "Confidentiality assured," Caroline said.

He glanced across the table at the elegant white-haired woman named Anne they had met earlier. She smiled and nodded knowingly as if she could hear their words.

"So let me ask you this…" Morgan said, returning his attention to Caroline. "Architecture…Why?"

"Perhaps the same reason you're a surgeon," she replied. Seeing his quizzical look, Caroline added, "Science and art together. Isn't that like surgery?"

The hairs on his neck tingled.

"Research, planning, and implementation…" she said.

"Neither field," Morgan finished her thought, "accepts conformity. Only how to improve on what's already been done."

"That's right," said Caroline, now sliding her hand affectionately down his arm.

The woman across from them smiled again.

Nibbling their way through dessert, they heard the band start up again. Caroline stroked his wrist.

"Wes…maybe…" She hesitated. "Would you…like to dance?"

"You *are* trying to make me self-conscious. My last dance lessons were in college," he confided, but hearing the quick downbeat he would dance with her even if his feet didn't comply. She wanted to—and so did he. "Hope I don't embarrass you."

"Not to worry," she countered with a playful smile. "No one will watch."

"Right." His eyebrows rose while his lips curled. "All *you* have to do is stand up." He gave her his hand.

On the dance floor, as he took her into his arms face to face, Morgan saw heads turn. The couple was impossible to miss. Caroline was taller than the other women he had known, and Morgan stood several inches above her. Looking into her eyes, he saw unhidden playfulness. She was enjoying this.

The music began again…and became faster. As their momentum grew, the candles and lights in the room became a blurred halo. He felt alone with her—and weightless.

The music finally slowed.

Locking his hands behind her waist, Morgan brought her close and smelled her warm skin through the perfume.

"One more?" he asked, not caring about anything but being with her.

"You'd better," she replied, her expression earnest, "or I'll never forgive you."

Caroline followed his lead in a harmony that was a perfect moment behind his, their bodies touching as the music told them how to move. When it stopped, Morgan took Caroline's hand to lead her off the floor. He swore her fingers were still dancing with his.

Janie was seated across the table, talking to the white-haired woman. Both women smiled at them.

"Ooo! My friend Anne said you talked to her! We're bridge partners!" said Janie. "We both think you dance…beautifully!" Her hands flapped in excitement over the table while her friend gave another knowing nod. "Wes, I knew you would be wonderful on a dance floor! You just never showed me!"

"Janie's well beyond Earth," Morgan whispered into Caroline's ear.

"Leaving Mars at least." She hid a giggle.

Morgan was overcome by the desire to dance with Caroline again.

"Want to go out there where it's quieter?" He asked her, tipping his head toward the dance floor.

"I'd love—"

"Ooo, Wes!" Janie continued interrupting Caroline's obliging smile. "Anne said you met George too!"

The dozing man was listing toward his wife.

"I'm sure he told you he's a surgeon!"

It was clear the wrinkled physician with closed eyes hadn't picked up a scalpel in a long time.

"If I do say…you're both darling when you dance," Anne said.

Her substantial diamond choker in a platinum setting emphasized what Morgan had learned earlier: their money had paid for the new lobby.

"George and I used to dance every Saturday night at our club." With enthusiasm in her voice, her fingers flitted together until she shook her head in disgust. "Then both of us got this damn arthritis." She looked at Janie, then Caroline, and grinned. "So when's the wedding?"

Holding a silent smile, Morgan searched for an answer that wouldn't cripple their infant relationship. Caroline was smart, good-looking, seemed to like *him*, and had come alone to a black-tie event. It was too unbelievable. Had he had that much to drink?

"Ooo...that would be fun!" began Janie. "I—"

Raising her palm to pause Janie's logorrhea, Caroline said to Anne, "You can't expect me to marry a surgeon."

Crap! Morgan thought.

"Good heavens, why not?" Anne countered. "Why don't you want a doctor?"

"He'd never be home," Caroline answered.

Morgan felt worse, until her hidden hand squeezed his.

"George came home." Anne stroked his hair. "Got me pregnant six times."

Morgan burst out laughing as Caroline grew beet red. Kissing his cheek, she lifted her clutch from the table.

"Time to powder, for poise," she said then whispered in his ear, "Stay alone."

Morgan watched intently as Caroline walked out of the ballroom. Janie came over and gave him a hug. Startled, his eyes pulled away from Caroline's invisible wake.

"Glad you're having fun! Cay's so sweet, isn't she? She likes you!" The next hug squeezed more. "Enough of me! There's more champagne out there...so I'll be moving on again! Time to look for a man! These parties are grand for that! Glad you're getting along so well! I'll call you tomorrow. Promise it won't be early...in case you have to sleep late."

She didn't need to add that. Missing his cheek, she kissed his ear. Her pungent perfume still cloyed in the air as it had two hours before.

"Tootles, dearie!" she said, waving.

"Janie loves a party. Especially when it's hers," said Anne. She righted her husband with a push to his shoulder. "Time for this one to go home. But I want to see your fiancée one more time! She has such sweet eyes...and what a grand figure! She'll spoil the dickens out of you! I know the look, because I've got nineteen great-grandchildren! You'll have a large family too...and...be able to afford good colleges!"

He had to escape.

Praying for her quick return, Morgan looked again at the direction Caroline had gone. He saw her walking and talking with a woman whose dress barely covered her thighs—and clearly had a longstanding relationship with a plastic surgeon.

The two women parted. Caroline came to him delivering a matter-of-fact smile.

"Her future husband's a major donor," said Morgan, rising to hold her chair. "She's going to be the fourth wife."

"I know." With a sly nod Caroline said, "I met number three at a foundation event a while back. Not as audacious—or bodacious, I might say. This one ought to stay indoors."

"Sorry?"

"A girlfriend's mom in prep school said it time and again—never leave the house looking like that."

"Is there anyone here you don't know something about," Morgan inquired, adding with caution, "like me?"

Caroline glanced around the room. "I don't think so." Smiling, she said, "You especially."

"Well then, thanks for coming back," said Morgan. A rush from her fresh perfume shot through his body as he discreetly pointed toward Anne. "And, even after you were bested by her."

"She was funny. Ah, the voice of experience," Caroline replied. "I admit, she got me...I'm rarely come up short for words."

"I'm learning that," said Morgan.

Leaning closer, her perfume intensified. "Wes…while I stepped out, I checked the auction. Sorry. You didn't get the Bears tickets."

He had forgotten. "That's okay." His shrug said more.

"Perhaps I can help you get over your disappointment, Dr. Morgan." Caroline's whisper caressed his ear. "I live in Lake Point Tower…A quick cab ride." His regret faded. "If you promise you won't fall asleep like George…you can join me for a drink."

———

Profiled by the glow of the skyline, the white sofa appeared buoyant on the plush oriental carpet that caressed the floor. Caroline spun a rheostat. Light from hidden ceiling fixtures quivered watercolor paintings to life.

He drew off her coat and removed his. While hanging both in the hall closet she asked, "Some Scotch?"

"Tell me where."

"On the antique chest." Caroline pointed toward the windows. "There are some snifters as well. Go ahead and pour." She gave him a quick peck on the lips. "Give me a minute."Walking down the hallway, her exposed back shimmered above the plunging fabric of her gown until she faded from sight.

Morgan looked around the serene living room. On a small table was a vase filled with fresh orchids. When he bent down to take in their aroma, his eyes looked at the picture beside them. Dressed in riding attire, a younger Caroline sat mounted on a horse while a distinguished man and elegant woman, both with blue eyes, stood alongside holding the reins.

"That's some gene pool," he uttered, his contemplation interrupted by a neighboring photograph. Caroline was grinning under a helmet, hooked by a rope to the side of a rock with nothing but sky above and green far below.

He felt queasy and shook his head. Any altitude above two stories terrified him.

Morgan moved to the chest. Averting his eyes to ignore the

thirty-three-story abyss outside the windows, he unsealed a bottle of fifteen-year-old Macallan Scotch and dribbled the amber liquid in one snifter then the other. He measured the amount with two fingers to avoid overpouring, not realizing Caroline saw the performance from across the room.

"Wes," she laughed, "an adult dose is okay."

Startled, he pulled the bottle away.

"Crap," he said, "spilled some."

His handkerchief blotted the puddle and went back in a tuxedo pocket.

"No worries, there's plenty," Caroline said. "I'll be in the kitchen for just a sec. Have a seat...get comfy."

He placed the glasses on the coffee table in front of the sofa and stood...waiting. Cabinet doors opened and closed, then came the quiet rustling of paper.

When Caroline reappeared, she had taken her hair down and tucked it behind her ears. The necklace and heels were gone. In one hand was a crystal plate decorated with truffles, in the other, a lighter. With a click, three candlewicks ignited in a tabletop steel candelabrum. Settling on the sofa, Caroline grabbed a snifter. The slit in her gown fell open above the knee.

"Wes...please...sit down," she implored him. "It won't break. Remember, I got it from Janie."

Her hand stroked the cushion, making the request irresistible. He sank into it. "Take your shoes off, if you'd like," she purred.

He did.

Caroline raised her glass, and Morgan did the same.

Clink.

"To outhouses," she said.

His glass remained high.

"Seriously?" he asked.

"Seems to me...a topic of mutual architectural fascination."

Her snifter came to her lips, hiding a smirk.

"In that case," Morgan replied, "we're both going to have to do research frequently." His snifter tapped hers. "To outhouses…Hope we study them often."

She unmasked the grin. "I'm onboard with everything but the last part." She sipped from her glass. "Please…Try the Macallan."

He tasted it twice. "That's delicious." He looked at the glass through the candle flame. "Doesn't one usually add water?"

"You can," she said, "but I prefer…undiluted pleasure."

She sipped again, moistening her lips with the liquid.

Morgan's tongue reflexively pinched between his molars before reminding himself he had to breathe.

Caroline raised the plate. "Here…try it with one of these. You'll see what I mean."

The bittersweet chocolate blended with the aftertaste of the rich whiskey.

"Until *now*…I was never a Scotch drinker," he said.

Retrieving the bottle, Caroline refilled his glass. "My daddy gave me the taste for it. The first time, I thought he poisoned me. But it didn't take me long to love it!" She took another sip and smiled. "Problem is, he drinks *really* old Scotch…and that makes it expensive. Unfortunately, that stuck too."

"I'm getting addicted quickly," Morgan grinned.

"Owning the habit won't take long," Caroline replied.

"That's your father in the picture," he said, pointing. "The eyes tell all."

"Amazing, I guess…" She laughed.

"Is that your horse?"

"Yes…Goethe," she said with affection. "A palomino gelding. He was a graduation present after college…just a fantastic animal. The best gaits imaginable! I taught him dressage."

"Where do you board him?" he asked. Every hair was tingling now.

"In central Virginia. My parents have a farm there. I went to college in Charlottesville, so…" The Scotch in her glass was almost gone. "Daddy and I would ride together whenever I came home, even during grad school. After I moved to New York, I couldn't get there much. Mother rides him, usually when she's bored from gardening, and daddy's done tending to his orchids."

"You miss him." Morgan already knew the answer from the tone in her voice.

"You mean Goethe? He's part of the family. The animal goes nuts when I come home!" She laughed. "Once, he came racing in from the pasture snorting and whinnying. Goodness! Then…he jumped over the fence and galloped to the car door! When I opened the window, he nestled his muzzle in my face! I had to give him a peppermint treat to persuade him to move enough so I could get out!"

Morgan poured another splash of Macallan into their glasses and asked, "When can you get home again?"

Caroline grew quieter, spinning the liquid in her glass. "Tuesday," she said. "I've got a few days off for Thanksgiving," adding quickly, "Planned it months ago."

"Goethe *and* your parents will be glad to see you…"

Morgan tried not to let the disappointment in his voice escape. He wasn't on call for the holiday—a rarity. As the only single surgeon in the department, he usually requested call for every holiday so his married colleagues could have time with their families. Ross had invited him over for their traditional barbecue, but Morgan had intruded too many times on Shandra's kindness. He declined, planning to do nothing except take a morning run along the lake and share another dinner she wouldn't remember with his mother in her memory care center. His brief thought of Thanksgiving dinner with Caroline was a fantasy too good to be true.

He didn't want the conversation to stumble, so he said, "I also noticed"—he cleared his throat with intent—"the picture of you mountain climbing. I could never do that. What's it like?"

"The first time…you're scared to death…but then for a while… it's exhilarating." Her amused expression left. "I don't need that excitement anymore. But I keep the rope under my bed so I can rappel down if there's a fire…or if I need to escape from a bad date."

His eyebrows rose. "Three hundred feet?"

"I'm teasing," she giggled, studying her finger while it encircled the snifter rim. "It's a keepsake. Some girls hang on to their teddy bears. For me it's my rope."

She looked away, out the windows.

"Wes…" She paused. "I really enjoyed tonight. You were wonderful company…the best."

"Thank you." His gaze followed hers to the distant lights. "So were you."

"I've been to more of those things than I care to admit," Caroline replied. "I like getting dressed up, but after four hours in heels, let me just say…I'm glad they're off." Her toes wiggled inside her hosiery. "Actually…I prefer jeans."

"I feel the same way about bow ties."

He undid the black noose so the silk tails drooped freely. Caroline added to their glasses again. Morgan read the label.

"So you normally drink Scotch this old?" he asked, his head spinning slightly.

"I bought it today before I had my hair done. Usually I just buy the twelve…" With downcast eyes, Caroline looked at her snifter, but it was too late.

"I sense a conspiracy in play," he chuckled. "Janie?"

"Yes," Caroline admitted timidly. "I told her about your tour, how you tried to impress me."

"And did I?"

"No…but it was cute when you wouldn't get off the elevator. I'd never imagine a surgeon to be helpless."

"I don't like heights." He squinted, contemplating what more there could be to the evening's plot. "Was Ross in on this?"

"I don't know."

"You don't lie as well as you think," he grinned.

"But…here we are," she replied.

As Caroline brought the final drops of Scotch to her lips, her eyelids closed. Morgan's willpower failed and he studied her leg. The examination ended too soon. She placed her snifter on the table and stepped to the windows.

"Come here," she said softly. He took several tentative steps until she cast a reassuring smile. "Don't be afraid, Dr. Morgan. I'll protect you."

The southern exposure presented a commanding view of downtown Chicago and Lake Michigan. The city lights simmered on the water's blackness, exposing the white-capped waves. He placed his hand on her shoulder.

"Spectacular," was all he could say. "The buildings just seem to… stick silently up in the air."

"Frozen music," she said.

The little hairs on Morgan's arms tickled. "I don't understand," he whispered.

"They embrace the wind," she whispered back. "Each…one is a note of a melody."

With an outstretched hand, Caroline traced the staves of the skyline. "Hear it?" she said, her voice barely audible. "Up here it's so calm…yet so alive…"

The heart of her perfume deepened, synthesizing with her words as her voice trailed off. "I hoped you'd come back here tonight."

His lips touched her neck and she became still. She turned to face him and they kissed, his fingers caressing the skin of her back. Their bodies drew tight, not wanting to release. Her breathing became faster.

"Caroline," he said. "I'd better go."

Reluctantly they retrieved his coat. She tugged at his collar and patted his lapels.

"Keep warm." She wrapped her fingers in his. "I'm flying to New York Monday. Work," she added. "Then Virginia…the following afternoon." Her eyes grew moist. "Please…call me."

Morgan kissed her again and went out the door.

THREE

Morgan's phone rang.

Damn it was early!

"Morning!" said the animated voice.

"Ugh. Hi, Janie...What the hell time is it?"

He looked at the clock. She could've waited a couple more hours. But there was no chance of that—not after last night.

"Ooo! Did I wake you? I thought nine a.m. was late for surgeons! Sorry! Not really! Did you drink that much?"

"No," he replied.

"Did you?" he asked, his voice hoarse.

"Oh, never!" she exclaimed.

A headache began boring through his skull. It didn't take a medical degree to remind him that champagne followed by wine and ending with Scotch was a bad thing. Janie's chipper shrill made matters worse.

"So did you have fun last night?" Janie asked, already answering for him. "I *know* you did! Isn't Cay beautiful?"

"Gorgeous."

Her perfume was still on his face.

"You know, even at rush hour she gets a taxi."

"No doubt."

He was definitely very hungover and needed to go back to sleep.

"Dearie…You went to her apartment! I saw you guys leave! Your hands probably wandered everywhere!"

"Janie, please!" Squeezing his eyelids, he then forced them to open.

"You'd be further along if you'd have let me set you two up earlier. But you told me no more blind dates."

"Caroline's not your typical—" was all he could say before she interrupted again.

"So when are you going to ask her out?"

"I don't know!"

He really needed to brush his teeth.

"Ooo! You should call her—this morning! This is so exciting! She really wanted to meet you. Oh, it was perfect! Anne was right. You should marry her. I'll plan the wedding! Do you want to use my country club in Glencoe? I'll get you a great price—and a hot band that rocks!"

"Janie! Shut the hell up!" The hammer pounding in his head was boring through another gross of invisible nails. "I love you…but please…shut up!"

"Sorry…it's just that…"

Oh shit… He forgot last night, and now he'd have to ask her. *Damn it to hell…*

"Janie…"

"What, dearie?"

"I need her number."

"You didn't get it? That's not like you! Don't you have a little book with—"

"I beg of you…please…just give it to me so I can go back to sleep."

"If she says yes, will you let me know?"

His head throbbed.

"Do you want me to tell her what to wear? I'll call her when we hang up!"

"Whatever! Please…have mercy and give it to me." It was clear any relationship with Caroline would require both of them getting unlisted numbers.

Fumbling around in the drawer of his bedside stand, his fingers found a pad of paper and a pen.

"Are you writing? You'll forget if you don't."

He scribbled the digits.

"Call her, Wes. I know she likes you!"

"Right now, however…bye," he grunted. He took some aspirin and went back to sleep.

———

By noon he felt better and summoned the courage to call Caroline. When she didn't answer, he left a message, trying not to sound disappointed. Reluctantly he went to shower, knowing her perfume would be washed away. While drying, his phone rang. He was sorry for only a moment it was Ross Merrimac.

"What's up?" Morgan asked.

"You alone?" Ross knew him too well.

"Uh-huh…."

"Good. She'd have to get home by herself anyway." Morgan heard the excitement grow in his voice. "Ready to go to work?"

"What we got?"

"Your transplant program's about to launch."

"Be there in a few."

"Clock's ticking, brother." A donated heart would survive only a few hours unless placed in a patient. "Word is we may have another after that, so I figure we're going to be at it for a while."

———

Lights flashing and horn honking, Morgan's black BMW sped south on Lake Shore Drive. He passed Lake Point Tower and started worrying. If Caroline happened to call while he was working he didn't want to miss her, but there was nothing he could do about it.

God, that woman's distracting me.

It was a great feeling—just bad timing.

The surgeries and caring for the kids afterwards in the ICU would go on for many hours, consuming every second Morgan had—and for how long? He wouldn't know until he got home. But he couldn't wait. He knew he'd love every minute of it.

Please call me back, Caroline, he prayed, *please…*

Dr. Morgan parked his car in the physicians' lot and ran.

Forty-eight hours passed, but Morgan paid no attention. He was focused. Year after year, through forgotten birthdays and foregone vacations, he had stood over an operating table, learning, thinking, and honing his skills waiting for these opportunities. He fed on the intensity, driven by the desire for the triumph—to return to the parents a child who was healthier than the one God had given them. (His final reward always came when he got home, threw on some running clothes and pounded his way up and down the trails of Lincoln Park.)

Today the discipline had paid off again. By Tuesday afternoon both of his tiny patients had new hearts that were beating without any problem.

Sitting on the bench beside his locker, Morgan checked his phone messages. Caroline had called three times. He touched the redial button.

"*Hi. This is Caroline Pruitt. I am unavailable. Please leave a message.*"

"Give me a little more time, Cay," he almost pleaded into the mouthpiece, and then remembered she was on her way to Virginia. He'd have to try later.

Morgan looked up when he heard Merrimac shut his locker door. "That was great!" he said to his boss.

"Textbook," Ross agreed. "You've done good, friend…as promised. The trustees will be pleased. Maybe I'll renew your contract for another year."

"Gee, thanks." Morgan gave him the finger. "Does that include a paycheck?"

"Only if you do what I do and go home," said Ross. "Don't you even think about going out tonight."

"Not a chance."

"Smart man. You and I both need sleep, so let's get this over with," Merrimac said. "Costume up with your white coat. We need to go do our duty and kumbaya with the press, so smile and remember not to use words they can't spell."

Haggard and unshaven, the surgeons gathered their teams and went to report to the media waiting in the hospital lobby.

Squinting from the intense light, Morgan thought he probably looked only semiconscious—a condition that was more true than not.

"It's been a long two days," he said, vaguely hearing cameras clicking in front of him. "Dr. Merrimac and I have some comments, we'll take a few questions, and...call it a day...or night, depending on one's perspective."

The reporters laughed.

"I think it's important to remember," Morgan began, "that our successes today and in the future come not just because of the dedicated teams of professionals standing behind me but also because of the broad financial support by many people in Chicago that made this program possible."

Merrimac smiled, adding a vigorous nod for the cameras.

The thirty-five minutes of questions and answers was pure tedium. Finally, the two men shook hands in the privacy of the locker room, both looking noticeably tired. They started to remove their scrubs.

"Crud!" Ross's stubbly black face grinned. "I forgot to ask...Did you have a nice evening with Caroline Pruitt?"

Morgan tossed his scrub pants into the dirty linen bag.

"You and Bonwitt arranged that, didn't you?"

"Yeah, guy. She called me. One of the perks of being in charge." Morgan's friend never stopped grinning. "Thinking up a reason to get you to that thing alone wasn't easy, so I just pulled rank. Simple, and it worked."

"Why didn't you just tell me?" Morgan's scrub shirt missed the bag and landed on the floor. He stumbled to pick it up. "Whatever happened to the band of brothers?"

"Catching you unaware was more fun." Merrimac exploded in laughter. "I didn't actually meet Caroline until a few weeks before you did, and I was impressed with her smarts."

"She's intelligent, all right," Morgan nodded.

Ross knew him better than that. "Good looking too."

"I hadn't noticed," Morgan lied.

"Bullshit, Morgan. You mentioned it once and a dozen times."

Morgan donned his jeans and pulled down a sweatshirt, covering his well-toned abdomen. He was in such a hurry when he left home two days earlier that he forgot his call bag. Fresh underwear would have to wait.

"So Janie called you…" Morgan was certain Merrimac was tired enough that little provocation was necessary to elicit the information.

"Soon after that tour you took of the hospital," Ross answered, "I guess Caroline said something *complimentary* about you to Bonwitt!" He made a skeptical face. "*That's* amazing in itself! Man! So Bonwitt called me at home. What a trip!" His whole body shuddered. "In the same endless sentence, she also worked in the notion about me persuading Queen that we should let her redo our place."

"That's Janie," said Morgan.

"Would never work." Merrimac said. "The Queen would throw Bonwitt out the window in two minutes." He finished buttoning his shirt. "Anyway that's the story, Dr. Morgan. So do *me* a favor and try not screw this one up. My conscience still bothers me that I was part of this scheme. Caroline's too good for you."

"Don't remind me."

Ross shook Morgan's hand again. "Heck of a job, Wes. Really. I can't thank you enough. Oh, and one more time: want to come for Thanksgiving?"

"Going to see Mom, but thanks," Morgan said, zipping his weathered bomber jacket part of the way up.

"Let's get out of here, brother."

"Yeah," agreed Morgan, admiring the uncultivated stubble blooming even on his wide cheeks. "I hate beards. Need a shave." He stuck his nose inside his jacket. "Mostly a shower."

His BMW got him home. Red from the hot shower, he wrapped himself in his bathrobe and lay on the bed. In the final moments before the exhaustion won, he felt himself falling into a cloud with Caroline. Whenever he touched her, she touched back. Her auburn hair was everywhere. Her breasts pressed tightly against his chest. Her legs…

An alarm?

What's the problem with that child?

The noise continued.

Somebody check that alarm!

Ringing...

Where's the nurse?

He knocked his phone to the floor and started groping for it.

"Hello?" he gurgled.

"Wes, it's Cay."

"Who's okay?" He was barely conscious.

"It's Caroline."

"Cay?"

Her voice was dreamy. Was she lying next to him?

"Yes, it's me! You're sleeping, aren't you?"

"Um...no...yes." His mental marbles were still rolling around searching for the correct slots. "What day...is it?"

"Tuesday. Almost six."

He'd been asleep just three hours.

"I heard it on the radio!" she said. "Are they doing all right?"

"I think...so." At least no one had called him to tell him otherwise. "Where...are you?" he asked.

"In Roanoke, at the airport...waiting for my father. Wes, I'm so excited for you!"

"Thanks." Recall of the last two days was coming back. "It was a real marathon."

"They're okay?"

"Troopers. So were the parents. Everybody was great." The phone clicked. "Cay?"

She came back. "Daddy's here. I need to go."

"Umm..."

"Wes?"

"Yeah?" He yawned, still not thinking clearly.

"Please get some sleep," she said sweetly. "Call me tomorrow."

"When?"

"Whenever you want to." Caroline added, "Please don't forget."

FOUR

Thanksgiving

Morgan ran along the lakefront to the north end of Chicago and back. No surprise other joggers and cyclists were out too. The morning was clear, the air crisp.

"Twelve miles! That's good!" Barely winded, he applauded himself while walking the last yards home.

Morgan had run the same distance many times before and made every effort to work out as regularly as possible, even training for marathons in the past—but he'd never actually run one.

If he were to compete, he'd want to win, and to win he'd have to do nothing but train. His growing workload now demanded so much of his time he often felt that he had to manage every minute. Still, despite those demands, he was able to schedule fairly regular exercise, and his life felt balanced—that was, until last Saturday night.

Feeling his muscles tighten, he paused to stretch and thought about Caroline again. "God, that woman's beautiful!" he said, alternating each leg in deep lunges. They had talked by phone the evening before, until Morgan heard her dozing off.

"*So your little transplant patients are okay?*" Caroline asked more than once.

"*They're just rolling along.*" Her interest pleased him to no end. "*Probably out of the ICU tomorrow.*"

"Doing anything for Thanksgiving?" The question was followed with a yawn and apology.

"Seeing my mother," but he wanted to say, *"Wish you were here."*

Cay yawned again.

"Tired?" he asked.

"Yeah... Goethe missed me, so Daddy and I... rode a long time... today... " The cadence of her words slowed more. *"We're going again... in the... morning... before dinner... even though my back's... pretty sore... "*

"Did you take anything for it?"

"Daddy gave me... " Her voice faded. *"A snifter of thirty-one-year-old Macallan."*

"That must have been tasty."

"You know, it's as old as I... "

"Ah! Scotch reveals a secret."

She was three years younger than Morgan.

"Please... don't tell anyone," she giggled.

"I don't know 'bout that... unless there's a bribe in it." Time to say goodnight. *"I better let you go."* He didn't want to. *"I'll call tomorrow after my run."*

Morgan closed his front door. Kicking off his running shoes, he got some water and looked at the time. She was probably already riding, but he'd try anyway. He wanted to check on her sore back.

"Lamest reason I ever came up with," he laughed while punching in her number.

"Hi. This is Caroline Pruitt. I am unavailable. Please leave a message."

"Um...hi...it's Wes. Back from my run...going to get cleaned up and go make rounds...then drive out and have dinner...with my mother. Try you again later."

By noon Morgan had left the hospital and was heading to La Grange where his mother lived in a skilled nursing facility. Her Alzheimer's had grown worse over the last few years and in the spring she tripped and broke her right hip. After surgery, rehab healed her body but the last of her fleeting memory had vanished.

Whenever Morgan visited he'd roll her wheelchair near a window where they would sit together looking at the broad expanse of gardens. While his mother sat silently, he would talk about his work or whatever else was new in his life. Today he would tell her about the heart transplants he'd done—and Caroline.

"Lizzie…you won't even know I came," he said sadly as he drove to one more never-ending good-bye.

She didn't remember anything now. Morgan wondered if she even knew she had a son.

When traffic slowed, he called Caroline again. She answered late into the rings.

"How's the back?" he asked cheerfully.

"It's okay." Caroline's melancholy sliced through him. "We'll talk later," she said.

"Cay…what's wrong?" he asked.

"I just don't…want to talk to you now."

Unlike last night's drowsy patter, she sounded disconnected and far away. The call ended.

"Aw, come on!" Morgan shouted at the windshield. "What the hell did I do?"

———

Cutting another piece of turkey, Morgan put the small forkful in his mother's mouth. He looked around the spacious dining room with its stylishly painted walls and crown molding. Most of the residents had families with them, and that was good. Some came to share Thanksgiving dinner, others just to visit. Over the holidays an occasional bored child would race away from a table with the mother following quickly. That never bothered Morgan. If they were running or getting into mischief, they were healthy—a very different reality from the hospital, where he often thought the entire world had only sick children.

"Chew, Mom," he said gently. "It's good."

She swallowed it. Morgan wiped a bit of cranberry relish from her chin.

"Remember when you made this at home?" Cornbread followed. "You cooked every Thanksgiving dinner…and you let me help."

His mother coughed slightly and for a moment seemed to recognize him.

"Dad..." she said.

Morgan gave her another bite.

"Dad's gone, Mom."

Lizzie Morgan was a good mother, forcing him in grade school to read more and write better than his classmates. She also spanked him when he misbehaved. That ended the day when Mary, his six year old baby sister, died. As a child Morgan never understood how it could happen, and then years later his father succumbed to a massive heart attack in his bank office, leaving just Morgan and Lizzie. With the payout from life insurance, Morgan went to college and medical school at Northwestern completing both in six years.

"I want to be a surgeon," he said to his mother while he was in medical school, *"a pediatric heart surgeon. They take care of babies and children like Mary."*

By the time he succeeded, Lizzie was already failing and rarely remembered him. With the remaining insurance money, Morgan found her a place where she'd be cared for and safe. Once he went into practice, any additional costs were no issue.

He kissed his mother's forehead. "I love you," he whispered. "Mom, I met a girl. She's an architect, and...she's really nice...and pretty. You'll like her. She's different from the others."

He had hoped to tell her that Caroline was maybe a serious prospect for marriage, but her recent abruptness on the phone pushed him into unfamiliar territory. Women had never made him feel insecure before. Perhaps the theater of the last few days was only to advance her position in the firm, or—*"Sorry...it was fun, but... oops...I forgot to mention..."*

Returning home Morgan accomplished little more than shuffling papers and pretending to read journal abstracts while the holiday football game created background noise. It was hopeless. All he could think about was Caroline. Her power over him was overwhelming. He was in a place he had never been before.

What had he done wrong?

He'd make it right—if he could.

Caroline called that evening.

"Hi," he said and took a long pull from a bottle of beer, waiting for the inevitable.

"How was dinner with your mom?"

"Okay, I guess."

"It's good of you to go see her," Caroline said. She sounded sincere.

"Mom's got Alzheimer's bad. At one time I thought, after my residency, she could live with me. I was going to hire help...but by then...that wasn't going to work. She needed assisted living... memory support. I got her in a place that's perfect."

Why was he going on like this? Was he afraid if he stopped talking, she'd hang up again?

"Sorry," Caroline said. "That's tough. Listen...I was very rude earlier."

"I figured I just caught you at a bad time," he lied.

"Wes..." she said, "You did, and I'm sorry. I've changed my flight. I'm coming back tomorrow."

"You said you were staying—"

"I need to see you," she replied. "Can you do dinner tomorrow night?"

He thought the request sounded like an invitation to attend a medical staff conference.

"The ORs are quiet tomorrow. I'll be off by early afternoon."

"So dinner?" she asked again.

"Where?" Morgan suspected the reservations had already been made.

"How about Leonardo's? Seven o'clock?"

"On Halsted?" Hoping to sound enthusiastic but not too eager he asked, "Would you like me to get you at the airport?"

"I'm coming in through O'Hare. That's a long way for you."

"Don't mind at all." Morgan had to try.

"No...but thank you." *Not negotiable* is what she didn't say. "I'll cab it."

Paranoia set in. While it wouldn't be his first brush-off, it *would* be the first time he cared. He felt sick.

"Can I at least drive us to dinner?" Instinct told him he wouldn't be drinking much alcohol.

"I'd like that. I'll be in the lobby at half past." She was sounding brighter. "Looking forward to seeing you."

Those few words helped, but Morgan still didn't sleep well that night.

———

Merrimac knew his friend was upset. Morgan's uncharacteristic detachment was apparent the moment they met outside a patient's room.

"Share it, brother," Ross said.

"Rounds first," replied Morgan, looking at the gathering crowd of medical students and residents. "Get it over with. We'll do coffee later."

Merrimac waved the growing assembly of physicians-in-training closer. "Let's get started," he said. "We've had an exciting week. Our now-famous Dr. Morgan will lead off the discussion about post-transplant surgical care."

Morgan smiled meekly then rambled on for several minutes. Obvious to all, the usually good-humored attending physician was fretting. Ross stepped forward to help. In silence, Morgan drifted to the back of the group.

Merrimac finally said, "I'm going to let the chief resident finish rounds. Dr. Morgan and I have a matter to take care of." His hand ushered the path down the corridor. "Wes…"

The friends walked to Merrimac's office, got coffee, and sat down.

"I'm lost, man," said Morgan.

"Let me guess her name," Ross replied with a grin.

Morgan told him about yesterday's phone call.

"You really got bit there, bro…and after only one less-than-intimate dinner?" Merrimac couldn't stop laughing. "So my friend's realizing there's more to life than just sex?"

Morgan mentioned his additional time at Lake Point Tower.

"You and women!" said Merrimac. "Don't blame this on me! Thought I was doing you a favor following that Bonwitt woman's suggestion. Seemed like a good idea at the time. Can you believe she's still bugging me about redecorating? Why don't you just call *her* and ask what's going on?"

"Call Janie? Suicide would be better."

"You got that right!" Ross laughed, stretching his arms back and forth before scratching his head. "Look. Wes. You—of all people— ought to know how enigmatic females are. Me? I've been married for years and still can't figure the Queen out. All I know is not to cross her. Wicked temper, know what I mean, brother?"

"You're not helping."

"All's not lost, my friend," replied Ross. "Despite the spell this girl's cast on hopefully more than what lives below your waist, keep in mind you had a great week! Tonight, at least, you'll know. Then if you still want to jump off the roof, you'll have a legit reason. Now, bolt! Go running, go drinking, but leave."

"Comforting bedside manner you've got." Morgan looked glum.

"Want me to throw your rear out myself?" Merrimac's thumb flipped toward the door.

———

Twenty minutes early, his BMW idled near Navy Pier. Finally he drove to the lobby door and got out, his overcoat tails flapping in the stiff wind.

"Wes Morgan for Caroline Pruitt," he said to the lobby attendant.

"Ah! Dr. Morgan! Ms. Pruitt told me to expect you. I'll let her know you're here, sir." The man raised the receiver and entered a few numbers. "Dr. Morgan is here…You're welcome, Ms. Pruitt." He hung up. "She's on her way."

"Your name, my friend, is…" Morgan asked.

"Robert, sir." The men shook hands.

Morgan stood on the oriental carpet watching the numbers decrease as the elevator descended. When he heard it slow, he straightened his back and took a deep breath.

Ding.

The door opened.

Caroline cast a serene smile with her lips and stepped toward him. Her white lambswool turtleneck accentuated her curves even more as she reached and took his wrist.

"Good evening, Dr. Morgan."

Her simple greeting was elegant and dignified, without a hint of concern.

"And to you...Ms. Pruitt."

Morgan was positive his voice cracked.

Raising her chin, she asked, "Hungry?"

"Of course!"

He wasn't sure he could eat anything right now.

Caroline handed him her lipstick-red swing coat. As the cashmere melted in his fingers, she turned to receive the sleeves. A pair of soft black gloves went on next.

"Nice-looking barrette," he said, noticing the inlaid silver clasp. It gathered her auburn hair into a refined mane. He realized the compliment sounded lame.

"Glad you like it."

He analyzed each of her words.

Robert held the lobby door for them and then opened the car door for Caroline.

"Thank you," she said before he shut it.

Robert hustled to the driver's side but Morgan was already getting in.

"Pleasure meeting you, Robert," he said, slipping a folded twenty-dollar bill into the doorman's hand.

"Enjoy your evening, Dr. Morgan," he said.

Trying his best to keep his fear hidden, Morgan buckled his seat belt and looked at Caroline. Moving closer, she kissed his cheek.

"Wes," she said, "you look wonderful."

———

The maître-d' ushered the couple through the overflow crowd at the bar to a secluded table. While Morgan held Caroline's chair, he couldn't miss the keen interest in the male faces around them. In the past he would have enjoyed escorting the most attractive woman in the restaurant, but now the noticeable stir she created made him tense.

Caroline seemed oblivious to the ardent attention, focusing only on Morgan. Their conversation during the drive to restaurant had equally unnerved him. They talked like they'd known each other for years, all the while Morgan searching for what hid behind.

A waiter brought them menus. "And to start?" he asked.

"Wes, shall we have wine or drinks?" she asked.

"Oh...wine, I think."

His angst grew.

Caroline's polished fingernail pointed to a spot on the wine list. "This Tuscan red, I think, and...sparkling water okay with you, Wes?" Her pale eyes projected an intensity that shot right through him but revealed nothing to be amiss.

"Fine." Morgan nodded.

"Very good," said the waiter.

Caroline sat back slowly, turned to one side, and crossed her legs. A black stiletto boot extended from under the tablecloth as her finger ran back and forth over the tops of the turquoise globes in her necklace.

"Glad this worked out," she began. "That we could get together."

The wine arrived.

"Wes, you taste it. Tell me if I did right," she said.

The waiter obliged.

Morgan performed the requisite swirling, smelling, and tasting, but none of his senses was working very well.

"Please," he said to the waiter.

A waterfall of Chianti splashed into both glasses.

Caroline raised hers first. "To your successes this week," she toasted, "and to the brave little ones and their parents."

"I appreciate that," Morgan said.

Caroline shifted slightly to one side. The bottom of her necklace slid across her breasts. Why was she teasing him?

"You said you were hungry. Maybe we should order..."

THE ARCHITECT OF REVENGE

As she studied the menu, her hand drew her mane forward so it flowed down a shoulder.

"A couple of appetizers?" she asked.

"Sounds good." His stomach suggested otherwise.

Before Caroline drew the waiter's attention she caught Morgan's crestfallen focus on his wine glass.

"What's the matter?" she asked.

"You tell me…"

"Oh dear…" Her hand came across the table and grasped his. "You're worried."

"Just get it over with." There! He said it and took a swallow of wine. "Saturday was a great time…we'll leave it at that. You have better things to do than waste time on me."

"Oh, Wes…No!" Her eyes teared.

"I feel terrible," he said with a glum face. "I was hoping this would go someplace."

"You're so wrong!" she said quickly. "It's not what you think. I really want to see you."

"Huh?" Morgan was more confused than ever.

"Yesterday…" She cleared her throat then took some wine. "I'd just gotten off the phone…" Her hand still lay on his. "Wes…there's a reason you didn't get those Bears tickets."

"You told me. I was outbid."

"By my former fiancé."

Of course a woman like Caroline would have been in such a situation. How recent was their relationship? Her past didn't bother him—well, maybe he was a *little* jealous of it—but what worried him was it might not be completely over.

Without expression he asked, "The guy at the reception you threw those lightning bolts at?"

"You saw that?"

"Couldn't miss it," Morgan replied. "You did it to Janie earlier also, when she called you *Cay*."

"Well, *that* was different," Caroline said delicately. "My nickname's special. Not many people can use it…at least early on."

"So why would your fiancé be at the Art Institute?" Morgan asked unable to conceal his apprehension.

"*Former* fiancé," she quickly corrected him. "He's one of the managing partners of my firm. His name's Avery—lives in New York."

"Oh…"

The waiter returned. "Would you like to order dinner?"

"Maybe in a minute," Caroline said.

"No rush," said the waiter. "I'll be back in a bit. Enjoy the wine!"

"There's more you need to know." Caroline looked at Morgan with guarded intent. "We met in the New York office when I was an intern." She was chewing on her lip. "There was a relationship… clandestine, of course. I shouldn't have, I know."

"It happens."

As a physician in a hospital, he knew such breeches occurred. Some worked out, most didn't.

"They hired me. I was so excited and happy." She shook her head. "More like naive and in love. Avery asked me to marry him. It was all storybook—Hamptons wedding, the whole drill." She took a sip of wine to sooth her voice. "A month before, I walk into his penthouse…he's in bed with the newest intern."

"That's pretty awful!"

His dread became relief—and anger. That anyone could hurt this beautiful soul was incomprehensible. Even in his relationships Morgan had never been so callous.

"It was so bad!" Caroline shifted in her chair. "I was devastated," but her voice grew defiant.

"I told the directors I was going to quit. By then they knew most of what had happened…and said they'd make me a full partner and move me to Chicago. I accepted…only if they'd let me finish the Downs project in New York."

"So that was it?" Morgan felt better…but exhausted. His hand now rested on hers.

"Before you joined Janie and me on Saturday, Avery took his first opportunity since our breakup to come over. Insisted on having drinks later. I told him no. I already had an escort." Her bleak grimace grew to a weak smile. "You didn't know it yet."

Her irritation returned and she shook her head in disbelief. "Later he saw you bidding."

"So the guy likes football…"

"Darling, you're so naive." Caroline's evolving smile confirmed what she just said. "He can get those tickets whenever he wants. My company donated them. You probably didn't notice that on the card."

"No, but I was incredibly distracted at the time."

"I called him Sunday morning, angry as a hornet. I told him I wanted those tickets. He was being a complete, total…" Despite her bitterness she didn't utter the word she obviously wanted to use. "He said he'd bring them over. What a fool I was!"

Morgan had never heard her voice rise before.

"He brought them, all right, but I was foolish enough to think we could interact like adults…that this thing was behind us." Her face filled with contempt. "Instead…he came on to me! As if nothing had changed! Then he heard my cell phone ring! He didn't know, but figured it was you! So he made threats!"

She was crying.

"I told him to leave, but…he wouldn't! So I called Robert. Bless him! He came up immediately and got him out." The tears continued. "When I calmed down, I listened to your message, but I didn't know what to do! I wanted to tell you what a gentleman you were. Thank you for a special evening…then you didn't call back."

"Sorry," was all he could think of to say. "I was tied up for a while. A surgeon's life sucks. Gets in the way of other important things."

Still, he was glad he went home that night. To have made love to Caroline the first evening would have probably ruined any chance of a real relationship.

"Darling," she said, "what you do *is* important…and I love that it's for children."Caroline's voice grew more controlled. "Thanksgiving morning after daddy and I returned from our ride, he called me and started in again. My father took the phone out of my hand and used words I hadn't heard him say before. Avery might try to mess with my head but knows better than to get on the wrong side of my father." Caroline sighed. "Anyway, he's out of my life forever. Good riddance."

"Cay...I'm sorry all this happened. But you could have just told me over the phone, stayed with your family."

"No."

The woman would not be deterred. She did things her way.

Caroline removed a blue linen envelope from her purse and gave it to him. He rubbed the gold embossed *C* in the top corner. With a mystified look, he opened it. Inside were the two tickets to the Bears game.

"Caroline," he said, "I don't want these anymore." Then he grinned ardently into her eyes. "Unless...of course, you have a warm enough coat to go with me. Soldier Field can be damn cold in December."

"I do." She nodded and wiped her nose discreetly in her napkin.

"Good, then it's all settled." He poured the remaining wine. With restored confidence, he said, "Nice to finally have the last word."

"I'm glad you think so." They shared a smile.

Swirling the wine, he studied its legs on the side of the glass. "One more thing..."

"Whether the coat is warm?" she asked without irony.

"No," he grinned.

"What then?"

"Could I..." He paused. "Kiss you in public?"

Caroline came in close from across the table. "Sweetheart, you'll have to try it to find out."

FIVE

Mid-December 2000

At the far end of the waiting room, the shared look of fear on the parents' faces vanished the moment Morgan smiled at them. It was a simple message that streamed like a banner: Everything went well.

"Your son's doing great! I'm proud of him," Morgan said, sitting down on a multicolored footstool designed to look like a mushroom. "Sorry it took all morning. These repairs take time, but we fixed it."

He pulled off his surgical cap and looked at the damp band where it clung to his forehead.

"Maybe I *did* sweat a little."

His laugh brought the first smile to both parents' faces.

"When can we see him?" asked the mother.

"The nurses will let you know," Morgan replied. "Right now they're getting him settled in."

Everything he said was crafted to encourage confidence. Such was the nature of the world he worked in. Rarely did he have to deliver bad news, but when it happened it was given in private, with other staff to assist with the grief that followed.

"Dr. Morgan..." Abby was behind him. He turned. "I apologize for interrupting," she said.

The surgeon stood up and introduced the senior surgical nurse to the parents. "This wonderful woman is my rock…and keeps my leash tight." There were handshakes. "What's up, Abby?"

"You left your phone on the side table again…almost vibrated to the floor." She smiled, handing it to him. "I took the call. I think it's important."

Morgan saw Caroline's number.

"Thanks, Abby." He winked at her and said to the parents, "We'll be checking in on your son a lot. Maybe after you've had a chance to see him, you should stretch your legs, get lunch. Worrying is our job. You and your family have a Merry Christmas!"

They shook hands and then Morgan and Abby walked together back to the surgery suites.

"You talked to Caroline?" he asked with caution, knowing Abby would speak her mind if she didn't approve.

Once she saw him vigorously kiss a woman near the entrance of the hospital.

Abby later scowled in private at Morgan and said, *"No lady wears a blouse that revealing in public. You can do better—much better."*

"And?" Morgan asked.

"My oh my…Polite!" Abby looked directly at him. "Ms. Caroline's a Southern woman…I can tell. She called me *ma'am.* Her mother and father raised her to be proper."

"So you approve, Grandma?" Morgan could only hope.

"What a sweet voice! She should be in our tabernacle choir!"

"Guess I better call her back right now!" Morgan tapped in her number.

"Don't you keep that girl waiting alone in the cafeteria!"

"Huh?" The phone was already ringing.

"Hi!" Caroline said into his ear.

"What are you doing here?"

"Other than stalking young doctors," she replied, "I'm doing some site work today, building your hospital. Remember? Architects do visit their edifices from time to time."

"Where are you?"

"Got a table for two by a window. Look for the candles and wine. You can have half of my turkey sandwich."

"Hang on, Cay," Morgan said, turning to Abby. "Do I have time to have lunch with her?"

"I don't think we'll be counting instruments for about an hour," Abby answered.

"My hair flat?" he asked.

"No," but she still used her fingers to fluff and comb his errant cowlick. "That's better."

"Thanks, bye, later." His voice rose as the distance between them grew. He hadn't had a chance to see her since the Bears game last Sunday.

"Hey, you!" Caroline said. Her tight ponytail bounced as she looked up.

He kissed her.

"That's enough for now," she said, breaking away. "You'll ruin your reputation."

"I don't care."

"Good afternoon, Dr. Morgan!" The unified greeting came from a moving cadre of white-coated residents clearing their trays.

"More scandal for you," Caroline said merrily.

Morgan scanned the crowded room. Diners were looking their way.

"I think we've succeeded already. Want to go to the staff dining room? Less crowded."

"Dressed like this? I don't think so."

Her sweatshirt and jeans were streaked with dust and grimy stains. She had a smudge near her right ear but freshly applied lip gloss. Her carefree beauty seemed so natural it took his breath away.

"Oh, I don't think anyone would mind if I took a construction worker to—"

"Nah," Cay said, "this is fine. Abby...we talked for a couple of minutes. She's really a dear woman! Knows you like a book!"

Morgan groaned.

"I assured her I wouldn't keep you long." She handed him an iced tea, a napkin, and her plate. "Here...I promised you half a sandwich."

"Hope you have a good lunch, Dr. Morgan."

The surgeon looked at the speaker—the nurse who circulated in his operating room. Wasn't she supposed to be setting up his next case?

Caroline smiled and said, "So what's the rest of your day looking like?"

"Have one more operation this afternoon."

He bit into the bread.

"I'll be done here about five." Caroline stroked her ponytail while she spoke. With each pass, her hand lingered just above her breast. "Can you do dinner?"

"Going to be later for me," he replied with a dazed pout.

"Hope you're having a pleasant lunch, Dr. Morgan."

He looked in the direction of the voices. A trio of operating-room staff kept moving, only to pause and wave at him a few feet behind Caroline.

"Popular fellow," Cay said.

"These people never leave the OR lunch room," Morgan confided. "Most brown-bag it."

"Another wave inbound," Caroline noted.

Several more OR staff dressed in pale green scrubs said hello in passing.

"Sweet of all your friends to stop by," she said as Morgan nodded to the group.

He shook his head. "Anyway...if we do dinner, it'll be late...but more private."

"I rarely go to sleep before midnight," she replied.

"We could eat at my place. It's clean, I think." His brow crinkled before he smiled confidently. "Yeah...It is...My housekeeper's been there."

Morgan was fastidious about keeping his home neat and organized, but without exception there was probably a pair of underwear that missed the basket or some dishes left in the sink. Henrietta righted those little things, cleaned the place and every week washed his sheets and remade the bed—good in any circumstance, but especially today if Caroline ended up in it.

"Hi there!" a voice behind him said.

Morgan turned around. "Abby, what are you doing here?"

He put down his sandwich and managed to formally introduce the two women. When Caroline rose to take Abby's hand, she towered over her.

"Pleasure, Abby." The women bonded immediately. "Wes speaks highly of you."

"Dr. Morgan and I have known each other a very long time," Abby replied.

"Some rich stories, I suspect," Caroline nodded.

Morgan felt perspiration accumulating rapidly under his arms. He held his breath.

"Dr. Morgan is a real joy to work with."

"That's wonderful to hear," said Caroline. "So...I guess, Dr. Morgan, Abby has come to reclaim you." Caroline looked at her. "I hope someday we can get together...share more."

"There's plenty to tell," Abby laughed not so subtly. "Take years, but I'd enjoy that."

"Hey, what happens in the OR stays, right?" Morgan reminded her as he answered his ringing cell phone and pulled on her arm. "Back to work for us, Abby."

"My boss here needs to take me away," she said. "Wonderful meeting you, Ms. Pruitt."

"Likewise," Caroline said.

"Cay..." Morgan really didn't want to go. "I'll call you when I break scrub, swing by and get you."

"That'll work. I'll bring the food. Call me when you leave."

Morgan and Abby walked back toward the elevators that would take them to the operating suite.

"How many people did you tell I'd be in the cafeteria...you know, with Caroline?"

"Lord have mercy, she's a beautiful girl!"

"You didn't answer my question."

Abby smiled. "I never gossip, Dr. Morgan."

"I know," Morgan said, aware hospitals were dry kindling and a bit of gossip would ignite an inferno of curiosity.

"You're going to marry her, I hope."

Abby was never this frank.

"It's only been a month. And she hasn't asked me yet," he replied.

His growing preoccupation with Caroline totally supplanted any desire to remain unattached. He had never felt this way before! He could only hope…

"Don't let her go," said Abby, pulling him from his thoughts. "She loves you."

———

"You shouldn't have gone to so much trouble. A pizza would have been fine."

Morgan meant it, but when he'd called to say he was on his way, Caroline said the cooking was done. All she had to do was warm the veal and construct the salad while he uncorked the wine and lit a fire. The entire time she moved around his kitchen, he watched, mesmerized, as she reached, bent, and stretched, opening cabinet doors.

After they finished eating, Caroline nestled against his shoulder as they sat on the sofa, enjoying the final drops of wine.

"I'll clear this," Morgan said, "because I've got to get the dessert."

The plates were soon stacked on the kitchen counter and he returned with his hands behind his back.

"Here," he said, presenting her with a bottle of eighteen-year-old Macallan.

"My goodness!" she said.

"It's the reason I was bit more late picking you up," he admitted. "I wanted to get you something special…with you cooking and all."

Her fingers ran over the label. "Wes, you shouldn't have. I know this really set you back."

"I don't care," he said and went rummaging through his glassware. "You only live once, and damn it, I'm enjoying this."

His confidence wilted as he searched his cabinets.

"Oh crap! Cay...I'm an idiot! I don't have any snifters."

Caroline joined him and found two highball glasses. Holding them up to the light, she shook her head.

"My! Crate and Barrel—good start! At least you're aware that glassware counts." She started washing them and grabbed a drying towel. "They'll do just fine...tonight."

Morgan opened the bottle and poured generously.

"You've learned proper dosing," she laughed and gave him a hug. "Turn off the lights and put on another log," she said. "This needs to be enjoyed with just firelight."

Morgan did as instructed then joined Caroline on the sofa.

After a deep sniff, she took a taste and looked again at the glass.

"Santa will be here soon." She gave him a kiss. "When I write him my letter, I tell him you've been nice...so maybe he'll bring you some real snifters. You'll have to promise him, though, that you'll use them only with me."

She rested her head again on his shoulder, pulling a throw blanket over them both. In warm silence, bathed in the serenity of the soothing fire, they sipped until their glasses were empty.

Morgan heard the dishwasher running and realized he had dozed off. Without waking him, Caroline had loaded and started the machine and come back under the blanket. He felt her bare breasts massaging his chest each time she breathed. The heat of their bodies heightened the scent of her perfume, generating a sublime sensuousness.

"Time for bed," she whispered.

———

The high-pitched whine of a small jet engine started and stopped and started again. Opening his eyes slightly, he realized he was in bed and wearing his pajamas. How he got undressed *and* in them was a mystery, but, more strange, his hairdryer was somehow intermittently turning itself on and off.

"Cay?" he called.

"In here."

He got up to see.

The shower door was beaded with water, and standing in front of the foggy mirror was Caroline, wearing his bathrobe. The dangling belt told Morgan the robe was undone in front. The entire scene was so extraordinary he remained unconvinced it was real.

"Wes, there's over a foot of snow outside, you need to get moving."

Her pragmatism blended with unruffled immodesty left him confused even more.

"What time is it?"

"Five thirty. You need to get me home. We both have to work."

She crumpled a scrap of plastic wrapper and tossed it in his wastebasket.

"You found the spare toothbrush," he said.

"Such a thoughtful touch. Makes a girl feel welcome."

It was now officially hers.

She spun around with the robe totally open. She hugged him tight.

"Kisses after you brush yours," she said.

He obeyed and returned for his reward.

"Now, go shower while I make coffee," she said. "You have coffee, yes?"

Morgan nodded, still dumbfounded.

By six he was warming up the BMW. Caroline closed the back door of his townhouse and climbed in. Snow was everywhere, its beauty marred only by the fact that he had to go to work, and that meant they'd be apart. Following in the tracks of a snowplow, their sparse conversation changed only when he stopped at her lobby entrance. His face desperate, Morgan took her hand.

"Caroline…"

"Cay…" she corrected him.

Morgan nodded and began again. "About last night..." He hesitated. "Maybe we had too much Scotch...I know I did."

He was worried he'd taken advantage of the situation.

"You don't snore, Wes," she confided.

Her words were affectionate but not reassuring.

"I got plenty of sleep and...you're a good cuddler."

"That's not what I—"

She cut him off with a kiss.

"Don't worry, Dr. Morgan. Again...you were a perfect gentleman." She gave him another kiss then opened the car door. "You'll get another opportunity."

SIX

December 2001

As the raw drizzle wept from the sky, tire spray splattered his windshield, creating a smeared glare of taillights with each pass of the wipers. Every automobile in front of him seemed intent on creeping toward the intersections then holding back long after the stoplights became green. The entire way home, his frustration grew, pounding his denial deeper into the pit of fatigue, until again grief and exhaustion became one.

Morgan parked the BMW in his garage and climbed the back steps to his townhouse, fumbling through the tears for the key. Once inside, rainwater dripping off his coat, he kicked the door shut with his heel while dropping his overnight bag where he stood. At least when he was at the hospital he was protected from his home's empty stillness.

He hung the coat on a hook and traced the final gray light of the day to a table and a neat stack of mail. Arranged by Henrietta, he knew the small pile contained the usual bills but no condolence cards. They had stopped coming weeks ago. There was little more anyone could say.

Morgan walked to the kitchen sink, turned on the water, and wet his throat. Only then did he see that Henrietta had placed the damp newspaper near the drain so it wouldn't water-spot any wood. He didn't care what happened to the wood—or the paper. It would never be read. The news was the same every day, more testimony to the cruel reality no one could believe.

From their last bottle of Macallan, Morgan poured a few ounces into one of the snifters Caroline had given him. Sitting down on the sofa, he watched the curtains of scotch stream to the bottom of the glass before tentatively taking a sip.

"See, darling," Cay had said. *"Daddy taught me that fine crystal makes Scotch taste even more delicious."* When Morgan filled his mouth with more, she removed a drop from his lips, tasting it with her finger. Tempting him to transgress, she whispered, *"You stay right here."*

Morgan's gaze held firm on the cold hearth. Its flames had cast their passionate shadows everywhere the first time they made love. He relived again Caroline standing in front of the prurient blaze, her hair decanting over the back of a white gossamer caftan that poured to the floor. With her face in smoldering repose, she placed her Scotch on the mantle, glanced his way while drawing the silk robe behind her buttocks to reveal fine lace underwear—all which remained between them. One of her long legs nudged forward.

"I'm really not this way," she said, submitting her open hand to him in anxious anticipation. *"I hope you're not disappointed."*

Morgan reflexively took a large swallow of the Scotch. A wave of nausea slammed him and he retched hard. Racing toward the sink, he vomited on the floor.

"You motherfucker!" Morgan burbled through the detritus. "Goddamn you!"

He spit out more globs while he turned on the faucet and stuck his head in the water.

He sneezed.

Using a finger to clean out his nose, he reached for a paper towel to dry his face.

"Goddamn you..." he said, pulling off his shirt, using it to wipe up the vomit on the floor. The balled-up cloth went into the garbage.

Morgan found the snifter miraculously upright and unbroken. Holding the glass at arm's length he walked to the sink to dump the liquid, and backed away to his bathroom.

He stripped off the rest of his clothes.

"You look like shit!" he grunted to the person in the mirror.

His wilted skin showed every rib. Even though he hadn't exercised since September, he'd still lost fifteen pounds. He needed a real haircut. With a chimpanzee grin he picked uselessly at his teeth before looking at his retracted, lifeless penis.

"Fuck me," he said with contempt. "You're pathetic. Throwing a rock at your TV? Is that all you can do?"

The video released by the Pentagon several days before showed a smiling Osama bin Laden stating how pleased he was that the Towers collapsed completely. Morgan erupted when he heard that and threw the marble paperweight on his desk at the television. The large LCD screen popped, sparked, and went dark. Since then the broken glass and polished green stone, given to him by Ross Merrimac with the engraved date of his first transplant, remained untouched on the hardwood floor.

He turned on the shower, hoping hot water and steam would help him concentrate on anything that might cloak his misery. He thought about an operation he performed the week before, one that changed the destiny of a child clinging to life. His OR team applauded him—said he'd done a stellar job—but he just shrugged off their accolades and walked away. His craft meant nothing to him anymore. It was only a distraction, something that consumed time and kept him away from his townhouse, but the long hours couldn't cover what Morgan knew. His interest in surgery was gone.

Merrimac had tried to help until yesterday when they had argued in the operating room. In front of everyone, Ross told him that his ability to make precise decisions—the glue that made him a surgeon—was dissolving. As Morgan stood there and listened, he realized didn't care what Merrimac thought. He didn't care what any of them thought.

A towel absorbed the cooling water, and Morgan collapsed into his bed between the threadbare sateen sheets he had shared with Caroline. They hadn't been washed since. His housekeeper had tried, but Morgan said he'd fire her if she did, so they stayed where they were. He'd never wash them. Caroline's essence was still on the pillows.

He pressed the button on his bedside CD player, and the room came alive with her dulcet tones. Retrieved by the phone company, her twelve words were all he had. He pressed the button again and again, filling the room with her words until his tears ran dry. As he waited in the darkness, he prayed for salvation.

None ever came.

"You motherfucker," he uttered in a hopeless whisper.

———

Morgan stared at the paralyzed ceiling fan, his body immersed in the residue of sleepless perspiration and its dried stench. Another night of torment had slowly passed. He smelled her pillow again.

"I'm exhausted. Did we get any sleep?"

"Since when do you need sleep?" she asked back.

They made love again. Afterwards, Caroline's head lay deep in the pillows with her blues eyes gazing at his. She touched the tip of his nose and gave a tender smile.

"Had enough?" she asked.

Morgan had to move.

He had to get to the hospital.

He walked into his bathroom to piss.

"What the fuck? You fucking asshole!"

His fists tightened as his rage swelled.

"Motherfucking bastard!"

He stumbled to the kitchen. From the soaked newspaper, the smell of Scotch hovered above the depth of the sink. He vomited on it again then groped his way to the sofa and lay down—his consumed body in the fetal position, shaking with each tear.

"Cay…Oh, Cay…I miss you so…"

He was empty. Drained. Ruined. His soul sucked dry. The bitter aftertaste of the unfathomable horror drowned him day and night.

Morgan showered, dressed, and went to work.

———

His stomach growled. After performing in the OR to everyone's usual expectations, Morgan threw away his damp surgical cap, buttoned his white coat over his sweaty scrubs, and headed for the hospital cafeteria. Perhaps today he'd be able to eat and keep some food down.

Cautiously balancing his tray, he picked his path through the confusion of the cafeteria, hastening his steps to the table where he and Caroline had shared her lunch. Whenever he could, Morgan tried to eat there, often waiting nearby until it was empty. Sometimes he'd just sit and nibble on a cookie and drink some water. Other times he picked at whatever he had scooped onto his plate, taking in a few bites because he knew he had to. But mostly he stared at the empty chair, remembering the day they shared a simple turkey sandwich and his heart melted like an ice cube into the warm lagoon of her eyes.

A group of surgical residents eating in the next section nodded to him, and Morgan did his best to acknowledge them back. When he looked down at his tray, his appetite vanished immediately. He forced himself to take a bite of an apple. As he chewed, its sourness intensified his exasperation.

Morgan overheard the residents' conversation.

"You could argue that Christians used force to impose their beliefs during the Crusades..."

The speaker was one of Morgan's favorite students, an enthusiastic young man from the Middle East who was typically private about his faith. Morgan trained his ears to hear better what the man was saying, but a group of laughing nurses passing between blocked any chance of that until they moved on.

"Islam is a religion of peace—"

Another crowd of people walked between them, talking loudly.

"When the Towers—"

Morgan's stomach twisted.

"Some people in my country cheered."

Blood rushed to Morgan's face. The responsibility of being a senior surgeon could no longer restrain him. Reacting viscerally, he threw his tray toward the resident, jumped across the aisle, and lunged at him, yelling, "You goddamn son of a bitch!"

The surgeon's fingers squeezed the young man's neck as the institutional cafeteria chair tipped backward. Both crashed to the floor with Morgan on top. The resident almost lost consciousness on impact.

"How can you talk like that?" Purple in the face, Morgan's grip around the man's neck grew tighter. "Fucking Bin Laden—and you bastards—killed Cay!"

Many hands pulled Morgan off and forced him into a chair. Food and broken dishes were strewn everywhere.

"I loved her…" His head bowed into his hands as everyone in the cafeteria stared in shock.

The resident stood up shakily and looked at his soiled white coat. When Morgan struggled to move, the terrified man recoiled and quickly stepped away, never taking his eyes off him.

———

Ross Merrimac paged Morgan and demanded he appear immediately at his office. Once Morgan arrived, Merrimac shut the door. An administrative assistant stood in a corner, monitoring the conversation.

The chief of surgery suspended his friend from surgery and further barred him from entering the hospital. He had to.

"Morgan, you'll be lucky if that resident doesn't file assault charges…and maybe he should."

Merrimac didn't offer him a chair.

"He deserved it," Morgan seethed through his teeth. Pumping his fists, Morgan had no intention of backing down.

"No he didn't!" Merrimac answered in an unusually loud voice. "The other residents said he was *condemning* the terrorists. But that makes no difference, Dr. Morgan." He was getting testier and it showed. "You almost strangled that kid."

Merrimac glared. "You're a damn doctor!" His forehead blood vessels bulged.

"They killed Cay…"

"I know how much you loved Cay, but that house officer didn't kill her! You know that! Attacking an innocent man is your approach to anger management? Are you crazy?" Merrimac's hands moved in underscored synchrony with his words.

"Why did I believe you?" Merrimac said, finally catching his breath. "Should have gone with my gut, insisted you get help weeks ago. But oh no! Damn surgeons and their egos! They can control everything!"

He continued through clenched teeth. "God almighty! Do you have any idea how bad this is? We've invested a fortune in you and this transplant program! I frigging know the chairman of the board is going to call me and ask why we have a bigoted lunatic on staff! How will this affect the hospital? Worse yet, the program we're trying to build!"

Merrimac's hands shot in the air. "What about our patients? Christ almighty!" With a final sway of his arm, Ross Merrimac motioned him toward the door. "Unlike the way you treated that kid, you get a fair hearing! We'll notify you about the date. Now... get the hell out of my face!"

To sever contact, he grabbed a surgery journal, opened it to a dog-eared page and started reading.

Escorted to his office by hospital security guards, Morgan collected whatever he could, packed it in his briefcase, surrendered his identification badge, and changed into street clothes. They flanked him to his BMW.

———

During the two weeks before his hearing, Morgan became a vagrant entombed in his own home. Eating little, sleeping less, and infrequently shaving, he moved aimlessly from room to room, snatching restless catnaps and doing little else. Cocooned in his misery, there was no escape.

"You were stupid for jumping that kid..." he said. Flushing the toilet, he'd argued the point with himself for days. "Nah...fuckin' prick deserved it."

His words suddenly softened. "Cay...You would've scolded me, I know." He thought the worst. "Been ashamed...I'm sorry."

Childlike, he started crying into the carpet where he lay haunted without pity.

———

Their jog through Grant Park had taken them a mile out in the lake at the end of Navy Pier. A leisurely stroll back gave them time to let their conversation drift.

"Why 'Cay'?" he asked. Morgan had been curious many times.

"Daddy called me that since I was little." She laughed, her face glowing even without makeup. *"Who knows why fathers do what they do?"* A shrug suggested acceptance. *"It just stuck."*

"You said not everyone's allowed to use it."

A sudden breeze swayed her ponytail. *"My nickname's very personal to me,"* she replied, begging the next question.

"So when you called me from the airport, and I called you Cay...you didn't correct me. Why?"

Caroline stopped and smiled at him, then said the words that would stay in his heart forever. *"I only let people I love call me that."*

Morgan couldn't believe it. She had loved him from the beginning.

"Come on," she said, *"let's go get cleaned up. Saturday's a-wasting."*

With shampooed hair tucked under a towel and her bathrobe open in the immodest style he loved, she gathered their running clothes and headed for the washing machine. He went toward her.

"Cay..." he stammered, *"Caroline...I love you. Will you marry me?"*

An overt sigh followed.

"You're going to need to work on your timing, Dr. Morgan." Nonplussed, Caroline loaded the clothes in the washer. *"Every girl dreams about this moment...and you realize, of course..."* She measured the soap and softener in exact detail and started the cycle. *"You've just asked me to marry you while I'm doing your laundry? Regardless..."* Her eyes twinkled above a smile and she threw her arms around him. *"My answer is... yes!"*

"Then we need to go shopping," he said.

The Michigan Avenue jewelry stores consumed them that afternoon. When the salesperson handed Caroline a loupe and a large diamond, she became restrained and asked for a minute alone with Morgan.

"Wes," she told him, *"no big diamonds."*

"I can afford them," he replied.

"No," she said firmly. *"I'm not your second wife…"*

———

"Oh, Cay," Morgan wept into the carpet. "You never knew I bought the ring! You never knew I was coming to surprise you…"

How he loved the secret planning! Even though they had spent the entire weekend making love at his townhouse, Caroline never had an inkling what he was up to.

His phone rang. He listened through the answering machine.

"Dr. Morgan," the unemotional woman said, "this is a reminder that your disciplinary hearing is at one p.m. this afternoon. Please be prompt. Thank you. Good-bye."

She hung up.

"I have nothing left," came his exhausted whisper after the click. Finally fulfilled by Caroline's presence in his life, his world had become perfect—until it was destroyed.

"Nothing…"

He was on his knees.

"Oh, Cay…"

The anger had beaten him. Exhausted, his mind, body, and soul were ruined.

"I can't do anything…"

He fell to the floor, weeping into his forearm.

"Oh god, Morgan…you're so fucking weak!"

The tears soaked his skin.

"A spineless jellyfish!"

He rolled onto his back, sucking mucus from his nose to the back of his throat.

"Fuck," he uttered, trying to swallow the tenacious slime. "Fuck…"

He started coughing. Propping up his head and neck against the side of the sofa, his vision wandered tiredly around the room.

On the shelf beside the fireplace were his surgical textbooks. Every chapter covered a problem in the human body and the ways to operate on it—an instruction manual without wasted words.

"Split the muscle in the direction of..."

"Insert the trocar through...."

"Close the wound by..."

In time a surgeon would learn every page. Someday the instructions would flow to the hands and fingers unmarred by hesitancy or self-doubt.

"Get up!"

His inner voice began speaking, commanding him to reality. Physicians heard this voice throughout their careers. Whether lying in bed, driving, working—anywhere—it would surface without warning and persist without mercy, besieging its owner until it forced atonement for a mistake or oversight.

"Get the fuck up!"

Morgan heard the silent command intensify, overwhelming him with the same severity as it had when one of his babies died.

He cleared the back of his throat and swallowed the glob.

Morgan walked to look out the back window. The building's garage light pried open the gloom, revealing calm pools of rainwater, the thermometer barely above freezing.

"I'm going running," he said.

Unused for months, he put on his track suit and shoes. The pants were so large he had to tighten the waistband. The jacket's sleeves slid beyond his wrists. He stepped outside and pulled the door shut. Lumbering several hundred years toward the lakefront path, his muscles ached from the sudden jolt of exercise—a cruel reminder of his months of idleness. He halted at a stone and masonry ledge in the park where molasses-thick muck oozed through the cracks. As the damp mist invaded his bones, Morgan stared beyond the mud to the brown grass where the winter before Caroline had laid down in the soft snow and flapped her arms and legs to make angels. At her urging and without protest, he had joined her to do the same.

He could still hear her laughing.

Morgan continued south, his moist breaths dissipating the quicker he ran. He didn't realize he had been sprinting until he looked up and saw the closed drapes of Cay's empty condominium. He slowed, coming as close to the building as he could. Craning his neck he saw the checkerboard of windows climb to the sky until they converged at a vanishing point, then he looked toward the lake.

His soggy track suit provided no shield from the winter morning, but he wasn't cold. His muscles ached, but he didn't feel them. The anger and pain were gone. There was only clarity.

"You fucking bastard," he said coolly. "Time to fix this. You're history."

———

The stone faces around the giant ellipsoid table offered epitaphs to the absurdity of the hearing. They thought they knew the outcome, but Morgan had already reached the verdict.

With unctuous authority, each of them in sequence described, discussed, and commented while also watching for the adulating nods of their peers. Occasionally they would look at Morgan's fixed gaze, his motionless hands and fingers entwined.

Over his bifocals the senior medical officer said, "Dr. Morgan, what happened was inexcusable, even considering your personal circumstances. Your behavior has generated legal problems for the hospital." He glared, waiting for an apology. Bristling when none came, his eyes rolled, "Dr. Morgan, are you listening?"

"Yes."

He wasn't.

"Dr. Merrimac"—the officer motioned to him—"any comments to Dr. Morgan?"

Ross Merrimac looked at his friend and studied the ill-fitting sport coat and the shirt collar that had grown too loose. The haphazardly knotted necktie displayed an out-of-character inattention to detail.

"Wes…I know you hurt," he said. "Life is full of tragedy. Look at what you do for a living. We all feel for you."

Merrimac tried to connect through the unspoken yet understood emotions of their world, but for Morgan his voice was just an irritation.

"You know your temper's very short, and that makes you unsafe. We're in a high-risk profession. We *cannot* have physicians who don't control their actions."

Morgan nodded but was oblivious to the words. He was problem solving—a habit ingrained over the years. As he considered the first elements of the new task ahead, those surrounding him at the table could only appreciate vacuity in the surgeon.

The senior officer asked, "Dr. Morgan, do you have any response to Dr. Merrimac, or any of us, for that matter?"

"No."

Merrimac shook his head in disbelief. What had he missed? A man could be hurt, but a surgeon rarely cracked like this. Death happened, and life went on. He was watching his friend's entire career fall apart. During the forty-five-minute meeting, Morgan had spoken only a few words and none in his defense.

"Dr. Morgan, please step outside," the officer said. "We'll call you back when we're ready."

Standing impatiently by a window, looking at the hospital Caroline had built, Morgan continued planning. In time he was again seated, staring in the same indistinct manner as before.

"Dr. Morgan," said the senior operating officer, "this committee has discussed the circumstances of your actions and considered your tragedy." His voice had become an annoying distraction. "You will receive a six-month suspension from all clinical activities. During this time you're prohibited from entering this hospital for any reason. In June this committee will meet to consider your reinstatement. If for any reason you do not comply, your hospital privileges will be terminated."

"Fine." Morgan's head never moved.

Several pieces of paper slid toward him. "Please sign these. One acknowledges the terms of your suspension; the other speaks to a required psychiatric evaluation and whatever treatment necessary. Take the copies with you."

"Fine."

He was on his feet and opening the door, only turning to acknowledge Merrimac's voice.

"Wes, you take care. You can call me day or night."

Morgan nodded once.

Outside the building he ground the papers in his fist, tossing the crumbled wad in the first trash container he saw. The surgeon had no interest in a couch, pills, or shock treatments.

Deaf to a speeding ambulance, he entered the university library and saw several coeds laughing quietly at a table near the entrance.

"Do any of you have a pen and paper I could buy?" Morgan asked them.

"I've got this," one of the women giggled, holding up a pink legal pad and pen topped with a feather.

"That'll be just fine," said Morgan, giving her twenty dollars.

She looked surprised. "Anything else you'd like?" She smiled.

"No," said Morgan, not playing to her suggestion. "This is all I need. Thanks."

He walked to the stairwell, climbed several flights, and found a cubicle where he wouldn't be noticed. He hung his raincoat on a nearby chair, tugged loose his necktie, and sat down. Occasionally he used a computer terminal or went to another floor to retrieve information, but mostly he sat and wrote, organizing his thoughts until closing time.

SEVEN

January 2002

Ross Merrimac didn't know what to think. Morgan had to be upset after the hearing, but needed to understand Merrimac was only doing *his* job. Morgan wasn't one to hold a grudge—he just wasn't that way. When the messages on Morgan's phone went unanswered, Merrimac hoped his friend was simply taking a long vacation someplace like the Bahamas, lost in both the liquor and sunshine. Still, he worried about his star surgeon, so he left the hospital one wintry afternoon and drove to Morgan's home. If there were no answer, Merrimac would tape prewritten notes to his front and back doors.

He rang the doorbell and waited.

When the door opened, Morgan's trim beard made for a dramatic change in his appearance. Surgeons at the hospital weren't allowed to have beards because whiskers could fall into the sterile field, but Morgan wouldn't be back for several months, so it was okay for now—just different.

It seemed odd he was dressed in only a T-shirt, running shorts, and leather sandals, because it was fourteen degrees outside. Maybe he kept his place warm, but that warm?

Morgan remained in the doorway. He tugged the speaker buds from his ears while the wind blew on his bare legs. Annoyed he let Merrimac come inside.

"Got any coffee?" Ross asked, seeing the mugs scattered around the living room.

"Got no cream," Morgan responded without enthusiasm, heading for the kitchen. "Only sugar."

"No problem."

Merrimac studied the room. The awards, photographs, and bric-a-brac that lined the shelves and mantle were gone except for a book wrapped in white cotton. On the floor nearby was a cardboard box with a hand-drawn red heart on it. Numerous maps lay strewn on the dining room table. On the seat cushion of an armchair a phone book had slips of paper jutting from the yellow pages. There were pads of legal paper everywhere, each top sheet covered with handwriting and dog-eared pages beneath. The coffee table had a pile of travel books; Morgan's laptop computer sat nearby. Before Merrimac could see the website that was open, it switched to screen-saver mode.

The furniture, shoved close to the walls, created space for a weight bench.

"Whatever you're up to, you're doing what you do best: multitasking." Merrimac was beyond curious.

"Going through all my old shit," said Morgan flatly as he gave Merrimac the coffee. "It accumulates."

That was interesting too. Morgan wasn't known to be a pack rat.

"Mind if I sit down?" Merrimac asked.

"I'm really busy. But for a few minutes, I guess," said Morgan.

Moving farther into the room, Merrimac found the single chair that wasn't stacked with books. Morgan stood leaning against the mantle, his unambiguous posture broaching disinterest.

Pointing at the bare shelves, Merrimac had to ask. "Where'd all the things go?"

"Redecorating," Morgan replied.

A quick excuse.

"Not a bad thing."

Merrimac wasn't convinced. He saw a bath towel on the floor placed at a strange angle to the room's corners.

"See you're working out. Good for you!"

"Trying to," Morgan said.

"Nice beard, by the way."

"Thanks." Morgan hated the thing but was learning to live with it.

"Why did you grow it?"

"Running," Morgan said. "My scarf."

It sounded legitimate.

"How's your mom doing?"

Merrimac was working hard to get Morgan away from simple sentences.

"Lizzie fell again."

"Sorry to hear that."

Morgan shook his head. "She'll be gone soon."

Even when talking about his mother, Morgan seemed disconnected. He had every reason to be numb—all that he loved in life had met tragic ends.

"We did a transplant the other day. Kid's doing super!"

Ross hoped mentioning Morgan's passion might lift his funk.

"Glad to hear it."

"Spoken to the Pruitts lately?"

"After the memorial service, in Cay's condo."

That was the truth. Morgan adored Jon and Connie but he didn't want to talk to anyone. All distracting entropy had to be controlled and eventually would be.

"So you're doing okay?" Merrimac got to the purpose of his visit.

"Fine," said Morgan.

"Where I come from, saying *fine* too many times doesn't mean jack, brother. So…are you actually *fine?*"

Merrimac's push for a deeper answer yielded only, "Yes…fine means fine."

"I don't believe you," said Merrimac.

"Believe what you want," said Morgan.

"Come on, friend. Talk to me! I'm your brother!" Merrimac's frustration grew to concern. "Are you okay? Did you see the shrink yet?"

"I have an appointment next week." It was a lie but might get rid of him quicker.

"Well…let me know how it goes." Merrimac put his cup on a side table. "I miss you, man. We all do. We need you back. Abby hasn't been the same."

"Tell her not to worry. Tell everybody that."

Morgan's wristwatch beeped. Instinctively, Merrimac looked at his. It was 1:08 in the afternoon—an odd time to mark. Morgan gave him the unsubtle hint it was time to leave.

"Ross…I just need my space right now."

"Okay, Wes." Merrimac wasn't satisfied but could do little more. "Stay in touch, will you?" He gave his friend a hug but Morgan reciprocated only weakly. "I'll be going, then."

Morgan opened the door. "Thanks for checking on me."

One more try.

"Maybe dinner sometime?"

"Could work."

Wouldn't happen.

When the door shut, Morgan stared at the lock. "Fuck me," he said. "I don't need this." He walked over to the towel, stuck the earbuds back in, and sat down on his knees.

Several minutes later he opened his bedroom door.

"Glad this shit was in here." Stacks of cardboard boxes were everywhere. "Time to get rid of this crap asap."

He noted it on a yellow pad then went to the table covered with the maps. For an hour he measured distances, performed a series of calculations and added the information to specific months of a calendar.

Morgan looked out a window. Snowflakes drifted past. That was good. Nobody would be out in this weather. He put on his long underwear, running suit, and knit cap, spun the dial on his iPod to the next program he needed, grabbed his gloves, and went for an eight mile run.

Jon Pruitt called. Caroline's condominium had a sales contract.

"Wes..." he said, "You can walk through one last time, if you'd like...see if there's anything more you might want that you missed."

The sadness in Jon's drawn voice worsened Morgan's trepidation. The fresh confrontation with the grim reality that ruined his life would be unpleasant, but he'd go. There was one thing he'd forgotten and wanted even more now.

Morgan felt sick as he parked the BMW outside Lake Point Tower. He got out of his car.

"Good to see you again, Dr. Morgan. Are Mr. and Mrs. Pruitt doing better?" asked Robert. He'd been so kind and helpful, escorting them after a hug to Cay's condominium.

For an hour after struggling with what to take, the Pruitts and Morgan each had a full box. Connie used a marker to draw a red heart on Morgan's.

"Here's the key, sir." Robert handed it to him and said, "Would you like me to go with you?"

"I'll be all right...only take a minute."

Morgan knew neither was true but got into the elevator alone anyway.

His fingers shook when the key moved the tumblers. When he opened the door, the air was stale.

Her scent lingered everywhere.

Morgan went to the window and drew one set of drapes. Immediately he saw the forgotten smudges on the glass. They were Cay's fingerprints.

Morgan sighed. She was so excited when the Fourth of July fireworks exploded over Navy Pier. She pointed at each brilliant burst of color. Later that night when the moon rose, she saw her handiwork and said, *"I'll get those in the morning."*

She forgot.

Morgan walked into the kitchen, passing the remaining furniture lining the bare walls.

"Goddamn it!"

His fist slammed on the counter. With the vibration, a cabinet drawer slid open. It was empty.

"I loved your cooking!" His teeth ground. "God, how I loved your cooking…" With his eyes closed he inhaled deeply. "I can still smell every meal…"

Even late at night when he came from the hospital, Cay never seemed to mind feeding him.

"Forever bred in the soul of a Southern girl," she disclosed once with pride. *"Keeps you coming back, doesn't it?"*

Every step closer to her bedroom became a struggle.

Morgan paused outside Cay's office. Her drafting table was gone. So was the orchid terrarium he had given her for Christmas. He had searched throughout Chicago for the antique copper and glass container, and the blue orchids inside. They were wilted but still alive.

"They'll be fine," Jon assured Morgan, while watering the plants. *"I'm a pro with these,"* he said and took the terrarium to his car.

A slash of red on the floor caught Morgan's attention. He went over and picked up Cay's reading glasses. They had been stepped on.

"You were so irritated when you wore them to bed."

"You never saw these," Cay had said as they vanished from her face.

The few feet into her bedroom stretched for miles. Morgan finally lay down on the bare mattress and gently rubbed his fingers back and forth where her body slept.

"Thanks for loving me," he said to where her head once rested.

For several minutes the tears flowed.

Morgan rolled to the floor and groped under the bed until he touched the braided fibers of Caroline's climbing rope. As he carried it back to the living room, his watch beeped.

He turned on his iPod and stared east through the window toward the lake's gray horizon. Standing on his tiptoes, he crammed his face against the glass, trying to look straight down. He held up the rope, gripped its coiled loops with both hands, and tugged hard. He looked east again.

"Motherfucking asshole," he said.

He closed the drapes and went to his car.

He'd never go back in there again.

———

Lizzie Morgan died three weeks later. She'd been in her facility's hospice unit after the recent fall. When Morgan received the call, he went and held her hand for an hour as her breathing slowed, then kissed her forehead.

"You're a great mom," he said as she slipped away.

He would do as she asked and donate her body for medical research. Years before, she had made him promise, despite his protest.

"Wes, what good am I to others if I'm in a box?"

She thought what she said was funny.

Morgan thanked the staff then found a private room and called his attorney. Ridding himself of another detail, Morgan had transferred executor powers to the lawyer at the first of the year.

"Whatever's left goes to her nursing home," Morgan reminded him.

"Will do," the man said. "I'll send your thank-you note when the time comes."

Morgan said his final good-bye and went outside to stand in the bright January sun. He put on his sunglasses and waited for the bank clock across the street to display the temperature.

-9 °F.

Morgan looked high in the crystal sky.

"Mom..." he said quietly, "I hope I don't...disappoint you." His teeth rubbed over his lips. "Say hi to Cay. Tell her I love her very much and...I'm sorry."

He made another phone call and went to his car. They'd be waiting for him at the DuPage County airport in an hour.

———

The air was smooth when the plane leveled off at nine thousand feet. Morgan was oblivious, lost in his thoughts.

With mom gone, I can move on it now...

His jump instructor opened the fuselage door. Morgan didn't hear or feel the rushing air.

Tapping her fingers on his helmet, his jump instructor shouted, "Hey...you in there?"

"Sorry. Thinking about things."

"Start thinking about this, okay? First solo isn't child's play!"

Counting his heartbeats, he was amazed. Each time he jumped, the rate decreased more.

"Get ready!"

The cold wind was fierce.

"Really want to do this?" she yelled. "Wind chill's makes it thirty below out there!"

"Spring weather!" Morgan shouted. He made certain his face mask covered his nose then gave a thumbs-up.

"Now remember...pulling earlier is better than later!" his instructor shouted back. "But never forget three thousand feet is a hard floor! Don't wait a second..."

Morgan jumped. He'd pull when he was ready.

EIGHT

March 2002

"Will they ever stop bothering me?" Morgan grunted, cradling the bar in the weight bench uprights. Glistening in sweat after finishing his third set of ten reps, he grabbed a towel to wipe his face.

"I'm coming!" he shouted when the doorbell rang another time.

Ross Merrimac invited himself in when Morgan opened the door. "Wes, time to talk," he said.

Morgan wiped his face with the same towel he had used for weeks. "What do you want?"

No pleasant banalities were exchanged.

"You know what it's about."

"I said I'd see the shrink," Morgan said. "I've been busy."

"For three months?" asked Merrimac.

"So?"

"You're running out of time! Plan on abandoning your career?" Merrimac's voice rose.

Morgan was silent.

Merrimac looked around the room. There were now barbells and weights scattered everywhere. The bookshelves were still empty—that hadn't changed.

"Are you trying out for the Olympics?" Merrimac asked.

"I'm able to press over two twenty-five now."

"I don't care! You're supposed to be in therapy! Is this"—Merrimac's arm swept over the living room—"the prescribed treatment?"

"Ross, I don't need you bitching me out. I've got things going on I need to take care of."

"Like what, pray tell? Is this going to be your new normal? What are you planning on doing...coming back to work looking like a buffed Hippocrates?"

"Enough!" Morgan said.

Merrimac could tell by looking at his friend's face that his attempt to be humorous backfired.

"I told you I'd see the psychiatrist, and I will."

Both men were losing their patience.

"Look, Wes," said Merrimac, "I know Caroline's death...this whole thing's pissed you off. It's pissed me off. In fact, it's pissed everybody off. It's going take time."

He put his hand on Morgan's shoulder. The muscles were thick from some serious physical training. "Will you do it for your friend... please? If you need longer, take it! You can teach when you come back. But please get help."

"Fine."

"You know what I've said before about that..."

"Ross! It's time to go! I said I'd take care of it. I can look out for myself."

Merrimac debated saying more but held back. There was nothing he could do. The demise of a successful physician's career was a terrible thing to watch. Merrimac wanted to Baker Act him, lock him up in the psych ward and get his brain fixed, but Morgan didn't sound suicidal. He was acting weird but not crazy. Merrimac would have to wait. That would be difficult. Wes was his friend.

"Can I check in with you maybe in a week?"

"I'll be on it by then."

"Good. I'll call you."

Morgan locked the door.

"One week. Shit..."

No more procrastination! He got his cell phone and called his attorney.

"Sell the townhouse," Morgan told him. "Take the best offer you get within sixty days. I'll send you the papers this afternoon."

The man couldn't talk him out of it.

"I'm also going to be sending you a cashier's check in a few days. Please hold it in your trust account."

"Wes…why are you doing this? Want to come in and talk for a while? Maybe have dinner and drinks?"

"I'm okay. Just simplifying. Life's short. Got things I need to do."

"I'll call you when the town—"

"No, *I'll* call you," Morgan replied. "Don't fret. If you need to get me, best to drop me a note." He gave him a PO Box number and address.

"Wes…I know you're not crazy."

"No, I'm not…just pissed."

———

Morgan waited in line at the post office to mail the documents. When the clerk called for the next customer, he didn't realize quickly enough she was speaking to him and a voice behind said loudly, "Move, goatfuck."

Morgan smiled. The insult was trivial, but a milestone nonetheless. His appearance was becoming more convincing.

His watch beeped and he glanced at it, thankful for the reminder. Pausing five times a day took effort, but eventually it would be ingrained in his head, as would everything else. Finishing with the clerk, he put his earbuds in, walked back to his car, and drove home.

He ran north that afternoon to Rogers Park. As he came back along the lake, he kept his eyes trained on the distant black silhouette of Lake Point Towers. He stopped once, staring east for several minutes, then continued running, his pace quickening until it was a near sprint. He wasn't tired, wasn't out of breath. He just kept going and thinking until he got to Diversey Harbor. He veered off the lakefront trail and went under the bridge, where he made his last cell phone call.

"I'll take the apartment. See you tomorrow at nine."

He dropped the cell phone into the dark water. The possibility of being tracked through it eliminated, he'd use a prepaid phone card to contact others, and only when necessary.

The next morning Morgan signed a contract for a tired third-floor studio in a Rogers Park walkup. He paid cash, adding a hefty security deposit that would make the building manager forget about him. Utilities were included, isolating him more. The L trains rattled the sash windows incessantly, but drapes bought from Goodwill would buffer some of the noise. A canvas cot went in a corner, while a metal chair and two long folding tables took up most of the room. Several cheap lamps would add light, and an old television would give him the news he needed while he ate microwaved food. His weights arrived next, then he brought the boxes of CDs, books, maps, and some clothes from his car.

Everything else that remained in the townhouse was now gratuitous; serving no purpose, so he left it all where is was—except for the box with Connie's red heart. He could never part with that. He placed it in the BMW's trunk next to the new carbon fiber bicycle that would provide additional exercise as he rode it throughout the city. He could dart everywhere, using alleys and one-way streets to allay anyone who might start looking for him.

Morgan's world was slowly becoming controlled.

NINE

April 2002

In April Morgan drove the BMW to the panhandle of Texas and spent three weeks on a ranch learning everything he could about sheep and goats. The Slavic owner was delighted to have a sturdy guest who was not only willing to pay him generously but also to help from dawn till dark with the chores. In return, when Morgan told the rancher he had inherited a farm that also included pigs, the man made certain Morgan learned about them too.

They were vile beasts, but worse were the sheep and goats, crapping wherever they walked. At every dinner the rancher's wife served cheese from both as a side dish. Morgan had always tried to avoid the putrid muck in restaurants, and after spending days with the animals it tasted even worse, but he would never insult his hosts.

"Delicious," he said, raising his plate to welcome more.

When his time at the ranch concluded, Morgan drove to Houston for several days. At every rest stop on the interstate, he'd go for a thirty-minute sprint through the sagebrush, dodging the occasional rattlesnake. Afterwards, he would wipe the sweat off with a damp towel, put on a dry T-shirt and get back in his car. He always sat on a plastic tarp with a CD playing and the cruise control on. He didn't want to get pulled over by state troopers for speeding. That would change everything.

Morgan checked in with his attorney from a campground payphone outside Houston.

"Your place sold," the lawyer said. "They don't want the furniture."

"Tell the buyers I'll take care of that by mid-week."

Morgan made a note.

"So you know, when the sale finalizes, you're total cash is going to be a little under five million."

"Take a fair fee," said Morgan.

"I'm not liking this," said his attorney.

"Don't worry," Morgan replied. "Just hold the money in your trust. After I get settled, you'll hear from me."

"Do *you* have enough for now?" the lawyer asked.

"Plenty," Morgan said.

"*When* again am I supposed to mail your letter to Dr. Merrimac?"

"Late May, about five weeks."

"You know, Wes…this is bothering me."

"I've done nothing but simplify my life," said Morgan. "I'm going to take a long vacation."

"And throw away your career in the process."

Morgan said, "Call it a sabbatical."

"I still don't like this," his attorney said again, referring to not only his client's recent decisions but also his cagy behavior.

Morgan replied, "The expression from your generation was, I think, *finding yourself.* That's what I'm doing."

"Okay," he conceded. The attorney had never lost an oral argument until he butted heads with this surgeon. "Before you go, I've got one more thing."

"Shoot," said Morgan.

"Jane Bonwitt called."

Morgan released a loud sigh. The woman was possessed!

"I told her to send you a letter and gave her your PO Box."

"Good," said Morgan.

"Wes…one more time, I—"

"Don't." Morgan didn't wait. "Good-bye."

———

Morgan arranged for Goodwill to remove everything in the townhouse. While he waited, he wandered in the rooms layered with dust, repressing each memory of the place that tried to distract him.

The doorbell rang. When the four men entered, they shook their heads in disbelief.

"Please get all this out of here," Morgan requested, "and no receipt is necessary."

"Man! Positive about that?" asked the supervisor. "No help from Uncle Sam?"

Morgan shook his head.

Soon only his bedroom furniture remained. He watched as they dismantled the bed, and finally it was gone from his life. One man opened a bureau drawer and found a silver picture frame. Morgan stared at their photograph from the Art Institute. He had forgotten to take it with him.

"Beautiful," said the man. "She yours?"

Morgan stared at Cay's exquisite face. It was impossible to imagine she was gone. His anger surged, but he calmed himself instantly and said, "Yes...once."

"She loved you, Wes." The voice was Janie's. "More than you'll ever know."

Shit!

The woman had to have been patrolling the neighborhood and saw the truck. She gave him a big hug before studying his square physique and strange hair. After rolling it between her fingers, she touched his beard.

He knew she would ask, so he said in a subdued voice, "I'm taking time off, nothing more." Morgan wasn't interested in casual conversation. "Getting my life back together."

"Where are you going?" she asked. Tears were imminent.

He wouldn't tell her, so the interrogation continued. Morgan picked up the silver-framed photograph and stuck it under his arm.

"I'm so sorry, Wes," sniffed Janie.

His inert hug offered no consolation to her.

"Don't worry about me," he said, scanning the space that once brought him so much happiness. He handed her the key. "Lock it up when they're done. Good-bye, Janie."

He went to his car and placed the box on the passenger's seat. Confused, she followed, trying to get him to lower the window, but Morgan ignored her. He had to clear his head. As he drove away he kept looking at the picture on the seat where Cay had sat and laughed, teased him, and said she loved him. At a stoplight, he lifted the photograph to gaze at the lips he would never kiss again. His anger fell as he looked in the rearview mirror.

"Morgan," he said, "get control. Pay attention!"

Janie's black Mercedes was following him. She was making no effort to conceal her intent.

"I'm taking you to O'Hare," he said. Driving through the airport's huge parking garage would loose her. Finally his world would be controlled, and he could work without interruption.

TEN

Moab, Utah June 2002

From the ground the fissures looked like smooth tears in cardboard—perceptible evidence of the power that ripped apart the Wingate sandstone. Inches from his nose, however, the rock had deviations that became rungs of a ladder. Some pock marks could take just one finger or toe, while others, several digits more. Sometimes a vertical slice was wide enough for one foot or hand to jam in alone. Others swallowed Morgan's entire body. Every hole, ledge, and gap owned a name, but to seasoned climbers they were simply called *cracks* and were used to lift a body higher, often one inch at a time.

Heated by the sunlight, updrafts enveloped his face as wind gusts whistled through the gashes, creating shrill howls.

"Man…if those were organ pipes…" The endorphins caused his mind to drift. "They'd need tuning…"

Morgan looked at his left index fingertip. It was bleeding again.

In the beginning he had taped his fingers, but eventually he ignored the red ooze, letting the lacerations callus to mittens—lone protection for what once passed delicate suture through tiny hearts.

"Fuck it," he said.

He was honed, leading the route to the top.

The maws of the monolith swallowed another chock, and the cam clicked open. He clipped a roped carabineer to it and tugged. The metal hook would hold if he lost contact, restraining six thousand pounds of tension in a hundred-foot fall. The problem was he was over a hundred sixty feet up. If his climbing instructor didn't belay him quickly enough, his accelerating body would break the rope. Earlier in the week, after a sudden sneeze, Morgan got an abrupt taste of what would happen. His foot lost a jam and he blew out fifteen feet of rope plus stretch before he was belayed. Over the seconds banging against the stone, he laughed at the distant ground until the swinging slowed.

"Dude," the man yelled directly to his face. *"That'll learn you! Hold that shit in!"*

"No kidding...Really?" Morgan said as he smiled back, clawed hands and toes into the nearest cracks, and began again. But he hurt like hell that night.

On a narrow ledge, Morgan paused before his final push to the rim. Barely two inches wide, it still offered welcome relief from gravity.

He looked at his BMW far below then studied the Utah horizon.

"Incredible..." he said.

How things had changed! He marveled at his ability to adapt. Altitude now bored him, and climbing was just vertical walking—only frustratingly slow. The endorphins surged again when the polyethylene rope tickled his calf.

"Cay...you'd be proud of me," he said to the vastness. He remembered how she laughed the cold Saturday they went to her health club and she watched him slip off every foothold on the rock-climbing wall.

But Caroline wasn't there to praise him. She wasn't there at all. Ten months had passed since he talked to her, and kissed her, and they'd made love. Not a second lapsed when he didn't long to hold her. He would never forget. How could he? Her memory floated on the deep water of his conviction.

"You motherfucker." He closed his eyes to let his anger escape.

Restraint took focus and discipline, but complete subjugation still eluded him. That couldn't happen much longer. His survival depended on absolute control. Any mistake would be lethal.

"Damn you!" his instructor shouted.

"Sorry, Tony," Morgan answered back. "Enjoying the view."

"You're going to pump out!" Tony was irritated, reminding him of the danger. Muscle fatigue happened quickly late in a climb.

Move your ass!

Morgan's internal command was severe—plus he had to piss. Some climbers just let it drip, but his bladder would hold. The end was minutes above, and the grip strength in his arms was dwindling.

The steep rock face separated, and the large crack flattened into a groove. Swinging his legs over the rim, Morgan stood up, dropped his harness, and gave a grim smile while he looked at the void. His assault of Coyne Crack at Indian Creek ended his climbing instruction.

There was no time for fanfare. Already impatient, Morgan wanted to get off the top and leave. He needed to. The hours seemed to shrink as the demands between his physical training competed with his studying, until the only thing he could sacrifice was sleep. That didn't bother him. Ritalin ordered from Canada with his medical license allowed him compact his activities into a tightly organized schedule. Day or night he could be outdoors exercising, doing research at home or the library, or working with language tutors. A gym in Wicker Park had boxing lessons at midnight. The men who trained there were tough. Morgan always returned home bruised, but he got used to it. He never tired.

Study and train.

Study and pain.

His instructor joined him at the top.

"You beat up those rocks good." The trident tattoo on the man's arm twisted as they shook hands. "So, Bill, what you think of it?" he asked.

When Morgan didn't respond, the man said again, "Bill, ya hear me?"

"Sorry," Morgan answered. It wasn't the first time he didn't immediately respond to his fictitious name. "Tame, I guess," Morgan said.

Together they stared at the distant red rock towers.

"Want to grab a beer when we get down? I know a great country bar about five miles from the base," said Tony.

"I'm not a very social person," replied Morgan.

"It's something more than that, I can tell," said Tony. "You're dialed into some serious shit."

Morgan grew concerned. Did this man know more about him then he thought? Hanging out with Tony for a while was probably a good idea.

———

Tony was intrigued when Morgan ordered a Coke, but he said nothing.

"So you think climbing that rock was…you said…*tame?*" Tony asked. "That's one of the toughest stones out there."

"Heights don't bother me," Morgan shrugged.

"Me neither. I jumped a lot in the navy," said Tony. "Once you HALO through a thousand feet a couple of times before pulling, you don't much think about heights anymore."

"I know," said Morgan. "Did it my first solo."

"Shit…A thousand feet? Problem with your primary chute?"

"No," said Morgan, "I just waited."

"Really." The guy had balls—especially because it was intentional. "If anything fucks up that low…man…you splat! And there's a mess to clean up. I've seen it." He scratched his bald scalp, trying not to amplify his curiosity. "So why'd you do that?"

"To see if I was afraid," said Morgan.

"Were you?"

Tony's ongoing assessment already told him the answer.

"I wasn't."

Tony looked at Morgan. He'd been his strongest student, enthusiastic in a calculating way, climbing hard and fast every day to the point of almost terminal fatigue. His persistent confrontation with death had a purpose, but what that was Tony didn't know.

The waitress returned, placing two frosty glasses on the table and stooping over in the process, revealing to Morgan even more cleavage. He glanced only briefly.

"Hot-looking babe," Tony said. "I believe she's sending you an invite."

"Flattered," replied Morgan, draining half the Coke. "Not interested."

"Got a woman?"

"Did," answered Morgan.

Tony cracked open another shell, ate the peanut, and tossed the hull to the floor. "I've held your life in my hands for two weeks, so want to talk about it?"

"My own personal hell."

"We've all been there," said Tony, gaining a little more insight into Morgan's despondency. "Have a picture?"

Morgan pulled one from his wallet. Every time he saw Cay's face his stomach churned.

Tony whistled. "God...she's gorgeous! Gonna marry her?"

"That was the plan."

"Tell me what happened. She's just too fuckin' beautiful to run away from. Another man?"

"No," Morgan said. "She's dead."

"What the fuck! How?"

"9/11..."

"You've got to be kidding!" Tony shouted. "You're fucking kidding me!"

"No. North Tower...I was on the street...Watched it all."

"Oh, you sorry bastard!" Tony moved closer to Morgan and put his arm around his shoulder. "My friend...I'm so fucking sorry! Ought to nuke a bunch of those fuckers!"

Morgan took the rubber band out of his hair and shook his head. His shoulder-length strands were stringy from the dust. He felt the pit inside grow larger.

"You got every right to feel fucked over," said Tony.

Morgan nodded dolefully. "I was in love with her."

Tony caught the waitress's attention. Wanting to hear more, he ordered a pizza.

"No sausage on my half please," Morgan added.

When she left, Tony said, "So…Bill…by climbing rocks and jumping out of airplanes…you think that brings you closer to your woman?"

"No. I'm learning to control…my fear…of everything."

"Hmm," said Tony. "You know, I was a SEAL. The training was brutal…more like terrifying…but I got immune." He grinned. "After that I realized…I can do anything."

"That's the plan," said Morgan.

"When I met you, your face looked beaten up, like you'd been fighting, maybe trying to learn how anyway."

"Yeah…boxing."

"What else you been doing these last couple of months?"

"Nothing."

"Not believing that." Tony shook his head and tipped back in his chair. "So far your menu's only seems full of some God-fearing shit."

"Something to do."

"Bill, Navy SEALs are a family," Tony began. "Brothers who'd rather take a bullet for a buddy than live without him. Know what I mean? We don't talk about it, but there's absolute trust among us. You can't imagine the secrets I neither could nor *ever would* share."

The pizza arrived. Morgan took a piece and started chewing as his watch beeped.

"Odd time to note," Tony observed, looking out the window at the sun before taking his own slice of piece. "My gut tells me deep inside you're principled. Clearly, you've got fuckin' discipline." His eyebrows rose. "You're angry as hell…but it's not focused enough."

Morgan looked at Tony dead in the eyes. "I want you to know… my name's not *Bill*," he said.

"Kind of guessed that," Tony grinned, taking a bite.

"*Wes*," Morgan said.

"Probably *Wesley*," replied Tony. "I can see why you shortened it."

"Easier to spell too."

"So…Wes…this is fun. Like I'm having a meal with two people, maybe more." He grinned. "What sort of work do you do?"

"I'm an architect," replied Morgan.

"I don't think so." Tony's scraggy fingertips pill rolled. "Hands don't lie," he confided. "The way you plug them into nubbins and the like...Too dexterous. They're ambitious, like you are—but not cocky. There's another thing."

"I know you're going to tell me," said Morgan.

"Architects your age don't have your money. But doctors do... surgeons in particular. I'm still pondering what kind."

"Pediatric heart surgery."

"So you want to ruin million-dollar hands crack climbing why?"

"That life is gone," said Morgan. "Working on a different career."

Tony looked out the window while Morgan watched him drain the last of his beer, sucking on the bottle as if he was hoping to find more hidden inside. Finally convinced it was empty, his fingernail picked at the paper label.

"Let me tell you, my friend. The way you're going about it isn't going to get you there."

Morgan stared silently.

"I've trained people to do some interesting shit." Tony held the rest of his words and chewed his tongue for a moment, then said, "Got time for another internship?"

"Last one took a year," said Morgan. "I survived it."

"Then this would be a cakewalk," he smirked. "Not—"

"I'll pay you well," Morgan offered.

"Who said anything about money? I'm on a pension." Tony spun the empty bottle on the table. "Maybe a gratuitous gift now and then might be a pleasant surprise."

"For expenses, of course," added Morgan.

"I'm never going to ask what you're doing...but I've a damn good idea what it is. I sure as hell just found out the *why* part." The navy SEAL smiled. "I'll say this once—what you're thinkin' about is really stupid."

"I was in love with her."

"Then, Doctor...in one year..." Tony came forward in his chair and firmly took Morgan's hands. "I'll make you the architect you need to be."

ELEVEN

September 2002

"Wes...we're square on the pickup location?" asked Tony. His truck was idling on the shoulder of the road west of Tucson at the edge of the Sonoran desert.

"Got my trusty sextant right here with me." Morgan held up his thumb and index finger wide. "Azimuth and declination calibrated to one degree of arc."

"Smart ass," Tony replied. "But you'd better be damn accurate, because if you aren't I won't find you until the buzzards circle."

"Maybe I'll play dead so I can roast one," Morgan replied.

"They taste like chicken, you know." Tony smiled then held out his Sig Sauer. "Hey. Want to take my piece? Two-legged coyotes portaging across the border don't like to be seen."

"No, señor." The Arizona sun was getting hot. "Besides...what the hell have I been paying you for these months? So I can cheat?" Morgan barely grinned. "No damn sport in that. And I've been shooting your toys for weeks and am sick of cleaning them." He patted his knife. "This'll do me just fine."

Tony pulled an icy beer from a cooler and laughed. "Cold one to start the journey?"

Morgan shook his head slightly.

"Consider it medicinal."

"Don't tempt me, infidel!" Morgan picked up his canteen of water and adjusted his hat. "I'm just going for a hike."

"That's the spirit," replied Tony.

"Got my iPod…" Morgan twirled his walking stick in his fingers. "What more could a nomad want?"

"Well, Wes, I could think of a few things more to take for pleasure—like a woman, maybe, or—"

"Not for me." Morgan pointed at the desolate horizon. "Time's wasting. See you in a week," he said, and he started walking west toward Yuma.

He had few provisions but wasn't concerned. Water was everywhere, and he knew how to find it. There were things to eat too—under rocks, in the dry arroyos, or scurrying on the ground. At night the desert floor would be his mattress and the stars his blanket. He was grateful for the solitude—and time to let his thoughts drift to Caroline. He fought to control the memories. As much as he hated it, he had to blot her out of his brain. Distractions might provide visible proof that he wasn't what he said he was.

"Tony…you've helped a lot," Morgan said quietly to the desert.

It was as though he had opened Morgan's head and impregnated his brain with abilities he'd never imagined existed. Even more profound, Tony had taught him how the same intuition he used while operating— his sixth sense of sharpened awareness at the surgical field—could be expanded with his other senses to more broadly analyze and understand his surroundings and dissect what might be erroneous or, as Tony said more than once, just plain strange. Using mnemonics like he had in medical school, to remember things like the cranial nerves and other anatomic structures, whenever Morgan rode his bicycle, he practiced, memorizing the transient ingredients of his surroundings—where cars were parked, the direction and distance of unexpected sounds, and the ebb and flow of pedestrians. Each time he passed the same location, he worked to recall what had been there in the past and how things had changed. After months of practice, Morgan learned how to absorb such information without even realizing it, the mental exercises becoming a game of analytical solitaire.

His watch beeped.

He took his shoes off, turned around to face east, and knelt to say the prayers. When finished, he dusted off his pants and took a sip of water. Empowered, he continued his trek.

A dome of blackness descended, and the stars became close enough to touch—offering themselves to guide him. He located the constellation Cassiopeia and drew an imaginary line to the North Star.

"Hello there, Polaris," he said and turned his body so he faced west.

His right arm rose until his closed fist hid the star, then he estimated the angle above the shoulder. He looked at his watch, converted the hour and minutes to Universal time, then looked at Andromeda suspended in the Southeast horizon.

Latitude and longitude—they were crude measurements, but all he would need.

"Tony, that's amazing," he said. "In position and on schedule."

He walked in the calm for several more hours until finally lying down on the hard-packed ground to rest.

———

In the predawn light, Morgan opened his eyes and realized he was not alone. Another predator had joined him. Both of them were motionless, except one produced an occasional sizzle.

"Come here," Morgan whispered into its glowing eyes.

The split tongue flicked and retracted.

"Closer," he taunted the snake. "Don't be afraid."

Inches away, he watched its nostrils flair as the thick rattlesnake coiled tighter.

"I'm not going to ask again," Morgan said.

Before the reptile could spring, the knife arched over and sliced off its head. The long trunk convulsed for almost a minute before falling still.

Skinned and filleted, Morgan cooked the meat in sage smoke. The knife brought another piece to his mouth.

"Tell the chef it needs pepper," he belched.

Tony took Morgan to his motel so he could shower. His student was very sunburned and a few pounds slighter but otherwise no worse for wear.

"Peaceful out there, isn't it?" he asked Morgan while he dried off.

"Seducing," he answered.

"You said you're going to visit the desert again next summer," Tony said.

"I can't wait."

He dropped Morgan at his car, which they'd left at the Tucson airport.

"When you return this winter, I've got some cold-weather playtime in store for you. Don't bring anything along."

"Don't have much *to* bring," Morgan responded.

"Remember: in Chicago keep your head low. Blend in," Tony admonished him. "My buddy knows you'll be calling him. Isaac will teach you what you also need to know." He smiled.

Morgan nodded and opened the door of Tony's pickup truck.

"There's another thing," the SEAL said. "Your Arabic…needs more work. Your inflections wander."

"Not an easy language," confided Morgan.

"Go to some services. That'll help."

Morgan had attended local mosques whenever he was in Chicago. Most congregations welcomed him openly, only a few were wary.

"Been doing that," said Morgan. "But thanks for the critique, I'll work on it."

The men shook hands.

"See you in two months," said Tony.

The BMW motor turned over.

The nonstop drive east to Chicago was once again grueling but productive. The highway became another classroom. Every second possible he would play CDs to refresh his knowledge. Hours and hours of concentration passed the time, interrupted only by the thirty-minute runs. Then he was home—whatever that meant.

Morgan drove the BMW into the gated storage locker. After Janie followed him that day, he took no chance of having the BMW seen. It came out from hiding only when necessary—and that was rare.

Opening the trunk, he placed the black ballistic nylon backpack on the cement and pulled his bicycle off the ceiling hook. Satisfied the tire pressure was okay, he slung the pack on his back and scanned the outside perimeter before pulling down and locking the roll-top door. Confident he wasn't observed, he rode toward the Rogers Park apartment. After a brief rest, he called Tony's friend. Morgan would meet him the next day at a private gym on the north side.

———

"Krav Maga is…" Isaac said, and hit Morgan in the gut.

Morgan buckled to the floor. Isaac helped him to his feet.

"That's a polite…" Morgan coughed, trying to breathe. "Introduction."

"As I was saying…" Isaac's fist hit Morgan's chest and he fell backward to the padded wall. He had only a moment before the sole of Isaac's foot smacked next to his ear. "Perhaps I'm not making myself—"

Morgan's fist came toward Isaac's face but was brushed away with a sweep of his arm while Isaac's other hand grabbed Morgan and pulled his body close.

"KM is the art of overcoming your opponent with natural, minimal movements, using anything available as a weapon," Isaac said.

Morgan sensed only tranquility in the man as his other hand rose and grabbed Morgan's throat gently.

"See," he said, "you were listening again…not acting. In my world, you're already dead."

Isaac's grips released.

"A human needs two seconds to process and react to external stimuli. Think how far a car travels at sixty miles per hour."

"Maybe...ninety feet," said Morgan wondering where he'd be smacked next.

"*Two seconds* is a very safe distance...if you use it to your advantage," Isaac reiterated. "Proximity is irrelevant. It's *time*. If *you* act first, *you* control what happens next...the knife, the bullet...your fist...your escape. Time becomes *your* tool—your *weapon*. So...give; *never* receive."

The unassuming middle-aged man offered a handshake. Morgan shook his head. Both men smiled in unison.

"Ah! Good! You *are* a quick study," said Isaac. "See...you're not dead."

"Marginally reassuring."

"Street-fighting choreography." Isaac's outstretched hand remained. "Now...shake."

It was no trick this time. His handshake was sincere.

"I know Tony would have mentioned the bond of trust. The same goes for you and me. That's how we work."

Morgan's whole body still smarted from the formal introduction.

"When we're done, you will become a machine that moves with deadly precision. Lesson two is tomorrow. Here. Same time," said Isaac. "By way of fair warning...cut off that little pony tail of yours. Or I'll use it to break your neck."

———

On a cold Sunday in October, Morgan ran the Chicago Marathon. He hadn't registered—he wouldn't have, of course—but he still planned to run the entire twenty-six miles. Morgan's grueling apprenticeship was no different from becoming a surgeon, consuming every second he lived. Maximizing his stamina remained of paramount importance, and north of the Mason-Dixon nobody would pay attention to a Middle Eastern-looking man inside a crowd of runners.

In the early morning, he rode the L downtown and waited several hundred yards upstream from where the marathon would start, joining the bulge of runners after the sprinters pulled ahead.

Until the final miles, Morgan held a determined pace. When Lake Point Tower loomed in the distance, his tempo quickened and he dashed forward of the pack. Morgan saw a local TV reporter direct her camera operator at him, so he covered his face and peeled into the crowd of cheering bystanders to slip away.

———

"Queenie, did you see that?" Ross Merrimac sprang to his feet from his easy chair.

"See what? I'm cooking dinner."

"I think I just saw Wes on TV," he said.

"Do tell…" Shandra came out from the kitchen. "Where?"

"I was watching the news…and I saw him…running in the marathon." He scratched his head. "Least I think it could have been him. His body was muscled and his skin was really dark."

"What? You don't think black people run marathons?"

"No! It was Wes! I saw him!"

"Why do you think he'd show up at the marathon? You don't drop out of touch with everyone just to train. You didn't have a margarita, did you?"

Shandra hadn't smelled any liquor on his breath, but she knew he snuck one now and then. And when she found out, she chastised him.

"No, Queenie, I haven't been drinking," Merrimac said with disgust, becoming sick to his stomach as he again relived Morgan's disappearance.

It had been five months since Morgan's resignation letter arrived, and the last time Merrimac had heard anything. The surgeon's departure had created serious havoc for the transplant service—a predicament Merrimac was resolving. Nevertheless, he still worried about his friend. Morgan had seemingly vanished, yet today he showed up running the Chicago Marathon? That wasn't right.

Shandra came to his side while her husband changed channels. "You said his townhouse was empty months ago…"

"Maybe we'll see him again on another replay," Merrimac said, only half listening.

"You could check with the marathon people," his wife suggested.

"Good idea," Merrimac said while scrolling through the channels. Until now he had held out hope that Morgan had disappeared to get the help he needed. But seeing him on TV made Merrimac realize he had rationalized the months away.

He called the race organizers on Monday. When Morgan's name wasn't listed, Merrimac went to the TV station. After reviewing the raw footage several times, the technician printed out the best image, and Merrimac took it to the local police precinct.

"You say you haven't talked to him in months...and now all you got is this picture?" said the detective, eyeing the image and shaking his head. "Did you...like...talk to his family? That'd be simple enough, don't you think? I mean, you don't need a detective to tell you that."

"His only family was his mother, and she died at the beginning of the year."

"That's some sorry shit probably going' on here, Doc." The man leaned back in his chair, pulled out a pack of cigarettes, and bumped one up before looking at the physician sitting across the desk. "Do you mind?"

"Go right ahead," said Merrimac. He wouldn't have even noticed.

"Screw it. I'll wait," said the detective, sticking the white roll behind his ear. "So. Morgan's mom—that's his name, right?"

Merrimac nodded.

"She dies. Who's doing the estate?"

"Probably Morgan's attorney," said Merrimac.

"Numb-nut lawyers...We bust our humps breaking a case, and those slimebags get them off. Ought to lock those assholes in the same cell as the perps..." He looked at the surgeon and said, "Cheap way to fix *their* hemorrhoids, right, Doc?"

"I think so..." replied Merrimac, hoping anything he said might encourage the detective to consider the matter more seriously.

"Did you talk to him?"

"I tried." Merrimac knew it had been a while ago.

"His attorney won't tell you shit, of course."

"That about covers it," answered Merrimac. "He gave me his PO Box, told me to write a letter."

"So…let me like…be clear on this," said the detective. "This doctor friend was supposed to see a shrink and didn't, you get a letter that says *fuck you*…and now you think you seen him running? So…because he didn't check in with *you*, he's missing?"

The detective rubbed his eyes. "With a PO Box and an attorney, he's not missing. You just can't find him, if you know what I mean." The detective pointed at the picture. "Sounds to me like he doesn't give a shit about you."

"If that isn't him in the picture…could he be dead maybe?" Until that moment Merrimac hadn't thought that likelihood possible.

"Need a body," said the officer. "Tell you what. We'll check it out… Pass it to *Missing Persons* if I don't find nothing." The detective concluded with, "I'll get back to you."

———

Merrimac sat alone in his office wondering if he should call Jane Bonwitt. She had called months ago looking for information when she found Morgan leaving his townhouse.

"Wes," he said out loud, "I'm doing this for you…"

He sighed and picked up the phone. From past dealings with her, he knew to start talking right away.

"Jane, I think I saw Wes on TV running the marathon…so I went to the police. They really didn't help…said he wasn't missing…but also said they would look into it. I doubt they will. Have you heard from Wes?"

Her response took several minutes. "Oh, my! Let me remember… Okay…After I saw Wes at his townhouse—he looked really hairy— and men were there who took out all the furniture! All the things he bought from me! Then he took the picture Cay gave him from their first night—she looked so beautiful! What a cute couple! Then Wes got in his car and drove off! He wouldn't talk to me! So I followed him to O'Hare, that's where I lost him…"

Good God! thought Merrimac. *How does she talk without breathing?*

"Jane—" he tried to interrupt.

"Then his townhouse sold—a real estate friend of mine told

me—so I talked to the new owners and they said the whole thing was handled by Wes's attorney. So they gave me that number and I called him. He said Wes has no phone number, just a *post office box*, and I'm supposed to send him a letter! So I did, several over the past months! What unmitigated gall that lawyer has! I'm Wes's friend! I warned him the head of the Illinois Bar was a—"

"Jane"—Merrimac engaged the ploy physicians often used—"There goes my beeper. They're paging me to surgery. Sounds like it's urgent."

"Oh, can't you wait? There's more. Only take a minute."

"Hurry, Jane."

"I didn't get a call or letter—nothing! So I've been driving to Berwyn, past all those yellow brick bungalows, row after row, and sitting in the post office parking lot for hours with my Mercedes running, waiting for him to come, and he never has! So I don't know where Wes is. I miss him. I miss Cay too. It's all so terrible."

"We all miss them," Merrimac interjected. "I don't know what to do to find him."

"You know what I'm going to do?" Bonwitt declared.

Uh-oh. Just when he thought he was getting rid of her.

"I'm going to find him myself! I'll hire a private investigator."

"Good idea. Let me know," Merrimac said, realizing the only way to compete with her was to never stop talking. "Janie, I've really got an emergency and need to run. Bye."

He'd wait a moment.

"Thank you for talking with me, Ross."

Merrimac hung up. "God almighty! Sweet savior come to me! Wes…maybe you should stay lost!"

TWELVE

May 2003

"Come on, you jerks..." Fred Brosinski barked at the radio.

The White Socks had struck out in the third inning. Well, they may be down on their luck, but finally *he* had the perfect job—getting paid since November to wait outside a post office for a black BMW, listening to sports and laying down bets on the ponies.

What did he care? The big woman with the mushroom-cloud hair and toxic perfume never flinched when she wrote the check while sitting at her polished desk with a view of the lakefront. It was the largest retainer the private investigator had ever received.

"I'm told you are the best," Bonwitt said before the ink dried. *"My friends—"*

"You heard right," he agreed, quickly learning to interrupt.

"Is this enough money to make Dr. Morgan your priority? Because cost is no object."

"When it's somebody you care about"—he was amazed he didn't laugh—*"it shouldn't be."* He tried not to look too long at the amount. *"This should be enough... to get me started."*

The first thing the Chicago-detective-turned-private-investigator did was swap a bottle of gin at the motor vehicle department for a favor. He learned the BMW was still registered to Morgan at the Lincoln Park address, with its city sticker renewed for two years.

A quick hello to the new townhouse owners confirmed they'd never seen the BMW or met Morgan, so the car had to be parked somewhere else. Finding it at random would be impossible. Unless Morgan got a ticket—a mistake Brosinski thought improbable—the bureaucratic morass in Chicago would take forever to discover the car was no longer at that address.

So Brosinski did what Bonwitt had, and idled outside the Berwyn post office waiting for Morgan to pick up his mail. With his expenses paid well beyond their true costs, Bonwitt's money filled his pockets. He even paid his part-time secretary to stop by so he could run to the bathroom in a nearby bank or drive half a block to get gas. He paid her extra for that, of course—and for other, more personal accommodations—but today her child was sick and home from school, so he was stuck with an expanding bladder.

A Sox pop fly ended the next inning.

"Is this fuckin' guy ever goin' to get his fuckin' mail?"

Parked across the street from the Berwyn post office, he shifted his corpulent backside in the seat of the dingy green Laredo with threadbare tires and stuck his hairy hand out the window to ash his cigar.

"I'm so fuckin' sick of sitting my ass here, day and fuckin' night." It had been the same routine for months. "Thank the fuckin' saints it ain't hot yet."

Smoking the cigar down to a stump, he ate another doughnut. Every other day he bought a dozen and kept them next to him for the local police if they pulled up. With a flip of his badge and a Dunkin' Donut, they'd talk sports and leave, reassuring him they'd call if they saw a black BMW. They never did.

"Shit." Brosinski had to take a leak. "Too much coffee."

He looked in the back then felt under the driver's seat.

"Shit."

No bottles. He shook his thermos. It was almost empty. He unscrewed the lid, gulped the last few ounces of coffee, and spread the newspaper over his lap. After unzipping his pants, he held the thermos low between his legs and with a relaxed smug looked out the window.

"Oh, fuck!"

The bottle dropped to the floor, the urine spilling on the front mat.

"Shit!"

A black BMW turned from a side street and parked in a diagonal space in front of the post office.

"Fuckin' A!"

The license plate belonged to Morgan. He waited for his mark to get out of the car and go inside.

With the newspaper still covering his fly, Brosinski jammed the Laredo into drive and backed into the street ahead of three moving cars, forcing himself over to the left turn lane. Forcing a U-turn into oncoming traffic, he parked on the passenger's side of the BMW and zipped up his pants.

Brosinski kept looking around as he turned on a billfold-sized GPS tracking device and opened his car door.

He crouched down so his left hand could stick the magnetized little box to the BMW's undercarriage.

He pulled himself inside, closed the door, and backed out. As he slowly drove away, he used his rearview mirror to track a dark-haired, bearded man carrying several white envelopes to the car.

Brosinski laughed. "We are fucking Siamese twins now!"

———

Morgan did a fast scan of the periphery, noting vehicle movement and pedestrians. His attention was directed to a green SUV with tinted windows, which seemed to be moving more slowly than the accelerated pace of traffic. He watched the vehicle until it was out of sight.

He drove to the storage locker and bicycled home in his usual random pattern so he couldn't be followed.

That afternoon, the GPS led Brosinski to the storage facility, but neither Morgan nor the BMW was anywhere to be seen. The PI went into the office to talk to the agent.

"Did you see if my buddy parked his BMW? He was gonna lend that baby to me tonight. My lady friend says I'll get lucky if she can have a ride."

"Not supposed to talk about clients," was the reply.

"Oh, come on, friend!" Ten dollars appeared. "Just tell me where my buddy parked it. He ain't answering his phone and forgot to tell me. See?" Brosinski said, dangling his keys with the Jeep logo hidden. "Got his keys."

The man took the money. "Locked up. Can only bust in if the owner says it's okay, like if they lose a key."

"Can you tell me when he left here?"

"Don't know. Been working inside all day," the agent said. "Give me your number and I'll give it to the manager. That work for you?"

"Right-o," said Brosinski. He wrote down a fictitious name and, after the area code, seven random numbers. "Thanks," he said, glad he only lost ten dollars.

———

"Son of a bitch!" Brosinski shouted, looking over his secretary's shoulder at his computer.

He had missed the GPS alert that the BMW had moved, and was now parked on the Midway of the University of Chicago.

"I need to go," he said as his secretary began wrestling with her halter top. She had come into the office with her hair a different color, wearing tight shorts and her tits falling out. It was all the advertisement he needed. His desk was the most immediate firm surface available.

Scrambling through the pouring rain without an umbrella, Brosinski raced to the spot where he had illegally parked, turned over the engine, and sped toward the campus.

"Well, Morgan," he said, listening to the wipers chafe back and forth, "guess the threat of a little bad weather put your pampered candy ass back in the seat of that fancy car."

This was the break Brosinski needed. Bonwitt insisted on proof he was getting closer to discovering where Morgan was living. More important to Brosinski—he wanted the easy money to keep coming.

The closer he got to campus, the harder it rained.

"Hope this fuckin' shit stops. I need a clear shot of your mug without sticking my camera up your nose."

He spotted the BMW parked near the crosswalk that led to the library. He drove past, came around on the opposing street, and stopped the Laredo across the open field about three hundred feet away. The telephoto lens would reach that far without a problem and provide the pictures he needed to clearly identify Morgan.

"If it just stops fuckin' raining," he said, lighting a cigar.

Brosinski waited all day. Disappointed there were few coeds he could take pictures of, he thought he'd go to Oak Street Beach on Memorial Day to get some shots of the season's first bikinis.

"If it doesn't fuckin' rain," he added.

———

Morgan's watch chirped.

He'd had enough studying for a while. The rest of the material could wait until later.

When he finished, he put his laptop and folders in the black backpack, took a drink of water from the fountain, and headed down the stairs to the main entrance.

Morgan paused on the steps. The rain had stopped, making visibility sharper.

"Know your world…" Tony's words echoed in his head. *"Separate the unusual from the normal chaos."*

In the periphery of his vision, his attention covertly appraised a distant green contour.

"Remember," Tony had said again and again, *"coincidences don't happen…"*

With his backpack in hand, he walked down the steps and continued on the path that ran through the gardens toward his car.

Through the camera Brosinski watched his progress.

"Thank you for finally getting your fuckin' ass out here." He started taking pictures. "You look like an Arab fuck." The lens kept clicking. "The fat woman will love these," he chortled. "How 'bout a big smile for her?"

Morgan opened the trunk with his key and took out his bicycle. Brosinski watched him pull out the front tire and lock it into the forks.

"Now you're fuckin' going bike riding?" he said.

Morgan placed the backpack in the trunk and closed it. He mounted the bicycle and rode away.

"Shit..." Even though he knew he'd have to wait, Brosinski smiled. "I know you ain't leaving that hottie car here overnight."

Fifteen minutes later, he saw Morgan return and dismount, leaving the bike on the grass while he opened his car trunk. The camera clicked away.

———

Morgan saw them walk from the garden to the sidewalk. One man was wearing a red baseball cap over a clump of long dreadlocks that covered broad shoulders, which ascended from a narrow waist and thicker legs. The second man, shorter and more squarely built, held a knife along the closer thigh. Both their strides lurched in synchronized rhythm.

Morgan stepped on the wet grass to get his bike, keeping them in sight.

The man with the baseball cap stopped just on the other side of the bicycle.

"What the hell?" Brosinski said while looking through the lens.

"Cool ride, motherfucker."

The dreadlocks fell forward as the man bent down and peered through the passenger window.

"Thank you," said Morgan calmly.

"Bet you get some finger-licking good pussy with that!"

The man stood up and put his hand on the bicycle seat.

"Not recently," Morgan laughed, placing his left foot on the derailleur.

"Sweet bike too, asshole."

"It's a good one," nodded Morgan. His left hand slowly rose to the level of the seat and turned palm up while directing a smile at the man with the knife.

"You're like Santa Claus, motherfucker," he said displaying his gold teeth, "bringing us such good shit, for an early Christm-*ass...*" The blade flashed. "Give my bro da' keys to that shit."

Brosinski continued taking pictures.

Morgan kept looking at the second man, but his head tipped away. "Your brother here's got some cool dreads."

The man in the baseball cap leaned over the bike to stare closer at Morgan. The dreadlocks followed.

"We taken all this shit," he announced.

Morgan grinned broadly at the man with the knife.

Through the camera lens, Brosinski saw the smile—a peculiar facial expression during an armed robbery, and one he hadn't expected. The automatic shutter kept cycling.

"By all means, have it," Morgan said, reaching for the keys with his right hand.

His foot pushed the bike forward. Grabbing the dreadlocks with his left hand, Morgan yanked the man's head down and drove his knee into his nose. The man fell backward to the ground.

Startled, the second man slipped on the wet grass. Before he could regain his balance, Morgan slammed the bicycle on him. The knife metal pinged on the sidewalk as Morgan rammed the BMW key protruding through his fist into the man's throat. The assailant crumpled.

Morgan turned to the first man. Blinded by tears and coughing blood, he tried to stand up. Morgan spun, smashing his foot into the side of the man's face. He dropped cold.

"Happy holidays, gentlemen," he said, not even winded.

Morgan removed the front wheel, put the bike in the car trunk, and drove off.

"Jesus H. Christ!" shouted Brosinski. An additional thirty-two pictures were all he had taken. He grimaced as he scanned the frames several times. "Only twelve seconds?"

He looked up and saw that the BMW was gone.

"How did you know how to do that, Doc?"

THIRTEEN

Early June 2003

Morgan did several quick turns, slipping through side streets, then double parked. Leaving the motor running, he got out and crawled around the car, using his hand to examine the underside of the chassis.

He touched a small box beneath the passenger door. With a yank, the GPS dropped into his hand.

As he left the library, he had seen the Laredo. There was nothing extraordinary about it except that it was old, green, dirty—and had tinted windows. A quick circuitous bike ride confirmed that the last number on the rear license plate was the same as the one that day in Berwyn.

That meant he was tagged at the post office, and whoever was driving the Laredo already knew about the storage garage. The BMW could never go back there again.

Morgan shut off the little box and drove deeper into the South side, finally backing into a shallow dead-end alley. He cracked the window and turned off the motor to wait until rush-hour traffic was thicker.

"Thanks, guys for your help today," Morgan said in a taciturn whisper, as if the window might broadcast his secrets. Tony and Isaac were good teachers.

His hand toyed with the GPS.

"Who's doing this?" he wondered.

The list was short, and Morgan suspected Janie was at the top. Tenacious in her quests, it would be just like her to hire someone to find him. Once discovered, Janie would come knocking.

"You're in for disappointment," he said.

The BMW's engine came to life. He drove to a public garage several miles from his home, left his car, and biked back.

That evening, a local TV station reported the special-interest story about two men who were seriously injured on the University of Chicago campus. Although their tattoos suggested they were gang members, the only man who could speak told the female reporter that he and his friend had just left church and were walking home when they were confronted by a large group of students who, without reason, mugged them.

Brosinski roared with laughter. "You have no idea, your moronic bitch!" he said at the television. He looked at the pictures again on his computer.

"Fuck, Morgan!" he said. "That's what I call taking out the trash."

His demeanor changed as he opened another beer. There hadn't been a GPS signal the rest of the day.

"Damn batteries must have slipped off the contacts," he said. "Irregardless, I'll still find your ass."

———

Morgan rode his bike to a large parking garage just off Michigan Avenue, locked it in a rack and then walked up to the building's top floor. He turned on the GPS. After jiggling it for several minutes, he shut it off and went back to the street to wait.

"Why did that damn GPS just start working? Try missing those fuckin' potholes, Morgan!" Brosinski groaned as the email message came through in his office. "And what the fuck are you shopping for there?"

He grabbed the keys to the Laredo.

"I'll catch your ass if it kills me."

Brosinski sped to the parking garage, snagged the ticket, and slowly drove behind the rows of automobiles. Morgan's black BMW wasn't there. A torrent of profanity escaped through his open window and was heard by two women walking to their car. Thinking the comment was meant for them, they turned and in unison gave him the finger.

"You'd be so lucky," he yelled, accelerating toward the exit ramp.

———

Frustrated, Brosinski started driving the Rogers Park neighborhoods and waiting in delivery zones near intersections. If Morgan had garaged the car here, it made sense he lived somewhere nearby. His instincts were confirmed when one afternoon Morgan stopped beside the Laredo, leaned his bicycle against a wall and walked into a convenience store as the detective tried to slide down in his seat. When Morgan emerged, he stood a few feet from the front bumper drinking a pint of milk.

"Got you," Brosinski whispered.

As Morgan rode away, Brosinski forced the Laredo into the traffic and chased his fleeting target down side streets. He finally saw Morgan shouldering his bike up some stairs and opening a door.

"Too easy!" A conceited grin waxed. "I'll check out your place mañana when you ain't there." There was no need to tell Bonwitt yet. He wanted the checks to keep coming, but he needed the proof just in case.

———

Brosinski waited in the oppressive June air. When he was confident Morgan wasn't home, he grabbed a grocery bag filled with newspaper balls and crowned with carrot tops and a stale loaf of French bread. After puffing up the stairs, he knocked on the door.

No answer.

He tapped again. "Hey, sugar…what gives?" He said to the wood. "Open up, baby. Brought your groceries…hope you saved some sweets for me."

He slipped on latex gloves. The lock was easy to pick.

The dark room was stuffy. His flashlight searched the seemingly empty space.

"Don't you fuckin' live here?"

There were no papers or books. A cot was wedged in a corner behind a bench that was stacked with weights. There was a table with two lamps. The bicycle rested against a wall.

"Where your fuckin' clothes?"

The closet was empty.

The kitchen cabinets, refrigerator, and microwave looked like they had never been used. There was no garbage of any kind. Brosinski walked to the bathroom.

The bathtub didn't even have a shower curtain.

"I ain't believing this shit," he said and removed an ultraviolet lamp from his pocket. The special light would allow him to scour for Morgan's prints or any DNA evidence.

"Let's see how clean this place is, you jerk."

There were no fingerprints on the bathroom mirror or fixtures. He kept looking. The lamp scanned the shower walls and tub.

"Didn't you ever yank the chicken?"

There wasn't a trace of sperm.

He looked around base of the toilet. "Well, well, well…"

Several black hairs were curled on the tile. Brosinski lifted them with tweezers into a small bottle.

"These might be useful…"

He illuminated the cot then looked underneath.

"Bingo."

Several more hairs went into a second bottle and Brosinski stopped to listen to the nervous quiet. He knew what might happen if Morgan caught him inside. The PI wouldn't want to pull his gun, so he left. There was nothing more to find.

Brosinski returned to his office and checked his computer. All morning long, GPS messages had plotted a path that ended in northern Wisconsin.

"What the hell are you doing up there?"

The detective entered the final coordinates—a small town west of Green Bay.

"Enough of this bullshit!"

After driving ninety miles an hour, he parked in the gravel lot of a humble one-story motel. He strode to the front desk and flashed his badge.

"Nobody by the name Morgan staying here," said the owner's wife. "I'm afraid we don't get many expensive cars like BMWs." She shook her head.

"Nothing else you remember, ma'am?" Brosinski said, proud of his professional performance, but he wasn't about to drive his weary ass back with just that one answer. The GPS had signaled from this spot. "Maybe a BMW stopped here so the driver could use your bathroom?"

"Now that you mention it, UPS did leave a small box here at lunchtime. The address was right, but it was sent to the name *BMW Spare Parts.*"

"Huh?"

"Didn't know what to do," she admitted, "so a bit ago my husband drove it to one of those drop boxes after writing on it: Return to the sender."

"Which was where?" Brosinski asked, his skin flushing with anger.

"Chicago. To a Jane—"

"Aw, fuck you, Morgan!" he shouted.

The woman jumped back to avoid his spit.

———

"Janie, you are relentless," Morgan said while he drove the BMW away from Chicago.

Since the beginning, even at her conniving worst, she meant well. The introduction to Caroline was proof of that. However, Janie's persistent meddling had become a tedious distraction. None-the-less, this final episode pleased Morgan. From the onset, ascertaining that the Laredo's appearances were not incidental made the entire contest with its driver a mismatch. Testing the skills Tony taught him, Morgan played aloof until his affairs in the city were concluded, and the time came for him to move on.

The white lines became unbroken as the BMW accelerated toward Morgan's last journey to the Southwest. He glanced in the rearview mirror, his dispassionate face cleansed of emotion. As he viewed the receding skyline, nothing there mattered—all that he had once been died with Caroline that September morning.

"Cay, I love you," he said, but would give up no more tears. The time for sentimentality was gone.

His new life would begin in the desert—the final test—one that would require absolute discipline. Tony had argued with him weeks before, insisting on providing support, but Morgan resolutely said no. He wasn't concerned, reassuring his mentor that the small locked coolers containing the necessary stores of water and food he'd hide in the hellish landscape would not be disturbed by any two or four-legged animals. All Morgan asked was that Tony drop him off at the starting place—the below-sea-level Badwater Salts Pools—and meet him at his BMW sixty hours and one hundred thirty-six miles later at the Mount Whitney Portal.

Tony still protested.

"I'm just going for a run in Death Valley," said Morgan.

"In July," Tony reminded him.

FOURTEEN

As the desert sun climbed behind him he watched his shadow emerge from the soft glow. In the gentle rays, they ran together, savoring the final traces of the delicious night air. With only momentary breaks for the last twenty-six hours, his muscles long ago ceased begging for pity. Morgan no longer knew if his legs existed.

He looked at his watch.

"Good pace," he said.

He found his next container a dozen yards off the highway. The coyotes had stayed away from that one too. His knife cut the seal on the cooler. He refilled his water pack with more electrolyte solution, changed his socks, and put on a UV-protective shirt. He drank a premade slur he had concocted of salty rice and sesame seeds mixed with tea and honey. Warm and pasty, his stomach quickly protested.

"So much for my Badwater libation," he grunted.

He looked around while pulling out his penis to pee.

"As if anybody's watching," he said.

Cola-colored urine splashed on the caked ground. Absorbing the liquid even before the final drops fell, only a shapeless brown smudge remained.

He started running again.

You can't stop...

The trite words dissipated as swiftly as they came.

The hills became brushed in orange. His silhouette slowly shrank until he was again alone on the carpet of heat. Hot became hotter until his perception of temperature was gone.

Shimmering walls of air engulfed him as the world coned tight to become a tunnel. Hypnotized, a monochrome orb ahead pulled him forward.

The heat will go away again…tonight, he was trying to think, *with the altitude…*

In the suffocating brilliance, he measured his progress in single footsteps. For a time he ran backward to look at the death that had missed him, but could find no rationale to acknowledge it again. He turned around.

By nightfall, miles ahead, the level road would ascend to Townes Pass in the distant hills, and he would cool off. There he would stop and pray. He couldn't remember how many times his watch reminded him. He couldn't remember anything.

———

Beneath the gibbous moon, he descended from the night air of the five-thousand-foot pass. In the desert glow he saw Mount Whitney touching a solitary flowering cloud. By dawn, he was well over half-way when the furnace returned for the final time.

His toes felt on fire, but he ignored the pain and kept his feet moving. He was back in the tunnel, where nothing mattered except survival. The end would come, eventually.

"Wes…"

The whisper had no volume. The seductive ripple drifted past like a chord of music plucked from its score. The heat was playing tricks on the brain.

"Wes…"

The music in his head receded again.

A speck in the pale sky carved lazy circles before vanishing in the sun.

"Morgan…" he spoke aloud, "it's a bird."

"Wes!"

Startled, he looked to his side. Blue wings flapped in time with his stride.

"Caroline…" Morgan spoke to the hallucination. "Why are you flying?"

The ethereal bird said, "Because I can, Wes…"

She flew away.

Hours passed.

Soaring even higher, the bird reappeared near the twin mountain peaks miles ahead.

"Wes…" she called, "watch!"

At its apogee, the bird pitched over and plunged toward the ground.

"Caroline! Don't!" He screamed at the dive-bombing bird. "Stop!"

Morgan halted to watch. With no comfort from the stifling oven, the only breeze in the claustrophobic sea of heat came from his breath.

———

As evening descended, iridescent sunlight reflected on the scorched pavement. Morgan had ignored the silvery mirages for two days, but as the sun sank, each morphed into a brilliant crimson puddle with a splatter of blue. He had never seen colors so vivid. Color was everywhere—brown and tan, gold and orange, and the black ribbon that stretched forever ahead under his feet. But *this* beautiful crimson was the color of—blood. Before this day Morgan had never appreciated its magnificence. With the dying sun, each puddle became scarlet and the blue became darker. Soon the puddles turned black at the edges, and the blue changed from indigo to violet.

At twilight the last puddle disappeared.

FIFTEEN

Morgan's ordeal ended at the campground below the Whitney Portal. Tony reclined in a chaise lounge by the tent and toasted his student's arrival with a beer.

"Not bad! An hour earlier than you predicted," he said, looking at his watch. "You didn't hitch a ride the last couple miles?"

Morgan didn't smile and barely shook his head.

"No."

A strong handshake followed, then Tony handed him a towel and a bottle of soap. "Go take a cold shower. Check for black toe."

Burns on the feet were an ever-present risk running long distances on superheated blacktop. Despite alternating pairs of shoes, all of Morgan's soles had melted a little. But he knew his feet hadn't suffered too badly.

When he returned, Tony asked if he was hungry.

"Not really," he said, but Tony had already warmed a meal over a small gas cook-top.

"Eat, Wes," he said, handing Morgan a plate of fish, potatoes, and corn. "You need calories and a serious recharge of your batteries."

Morgan did as he was told, stretching out on a second chaise lounge with his feet and legs exposed to the cooling air. While Morgan ate and gulped iced tea, Tony opened another beer.

After letting the silence command the space for a while, Tony smiled.

"I'm only going to ask you one question…as a final exam thing," Tony said while Morgan chewed. "How do you feel?"

As he finished his food, Morgan reflected to the beginning, back to a person who no longer existed, and realized now he didn't feel much at all. He felt hollow, stripped of any capacity for worry, pleasure—anything that made a person normal. His inside was dead—but his body was alive and ready to kill.

"Fine," Morgan said without forethought. This time, he meant it.

Tony stared at his sunburned student.

"Then, my friend…our time together is done," he said.

———

At dawn the two men silently folded the tent. Before they placed it in the BMW's trunk, Morgan lifted the carpet over the spare tire and handed Tony a bulging envelope.

"No charge, man," said Tony, giving it back. "This last part's been on me."

"No," said Morgan. "You take this." He crammed the envelope in Tony's pocket. "That was the deal. Too many greenbacks won't do me any good where I'm going."

"I don't suppose I can persuade you…" began Tony.

"No," replied Morgan.

Both men knew this would be the last time they met.

"Don't expect them to canonize you," Tony said with a smile.

"Not my intention," said Morgan.

The men shook hands a final time.

"Then may your arrow," Tony said, "fly straight and true."

———

After a sound night's sleep, Morgan started east. His brain had recovered from the heat and he could think again. The CD player came alive. It would be that way for many hours. When he stopped for gas the first time, he threw away all his papers and unnecessary clothes and shoes. At the next fill-up, his smashed iPod and destroyed laptop hard drive went into an oily bin. In central Texas his final language

CD met the same fate, and the shards of his training were gone. The only things remaining in his life were what he had compressed into his brain, his physical training, and the purified calm earned in the desert. His thoughts focused on his next destination—the Port of Houston Turning Basin.

A boat tour the year before had allowed him to mentally catalogue the freighter terminal configurations, dock activity, and the pattern of the crews and shore personnel as they made their way in and out of the wharfs. The time spent driving the roads flanking the filthy water allowed him to determine the best locations to study the inbound freighter traffic. The big ships came from all over the planet, and their crews came from everywhere too. Finding the right ship would take only patience.

Prepaying in cash, Morgan checked into a nearby campground and pitched his tent. He attached Houston Astros stickers to the BMW's front and rear bumpers and exchanged his front license plate with the same logo. Wearing an Astros baseball cap, he drove to a neighborhood and parked, spreading an Astros sunshield across the windshield. A passerby might notice the Illinois plate but would quickly relish that fans lived everywhere and ignore the car and its driver.

Walking with an Astros bag that held water and a pair of small binoculars, Morgan paused on a bridge overpass to read an incoming ship's name and home port. He strolled several blocks until another ship appeared then walked to a different overpass to look. In the late evening, soaked from the dense humidity, he drove back to the campground to rest. For several days, he repeated the process, each time leaving the BMW on a different street.

Morgan got his reward when he heard a freighter crew shouting over the engine noise. He looked at the house flag announcing her country of registry and the pennants on the dressing lines boasting of her journeys. The courtesy Stars and Stripes fluttered, respecting the host country as he studied the stern and surveyed the crew.

The *Shindu Sagar* would do just fine.

He watched where the ship berthed.

Morgan drove to a T-shirt shop and had the ship's name silkscreened on a green shirt with large white letters, then had the BMW washed and the inside thoroughly detailed. He asked the young attendant to spread a fresh plastic tarp over the driver's seat and carpet, then handed him a nice tip.

"Selling it?" asked the teenager with curious jealousy.

"Yeah," Morgan replied, "want it looking like new when I trade it in." The kid nodded.

"Hey, do me a favor," Morgan said to him. "Don't want to leave my sweaty fingerprints on the handle. Shut the door for me, will you?"

Morgan put on driving gloves and drove off.

With the BMW facing the campground office, he polished the windshield with an auto-glass compound until the sun dazzled off the luster. The manager saw the reflection and pumped his fist in approval, not understanding its true purpose of blinding a camera that soon would take Morgan's picture.

Morgan returned the man's enthusiasm with a big wave.

With the trunk raised so the manager couldn't watch, Morgan swapped his rear license plate with one he'd pilfered before leaving Chicago, then used a wire cutter to destroy his Illinois plates. Some of those metal pieces as well as the tool, his tent, binoculars, auto-glass cleaner and the Astros bag—whatever traces of his former self that remained—ended in the Dumpster on his way to the camp shower.

When he emerged, he wore aviator sunglasses, a different baseball cap, and fresh clothes. The towel and any remaining clothes joined the rest of the trash.

He drove to the long-term parking lot at Bush International Airport. Pausing just before he pulled up to the security gate, he tipped his head down so the cap's beak covered most of his face, lowered the window, and pulled the ticket from the automatic dispenser.

Driving around the lot, he carefully surveyed the ocean of automobiles before choosing a space with a rear cement wall. He backed the BMW in and shut off the motor for the last time.

Morgan put up the sunshield and released the trunk lid. As he got out, he removed the tarp, folding it into a small rectangle. He lifted the backpack from the trunk, strapped it on, and locked the car.

At the nearby airport bus stop, he dropped the tarp and remaining license plate parts in a trash can. A second can received the gloves and the shredded parking ticket.

He drew a deep breath.

Morgan's only possessions now were what he had learned, carried, and the guile to believe he might succeed—or die trying.

Boarding the bus, he took a seat in the middle, scrutinizing the smudge on the window. The backpack sat on his lap.

At the next stop, a man got on, looked at all the empty seats, and came up to Morgan.

"Hey! Rag-boy!" he said loudly. The man's halitosis was indescribable, but his body odor was worse. "Move the fuck out of my seat!"

Without protest, Morgan went farther back and sat motionless until arriving downtown, where he waited to transfer to the bus that went to the wharf.

The bus left him near a large plywood wall plastered with handbills for nearby restaurants, massage services, and gentlemen's clubs. He smiled. All men had the same needs.

Weaving through the large overfilled parking lot toward the port's main security entrance, he casually knocked the cap off his head. Bending down to pick it up, he tossed the sunglasses under a car and kept walking. A few cars later, he dropped his head to sneeze, leaving the cap wedged behind a truck tire.

In his frayed oxford shirt tucked into tattered jeans, his running shoes pressing in the cracked pavement, he leaned against a chain-link fence with the backpack at his feet, dawdling in the torpid air. He rubbed his hands across his leathery skin, waiting.

At shift change, exiting workers milled past him, dispersing to the parking lot. From every direction he heard beer cans pop open. Interspersed among the noises were the crews coming for shore leave. Morgan studied their faces.

Three men exited the security gate, one using a black walking stick to balance an ungainly limp. The person who gripped the dervish-style carved wood stick with streaks of inlaid ivory had caught Morgan's attention as he'd evaluated the incoming *Sagar* that morning. He was pleased to see the man with the gimpy walk coming his way.

Morgan studied the man's two companions. One was tall, bald, and very dark skinned; the other was shorter and more round.

Morgan unbuttoned the oxford to display the T-shirt. After scratching his neck, he used an index finger to rub his eye. With a slight grimace he shook his head.

The men approached him.

Touching his lowered brow, Morgan said in Arabic, "As-salaamu 'alay-kom." *Peace be with you.*

With a raise of his open hand, the man with the walking stick returned the greeting.

"Enta Wasalt a'la *Shindu Sagar*?" Morgan asked, wrinkling the space between his eyebrows. *Have you arrived on the* Shindu Sagar?

"Na'am," the man replied. *Yes.*

"Hal Fouad Mutallah a'la elmarkab?" Morgan added a hopeful smile. *Is Fouad Mutallah aboard?*

"I do...not know...him," the man said in broken English and looked at the other crewmen. "You...know him?" he asked.

They shook their heads.

"I'm expecting to join him," said Morgan. He looked into the sky, exhaling frustrated breath. "Patience is difficult. I do not know what to do. I do not wish to remain in this country."

The man gave a sympathetic nod. "What is your name, friend?" he asked.

"Barif," said Morgan. "Barif Ali."

"I am Jamil." He used no surname.

The two men shook hands, and Jamil introduced the others. The big man was called Hamid, a Somali; the other was Nidal, from the southern Philippines.

Jamil asked, "How long...have you...been—"

Hamid interrupted. "Blond girl!" he said loudly. "No dress…" Placing a finger on his head, he spun once underneath. "Dance!" he shouted, cupping his hands over his chest to imply large breasts.

Nidal agreed excitedly.

Jamil smiled. "Neither man has ever been in this country. They see such things in American movies only."

Morgan frowned.

"Perhaps such wickedness…is good to share with our new friend." Jamil looked at his watch. "Only three hours…"

He raised the stick and pointed toward the wharf.

Morgan nodded, his lips sliding into a grin. "We will find a place close." He pulled a crumpled wad of American money from a pocket. "What better but to give this garbage to vile whores."

Suddenly immersed in laughter, the trio paid no attention to the harsh rattle of a diesel motor until its horn bellowed. Everyone but Morgan jumped.

"Move, cocksuckers," a voice shouted from the window of the huge pickup truck. A hand extended, gripping a large-bore revolver, the decisive authority for the order. "Or I'll blow your little brown dicks to Allah."

Morgan motioned to the others with the tilt of his head.

"Time to go," he said.

The opportunity to rescue them was the break he needed. Hopefully, they would repay the favor.

SIXTEEN

Strapping his backpack over a shoulder, Morgan said, "Follow me," and led them to the signboard. He pretended to study them carefully before pointing at one.

Hamid brought his eyes close to the small picture, looked at the woman's breasts, and kissed the image.

"Close," Morgan said to Jamil and hailed a taxi.

Eager to help any sailor part with money, the driver briskly jostled the cab around pedestrians and pulled close to the curb. Assuring the driver there would be a good tip if he got to the address quickly, they sped off.

The cabbie dropped them in front of a building designed to look like a western ranch, with a surrounding wooden porch and beam railings. In the middle of the circular driveway, the neon figure of a cowgirl revolved around an illuminated pole while a speaker at the top shrieked, *"Puss 'n Boots wants ya'll to come right on in!"*

Morgan and Jamil looked at the jammed parking lot filled mostly with pickup trucks. Every man entering or leaving wore a cowboy hat.

"Barif," Jamil said to him, a worried expression crossing his face, "is this a good—"

Hamid and Nidal were already near the door, shouting for the others to join them. Halting their entrance was a large threatening bouncer. Morgan paid the cover charges and they went in.

The music was deafening and the smoke was thick. On runways, women in various stages of undress were constantly appearing and disappearing from the dark ends of the platforms. Some would whirl around poles like erotic tornados. Others would pretend to mount the poles, moving up and down, faster and faster until their bodies contorted in counterfeit orgasms.

Eventually each woman would move to the edge of the stage and present her gartered leg to collect bills offered by probing fingers. For a large enough sum, she would slowly ripple her fingers across the wedged-shape strings covering her crotch, turn away, bend over, and deliver a smile from between her open legs.

Ushered to a table close to the stage, Morgan heard profane barbs indiscreetly sent their way. He squinted to find the exits as they sat down. Jamil rested his cane against the chair, took in the scene, and gave Morgan another worried look. With his backpack between his feet, Morgan sat and spread his money on the table.

A tank-topped waitress appeared. Hamid's pupils dilated as he stared at her nipples poking through the sheer fabric. His jaw dropped when he looked at her tight hot pants.

"Four Cokes, please," Morgan said.

She scowled.

"Beer!" Nidal and Hamid shouted together.

Morgan looked at Jamil and they smiled in unison.

"But two Cokes," he said, holding up the same number of fingers.

Soon, a bucket filled with ice and six longneck beers arrived. By the time the two men were into the second bucket, they were drunk. Morgan kept a watchful eye on them, but before he could catch him, Hamid grabbed a dollar bill from the change and shoved his way toward the stage. A blond dancer saw him approach and thrust out her gartered thigh. When she saw that it was a dollar, she gave him the finger and strutted away. Hamid started to climb after her, but Morgan grabbed his belt and pulled him back.

The man with the revolver at the shipyard had sidled up to the table. Morgan had seen him sitting with friends when they arrived and had kept a wary eye on him.

"You dumb pricks. I thought I told you earlier to fuck off."

The cowboy grabbed Jamil's cup and took a big swig.

"Coke?" he said, finishing what was left, spitting the ice out of his mouth. "Figures you A-rab pukes would drink soda pop." He stroked the face of one of Morgan's twenty-dollar bills. "Listen, you faggot dipshits. In the U-S-A, we don't insult *our ladies* with a dollar. We give them one of these babies."

He snapped the bill close to Hamid's face and ambled to the stage. Inserting it in the garter of the nearest dancer, she responded by stoking her fingers several times across her G-string. When he returned, he growled, "That's how we do it here, *fuckers.*"

With a big-toothed grin, Hamid looped his arm over the cowboy's shoulder, jostling the Stetson down his face. The Texan shot fire from his bloodshot eyes.

The last thing Morgan wanted was a bar fight. Motioning the others to stay seated, he rose slowly, waving to get a server's attention. When she came over, he said, "Please get this man and his friends some beers and a table dance on me." He handed her fifty dollars.

"No thanks, asshole," said the cowboy. "I don't take no fuckin' charity from any fuckin' A-rab cocksucking faggot, and I ain't fuckin' drinking your beer. Maybe you homos want to go outside to get a taste of what American firepower can do to your shriveled—"

Morgan whispered in Arabic to Jamil, "We need to leave now!"

Grabbing his backpack, Morgan pocketed an unopened bottle of beer from the bucket and pointed toward the nearest exit. They got to the parking lot before the cowboy stumbled out behind them and headed for his truck. Morgan knew the gun was likely to appear soon.

Laughing, Hamid lurched toward the cowboy. Morgan shouted for him to stop.

He didn't.

"Go get him!" Morgan said to the others. "I'll talk to this man."

The pair raced to Hamid, dragging him behind a Hummer.

The cowboy fumbled for his key and the truck door opened. The man leaned inside. He was going for the gun.

"Hey!"

The man turned toward the sound, exposing his right flank. Morgan uncoiled his leg. Spinning horizontally, his shoe slammed into the cowboy's side. Lost for breath, he dropped to the gravel and passed out.

In a muted yell, Morgan said, "Come here!"

The four men lifted the Texan into the truck's front seat. Hamid wedged himself in on the passenger's side to keep the unconscious man upright, while Jamil and Nidal climbed into the small backseat. Handing them his backpack, Morgan got into the driver's seat, opened the bottle of beer, put it in the cup holder, and started the motor.

The Somali reached for beer.

"*Laa!*" Morgan said, whacking away his hand. *No!*

Morgan drove close to the wharf's security entrance and let the three crewmen out. In a hushed voice he spoke to Jamil, who nodded and said, "I will see you shortly."

With the truck parked deep in the lot, Morgan rummaged under the front seat finding the gun and a box of bullets. He placed them in the backpack, cracked a rear window for air, and got out. Morgan swung the cowboy's legs in the driver's well, sliding him into the seat.

Removing the microfiber towel from his pack, Morgan soaked it in the beer. He wiped down the steering wheel and door.

"Got you to work early, cowboy," Morgan said to the unconscious man. "Sorry about this."

He crammed the Stetson over the man's brow, tossed the keys in his lap, and locked the door. By the time the man was sober, the freighter—hopefully, with Morgan aboard—would be gone.

Throwing the towel under a car, Morgan walked toward the dock's entrance where he saw Jamil waiting outside the gate. He smiled, handing Morgan a security pass. As they went through, Morgan saw a camera and raised his arm to run his fingers through his hair, covering his face. A few hundred feet farther, they left the quay and boarded the ship.

Jamil introduced Morgan to the captain—a sweaty tanned man named Arwan whose nationality Morgan couldn't immediately place. When he tried to shake the captain's hand, Arwan barked, "Passport."

Digging deep into the backpack, Morgan produced the requested document, watching Arwan's face frown as he looked at it. At the time, the black-market Pakistani document was the best Tony could help him get.

"The stamps are wrong," growled Arwan. "In Trinidad, your fucking ass goes to a place I send you, and you pay whatever the man asks. Don't fucking come back without a good one!" When he cocked his head, the sweat dropped from his jaw to his collar. "Or the fucking sharks for you."

The captain's next orders were as unambiguous as the first.

"No free ride. You work ass off."

He squeezed Morgan's shoulder firmly.

"Jamil, show him where he sleeps. Then make him do your job also."

The welcome was over.

Jamil took Morgan to the crew quarters, pointing to an upper birth. Morgan climbed up, shoving his backpack against the bulkhead. Distracting him with profuse thanks, Morgan reached in the unzipped bag and slipped the gun and bullets under the far corner of the mattress. He shimmied down, leaving the backpack in easy reach.

The engine rumble increased. The *Sagar* was shuddering to life.

They returned topside. The tugboats were nudging the cargo-heavy ship, encouraging her to turn. Morgan smiled. All that mattered was that the captain had agreed. Grasping Jamil's shoulders, Morgan gave him a brotherly kiss.

During the first mate's next announcement over the ship's loudspeakers, no one saw Morgan reach in his pocket. Clasping the BMW keys, he placed his arm over the railing and released them to the fetid silt of the Houston Shipping Channel.

SEVENTEEN

Late August 2003

"**S**túpido," the security guard mumbled, watching the heat rise off the rows of automobiles in the sprawling airport lot.

Cars might be left for only a few days, others would bake for weeks. He got to know them. Some would be only short acquaintances, while others, if they stayed longer, became friends. He often wondered what their owners were thinking when they left them in the Texas sun. The more expensive the vehicles, the less likely it seemed they protected them.

The black BMW with the Astros sunshield was one of the exceptions. It had spent almost a month in the same spot. The car had been washed before it first arrived, but the driver wasted that money by leaving it outside for so long. With each rain, the guard had watched the handsome finish with the accumulating dust streak deeper. True, the cost of covered parking over the month would be more expensive, but the owner could afford a BMW. Still, why didn't he take a limousine to the airport, or have somebody drive him?

As Labor Day weekend approached, the temperature swings between the day's heat and the night's relative cooling finally flattened one of the BMW's front tires. The guard saw the car listing and got out of his vehicle. Squeezing between the BMW and a truck, he looked at the Illinois license plate covered with a plastic shield that blinded the gate camera to the raised numbers. He called in the tag to the office.

"Not recognized," a woman responded over his radio.

"Ten-four. It's not going anywhere. I'll call you later with the VIN. Out."

The backlog at the Illinois Department of Motor Vehicles in Springfield finally cleared on Tuesday. The plate belonged on a Jeep Laredo registered to a former Chicago police officer with an ancient DUI—all charges dropped. What was wrong was the vehicle identification didn't match the plate.

———

Brosinski's phone rang that afternoon, but his secretary told the caller he was gone for the day—the Sox were playing Boston at home. When the call came again the following morning, the voice was an unpleasant reminder from his past.

"Hey, Brosinski?"

"Yeah."

"How the hell are you?" His precinct captain had hated him. The feeling was mutual.

"Fine." *Asshole...*

"How's that secretary of yours?"

"Wears shorter skirts than yours," Brosinski said, hoping the call interrupting an otherwise empty morning would end fast.

"How's business?"

"Great," he lied.

In reality it had been off since his only major client—Bonwitt—gave him the boot after receiving the GPS at her office. He tried to redeem himself by taking Bonwitt to Morgan's apartment building. Face to face, the property manager reiterated—as he had over the phone—that the unit had a new tenant. The prior renter had abandoned the furniture and mailed a typed letter stating he had moved out, instructing the manager to keep the remaining deposit. No forwarding information was included. In front of the agent, Bonwitt told the private investigator to never contact her again and stormed to her Mercedes. For once she said nothing else.

"What the hell do you want, Oscar?"

"Ever heard of a Wesley Randall Morgan?"

"Don't think so. Should I?" he added quickly. Brosinski's brow grew wet.

"He's some hotshot baby heart surgeon at Potts who hasn't talked to anybody or been seen for months."

"You're boring me," he lied again.

"His boss got worried, so last October he visited his local precinct, talked to one of the detectives."

Brosinski faked indifference. "Who gives a shit?"

"The other day the airport security folks in Houston impounded his BMW. Turns out it sat in the parking lot over a month."

"Why the fuck are you wasting my time telling me this?" Brosinski's curiosity reached its zenith.

"You're positive you don't know this Dr. Morgan?"

"Don't think so," he repeated again.

"Interesting." The bait had been cast and the fat fish had swallowed it. The captain continued, "Your license plate's screwed onto the BMW's rear."

Fuck! Brosinski suddenly realized he'd been set up.

In July the police had pulled him over for the missing front plate. *"A sum bitch stole it,"* he said at the time, after showing his badge. The officer laughed. *"Damn state hasn't sent me one yet,"* he added quickly.

"Usual story," said the officer while writing the warning ticket.

As the PI had rifled through Morgan's apartment, the transformed physician had slid under the Jeep and removed the plate.

"Fred, why don't you drop by here...tomorrow...if it's not too inconvenient," said Oscar. "Let's make it 0900 sharp...well before the game starts."

Brosinski grunted.

"For old time's sake," said the captain and hung up.

EIGHTEEN

Pruitt Farm Early September 2003

Jon Pruitt reclined in his favorite armchair, where his giggling little daughter had often climbed on his knees.

"Cay... Cay... Cay... " the three-year old would sing, hiccupping as she bounced. Her father drew her arms back and forth over her head, pretending to dance with her.

"I think that's what she wants to be called," he said to Connie.

His wife shook her head. *"She needs a nickname at this age?"*

"I don't know," he laughed, enjoying another swallow of after-dinner Scotch. *"It works."*

"Daddy!" Caroline exclaimed. *"I try?"*

The father felt her mother's disapproval without even looking.

"No, sweetheart," he said. *"Not till you're older."*

Caroline's pout melted his heart.

Returning to the present, Pruitt stared at the window sheers bulging into his office with each gust of the fall breeze. One of the horses whinnied in the stable.

"Goethe..." he sighed.

He remembered saddling up that Thanksgiving morning.

She hardly knew Wes—but already loved him! Just like what happened when he first met Connie! Cay's aura was renewed after months of her feeling confused, inadequate, rejected, and defiled.

She was giddy.

Why the hell did that asshole former fiancé have to call later that morning and ruin it?

He had never heard his daughter use pejoratives before when she spoke to him on the phone.

Then it was my turn to tell him off!

After that, all she wanted to do was go back to Chicago to see Wes—that night! He remembered thinking: if the spark is mutual... God save him! Wes is a goner!

Then Wes came for a visit!

They were standing on the sprawling plantation porch getting acquainted.

"Cay, honey...it's a delightful afternoon. Why don't we relax out here for a bit?" He could tell Morgan's nerves were on edge. *"Sun's going down. There's a breeze. Give your Yankee boyfriend a taste of Virginia old-time charm."*

"Daddy, don't embarrass yourself!" Caroline swatted her father's arm. *"Wes knows you're from Connecticut, for God's sake."*

She put her arm around Morgan's waist and kissed his cheek.

"I'm a real Southern gal." The twang poured out. *"Sugar-pie, why don't we set right down on these here comfy wicker rockin' chairs, and spin out the tale to my country folk about our big jet airplane ride? Mom will serve you up some sweet potato pie and iced tea."*

"The hell she will," he had said, recalling he was already on the move into the house. *"We're drinking Macallan."*

"Then you'd better bring one of your old bottles, Daddy," Cay suggested.

"You know I will, sweetheart."

"That's not necess—" he heard Morgan say, but Caroline interrupted him.

"Didn't you once say you wanted to understand all my bad habits?"

He returned with a tray with four antique snifters, a small silver pitcher with spring water, and an unopened bottle.

Caroline seemed surprised by his immediate return. *"That fast?"*

"Had the fifty-year-old handy."

"Always organizing," Connie said. *"Planning this for days."*

"Daddy treats drinking scotch like a sacrament," Cay said to Wes.

"Oh, and you don't?" Morgan stated.

"Obligated to pass on a family tradition." He filled three of the glasses generously, the fourth less so, handing it to Connie.

"I understand now who taught Cay to pour." Morgan laughed.

"Jon has many better traits," said Connie. *"This is not what I'd call an ideal first impression."*

"I have to admit, in a way I already feel like we've met," said Morgan. *"Cay's been a good proxy."*

"Like father, like daughter! He raised his glass. *"Cheers!"*

"And, my Scotch education advances," said Morgan, smelling it several times before taking a communion-sized taste. *"Mr. Pruitt, that's very good."*

"It's Jon...and don't chinch your taste buds. Still have another case of this in the cellar."

When he saw Morgan's incredulous glance at Cay, he looked at his daughter, curled the corner of his mouth in satisfaction, and gave her an approving nod. She hadn't told Morgan about their wealth. He loved her for the right reasons, not just the old man's money—unlike that other SOB.

"So...Cay...honey...I'm glad you didn't pull your luggage from the car. You're going to stay in the cabin."

Caroline blushed.

"It was mom's idea."

"Jon..." The mother's firm look softened. *"You know that's not true."*

"All right, I confess...I persuaded your mother it was the right thing to do. And, Wes, I know you'll like the privacy."

With a timid smile, Caroline looked at Wes. *"When I was a teenager, we used to have sleepovers there. It's hidden from the lane by almond trees. When the patio door's open, there's a sweet breeze. The birds sing at sunrise!"*

"Actually, we wanted to have you stay in the house"—he was savoring a rare opportunity to torment his daughter—*"but decided that neither of us wants to hear you."*

"Daddy!"

Caroline lost most of her drink to the floor. Connie's mouth fell open in synchrony.

How lucky you are…" he grinned, knowing Morgan's interest was piqued. *"Connie did mention that I have better traits."*

Caroline's head sank into her folded arms. *"Oh no…"* she groaned, her remaining Scotch spilling to the porch.

"Jon…" Connie's warned.

"As I was saying…"

"No…no…no!" cried Caroline, her face burrowing deeper into her arms. *"Oh, this is so embarrassing!"*

"Wes, just so you know…" He wouldn't let either woman win this round. *"Cay has the same hormones as her father."*

"Oh, Daddy!" she cried out from beneath her auburn hair.

As Connie glared in horror, Morgan nudged Caroline's shoulder. *"I would never have guessed that about you,"* he said with a smirk.

———

The ringing phone pulled Pruitt from his trance.

"Jon?" Connie stood at the threshold of his study, her palm covering the mouthpiece. With a confused crinkle of her mouth, she said, "Airport Security…in Houston?"

His face gave a similar look, then he took the phone. His wife sat near him on the ottoman.

"Hello, Jon Pruitt. Who's this?"

"Mr. Pruitt, my name is Sandra Rodriguez." The voice was authoritative, familiar after years of working with the military and government agencies. "I'm the Director of Airport Security at the Bush International Airport."

He looked for the caller name and number. "Ms. Rodriguez, your caller ID is blocked. May I have your number please?"

There would be no conversation until he was confident that what the woman said was true. Although much time separated him from his former associates, he still worried about deception and maintained the habit years later.

"Certainly. Let me give it to you."

Pruitt jotted the number. "I'll call this number immediately."

He disconnected and tapped in the digits.

"IAH Security."

"Sandra Rodriguez, please."

"Transferring…"

The connection was immediate.

"Sandra Rodriguez."

"This is Jon Pruitt. So how may I help you?"

"Sir, we've impounded a vehicle here that's been abandoned for more than a month. It's registered to Wesley Randall Morgan of Chicago."

Pruitt said nothing. Years of contract negotiations taught him it was best at first to let the other party talk.

"We saw it had a flat tire and then discovered the car's license plate didn't match the VIN. We were unable to contact the owner, so we obtained a warrant and searched it."

The information was troubling, but as Rodriguez spoke more, Pruitt's worry compounded.

"In the trunk was a cardboard box with your name, address, and necessary postage…and a hand-drawn red heart on the outside. We have no information about Mr. Morgan's whereabouts. How do you know him?"

"He and my daughter were in a serious relationship, possibly moving toward marriage."

"Were?"

"She died two years ago." He could barely speak.

"I'm sorry, sir. I apologize for having to ask," said Rodriguez. "Have you had any contact with Dr. Morgan recently?"

"Not for several months, I think." Pruitt tried to remember exactly when the last time was.

"Do you know where he might be?"

"No."

He whispered to his bride of thirty-seven years, "Wes is missing."

Her face immediately showed the despondency he felt. "Oh, dear," she sighed.

It was his turn to question. Perhaps it might provoke a forgotten statement that Wes made sometime earlier, giving Pruitt a hint.

"What's in the box?" he asked.

"I can share that," said Rodriguez. "Let's see…a picture of a man and woman formally dressed…a small painting of a house…broken reading glasses…a hairbrush…two crystal glasses…a half-full bottle of Scotch…a box from Cartier containing a large diamond ring…and a CD."

"A CD of what?" Pruitt was afraid of the answer.

"A woman's voice…sounds like a cell phone greeting."

"Oh God…" The pain was growing unbearable. "Anything else?" Pruitt asked.

His mind started hunting for explanations.

The agent continued. "Also, inside were two envelopes…one with his birth certificate and his Social Security card, the other a brief note to you and your wife."

This was all bad.

"Sir," asked Rodriguez, "do you know why Dr. Morgan would leave his car here?"

"I can only suspect he left Houston for a vacation. He's got a lot on his mind, as you can understand."

As much as he hoped, Pruitt didn't believe an extended holiday was the reason, but until he had more time to ponder, he wanted to emphasize to the agent the least worrisome scenario.

"I would hope that's right, but as I'm certain you will understand," Rodriguez said, "we'll have to do a more checking. If you hear or think of anything—"

"My wife and I will be in touch." Pruitt was about to disconnect when he asked, "Would you be able to send us the box?"

"Not yet." Her words offered no guarantee when that might happen. "I promise…I'll do my best to see that it gets to you at some point."

Pruitt sat with his elbow resting on the chair arm, his index finger supporting his nose. He retold the entire conversation to Connie. Before speculating, he walked to an inlaid walnut door.

"I need to think."

His finger traced along the long row of bottles until he found the one he wanted. Pouring several ounces of the fifty-year-old single malt in a crystal snifter, he offered a taste to Connie then nursed the golden whiskey until only the smoky aroma remained.

"Wes did call us...regularly...then he stopped." Jon Pruitt tore away from his brooding. "That woman got me thinking. Wes always asked...*do your friends know where bin Laden is?*"

"Everybody wants to know that," said Connie.

"Why would he ask each time?"

"Wes certainly has a good reason," she countered. "*You* told him some things about your company. I suspect he was hoping a friend of yours might know if bin Laden was close to capture."

Pruitt frowned.

"Remember..." he started to say but held his words as he went to refill his glass. "Remember...I said Wes's voice sounded different. I recognized that...but why?"

"I don't know, Blue," she said, using his pet name and affectionately touching his hand. "Do you think Jane Bonwitt might know?"

"We haven't spoken since the memorial service. Worth a try, I guess." He rolled his eyes. "Once she gets talking, though, it'll take me the rest of the day to get off the phone."

He scrolled through his directory. The thirty-minute conversation yielded minimal information. Connie got the edited version.

"She saw him at his townhouse after he sold it. Said Wes looked *foreign.* That was the word she used. Dark and shaggy..." Pruitt tried a smile. "She talked to him, but he was vague and...just took off in his car. That's odd. Anyway, she hired a private investigator. I guess he found Wes but then lost him. She mentioned a GPS...hard to understand that part."

He looked at the ceiling. "She wasn't too clear, never has been. In any event, nothing more has transpired there." Pruitt's despondency worsened. "I hope Wes isn't lost to mescal tequila in a Mexican gutter."

"I remember," Connie said, "Ross Merrimac called, asking if we'd seen or heard Wes."

"Come to think of it, he did, didn't he? That was a while ago, and we told him maybe just a phone call. I don't remember." Pruitt sucked air through closed lips as his open eyes flared wider. "So Wes never went back to work…"

Connie nodded.

"At the time I figured the poor guy just needed more space. I mean, we felt miserable for months. Still do."

The parents had shared tears, but their overt despair quieted as each developed separate ways to reflect—Connie replanting or weeding the numerous flower beds surrounding their home and Jon tending to Cay's blue orchids or currycombing Goethe and the mare.

"I can only imagine how distraught Wes is," Jon continued. "I just wish he'd shared it. Damn surgeons…Maybe we could have gotten him some counseling." His face grimaced. "Without more, at this point…I just don't know what to think. Or where to start, for that matter."

"Blue, darling, could any of your friends help?"

Her husband shrugged. Retired from a technology company he founded and sold, he had stayed in touch with his associates, but as they retired also, everyone's contacts in the intelligence agencies dwindled.

"I don't know who I'd call or…how to explain it." His chin now rested on his clasped hands. "When I was inside, it was just a finger snap."

Cornelia tapped his kneecap. "How about Zach?"

"I can't do that."

"Darling, you've been friends for years, longer than you've known me. You helped him all the way."

"That's not a small call." He looked at the empty snifter. "Zach's got a lot on his plate right now."

"Jon, listen to me!" Connie's voiced raised—a rarity. "What do *you* think Cay would say? *'Fine, Dad! Abandon him!'* We owe her more." Connie began crying. "She *loved* Wes, and we do too…"

His wife gave him her unyielding look, one he understood.

"Zach called you the first chance he could…the next day! He's your friend and he'll help you…as a friend."

"Okay." It was the best solution but still difficult. "Okay, sweetheart… of course…for Cay."

John Pruitt knew his daughter would have insisted, never giving her father a moment's peace, pestering him until he had exhausted every option. Cay's love for Wes was intense.

He went to his safe, removed a file, and called the private exchange. A professional voice answered.

"Jon Pruitt calling for President Reeves, if he's available."

"Please hold, sir. I'll see if the president can take your call."

NINETEEN

Western Mediterranean Sea Early September 2003

"A 'safeer batnee bitsawsaw." *The birds of my stomach are singing.* Morgan squeezed the water out of the mop. He was getting ravenous even after scrubbing the heads.

Jamil gave an approving smile as Morgan refilled the bucket with fresh detergent and water.

"Barif, your Arabic is better," he said.

Jamil took pride in polishing Morgan's syntax and idioms, reminding him daily how being raised in America had deprived him of his heritage. The tutoring also helped pass the tedium of the long voyage.

"Shukran." *Thank you.*

From his years of surgery training and more recently working with Tony, Morgan knew there remained no substitute for learning other than total immersion. The thousands of hours he'd spent listening to the language on his iPod and car stereo, working with a tutor, and attending the mosques had laid a solid foundation, but it wasn't like conversing in it all day long. He was getting more fluent. Reading the cursive glyphs right to left, however, still remained damn near impossible.

Morgan grinned at Jamil, pleased that what started with the T-shirt calling card, revolver flash, and strip-club near-calamity forged the camaraderie that had gotten Morgan aboard the *Sagar.* The most reassuring component, however, was that Morgan hadn't ended up as trolling bait off the stern. Captain Arwan still made it clear he didn't trust him, even though Morgan used his last American money in Trinidad to buy a real passport—at least, a real *counterfeit* one. The Lebanese document had all the necessary stamps.

Morgan suspected it wasn't the first time the shopkeeper had assisted Arwan. The store was nestled deep in a side alley with liquor bottles and cigarette cartons covering the small window. For the hour Morgan had waited, the owner's daughter helped only one other customer. Once the shop emptied, she offered Morgan a pipe packed with fragrant marijuana buds and pulled aside a hanging dolphin-festooned beach towel, motioning for him to join her inside the closet-size space.

Morgan shook his head politely. He wasn't interested in the slightest.

———

After the prayers we eat," said Jamil as Morgan again wrung out the mop with his calloused and muscled hands. Morgan knew the Dhuhr was approaching. He had learned during his training to sense the time. He looked forward to the prayers—their powers had become consuming, the private minutes reflective.

The men washed their hands and feet in preparation, removed their shoes, and faced the bow, praying together. When they finished, both men sat on their rears to stretch their legs.

Jamil laughed. "I'm certain when you tell Arwan his toilet is clean, he'll piss all over it immediately so he can command you to clean it again."

"I don't mind," said Morgan.

"The captain is vermin," Jamil stated. "But God uses people to his purpose, revealed when He alone decides."

During the midday meal, a crewmember asked Morgan about his family.

"My father was a dog," Morgan began.

To demean a father with such words was a severe insult that drew everyone's attention in the mess. Morgan told his scripted lie about the newlyweds who immigrated to Chicago from Pakistan in the 1960s.

"The dog learned the tongue of the infidel and forbade my mother to speak Arabic near me." The story was composed to create intrigue but self-adulation. "He never knew, but I *did* hear it," he boasted. "I was not American," he confessed, "and wanted to know more about my ancestors and their faith…even if some of my learning was in English."

They praised him but condemned his father.

"My parents," Morgan continued, "sent me to a school thick with Zionists."

That created murmurs throughout the mess. Morgan occasionally made provocative statements to ferret out his shipmate's sympathies.

"After my beautiful mother died, the dog turned to alcohol and to death," he continued without remorse. "With the freedom to open my eyes fully, I sought more spiritual nourishment."Some around him clapped.

"After witnessing the unclean ways of America, I wanted a better path."

"Will you ever go back?" one of his shipmates asked.

With a puffed chest Morgan said, "For jihad."

The captain belched.

Gruff and bellicose, Arwan usually kept apart from the crew, except during meals. He listened, hoping he might hear a reason to throw Ali overboard, but by the time the *Sagar* passed Cape Verde, he begrudgingly appreciated his new deckhand, watching Morgan relentlessly scrub the toilets with undue pride for such a menial task. Arwan acknowledged to his first mate that Barif Ali must have been a hell of a school janitor in America. The man worked without complaints and never tired.

Despite Jamil's sponsor, Arwan was never convinced that Ali was what he claimed to be.

"He asked about a person who has never been aboard this ship," Arwan said to Jamil after the *Sagar* got into open water outside Houston. *"He had an adulterated passport."*

"Does it matter?" Jamil questioned. *"He wanted to leave America and has been honest about his desire. You have transported others less forthright. Ali works hard and obeys orders."*

"He could be running from the American authorities," the captain replied. *"We could be detained at a port. That could endanger the Sagar and what I'm doing for you—and could cost me money."*

"I searched his bag after he came aboard," said Jamil.

That investigation yielded little—a worn waterproof backpack with a change of clothes, a woven rope satchel, nylon workout shorts, and varied denominations of American money totaling five hundred dollars.

"If he was a thief," Jamil said, *"there'd be more. His Koran was printed in 1970."*

"I still do not trust him," said Arwan. *"Because your presence alone makes my ship vulnerable."*

"You are being paid well for that," said Jamil sternly. *"I will watch Ali for you."*

Sensing the distrust, Morgan remained amidships in the presence of the others. After two weeks at sea, Jamil gave him a tour of the lower holds. Morgan learned the repainted *handy-size* freighter was built three decades earlier in China and bought the year before by a Pakistani corporation that registered her in the Maldives. The engine room was fascinating, but the ship's belly revealed discreet secrets in several hidden boxes—liquor, rifles, small bricks of marijuana and cocaine—telltale markers that the *Sagar* was adept at transferring illicit goods as well as legal items.

He had chosen well.

Eventually Morgan began weaving around the cargo containers to the bow. The trip was a precarious undertaking. In the beginning a curious crewman followed him, watching Morgan fill two buckets with fire-hose water, hang them on a pipe, and perform three sets of ten squats and chest presses, plus a hundred push-ups, while the sea rolled underneath.

When the man returned with several more of the crew, they found Morgan straight-boarding, planked with his feet high against the bulkhead, resting on his elbows and reading his Koran as it lay on white cotton. When Morgan kneeled down to take a break, Hamid came over, laughing, and asked to use the equipment. When he discovered he didn't have the strength to lift half of Morgan's load, he rejoined the others who cheered and counted the repetitions as Morgan began his routine again.

After that no one ventured forward again while at sea, and Morgan was left alone. They would use the loudspeaker to call him to task or to prayers. Even Arwan encouraged him to stay on the forward deck whenever possible, making it no secret he hoped a random thirty-meter swell would drop a container on him and rid his ship of a passenger he was compelled to accept but never welcomed.

The bow was also important to Morgan for more than just exercise and reading. Close to the gunwales, an access hatch sealed a cave beneath, where no one entered willingly. He kept his backpack in there, hung behind a thick bundle of wires—its contents hidden until the time came for Morgan to disembark.

———

Chicken was frequently on the menu and Morgan enjoyed helping Nidal butcher then. He liked the round cook from the Philippines who always restocked the pens at their most recent port of call. One afternoon the breeze shifted so they had an opportunity to talk without being engulfed in the stink.

Morgan asked him about his family. Nidal spoke about the Southern Philippines and how his mother taught him to cook and season food.

Morgan asked about his father.

Nidal said angrily, "Dead. Most fathers are dead."

"Why?"

Nidal spit over the side.

"Americans and Filipino government try to kill us. Rid islands, they say. But they not succeed!" His bitterness was explicit.

"The swine are relentless," Morgan concurred, grabbing another chicken and swinging it by its neck until he heard a crack. Squeezing tight to seal the blood vessels, he laid the bird on a cutting board and used one of Nidal's knives to lop off its head. The wings beat fiercely as he lifted the body by the feet and held it over the water, directing the neck away from the railing. His hand relaxed. The blood spurted in pulses until finally slowing to a drip. The wings became still.

"Guns, drugs, bombs," Nidal continued. "Ships like this are just one tool that will get our weapons to reach the enemy. We will kill the cowards when they sleep or lie awake! Hiding in the shadows will give them no victory..."

With the bird carcass draped over both hands, Morgan elevated it above their heads before offering it to Nidal. "We will spew the blood of their children in the streets and drink the tears their harlot mothers weep."

Barif Ali flicked the chicken head out to sea and reached in the cage for another.

TWENTY

Mid-September 2003

The phone call came from the top floor of the concrete trapezium on Pennsylvania Avenue in Washington, DC. The director in the Chicago office made little circles on the desktop with his fingers to pass the time until the one-sided conversation with the FBI director ended. There was little information included with the request—there didn't have to be. All responsibility would fall to the agent assigned. The order had the highest priority and there would be no debate. The local chief already had an idea who he was going to dump this one on.

"Finding a missing doctor? You're fucking kidding me, right?" Special Agent Paul Cotsworth said again. "You chose me why?"

"You're the best I've ever had."

"Not that way, pal," retorted Cotsworth. "Never been that drunk."

His boss would offer no more laudatory remarks, only the succinct reason.

"It's a favor for a Company friend. Naturally, that person wants a quick answer."

"I'd like to know who the hell *that* friend is."

Only someone in the top tier could insist on such an expedited request. And that made his ulcer hurt more. No good ever came to an agent who was handed this sort of investigation. Long ago Cotsworth was assured his days in the field were over.

"I'm not the police, damn it," he said.

"Get on it, Paul. Protesting is a waste of time. You know that." The director gave an unsympathetic laugh. "Moses tried, but he still did what God told him to do. And his reward wasn't the Promised Land." He laughed again, the same irritating way. "Don't worry, though. If you screw up, I'll fire you." He shrugged. "Bye."

Paul Cotsworth was pissed.

———

"Agent Cotsworth...a pleasure."

Ross Merrimac's spirited handshake was as jovial as his voice. Cotsworth appreciated immediately that the surgeon was a man to be both admired and respected. Still, the agent wondered how those huge hands fit inside a kid's chest.

"Please, Dr. Merrimac," said Cotsworth, "I'm not in the office. Call me *Paul*."

"And I'm *Ross*." The black man grinned. "Too much formality for me. I let the kids call me *Dr. Ross*. We're caretakers of God's creations, not our egos."

He kept grinning. "Only my wife calls me *Dr. Merrimac*, usually because I wash darks with lights. Whatever she says after that I just agree and promise not to do it again."

"Isn't that the truth!"

Both men laughed together. They were off to a good start.

"Coffee?" Merrimac asked. "Before you say yes, you have every right to be skeptical about hospital coffee."

"I'll trust your decision," Cotsworth laughed. "Show me the way."

The men talked as Merrimac led him from the hospital lobby to the new café. Lattes in hand, they found a secluded table and sat down. Merrimac stretched back and looked around.

"They designed this, you know," he said with exaggerated pride.

"You mean Pruitt and Morgan?" asked Cotsworth.

"I'm being indulgent, of course. But in a very real way, yes," Merrimac answered.

"How so? You said she designed the ventilation systems and the like, and he had some hand in the operating rooms. Is there more?" Cotsworth didn't understand.

"Hard to explain," said Merrimac. "It's like these buildings have a collective energy all their own. Everyone, in a sense, who creates, works in one, or has been a patient adds to its soul." Merrimac smiled. "Sometimes I feel Caroline's spirit circulates in the ductwork, and Wes, well…his devotion to his patients and maybe even his love for Cay, was the force that made it all come together."

He sighed. "Paul, I can already guess what you're thinking… sharing these repressed thoughts of mine." Merrimac chuckled. "I admit, I did enjoy reading Freud in college…probably too much."

"Me too," Cotsworth admitted with a laugh, while pulling a legal pad and pen from his valise. "I'm going to write as we talk, okay?"

"I would expect as much," said Merrimac. "Before we really dig in, let me ask…How did you get involved in this? I mean, I spoke to the police a year ago. Did it take this long for their report to filter up to you?"

Cotsworth shook his head. "It didn't come from the police. To be frank, I don't really know."

In the first week, the agent received four follow-up calls— three from his local director and one from the director himself in Washington. Somebody wanted an answer.

"I'm glad you're on it," said Merrimac. "Go ahead and write away. Don't worry 'bout time. Got nothing scheduled until after lunch."

"Thank you." Cotsworth reviewed his notes. "So…you told me about Morgan's family. His mother died?"

"The last time we spoke, Wes had said she was close. When I called the place in La Grange…oh, last fall…thinking they might have a contact number for Wes, all I found out was that the final arrangements, the estate and the like, were handled through his attorney. I've got his number somewhere."

"I'll find it." Cotsworth wrote—*Call lawyer.* Not that it would do him much good. Client privilege was the bane of his work.

"His sister died too, correct?"

"As a child...in the operating room...during surgery for her Tetralogy of Fallot, or *blue baby* as it used to be called."

The agent sensed the surgeon's frustration.

Merrimac continued. "We fix it so routinely these days it's hard to remember a time when it wasn't so easy. When Wes interviewed for the job, he told me..." Merrimac's tone became nurturing. "He became a pediatric heart surgeon so other sisters could live. Childlike reason, I know, but sincere. And darn if the man didn't devote years learning how to do just that. That devotion I mentioned earlier... When one of his patients died—and that was rare—well, he told me he reminisced about his sister."

"Friends?" asked Cotsworth, moved by what he had just heard.

"Not really. Me, I guess."

Cotsworth made a note while Merrimac continued.

"No...Morgan's best friend was probably surgery. Maybe more like an enslaving paramour, that is, until he met Caroline. She changed him completely...and for the better."

"Tell me."

"Wes was smitten—I mean *in love*." A reflective smile evolved. "Shandra—that's my wife—and I went out a couple of times with them." Merrimac then whispered a private admission, "Paul, if I'd been single, I'd have married her. She was impossibly beautiful... sexy as all get out with that Virginian drawl, and smart too!"

Cotsworth whistled, sitting back in his chair with his fingers fanning wide outside his open palms.

"Cay never flaunted it. She'd stand with him at our boring staff get-togethers and make chitchat...letting Wes stay center stage."

Cotsworth was enjoying the tale.

"Funny," Merrimac added. "Morgan's wayward reputation didn't bother her, because when he met that girl...Lord have mercy!" Another laugh. "From what I gather, Caroline fell just as hard too. Once they connected, man! Their single days were over."

"And...she died on September 11," said Cotsworth.

"Yes." His voice grew muted. "Caroline had finished a project she started in New York before she moved here, and was at Windows of the World attending a breakfast celebration."

"Oh, Jesus..." Cotsworth felt his sympathy swell.

"Wes planned to surprise her at the reception. He going to give her a ring later too, so...he tried to get up there late Monday afternoon. As usual, he got stuck in the OR. Our secretary kept rearranging his flights."

He held a woeful look. "He finally got out of Chicago late only to wait in airport after airport, getting to Newark by morning."

What Merrimac said next was worse than Cotsworth could imagine.

"His cab hit gridlock...he saw the smoke and ran toward it, thinking of course he could rescue her..." The surgeon sighed. "Then...he saw...well...her red suit." Merrimac's eyes closed briefly as if he was offering a prayer. "Later, Wes walked all the way to the Plaza Hotel where Caroline was staying. Out of humanity, the concierge finally agreed to let him into her hotel room. The poor guy sat in there alone until the planes flew again. If he ate at all, it was probably crackers from the minibar."

Merrimac's voice grew lifeless.

"Shandra and I picked him up at Midway airport. He looked like a zombie dug from a grave...clutching her suitcase like a child grasps a teddy bear." The man wiped a tear. "The dust...it was all over his clothes. When we got him to our place, he sat on the sofa and said nothing. Shandra finally put him to bed."

"I'm sorry," said Cotsworth. "You could've lost him too."

"I know," replied the surgeon. "He could have perished with her." He sighed again in despair. "Maybe I lost him anyway."

———————

The next call Cotsworth didn't want to make.

"Sir, let me say first how sorry I am for your loss."

"Much appreciated."

Pruitt was amazed how rapidly the bureau responded. Zach must have called the director when he hung up. Connie was right—as usual.

The FBI agent went through his list of questions. When he asked about the corporation Pruitt had owned outside Washington, the father became aloof. Not wanting the agent to suspect he was the link to the FBI's involvement, Pruitt redirected Cotsworth's attention.

"Agent Cotsworth," Pruitt said with a stressed voice, "let me give you the number of Jane Bonwitt. She knew both Cay and Wes...set them up on their first date....also hired a private investigator to try to find him after she lost him at O'Hare." *God help you when you call her*, Pruitt didn't say.

———

Cotsworth covered his mouth to hide another yawn. He spent a tedious hour in Bonwitt's office, watching her blow her nose and blot tears, the only things that prevented the woman from talking continuously. When Cotsworth was finally able to inject a question about the private investigator, she launched into another commercial-free diatribe, concluding with the story of the GPS delivery, handing him the receipt.

He tried not to laugh while writing down Brosinski's phone number. The private investigator's clumsiness wasn't reassuring, but he would probably have—Cotsworth hoped, at least—some sort of usable facts. So far he had nothing more than a growing list of questions that filled the lines of pages of a yellow legal pad.

Cotsworth called Brosinski's former captain Oscar Jefferson and asked him to set up a meeting. The phone conversation ended with laughter when Jefferson told of the lost and rediscovered license plate.

"The idiot earns a living investigating people?" was all Cotsworth could add. His confidence in the detective's helpfulness dwindled more.

Jefferson told the agent that he'd have Brosinski there for the meeting—in cuffs if need be. He wasn't joking.

———

"Going down to District Eight," Cotsworth called to the pool secretary, putting his suit jacket on to cover the shoulder holster.

She waved without looking up from her computer. If they needed him, she'd call.

Cotsworth parked, flashed his badge at the entrance guard, and was directed to Jefferson's office.

Brosinski didn't stand when he came in. The limp handshake suggested the morning meeting would drag from the start.

"I searched his flat in Rogers Park," said Brosinski.

"You mean *breaking and entering*," said the chief.

"Warrants ain't no ass pain for me," said Brosinski. "Only you guys."

Oh, geez, thought Cotsworth. Nothing was needed to understand why Brosinski no longer worked for Chicago's finest.

"So what did you find?" asked Cotsworth.

"Wasn't much there," said Brosinski. "A cot, weights, cheap table and chair...shit like that."

"Did you say *cot?*"

"The good doctor lived rather austerely."

"Why?"

"No fucking clue."

The FBI agent rubbed both eyes, yawning in frustration. "Anything on it?"

"Not even stains, if that's what you mean," answered Brosinski. "Like he slept on plastic sheets."

"Hmm..." Cotsworth added another thing to ponder. "Fingerprints anywhere?"

"Every surface was clean. Had to be some somewhere, but...I mean the place was fuckin' *clean*. But he lived there, I know it."

"What makes you believe that?" asked Cotsworth.

"I saw him go in the day before."

"Doesn't mean anything," said Oscar.

"Yes it does. Here." The PI handed a baggie with two sealed vials to Cotsworth then tried to sound professional. "I got these from his floor and bathroom."

Cotsworth held the vials up to the light. "What's this?"

"Morgan has dark hair. These are his," said Brosinski, his voice overflowing with conceit.

"Did you process these?" asked Cotsworth.

"Nope."

The FBI agent stared at him, his frustration fermenting. The PI's brute arrogance reminded him why he didn't miss fieldwork. "Why the hell not?"

"Ain't pinball money for my ass like it is for you Feds. And the fat lady stopped paying me," said Brosinski, avoiding any comment about the GPS. Cotsworth's sarcastic smile suggested he knew.

"Besides," Brosinski added, "I didn't see Morgan doing no fuckin' crime."

"Abandoning a car with a stolen license plate isn't suspicious?" asked the agent, not expecting an answer.

Brosinski glared at Jefferson.

"I didn't know the fucker had taken it," he retorted.

"What Fred says is true," Jefferson conceded, adding, "but Agent Cotsworth and I laughed hard when Morgan whipped you at your own job."

Brosinski wanted to tell both men to go blow themselves.

"Anyway, Fred…you watched him…" said Cotsworth. "What the hell do you think he's doing?"

Brosinski had contemplated that as Jane Bonwitt blew the ink dry on the first check. "You're assuming Dr. Morgan's alive," he replied.

"For the moment, yes. And it sounds like he's done an effective job leaving no traces. The license plate would suggest that."

Brosinski held his words.

"What was his behavior like?" asked Cotsworth.

"Unstructured, and that's no fuckin' lie. Took a long time to find him. Had to sit outside the fuckin' Berwyn post office for months… watching all those fat-assed bitches go in and out." Brosinski didn't mention there had been a couple of good-looking ones he had taken pictures of for his collection.

"Okay, what else?" asked Cotsworth.

"Went to the *libary* fuckin' more than college fags."

"There had to be a reason. Did you ever go in, try to see what he was looking at?"

"No. Hate *libaries*."

That information would have been very helpful, you idiot, Cotsworth didn't say.

"What else, Mr. PI?"

"Dude's athletic, but even more. Physically strong, tough-like."

"I do not understand," said Cotsworth.

"A buddy of mine at marine patrol found him swimming in the lake."

Cotsworth produced an unsatisfied expression. "So?"

"It was fuckin' two in the morning."

"Where was he?"

"You won't believe it," said Brosinski. "Outside the breakwater north of Navy Pier. Somebody on a sailboat called it in. A police boat found him."

"What the hell was a sailboat doing out there at two a.m.?"

"The owner was screwing his girlfriend over the railing when the asshole backstroked alongside, embarrassing them to hell. How the fuck am I supposed to know?"

"When was this?"

"Shit, last year sometime. Don't remember."

The questioning persisted. "Did your buddy ask Morgan what he was doing in the lake?"

"Training for some thing called Ironman."

"Okay," said Cotsworth, "I'd buy that at the time, but not now... not in the present context. Did they pick him up?"

"No."

"Why the hell not?"

"Guess they thought he wasn't doing anything wrong, just being stupid maybe. Cops probably flushed it away like all the other random crap in this city."

Oscar Jefferson cleared his throat.

"You didn't look into it?" asked the agent.

"Give me a break!" protested Brosinski. "I didn't even know about it until recently! I was drinking beers and shootin' the shit with the guy after a ballgame. Total frigging coincidence. Those Sox bastards had lost again."

"Anything else, Detective?"

Brosinski had been saving the best for last. "Well, he did deck two"—he glanced at the African-American police chief before resuming—"gentlemen of color on the Midway." It remained one of Brosinski's most cherished memories of the case. "Damn near killed one of them...clean and efficient." Brosinski handed over a disc with the pictures. "You'll find these entertaining."

"Drugs?"

"No. Looks like they wanted his car." Brosinski's lips bulged. "It was pure self-defense on Morgan's part. He kicked—and I mean he *kicked*—the fuckin' shit out of them."

Cotsworth shook his head with incredulity. "Strange for a doctor."

"Fuckin' weird."

The agent had heard enough. The meeting concluded with the usual drivel about sharing information and working together. The business cards would get lost in the drawers.

The FBI agent made it a few feet out of the office before Brosinski called out, "Hey...Cotsworth..."

"Yeah?"

"April...last year."

"What was?"

"The swim," said Brosinski.

"Sounds invigorating. Was he wearing a wetsuit?"

"A thin shorty." The temptation was too great for Brosinski. "Tiger striped with pink booties."

Cotsworth felt an immediate desire to shoot him but instead replied, "Ambient air temperature's probably no more than forty degrees."

"My buddy put in his report that the captain and his deckhand wore their sweaters while they were banging."

Cotsworth shook his head and walked to his car.

Shifting the characterless sedan to reverse, it remained motionless as the agent's foot pressed the brake for an indefinite time.

Invigorating? Michigan was damn near freezing in April. Not even an Ironman competitor required that.

But navy SEALS do...

For five minutes he sat, thinking, before adding another question to the list.

TWENTY-ONE

September 20, 2003

B erbera, Somaliland, was the *Sagar*'s first port of call after passing through the Suez Canal. At dawn Arwan and Jamil disembarked and got into a car, its driver honking continuously to open a path through the swollen crowd. Morgan watched it creep away.

With the off-loading done, Morgan wandered the open street markets near the wharf. The carcasses of abandoned boards and boxes from the day before were now tables that displayed wares to be exchanged, bartered, or sold. In all the ports, the bazaars offered local foods and goods, legitimate or stolen—and always drugs.

In Berbera one of those offerings was khat. Flown in daily from Ethiopia, eager customers would swarm the tarmac to be first in line to buy a bundle of the slender purple and green stalks. What those peddlers didn't sell they'd chew to add to their own tombstone-eyed euphoria. Watching the locals grind the plants with decaying teeth, oozing olive saliva, reminded Morgan of goats frozen in place, contently munching cud. He declined offers to indulge and headed back to the ship, waiting on the dock near the gangway.

Belching filthy exhaust, four semitrailer trucks pushed through the tumult and stopped abreast of each other near the freighter's stern. The air horn of the first truck drew Morgan's attention to

Arwan's face as it stuck out the passenger's window. Peppered with his usual sacrilegious profanity, he shouted at the crew to quickly get their asses down to the quay.

Using his stick to support him, Jamil dropped from the second cab and waved Morgan over. "Two bundles of khat in my truck. Take them aboard," he shouted over the noise, adding the hasty explanation, "gifts for friends in Yemen tomorrow."

Morgan hid his frown as he removed the huge burlap bags. Backtracking north was an unscheduled change in the itinerary, which would delay even more his arrival in Pakistan. That worried him. The BMW had been at the airport for almost two months. The pilfered license plate would only slow the authorities so long. Eventually the car would be considered abandoned and impounded—and searched. They would find the box.

The Pruitts would be contacted and at some point hopefully receive its contents. Given Jon's placid but persistent temperament, he would do what Janie had tried and failed to do and doggedly search for him. In time Interpol could be alerted.

Morgan needed to get off the *Sagar*.

He carried the bundles into a storage room then climbed to the freighter's bridge deck. In the drenching humidity, his arms resting on the railing, Morgan saw Jamil point his deverish stick at each truck, apply a numerical sequence for unloading acknowledged by the drivers with nods seen through the windshields, then limp a dozen yards farther in front of the truck cabs. While holding his stick like a conductor's baton preparing to cue an orchestra, Jamil stood in the shade under a shanty roof and monitored his wristwatch, waiting by Morgan's estimate at least two minutes.

The spear tip dramatically reached and pointed at the truck instructed to move first. It pulled forward alongside the freighter. The *Sagar*'s huge crane turned and began lowering its heavy cables.

Arwan came up to the bridge, passing Morgan without acknowledging his existence. Through the window Morgan saw him holding beer bottles in each hand. At first he was amazed that Jamil and Arwan hadn't killed each other during their road trip but the explanation had to be within the large brick-colored containers being lifted to the freighter's deck. Morgan continued to study the on-loading symphony.

After the first two containers were aboard and secured on the deck, the crane operator lifted the next one from the third truck, moving it over until it swayed gently a few feet above the first container.

Morgan saw Hamid scamper onto the upper surface of the container beneath with a tank on his back and a nozzle in his hand. Hidden briefly from Morgan's sight, Hamid emerged spray-painting the final top square yards a different color brown and climbed down. The crane operator lowered and mated the containers, and several crewmen secured them. The sequence repeated itself as the fourth and final container was brought aboard the ship.

They're hiding a big investment, thought Morgan, and until the huge boxes were delivered to wherever the hell they were going, Jamil was in charge—of everything.

————

To Morgan's relief, the passage back across the languid Gulf of Aden took less than a day. He could hear the turbines forcing the propellers to chew through the water, pushing the hull with determination. In the Red Sea near the island of Perim, the *Sagar* idled until high tide to slip into the abandoned shallow-water port.

"Barif, bring the bags down and say nothing," Jamil instructed, "then return to the ship."

Two flatbed trucks were waiting, their exhaust stacks exhaling black fumes.

Morgan did as instructed and then went to the bridge deck. With the engines rumbling below, blinded by the brightness of the decaying concrete quay, Morgan squinted under a straw hat, watching the action.

A man with a flowing white beard got out of a Mercedes with tinted windows. Jamil greeted him with a strong hug and quick kiss. Introducing the captain, the three men spoke as the top containers from Berbera were loaded and fastened onto the truck beds by men who emerged from the passenger doors of the cabs. In the withering heat they moved with efficiency, speaking little. When they had finished and gone back inside, the old man went to the car, removed a briefcase, and handed it to the captain. Arwan shook his hand and returned to the bridge.

Limping to one truck then the other, Jamil tapped on drivers' windows. With automatic pistols strapped to their thighs, each driver got out, picked up a sack of khat, and climbed back in. The trucks spit smoke and rolled away.

Jamil and the white-bearded man shook hands a final time then Jamil boarded the *Sagar* as the thick lines retracted from the rusting bollards. Just as they were fully winched aboard, thrusters pushed the ship away. The time at the wharf was fifteen minutes.

The first mate emerged from the pilothouse to get a clearer view of the ship's progress. Before going back inside, he said to Morgan, "Tractors."

The door latched behind him.

"No fucking chance," Morgan said under his breath while examining the tops of the other two containers.

TWENTY-TWO

National Geospatial Agency (NGA)
Springfield, Virginia September 22, 2003

The first hint had come after five years of monitoring electronic chatter of the Iranian trade group. Nothing was unusual in the e-mail communiqué—just a routine intelligence intercept, one of billions a day. The trade group wanted equipment from South Africa. The negotiated materials were never mentioned.

A subsequent e-mail confirming a significant deposit of deutsche marks in a Maldivian bank triggered more scrutiny. Linked to the account was the name of a former senior member of the South African nuclear organization who was fired for corruption. The man's niche trade—dealing in maraging steel used in the construction of high-speed centrifuges for uranium enrichment—was not sanctioned by the International Atomic Energy Commission nor looked on with any favor by the US government.

The final e-mail noted the shipping date, manifest, and the physical description of the containers. The National Security Agency (NSA) published its report electronically to authorized government customers. The recipients—the military, the Defense Intelligence Agency, CIA, and the NGA—were looking for clandestine nuclear activity. The request was implicit with the report: determine the container contents and their final destinations.

"We keep looking the wrong way!" Glen Sorenson said in a tone louder than his normal voice. In frustration the junior analyst pushed his desk chair away from his computer and pulled off his rimless glasses. Rubbing the inside corners of his eyes, he added, "Damn it!"

He put his glasses back on and looked around to see if his superior overheard him. The Middle Eastern Nuclear Division office worked under her strict rules, and she didn't accept even minor profanity.

Certain he hadn't been overheard, he went back to work.

Son of a bitch! I wish we looked at Africa more!

Despite their increasing numbers, the constellation of spy satellites was used for more important searches than what was considered the irrelevant continent of Africa. Sorenson had reviewed the data from subsequent passes and still could not find the freighter. The last satellite picture taken two days earlier showed the containers on their trailer trucks next to a ship—their violent overland journey concluded.

Where did you go? You sneaky little bastard! The analyst was irked. Pausing to think, his hand left the keyboard so his fingernails could comb the sides of his relaxed ash-brown hair. *Bet you turned northwest...*

Unable to resolve his assertion, Sorenson bought a day-old satellite images from a French company. His growing smile confirmed his suspicion.

Hi, guys! You can't hide from me!

The ghost freighter had docked at a rarely used port on the western coast of Yemen. Viewed from three hundred miles above, the distinctive scratches on the two off-loaded cargo containers were telltale tattoos—and identical to those a Crystal spy satellite saw in South Africa earlier in the month, then outside a refugee camp at Mogadishu, and finally at the port. If the other two containers were still aboard, Sorenson was yet unable to identify them.

When Sorenson switched to thermal imaging, he knew the errant freighter was up to no good. He paged his supervisor to come to his workspace.

"Ma'am, remember that freighter I've been looking for? The one that loaded those containers in Barbera?"

Commander Elaine Jericho nodded.

"I've found it," he said.

The naval officer grimaced. A ship was a *she*, even a scow like the one undergoing scrutiny, but her new analyst was so determined Jericho just said, "What have you discovered?"

"This is from Yemen yesterday. Check it out."

She glanced at the satellite's name and coordinates, its orbital orientation, downlink data rate, and frequency. Glen enlarged the image until the freighter filled the frame.

"Commercial," she said. "Why?"

"No other images are available," replied Sorenson. "Lucky I found this one. The Saudis are conducting a Red Sea coastal erosion study."

"At least somebody got a picture." She said quietly. "Anyway... there's no legitimate reason for *her* to be at Mukha."

"I agree. My assessment is that the freighter's dimensions make it a *handy-size*," Sorenson continued, "Less than thirty-thousand tons with a deadweight draft maybe ten meters. It was high tide down there when this was taken. Please look at this IR image."

A simple click, and varying shades of gray blossomed to a garden of magenta expanding from a red core. The hot rainbow flowed forward through the bulkheads then streamed up the stack to a colossal plume.

"Ma'am, those engines are acting like an agitated bull waiting for the rodeo gate to open. Slipping that puppy in and out left no margin for error. They were in a hurry."

Whatever activity the ship and its crew were engaged in, it was clear they couldn't risk running aground. Getting trapped would make it suspect to the patrols in the Red Sea. The Egyptian navy was full of badasses, the Saudis worse.

"The captain must have planned this to the minute," she noted. Her fine eyebrows arched as full lips shaped the familiar pleasant yet firm smile. "Do you see the containers?"

He scrolled out to show her the trucks.

"The visible markings on these two are the same as in Berbera," he said sitting back to briefly rest his eyes. "The other containers—I can't identify them in this image, but they *should* be there. With the time interval between Berbera and Mukha, it's difficult to imagine another stop in between."

She leaned forward, bringing her jade green eyes closer to the screen. Sorenson tried to avoid looking at the profile of her eye-catching face. The taut bun pulling her deep jasper-hued red hair tight accentuated her petite nose and scattered freckles. A starched white military blouse offered nothing but a slight distortion of her breasts, and her creased regulation slacks almost concealed the outline of her hips. Sorenson smelled no perfume, hairspray, or body soap. Although she had left her officer's cap on her desk, not one of the analysts was ever fooled by this frequent yet trivial lapse of formality. The blue and gold epaulets had been duly earned. Jericho was in charge of managing the complex affairs of collecting and analyzing nuclear Middle East satellite intelligence for the Department of Defense.

Don't screw with me, her persona warned.

Nobody did.

From a pocket Jericho extracted a pen and pointed at the LED screen. "Glen, what do you think that thick black-and-white thing is that man is holding?"

Sorenson expanded the image to the maximum resolution, showing details in objects larger than eight inches. The picture degraded little between the satellite's camera and the surface. With no clouds, the angle of the late-morning sun made whatever the line was glow intensely.

"A fishing pole?" His hasty speculation came with an unsettled grin. She wasn't one for flippancy.

"Pointing it like one, but it's too short," she said, letting the comment go.

"A walking stick, I think." Sorenson did what he could to enhance the image. "The man holding it seems to be standing a little lopsided…In one of our images, I think I saw the end of a similarly patterned stick jutting out from under a roof line in Berbera."

"Show me," Jericho said.

Sorenson minimized the current image and opened the other picture from a file. Using the cursor, he drew a box around the tip of the stick and expanded it to the resolution of two inches.

"Maybe the same," the naval commander said.

"I'll see what I can do, Commander," he said.

"Let's go back to the other picture," she requested. Her head angled sideways as she looked again at the man on the quay in Mukha. "He has to be in somebody's database…"

"I'll work on it," Sorenson replied.

In time he'd understand each element. He had been trained to collect, exploit, and analyze. His ability to solve such paradoxes was one of the key reasons people like Sorenson were sought after graduate school. If need be, he'd work with the other analysts.

"There's someone who looks like the captain and another who looks like a sheik."

Sorenson focused on the car. "That's an older Mercedes, an SEL. Can't see the plates. The windows are tinted, and infrared shows"— he made a sucking sound through his cheeks—"it's air-conditioned, 'cause it's searing hot outside."

He continued. "As you can see, somebody's working the cargo crane." The dense megapixel snapshot caught the second container in the process of being loaded on a flatbed truck.

The cursor moved back to the freighter.

"There's a man on the bridge deck, with a straw hat, probably one of the lackeys…got some really sunburned arms." Sorenson shook his head. "Can't see inside the bridge, but somebody's got to be holding that ship tight to the pier."

The cursor raced over the screen while Sorenson tallied the number with his fingers. "I count maybe twenty-one people…maybe seven or eight of them are landlubbers, so the remaining twelve are crew, plus there have to be a few more we can't see."

"That sounds about right," Jericho said.

More mouse movements.

"Considering the consistency of our intelligence about those container boxes, that stuff needed to get somewhere," said Sorenson, "and we know it's not refrigerators. That they skedaddled like this assures it."

She frowned. "Why Yemen? I don't suppose you can generate a three-dimensional image to see if the other containers are aboard?"

"No, sorry, ma'am...not from this." Sorenson tried not to let his exasperation show.

"They might have been taken off after this image, but with only two trucks present, I think we should assume they were still onboard, especially with the timelines I noted."

Jericho's tacit nod suggested agreement.

"There's another issue," he said. "Their transponder's been off since Berbera." That made the freighter more invisible, but with bribes to the port authority that violation of maritime law wouldn't even be noticed.

"Illegal, but I'm not surprised," Jericho replied.

"Fortunately," Sorenson said, "after several orbits we were able to radar-paint surface traffic exiting the Red Sea since yesterday."

Sorenson single-clicked on the toolbar. Radar profiles of ships appeared.

"This one," he pointed, "too small, probably a plump fishing trawler." The cursor seemed to move in all directions at the same time. "This one's an ARAMCO tanker southeast bound."

The cursor swept another erratic loop until he highlighted an image.

"This one was on a...70.819 *true* heading that would fit the timeline," he said with grin.

"Toward Iran...or Pakistan..." Jericho said. "Hmm..."

Sorenson looked at her. "The signature matches the one in Yemen."

It was clear Glen was excited by his first serious engagement as an imagery analyst.

"What will it take for you to find *her*?" she asked. The woman's demanding nature expected nothing but results if her analyst continued to invest resources. She scorned wasted time.

"Ma'am, if we can cue some assets to hunt for this bogey—I can ascertain a lot more about its ports of call, and those containers." He looked at her confidently. "I bet I can even get the name on the stern."

"*If* always rules," she replied, knowing targeting satellites wasn't an insignificant request. Billion-dollar space vehicles were engaged based on hierarchy of need and reliable data—not fungible information.

"I'll write up the report immediately," he said.

"Good work, Glen."

Jericho gave her usual precise nod but felt unsure. Finding the ship many hours later would still be difficult, even with satellites directed to hunt. She'd review his report and make any corrections before publishing it, along with the targeting request, under both their names. Requesting an immediate satellite search for a freighter, especially departing a country beneath suspicion like Yemen, had to be labeled properly. That was *her* job.

Jericho sighed.

America had been attacked and people had died. Despite political rhetoric to the contrary, the frustrations of working through the silos of a fragmented bureaucracy with egotistical vanities hadn't quelled.

Jericho would be resolute. If the request were denied, she'd call the director. The admiral would push the CIA so Glen could get his satellite survey and she'd help him find his ship.

TWENTY-THREE

September 23, 2003

Tensing his core muscles, Morgan gripped a pipe with buckets of water hanging from each end and squatted. His legs pushed the load back to vertical.

Beards suck...

Squat.

Up.

Damn pimples...

Down.

Jamil...helpful...

Up.

Squat.

Up.

He knows more...

Squat.

Squat.

One hundred eighty squats a day—every day.

Drenched in perspiration, Morgan stowed the equipment and got on his knees. Edging his toes up the bulkhead, they came to rest on the flat ledge. He forced his torso into a frozen push-up with his Koran open in front on the white cotton. As he read, the sweat collected in the dimple of his lower back. When the depression was full, the puddle would trickle to the deck.

When he finished exercising, he held the Koran in his hands for a while.

"Damn, if I've not learned to understand this," he said.

He had studied its verses for two years. When he was young, he had read the Bible in Sunday school with the same intensity.

"Another faith hijacked by a few," he sighed.

Love your enemies and do good to those who hate you, Luke's Gospel said.

Repel evil with goodness and enemies will become the closest of friends, as said in the Koran 43:34.

Morgan wasn't surrendering to either notion.

Cay was dead.

He wrapped the Koran in the cotton, placed it in his backpack hanging beneath the hatch, and walked aft. Jamil and the engineer were standing outside the door of the crew quarters as he approached.

"Barif, I continue to admire your discipline and devotion," Jamil said, "considering your upbringing."

"You are infected with a desire to fight," the engineer said, taking a drag from a cigarette, the filtered end glued to his lower lip, allowing both hands the freedom to exaggerate his words. "You slipped through the fingers of the American stooges but will return to them someday and cause much fear."

"My friends, thank you," said Morgan.

Jamil nodded but said nothing, pointing with his head toward Hamid, who stopped to greet them before ascending the stairs to the bridge. Arwan followed him less than a minute later, grunting when he passed.

When he was gone, Jamil said to Morgan, "Barif, my brother, Omar, and I will speak soon. I know he will help you in your journey... Inshallah."

———

Paul Cotsworth tipped back from his desk to put his feet up. The police report filed the year earlier by Ross Merrimac couldn't be found. Cotsworth doubted there would be much in it anyway. The man wasn't missing then—only misplaced, and only to his friends. Morgan wasn't the usual 'he'll turn up dead' story.

Cotsworth's interview with Henrietta revealed only that until Morgan released her with a large severance check, she had watched him grow more reclusive...finding him at home often wearing just underwear. Many guys did that.

"Doesn't look like you decided to take a vacation," the agent said reviewing his notes. "No cell phone...no credit card activity for... eighteen months. So you went to cash..."

Cotsworth jiggled his head in disbelief, recalling his useless phone call to Morgan's attorney. The attorney cited client privilege but nonetheless confided he hadn't had contact with the surgeon for many months.

"So you cleaned up all the bills, sold the townhouse, and paid all the taxes," Cotsworth had said to him.

No comment.

"Fucking lawyers..." Cotsworth said after hanging up.

Next he had checked with the IRS. Morgan had posted no income for that year.

"Where's the money?" The agent unconsciously chewed on a pencil gripped across his teeth. "Bet the lawyer's holding it in a trust fund, along with other assets."

Another thing to research... It just went on and on.

Cotsworth studied the pictures Brosinski had given him.

"Man! We learned that shit at Quantico." The two men sprawled on the ground were seriously injured. Their medical records confirmed that. "That took big cojones."

How did a doctor go from saving kids' lives to kicking the shit out of thugs?

"Not *how*. *Why* is the question."

Cotsworth's finger rubbed his lip while he again opened the glossy brochure about Pruitt's architectural firm stopping at the section Merrimac had paper clipped.

Caroline Pruitt received her master's degree in architecture from the University of Virginia. After contributing to many successful projects in our New York office, Ms. Pruitt eagerly accepted the opportunity to grow our Chicago presence. The energetic Windy City, with its strong tradition of architectural firsts, a cornucopia of imaginative designs and visionary styles, offers many exciting...

"My God!"

Each time Cotsworth saw Pruitt's photograph, he reacted with the same intensity. The woman's face was daunting, her eyes unimaginably as she stood in the back row with her taller male associates.

"What was she...five eight, without heels?" he exclaimed. "I didn't know architects looked like that! I bet Morgan just..."

Of course, he did...

Cotsworth opened the file on the BMW, frowning when he read the forensics report. The three-year-old automobile had forty-six thousand miles—much more than expected from daily commuting in Chicago. There were no recent repair records, but the oil was clean and the tires had deep treads. The serial numbers might tell him where Morgan bought them.

"I don't think so," Cotsworth muttered. "Not a chance."

Maintenance had been off the books, and there were no fingerprints.

"Wiped clean...just like the apartment..."

But, then, why leave the box?

DNA analysis of the items inside was underway. The specifics would be entered in the CODIS database to help identify his body—if it was ever found.

"Ain't happening in a million years," said Cotsworth.

Pulling the stopper from the Scotch, he took a long whiff, passed on the temptation for a taste, and recorked the Macallan. The pair of crystal brandy snifters rested on his desk while he picked up a magnifying glass and examined the diamond setting. The center stone had to be over two carats and was flawless.

"This wasn't cheap…"

The framed photograph of the couple in formal wear confirmed again why cost was no object. He removed the CD from its plastic sleeve and played the short message several times.

"Sexy voice," he said. "He must have lost his mind listening to this…"

Then he read the letter…

> Jon and Connie,
> Please keep these for Cay and me.
> With love, your son

"Maybe you killed yourself…Had every reason to, I guess."

Cotsworth rubbed his forehead, wrote *suicide* on his pad, paused and scratched a line through the word.

"I'm not going there…not yet, anyway."

He scrounged through his desk for a ruler. Across the horizontal side of a piece of paper he penciled *Timeline*, then he drew perpendicular lines and placed pieces of information where they fit the best. The gaps were plentiful, but one thing was clear: beginning months earlier, the physician's life was heading off the grid. Unless Morgan left subsequent evidence, the BMW was probably his last contact point. In Cotsworth's line of work, the recent two-month gap was a colossal vacuum of lost data.

The phone interrupted his meditations.

"Agent Paul Cotsworth," he answered.

"Morning. Jerry Horowitz, DNA Forensics."

The guy's accent was instantly recognizable. He had to have grown up in Brooklyn.

Cotsworth jotted the name and number. "What's up?"

"Processed both of those hair specimens." He read the letters and numbers of the file code. "Labeled Morgan, right?"

"Yes," Cotsworth said—*Brosinski's crap.* "I guess they didn't get lost in transit."

"Who collected this material?"

"A third party," answered Cotsworth.

"Reliable?"

"Certainly." Cotsworth's response was the opposite of what he believed.

"Interesting," admitted Horowitz. "Positive it wasn't contaminated?"

"Why?"

"I've done some preliminary DNA evaluations of both particle types before digging into the MT and STR analysis."

"I know how it works." Cotsworth didn't remember, but it was no matter.

"Okay. From what I've analyzed, the subject is a mammal and male," said Horowitz.

"That's reassuring."

"There's a problem," said Horowitz. "The chromosome count is wrong."

The FBI agent sat forward. "How so?"

"I count thirty-eight, nineteen pairs, including XY."

"Humans have…"

"Forty-six."

"Both specimens?" asked Cotsworth.

"Right again," said Horowitz.

"So what the hell is that supposed to mean?"

"Probably an animal contaminant," said Horowitz.

"Like what? A cat?"

"No."

"How about a dog?"

"No, they have seventy-eight."

Do they need that many?

"So what the hell is it?" Cotsworth was fuming. Brosinski had to be playing a joke on him.

"To tell, I'm going to have to outsource the specimens."

"Where?"

"Purdue has the most complete animal database. It'll take two weeks, maybe less."

"Crap, that long?" Cotsworth couldn't wait. The director personally called him every other day.

"I'll let *you* know when *I* know," said Horowitz. "Have a nice day."

Cotsworth slammed the phone. "If you're screwing with me, Brosinski…"

Sliding his notes in a folder, he dropped the sleeve in a drawer and pushed back his chair. The bar at the Berghoff was two blocks away and he wanted some sauerbraten—and a beer.

TWENTY-FOUR

Badar-e-Abbas, Iran September 24, 2003

Jamil and Morgan said good-bye at the Iranian port terminal. There the two remaining cargo containers from Berbera were off-loaded.

"My destiny takes me farther, my friend," said Morgan.

"Mine also." Jamil handed him a small piece of paper with a name and address. "My brother, Omar. God willing, your journey takes you to him. He will help as he has helped many."

Morgan memorized the information and tore the paper in tiny pieces, which fluttered to the water.

When they embraced a final time, Jamil said in his ear, "Beware of the captain. His god is money and worldly pleasure, not the true Paradise we seek."

"Peace be with you," said Morgan and watched Jamil descend the gangplank and turn for a final wave with his dervish cane in hand. He boarded a large sport utility vehicle with dark windows that in moments became part of the endless traffic.

After the *Sagar* pushed out to sea, Morgan climbed to the bridge deck and stared at the distant coastline, softening in the darkness. Only a distant lighthouse beacon confirmed that land was still there.

"Barif, come in," the first officer called after Morgan knocked. He never entered the control center unless invited. He saw Arwan swooning on a couch as several empty bottles of Dutch beer rolled on a nearby table with each sway of the ship.

"I suppose you're here to use the loudspeaker again…for those damn prayers." Arwan's drunken eyes glared with contempt. "You people should have some fun…fuck camels or—"

The first officer cut him off. "When are you leaving us, Barif, now that Jamil is gone?"

"Soon, I hope," the captain answered for him.

"Yes, soon," Morgan replied.

The first officer continued. "Barif, you're a fine sailor. I will hate to see you go."

"I fucking won't," said Arwan.

The first officer glanced at the hull speed then performed the simple long division. "If the seas stay calm, the *Sagar* will be in Karachi…perhaps 0300 the day after tomorrow."

Morgan drifted beyond the center console, stopping outside the chart room. "May I go in?"

"Of course," the officer laughed.

"Stay away from the *Playboys* in there," grumbled Arwan. "Keep your dick in your pants, 'cause if I find you beat all over them, I'll personally stick mine up your little ass," he said.

"I won't touch them," Morgan said, entering the calm space used to plot navigational courses.

The door shut. Aglow in red light, he waited for his eyes to adjust. Locating a chart for the coast of Pakistan, Morgan took his time studying the sea lanes and water depths.

Dripping with sweat, Morgan paused to look over the railing at the fan of light spreading up from the explosive late-September sunset. With nothing left to do but remove the backpack from below the hatch and get his remaining clothes from his bunk, he continued exercising long after dusk. He'd be off the Sagar soon. For that he was grateful. He'd had enough of the crew, especially Arwan. But the freighter had served his purpose.

"Jamil was very accommodating…"

Perhaps in another life Morgan would have called him a true friend, but even in Houston his actions portrayed authority—and intent. Berbera, Perim, and Badar-e-Abbas confirmed it.

Morgan would find Omar.

Groaning in rhythm with each wave, the guy-wires hummed in the wind above the containers. Across the bow the shore beacon winked twice every nine seconds, confirming what Morgan had learned from the chart. The Cape Monze lighthouse was thirty miles west of Karachi, leaving only two more hours at sea.

He threw his exercise equipment overboard then sat on a box in his sweaty workout shirt and shorts to look at the nebula over the port city. With a crescent moon hiding hours beneath Earth, even the stars seemed extraordinarily bright. He relaxed, thankful that the first mate had forgotten to switch on the lights. That never happened at night when the freighter was underway. His face washed by the sea air's shifting texture, his thoughts drifted into the distraction of what would never be.

"Tomorrow's your birthday, Cay," he sighed.

They never had the opportunity to celebrate it even once.

"Happy birthday, sweetheart."

He glowered.

To his right he heard a sound that wasn't metallic. His auditory perception focused in the direction of the noise. He glanced that way but saw nothing,

A quartet of soft thumps came from the port side. He knew the ship made peculiar noises, all boats did. When he studied the grayness around him again, his adrenalin surged.

The lights were never supposed to be off.

A blade tip pressed between his ribs. Fast, foul, heavy breathing came from above his head. Only one person on board was that tall.

"Captain sell you as a fuck slave." Hamid released a putrid laugh. "Split the money with me."

The blade persuaded Morgan to stand. As he slowly rose, a face coalesced in front of him.

Oozing fury, Arwan's bitter visage spoke.

"Sorry your friend Jamil isn't here to play too." The captain was drunk. "Hamid...go ahead...See if his asshole's big enough."

Hamid pinched the blade tip in Morgan's side, forcing him to bend over. Pulling down his workout shorts, Morgan glanced at the bulkhead. He would have to be patient. A firm, thick penis began its probing. The sensation grew painful when Hamid forced in the erection.

The pumping started.

Arwan unzipped his pants. Before they landed at his ankles his reeking penis rubbed across Morgan's lips.

"Suck hard!" he commanded and moaned when the organ pushed deep in Morgan's mouth.

Hamid pumped faster. The knife pressure softened.

Morgan waited.

Hamid's sharp jabbing ended as he became consumed in orgasm. Morgan clamped his teeth hard on the captain's penis. He screamed as he tried to pull out. Morgan opened his mouth and with two quick steps yanked the pickax off its bulkhead mountings.

Hamid never felt the four-inch steel tip sink through his ear. As swiftly as the spike went deep in his brain, it came out. Morgan turned toward the captain, crumpled in agony. Swinging in an underhand arch, Morgan impaled the pick below Arwan's breastbone, driving it into the bottom of his heart. The captain became upright.

His breathing stopped.

Morgan moved his hand down the ax handle to pull the man closer. The captain tried to focus but the eclipse at the outer rims of his eyes was rapidly migrating inward. Before his vision dissolved to static, he stared at the halcyon eyes of the passenger named Barif Ali and saw a blankness he hadn't appreciated before.

Morgan never blinked as he tugged the handle up.

TWENTY-FIVE

Latitude 24.76 Longitude 66.85 September 26, 2003 0218 Pakistani Standard Time

Morgan let his grip relax, allowing the ax handle to slide through his fist until the sagging body lay on the deck. He scanned the space around him. He was alone, the stillness interrupted only by the wind. What light there was came from the muted glow of the bridge house, splintered into penumbras by the derricks, containers, and rigging. The Monze lighthouse was barely visible, but the one near the port channel was much brighter. Obscurity wouldn't last long.

Morgan hacked and spit. The foul taste stuck in his throat, but relief would have to wait. He turned to the immediate task.

The impaled ax handle rocked with the panting sea. Soon the force would rent the tissue and there would be blood—and a mess. Morgan's night-adapted eyes guided him to the hatch near the gunwale. Spinning the wheel, he opened the lid and reached in among the wires. He lifted the backpack from its hook and set it on the deck.

Morgan removed the ax pick from Arwan and dragged the body until the head and shoulders sagged into the hole. Elevating the captain by the legs, gravity ultimately swallowed the rest.

The Somali followed.

Deep inside the double hull, they'd remain interred for months. No one ever descended into the airless catacomb unless an electrical short required such an exploration.

"You bastards," he whispered. "All I wanted to do was get off this damn boat."

It would be their only epitaph. As sweat poured from Morgan's body, he dogged the hatch shut.

Morgan looked across the water for the port channel. Little time remained.

He stuck the stiletto in the outer mesh of the backpack and strapped the bag on. Pulling out some fire hose, he opened the valve a little, gargled and spit out the seawater.

It didn't help.

Increasing the water pressure, Morgan washed the deck, hatch, and ax and carefully scrutinized the area. No evidence of any struggle existed. The crew would shortly discover three men were missing, and it was imperative to keep them confused. Without bodies no one would know what happened—at least until Morgan was long gone.

"Shit…"

He'd have to leave behind the clothes on his bunk.

"I got to get the fuck outta here," he said, heading aft.

———

Sitting at the bottom of a rope loop, Morgan hurtled forward again.

Crash!

His cocked knees absorbed another blow as the *Sagar* pitched forward in the waves. Once again his head missed smashing against the transom. Hooked through a steel eyelet forty-five feet above, the rope was a rattail whip with Morgan at the end, holding on.

Between each swell he struggled. The unbalanced backpack contributing to his precarious position, he fought to regain his orientation before the next pitch. The life of the old pair of running shoes would soon be over, but right now they were all he had to protect his feet from the razor-sharp barnacles. The rolling sea and lingering foul taste made him nauseous. He breathed deeply, sucking in as much air he could.

Crash!

The ship descended suddenly, the stern crushing the crest of a wave. Thousands of gallons of cold water shot upward, drenching him. He shivered as the foam blew off in the wind. The harsh turbulence burrowed the square knot he had tied deeper into his violated ass. He accelerated forward again, holding the rope arms tighter and vomiting.

"Captain Arwan to the bridge please," the first office called over the loudspeakers, screaming life into the ship. Morgan looked at the water and saw no shadow. He was invisible.

The *Sagar*'s heading changed, and with it, the wave beat.

"Captain Arwan to the bridge," the first officer called again.

As the ship turned toward the channel, the relentless pitching subsided more. Waves rolled lengthwise under the hull, sweeping Morgan gently back and forth. City lights filled the starboard sky.

He had two miles to wait.

Seconds passed.

"Captain Arwan to the bridge!" The first officer's voice was distorted. "Hamid! Barif! On deck...immediately!"

The growling engines dropped an octave, diminishing the wake. Their rumble grew even deeper.

Moments later came three prolonged blasts from the ship's horn and a general alarm.

Man overboard!

Beams from searchlights pared the darkness. Voices shouted above Morgan. The poop deck's lantern scattered off the choppy backwash, surveying the sea.

The hull speed decreased again, but Morgan knew the ship couldn't slow much more. If the *Sagar* lost steerage this close to the channel's mouth, she'd run into the rocky breakwater before the tugboats arrived. He looked at the water moving below.

Only a minute more...

He listened, knowing a search-and-rescue helicopter would come soon. Dissecting the noise, he soon heard the sound of chopping air echo off the water. Under a brilliant spotlight, the search would begin at the bow, progress aft, and continue in the wake.

Morgan pulled up so his shoes straddled the knot. Above his head one hand gripped both lines together as his other hand used the stiletto to gnaw through the rope close to his waist. When the knot fell away, the downward pull became immense. The knife fell into the water and his free hand joined the other. Hanging by both arms, Morgan glanced to his left and right. The quarter-mile-long breakwater was imminent.

Looking up beyond the white letters *Shindu Sagar,* beyond the poop deck through the diffused light spilling over the edge, he inhaled and stared at the heavens.

He could smell Caroline as their lips riveted together, his fingertips running through her hair. She smiled—her eyes radiant, telling him what he longed to hear but never would again.

His right hand joined his left, and the rope's free end sped up and out of the steel ring. Dr. Morgan slid into the disturbed charcoal sea.

TWENTY-SIX

Even at slack tide, swimming out of the ship's wake was a bitch. Wearing a buoyant backpack made it damn near impossible. Cursing the added drag with the slap of every wave, his arms fought to pull him farther away while his cupped hands tried to clear an opening through the floating effluence.

The searchlight brushed over him. He unclipped the bag and submerged, gripping one of the straps. The beam returned and paused trying to pierce the turgid water, then moved away for good.

The current pushing him where he couldn't go, Morgan knew the breakwater pilings had to be close. If he got swept into them, his injuries would be lethal, but he stayed below the surface until his lungs screamed for air, then he swam like hell. The waves pounced, rolling him with added offense. But the turbulence gradually eased, and he paused to tread water to inventory what he saw.

The helicopter was low on the horizon, tracing the phosphorescent plankton wake. Several patrol boats were out of the channel in the open water, their lights surveying intensely for human outlines. The pulsating bursts of brightness from the lighthouse illuminated an empty beach.

Morgan swam another hundred yards then treaded water again. Waves crashed on the deserted beach.

Removing his backpack, he sank several feet beneath the surface. His shoes made contact. With the black bag in front to hide his face, he followed a small spiller in, pausing in neck-deep water to look around.

"Ouch…"

His right leg became instantly on fire. He touched the throbbing blaze. His skin was intact.

Jellyfish…

Constraining each breath, he struggled up the steep underwater terrace, his feet sinking in the gravel. He crawled onto the beach and lay flush on the sand, studying his surroundings again.

The helicopter was miles away, so were the patrol boats and…

God, how his leg hurt!

No time to think about it.

Morgan sat and pulled the backpack close, opening it. It was dry inside. The dual zippers had maintained their seals. He removed a gray satchel and laid it on the sand, scooped a few rocks into the backpack, and zipped it partly. Returning to waist-deep water, he heaved the bag as far as he could. This reliable accomplice, bought long before his fingers ever jammed a crack, burbled and sank.

After another scan of the beach, he emerged from the water and urinated on his leg. The soothing liquid soon dried. The breeze made his skin burn again.

The thin moon had risen. To the west Mars was minutes above the horizon, making dawn three hours away.

Morgan opened the satchel and removed a black salwar kameez that he put on over new cotton underwear. His feet slipped into supple leather sandals. He picked up his running shoes, nylon shorts, and T-shirt and stood in the quiet strangeness. Bathed in a cool sea breeze, an odd tranquility came over him—the last few minutes on the ship's foredeck a remorseless memory.

He smiled impassively. Six miles ahead were millions of Karachi citizens, and by sunrise he would plan to disappear in the faceless throngs.

With the satchel slung over a shoulder, Morgan walked along the island road. One shoe found a trash can, the other landed in a mangrove swamp. Everything else was lost to a cluster of bushes.

He found a bicycle outside a dark house. A mile down the sand-swept road, past the hanging fishing nets, the bicycle seat pressing into his chafed rear, he heard the pitch deepen and smother the world in a clamoring roar. The Sea King search-and-rescue helicopter was returning home. The searchlight was off—its mission futile.

Barif Ali rode on as the machine flew overhead.

———

Before dawn Morgan abandoned the bicycle against a crumbling wall and walked the last mile until he found a stone bench near the Old City Street Market. His body craved both food and water, and he knew he could find whatever he needed there—after dawn. He waited, the pain in his abraded anus made worse from the worn bicycle seat, while his leg, inflamed from the jellyfish stingers, burned.

A dense cloud of cannabis drifted toward him from a hidden source. Morgan held his breath waiting for it to pass, then with slowed breathing let the purity of his training relax his body to soothe the pain. Even in his prime as a surgeon he was never able to completely reduce the tension that crept through his neck and shoulders when he leaned over the operating table. Now not a single thought or calorie was directed toward feeling relief, worry, or anything at all. His concerns were only practical. The notion of congratulating himself for doing what years ago would have been impossible never even occurred to him. All he thought was: *At least I'm off that piece of shit boat...*

Fuck 'em," he said under his breath.

They were dead and he wasn't, and nobody would know what happened.

Listening for noises where his eyes could not see, his intense focus finally brought enough reassurance that he allowed his senses to submit to the aroma of baking breads and sizzling lamb with curry and onions. As sunlight seeped between the buildings, loudspeakers from rooftops projected the muezzin's atonal chant, calling the city to prayer. Minutes later the market came alive with the music of Qawwali, hip-hop, even American pop.

Withered children soon paraded everywhere, carrying fruits, vegetables, and burlap bags of rice. Working as slaves for the vendors, the little ones did as commanded, hoping their devotion would produce a morsel to feed their empty stomachs. Around them traffic increased, accelerating the world. A medley of horns blared, while from automobiles, tongas, and rickshaws, greetings flew back and forth, all in the male voice.

Morgan waited for the crowds to thicken. The local mafias controlled the markets, and their lookouts assembled early to watch the patrons, marking new punters who flashed rupees or didn't barter, making them suspect, in need of more scrutiny.

He'd have to wait just a little longer...

———

The mango shake was sweet and dense, filled with brown sugar, honey, fresh milk, and eggs. Morgan fought the desire to gulp the syrupy fluid and drank it slowly. He placed bottles of green tea in his satchel.

A vendor plucked a steaming chicken marinated in spices from a spit above a charcoal fire and tossed it on a board. Without repositioning his fingers, the cook swung a cleaver with precision, severing the bird in half. Morgan nodded with respect. Placing the meat on a sheet of waxed paper, the cook ladled coriander chutney on it.

"Shokran," said Morgan. *Thank you.* Speaking first in Arabic would give him the chance to see how convincing he sounded. If he had to, he could easily convert to English, which was prevalent in Pakistan, without raising suspicion.

After a taste he licked his fingers and belched—the most sincere compliment possible.

The man leaned toward Morgan until their faces were inches apart. "You come from Egypt?" the man asked in English.

"No," Morgan replied. "Lebanon."

"What is your name, friend?"

"Barif."

"You remind me of my cousin," he grinned.

"That's an honor to me," Morgan said with a broad smile that pushed his cheeks high. He was exhausted, but after what had just happened, taking time for ordinary conversation with a courteous local was a satisfying introduction to the country.

Morgan belched again and said, "I must be off."

"You must be staying and telling me more, please," the man requested.

"Next time, my friend," Morgan promised. He shook the man's hand and moved on.

As Morgan sat on another bench, devouring the bird, a mangy dog hobbled from a passageway, whimpering for a treat. The animal rubbed his flanks against Morgan's leg. Ignored, the mongrel kept pestering.

With a snap of his toes to its underbelly, the dog sulked away. No one watching would think anything of the jab.

Morgan shifted pressure off his buttocks. Finding some salve with zinc or rosemary was paramount to reduce the inflammation and risk of infection. He eyed a little stall across the market that sold herbal remedies. It would be his next stop before he went farther into the city.

———

Morgan found a hostel where he could shower and rest. Sucking on a cigarette painted with hash oil, his eyes transfixed on a televised soccer match, the desk clerk never looked at Morgan's passport while he took a calculator from a drawer.

"Twenty-four hundred rupees a—"

"Fifteen," said Morgan.

The clerk looked at him with bloodshot eyes.

"No, no, no," he said. "Twenty."

"Seventeen," said Morgan.

"For how long?" asked the man, returning his attention to the television.

"I don't know."

The clerk took another hit. Holding the smoke in his lungs he exhaled a little and offered the smoldering roach to Morgan.

He shook his head and said, "I'll pay you for three weeks."

The clerk exhaled into Morgan's face and tried to turn on the calculator but the battery was dead, so he used his fingers.

"Eleven...thousand..." He wrote the number on his hand.

Morgan smiled patiently and started watching the soccer game.

"Nine hundred..." Morgan countered.

More ink went next to the first number. Finally he showed Morgan the amount. As the hashish weighed the man's ability to think, he started laughing uncontrollably.

One hundred forty dollars—Morgan loved bartering.

"Up," the man pointed and handed him a key.

Climbing the creaking stairs, Morgan walked down a hallway, passing a door that couldn't hide the smell of marijuana or moans of carnal pleasure. It wouldn't bother him. He was going to do something he hadn't done in years—sleep.

The hunt would begin in the morning.

TWENTY-SEVEN

NGA September 26, 2003 0830 Eastern Daylight Time

After the final identification check, Sorenson entered his alternate world—a place that had no day or night, where the hands on his watch became an irrelevant illusion. Spy satellites worked in the instant, zipping in tandem circles around Earth in sun-synchronous orbits. Every ninety-nine minutes each would fly over the same latitude, but looking down a little farther west because of the planet's axial spin. In endless twenty-four-hour loops, the data downloaded to an ever-expanding library of information.

"Morning, Z!" He greeted his colleague Zand Zamani at the coffeepot. "Wife and kids okay?"

"Yuppers! And I'm off tonight!" said the former Desert Shield marine, whose family had escaped Iran in 1979. "Taking the brood to Chuck E. Cheese."

"A night away from here?" said Sorenson. "Is that a first?"

With an extensive background in Middle Eastern military strategy, Jericho hired Zamani to manage night-shift data analysis. Enjoying the solitude, Z, as they nicknamed him, had remained in that position long after seniority dictated otherwise. Though he was willing to stay into the morning to help scrutinize fresh data, few day-shift analysts ever wanted to detain him. They knew he enjoyed getting his kids to school so he could spend time alone with his wife.

That was no surprise. Sorenson understood the first time they met at a party. With a honeyed voice, the articulate Muslim woman stunned everyone in her black dress and head scarf. The couple met at the CIA, where she translated Iranian government communication intercepts from Farsi into English. Rumor was they took their breaks together. After they were married, their passel of children grew larger every other year. No one doubted the reason.

"Bed might be a novel experience." Zamani gave an expectant nod. "In the dark for a change."

"I bet," said Sorenson.

"Probably mess up my biorhythms bad."

"You marines can tough it out." Sorenson laughed. "Hope you get some sleep…sometime."

He looked toward the door. Jericho had entered with her usual china cup filled with freshly steeped tea.

"I'm off to observe from my perch in the sky," he said.

Standing at his workstation, Sorenson waited as his computer booted. Past the piles of books, maps, and thumbtacked cartoons, he watched his colleagues preparing to download their own morning pulls. Eventually they'd collaborate on what they were seeing and learning. Top-secret security clearances allowed them to share that much, but sources—the wellsprings of their information—were never revealed. Intelligence sources were critical to their work, and identities were protected, concealed in an unwritten trust. No matter how high one climbed in the intelligence tree—even those with Special Access Clearance (SAC)—those persons knew more, but never everything.

As a rule, every morning Elaine Jericho would round on each of her analysts to stop and casually talk, asking questions about their families and what they did the night before. Her ritual offered more than just polite conversations. She had done the same as a surface officer, touring the ship with regularity, wishing all hands well but studying every face. Clearances were no substitute for personal corroboration—an added intuitive assurance security that wasn't breached.

"Ready for a good day, Mr. Sorenson?"

"Good morning, ma'am," Glen said in his typical mellow voice that only grew animated if he drank coffee.

He could only glance at her. Her regulation wool sweater was more flattering than her usual blouse. Her heels tipped her hips forward ever so slightly. No one in the room thought Jericho appreciated how attractive she was, and nobody believed she dated. What a shame to have such assets wasted!

"Do anything interesting last night?" she asked.

"Naw. Love to admit I'm too hungover to think…but just went home and read some journals. Thinking of going for my PhD."

"You can never have too much education," she said with an approving grin.

"I guess."

The image of Bugs Bunny expanded out a hole from the center of his computer screen.

"What's up, Doc?" asked the rabbit.

She laughed lightly when she saw his splash page.

Even after ten months on the job, her presence still intimidated him. It wasn't just her rank. The women in graduate school at UCLA never looked this good.

"Getting ready to open my *pulls*," said Sorenson.

"Glen…thanks for what you do," she said sweetly. "Let me know how your day goes. And if there's anything I can do to help…"

She moved on to say good-bye to Zamani, who was closing down his workspace.

Sorenson entered more passwords. As the data downloaded, he got a fresh cup of coffee from the break room. Studying the orphaned doughnut in the box, he yielded to the hunger pangs in his stomach and took it back to his desk. The chocolate was soon on his fingers and smeared around the corners of his mouth.

The analyst waited as the attachments opened. He wanted to yelp when he saw that the NGA had fulfilled his request. Sorenson studied the images, radar footprint, and freighter's coordinates from three days before. The ship had passed through the Straits of Hormuz and had then turned due east.

"Commander Jericho suspected correctly," he said as his fingers manipulated the data. "You went to Iran…and then…" He looked at the coordinates and heading of the ship on the final image. "Headed into Karachi." He smiled respectfully at a picture stapled to his wall. "Thank you, Thomas Bayes."

The seventeenth-century minister had devised the mathematical theory the spy world used to filter probabilities. As information accumulated, the odds that the assumption was correct became more likely. All one had to do was enter the known data, and the program would constantly refine how the satellites searched. In time they located everything they were asked to find.

"Crud, still can't see the name." He did some quick calculations. "But you got into the port in Karachi at…" Sorenson clicked on the image's UCT (Universal Coordinated Time). Immediately converted to Eastern time, he looked at his watch.

"Hmm…fifteen hours ago."

He crammed the remaining piece of doughnut into his mouth, switched to infrared spectral imaging, and almost choked.

"Holy shit!" Spitting the damp pastry in his hand, he shouted louder, "What the hell is this?"

Jericho and Zamani stopped talking. With a bit more noise, his outburst would have been hidden, but everyone in the room heard it and peeked over their cubicles trying to see what would happen. If the redheaded officer said anything, they'd make fun of Glen later.

"Mr. Sorenson!" Jericho barely raised her voice above her characteristic sanguine tone.

The analyst didn't acknowledge that his superior had even spoken.

"Mr. Sorenson! I am talking to you, sir!"

To everyone's horror, he trivialized her directive with a frivolous wave-off, hypnotized by his computer screen.

"Hey, Z! Come here, man! Check this out!"

Zamani and Jericho were at his side immediately, with the other analysts soon crowding behind the trio. Sorenson looked up when the creased slacks halted inches from his face. He discarded the remains of the doughnut in his wastebasket, wiped his hand on his pants, and picked up a pencil.

"That freighter…" The eraser tip bounced rapidly on the screen. "Here's its radar image…caught broadside in the Karachi channel." A few more mouse clicks, and a more distinct infrared image appeared. "Commander Jericho…look at this!" He directed them to a pale gray and white cloud.

"Glen, what is that?" she asked.

"I think…a man."

"What?"

"That was *my* initial response too, a minute ago." Sorenson looked at Zamani. "What do you think?"

Several clicks revealed more.

"Looks that way, Glen," he said. The other analysts crowded even closer.

"What's he doing?" Jericho asked.

"Whoever he is"—Sorenson used software to tweak the image even more—"he made somebody mad. Looks like he's hanging from the stern."

"Can you guess how long he's been there?" asked Zamani.

"It appears here he's still warm…that means probably alive, at least when this was taken. There's more."

"What?" asked Jericho.

"An image distortion on his back…let's see…"

"Speculate." Jericho was impressed.

"No evidence of radiant heat from it." His hands drummed in unison on his desktop, causing his coffee to slosh, then Sorenson laughed cautiously. After a glance at the other analysts, his eyes held on Jericho. "Considering his circumstances, Commander…I'd say it's ballast."

"They probably"—Zamani's laugh infected them—"wanted to make sure he sank."

TWENTY-EIGHT

Jericho called the person who could help her the quickest. She imagined him tipping back in his chair, smiling beneath his receding hairline at the pictures of his grandchildren adorning the desk, the phone lodged between his jowls and shoulder, a coffee mug in one hand and a ballpoint pen clicking in the other.

"Good morning, Admiral."

"You're sounding all bright and cheery. What's up, Lainey darlin'?"

The naval commander took no offense. From Alabama, the soft-spoken Cottrell Herndon had talked this way to her in private since recruiting her. Forged in steel, the no-nonsense vice admiral was an affable Southern gentleman who understood military formality had its time and place, but not when he was consulting someone that he considered his equal.

"Admiral, go secure please."

She pressed a button on the STU-III. They'd speak again in fifteen seconds. The words *SECURE TO CODE WORD LEVEL* scrolled across the panel.

"So, Lainey, how was your electronic trip through space?"

"Good morning again, Admiral." She heard the pen clicking. "Interesting development. My new analyst found the freighter. Thanks to your help."

"Glad to be of assistance. Don't want the CIA Russia watchers stealing all the bandwidth."

That agency's fixation with the prior Cold War enemy remained a nagging hangover, frustrating other intelligence gathering. Negotiating satellite time required persistent effort.

"Sir, the ship moved the containers from Berbera to Mukha through a well-executed plan devised for deception."

"Darn those satellite viewers," Herndon commented.

No matter how secret, after every Vandenberg rocket launch, observers would monitor the trajectories, send the information to specific websites, and the calculations would begin. In days the satellite's orbit would be available to anyone with a computer. The information was so accurate, any illicit activity on the ground could be planned accordingly, hiding it from the probing sensors high above.

"Your man Sorenson did a fine job. Got some good folks working there. They make America proud." His chuckling fuzzed as his words were encrypted, transmitted, and reconstituted.

"Thank you, Admiral. They're all dedicated."

Herndon had given his highest recommendation that Jericho be assigned the senior analyst position. He admired her devotion to duty—a trait that had rubbed off on her staff.

"Gawd. Lainey darlin', I've told you to call me *Cotty*. We are encrypted…"

His unrelenting request was difficult for the starched officer. Ignoring him, she continued, "Sir, the IR image as the ship entered Karachi shows a person hanging off the stern," she paused, "probably alive."

"Trolling for tuna?" A folksy laugh followed.

"Please, Cotty." Maybe if she said his first name, he'd back off his droll humor for the rest of the conversation. "A more recent image shows the ship's still in port for too long when she should be underway. There's just low infrared from the engines and…no cargo's moving."

"Interesting," he said.

"I doubt we're going to have any more success from above getting her identity, but maybe we still have an opportunity from ground level. Perhaps a faster way…"

"Let me call a friend at CINCMED," he interrupted. "See if anybody's got a ship in that cesspool to take an eyeball gander. Heck, I'll tell him it's a *Priority One* request just to raise his blood pressure but let him know he'll get a case of Kentucky single barrel if he makes good. That will put fire to his behind." The man laughed.

"Thank y—"

He was gone. Jericho knew he was already calling the fleet admiral in charge of Mediterranean operations.

"A case of bourbon…" She shook her head at the peculiar interactions between the upper echelons, while staring at the dingy ceiling tiles then at the worn carpeting that hid a floor filled with miles of electronic cables.

Jericho reached down and chased a dust bunny with her fingers.

"Hmm. Been a long time…"

She smiled, remembering early in her tenure when the director of janitorial services caught her vacuuming her office. The blushing officer moved a displaced clump of red hair away from her eyes, tripped over the power cord, and stumbled into his arms. They both laughed. After that Jericho baked Christmas cookies for his children and never crossed onto the wrong turf again.

A yawn followed the memory. Jericho wondered if anyone the admiral contacted would really be able to get the freighter's name. Even in the spy world, nothing worked quickly. She didn't want Sorenson to be disappointed. With no other alternative but to wait, she began reading stacks of administrative and intelligence reports, performance appraisals, and directives. Each was stamped *ASAP.*

———

"Hey, Lainey…got some chicory?"

Herndon stuck his head through the door, knocking when he was already inside. Startled by the unplanned appearance, Jericho started to rise.

THE ARCHITECT OF REVENGE

"As you were, Commander," he said sweetly. "Keep your shoes off."

Relieved, Jericho relaxed. Never wanting to appear casual, she worried that stockinged feet could be provocative to male staff, even an admiral with a father's affection. Settling in her chair, her toes still groped for the shoes.

"You Southerners," she said. "How about just regular coffee? Is that good enough...sir?"

"That'll do," he said, adding a broad grin. "And don't you go worrying about your ol' freighter. She isn't upping anchor anytime soon. Tell you why."

"Hold on, let me get Glen here. He deserves to hear this. Just temper your words, Admiral. Also, please don't call me by my first name. The kid will get the wrong message."

"Bring him on in. I love to share."

Sorenson was visibly uneasy as he shook the admiral's hand.

"Excellent job, Glen. Used your noggin. Commander Jericho speaks highly of you."

Sorenson stood paralyzed.

"Could use you in navy intelligence. Ever think of signing up?"

"Sir, he's all mine." Jericho smiled at the admiral. "Glen, you can relax. This isn't a firing squad. It's about your freighter."

The young analyst remained frozen. Closing her office door, Jericho motioned for him to sit. He waited until Herndon dropped in the closest chair. It released a worrisome groan.

The admiral's ballpoint pen started clicking. "Glen, I got a call from a good sailor. Too bad they give them desk jobs. Known him since—"

Jericho politely coughed to break up what would become a prolonged monologue.

"Anyway your ship's name is *Shindu Sagar.* Maritime commission's already doing background. The tidbit came from a Brit frigate laying over for fuel. The crew was disappointed, as you might guess, as the sailors were hoping for liberty where...you know...the girls wear a little less and serve rum in coconuts."

Jericho winced. Sorenson didn't even venture a smile.

"There's more to tell, ya'll," said Herndon.

"Not about shore leave," she retorted.

"No, no, no! Just trying to tempt your Glen one more time about the navy!" Herndon laughed. "So this morning at about 0200, VHF starts squawking about a Mayday. Maybe twenty-one, twenty-two minutes later, a helicopter hammers over the frigate, rattling their bones. The Sea King's heading out to get wet feet, and darn if the Brits don't record the whole shebang!"

"Lucky break," Jericho added.

"The freighter's first officer's hysterical." Herndon continued, "Reports *men* overboard."

"*Men* overboard?" she said.

"Yes, ma'am. Tres amigos."

"Seriously?"

"How about those apples?" laughed the admiral.

"Three men overboard?" Jericho needed to say it herself to believe it. The ship was a lumbering freighter. "Calm seas?"

"Moderate at best. No weather." His pen was clicking furiously. "Get this. One's el capitano."

Jericho raised an eyebrow to see Sorenson ready to explode with questions.

"The helicopter inspected the ship then spent an hour checking the wake. Patrol boats too! Can you believe that?"

"Would a garnet laser have shown anything, Glen?" she inquired.

"Yes, Commander Jericho," he replied, "if we'd known. Could possibly have caught the splashes." He felt a disturbing sensation that another question was coming.

"That IR image you studied. It was close to the Mayday, correct?"

"Yes, ma'am. The interval was narrow."

"This doesn't make any sense," she said.

"I know," the admiral said. "Maybe they just lost the oscars."

Jericho translated for Sorenson. "A nickname for dummies thrown overboard to practice search and rescue."

"Oh."

"It may look that way," she theorized, "but that assumption conflicts with logic and the facts."

"Go on, Commander," said Herndon.

"You wouldn't dump bodies approaching a port, especially in normal swells, and call for search and rescue. You'd pitch them in deeper water. They're begging for an inquiry, even if the victims are weighted to sink. They didn't find them, did they?"

"Probably not," said Herndon.

The clicking pen made Sorenson frantic.

"So you think the crew killed them and sounded the alarm to make it look like an accident?"

"That makes no sense either…especially that close." She looked at Sorenson. "Glen, you're confident the man hanging off the stern was alive?"

"Seawater washing over a dead body would cool it promptly, so I suspect he was…ma'am," he added.

"Elaine"—Jericho glared at the admiral. Realizing what he had just said made him only grin more—"would you call a Mayday with a body dangling off your stern?"

"Strange, don't you think?" Even to a senior officer she knew well, speaking rhetorically with her junior civilian analyst present was disconcerting.

"Unless you didn't know," Sorenson interjected. "Sorry. Didn't mean to interrupt."

"That's what I think too, son," said the admiral, unfazed.

"So where are the bodies?" Jericho asked Sorenson.

"We know where one was…or is. That leaves two unaccounted for," said Sorenson, again adding, "ma'am."

"In the water, I reckon," concluded the admiral.

Jericho wasn't satisfied. "Still, the mystery is why. It's got to be something to do with those containers."

Strangely, the admiral's pen had fallen silent. His fatigued grin came from years of work and worry. "Maybe we need to…"

Jericho held up her hand to silence him. "Glen, would you excuse us, please? We're going to be talking a notch above for a bit. Thanks for your insights."

"You're welcome, ma'am. Admiral…" He jumped for the door and left.

"Smart guy," said Herndon.

"Mastered in optics and lasers."

"Don't lose him." His pen started clicking again. "Lainey, I'm thinking we've got too many questions. I'd call this a hot item. Warrants a spot on this week's nuclear agenda. Expensive resources have been wagered. You know Priscilla doesn't like unhappy endings."

"So you're reminding me *again* to be prepared?"

Jericho knew the woman well. Priscilla Rushworth was her superior in every regard. The CIA Division Chief and Chair of the Nuclear Committee arrayed her appointment like the winning sash at a beauty pageant. The woman demanded answers to any question she asked.

"That obsessive nature of yours assures it," grinned Herndon.

"I won't grate her, if that's what you mean. Just facts and our best estimates," said Jericho.

With a wrinkled brow, Herndon lowered his head. "Every picture has a story, Elaine. Question is what is going on *behind* the camera. One thing's for certain: it's usually bad. Terrorism's darn dirty. No uniforms. No honor. The vilest of devils." A gloom brushed across his face. "I've lived too long, I reckon."

The admiral saluted first as he walked out.

TWENTY-NINE

Virginia September 29, 2003

The civilian clothes were a welcome deception as she headed by train to the Foggy Bottom office building in Crystal City. On permanent lease to the CIA, the name on the portico was fictitious, but the armed guards inside the doors were not. Jericho turned off her cell phone and handed it to an impassive woman at a desk who placed it in an envelope then gave her a claim slip like she had just checked her coat. Jericho's credentials were reviewed and she walked through the body scanner.

"Tenth floor, ma'am," the woman said.

Stepping from the elevator, she passed through another checkpoint into a sterile complex, impermeable to usable wavelengths. Overhead, surveillance cameras watched all activity. Cottrell Herndon was waiting when she came out of the washroom. Reflexively her arm came to a salute. He grinned.

"Stop, Elaine, you'll scare the civilians." Her arm fell.

"Sorry, Admiral. Habit."

"That outfit flatters you," said Herndon. "I bet it makes you want to muster out and work for one of those K Street think tanks. Burn those uniforms…"

"Cottrell, how about a simple *hello* and *you look nice?*"

A firm smile followed, but Jericho knew the admiral couldn't help himself. He pestered her endlessly to get out in the world,

205

removed from the drabness of dispassionate satellite reconnaissance. He meant well, but she wasn't interested. America was at war.

"Okay," he said, his smile answering hers. "Hello, you look nice,"

"That's better." Jericho laughed. "Keep practicing, Grandpa. Now, is there anything more I need to know for the meeting?"

"I hear Priscilla's in rare form today." He rarely missed an opportunity to chide the woman's behavior. "Don't worry," he whispered, straight faced. "The room needs more estrogen. Maybe your sweetness will rub off." He patted her shoulder. "Ready?"

"Of course," Jericho said, heading inside the meeting room.

She found her name card.

Cdr. E. Jericho, USN
NGA Senior Analyst
Middle Eastern Division
Nuclear Committee

After preparing her remarks for the last four hours at home, she settled in the appointed chair. Her toes ached. When she noticed that the table skirt touched the floor, her heels came off. Her green eyes scrutinized the room, meeting the porous looks of other members. Seemingly wallpapered, there were more silent bodies—the true experts with immediate answers to anything asked. There were four women in the room, but just one counted.

The doors sealed shut.

A man spoke into the ear of a well-dressed woman whose makeup was applied with an engineer's precision. Priscilla Rushworth's slight smile didn't fool anyone. Her pencil clinked against a water glass.

"Good morning," she announced.

Silence came rapidly.

"We are secure," she said, smashing a gavel on a sound block. A transcriptionist's fingers danced on the keys as voice and video equipment created an additional record of the proceedings. The smile left. "This committee will come to order."

Priscilla Rushworth was in charge.

Every meeting began with praise to the White House and Congress, a flattering remark offered about the intelligence community, always including the CIA, and concluded with the importance *her* committee played in America's fight against terrorism. She never used notes. She didn't have to. She knew her script by heart. They all did.

Controlling each agenda item with her insistent style, Rushworth goaded everyone for information. The owners of unfinished old business received a saccharin-coated verbal flogging when assignments slipped past the finish date.

Once, when Jericho passed two committee members speaking quietly to each other in the hallway, she overheard the words that summarized the woman's personality: *"The sweetest bitch you never want to meet."* Jericho understood the sentiment from their first meeting.

"NGA update," Rushworth said. "Commander Jericho, please?"

There was just enough charisma in her voice to make Cottrell Hendon roll his eyes.

Jericho presented data regarding her division's most recent intelligence estimates, concluding with a summary and update on the status of the elusive freighter that was suspected of transporting elicit materials out of South Africa.

"Madame Chair," said Jericho, "my analyst tracking the ship surmised her next port of call after Yemen was Abbas. Now, those first two containers offloaded in Mukha might've been empty or had their contents moved"—Jericho was speculating, something she tried to avoid in a formal briefing unless there was no choice—"We know Iran is pushing hard to go nuclear, and *we* believe the ship still had the other two containers aboard when she got there."

"So you're suggesting they were delivered to Iran?" Rushworth asked.

"We have no specific image confirming that, but two containers that were visible before the stop in Iran were no longer present in the later downloads."

"Thank you, Commander Jericho," Rushworth said, "for the work you've done."

Herndon audibly sniffed.

"Thank you, Madame Chair, from *my* whole team."

Rushworth ignored the rejoinder. Jericho saw Herndon wink at her from across the table.

"Richard Fields." Rushworth motioned to her personal assistant. "More thoughts?"

"NSA is emphatic that the containers from South Africa held maraging steel for centrifuges," he replied. "The reason two of containers went inland in Yemen is unclear."

And it makes no strategic sense, thought Jericho. She had visited Yemen during a tour on the Horn of Africa Joint Task Force Command. The country was rural, and the common people barely literate. Al Qaeda only had a small presence there. *Why would that country be a nexus for nuclear materials?*

Cottrell Herndon spoke without waiting for the nod of approval from Rushworth. She couldn't prevent him, and the admiral wouldn't stop if she tried.

"Maybe the two boxes had surface missiles in them, bound for Oman. Nailing a tanker in the straits would send oil prices to the moon. Nice little run-up for the crude market would make people in the know very rich."

Rushworth's impatience was noticeable. "I don't like guessing," she replied.

Jericho interjected quickly. "I recommend we survey from the Yemeni highlands east to hunt for—"

"Order it," Rushworth said tersely, pointing to an air force attaché. "And, you may sit down, Commander Jericho."

Jericho returned to her seat as the door opened and a messenger handed Fields an envelope. He read its contents twice before speaking. "Seems we've got fresh intelligence."

Rushworth loathed information revealed this way—things she couldn't review prior. It made her capacity to immolate the committee members more difficult.

"Richard...if you please..." Her politeness veiled irritation.

"Thank you, Madame Chair." Fields reread the information before speaking. "Our sources report that this past July when the

Sagar laid over in Houston, one of the crew was Jamil Sayyaf. If you recall, he's been trying to secure a nuke for al Qaeda. A port guard confirmed his presence because he walked with a limp—a bullet injury that unfortunately missed a more vital spot—and used a black stick for support. The images over Berbera and Mukha suggests Sayyaf was—"

"Didn't Houston detain him?" Rushworth interrupted.

"They didn't know," he replied.

"Oh, for God's sake! That's ridiculous!" Rushworth looked around the table, shaking her head. "Keep going," she sighed noisily.

"Sayyaf wasn't aboard the *Sagar* in Karachi, neither were three other men. But there are many pieces that we just don't know at this point." Fields looked at the document again, pausing to organize his thoughts. "As Commander Jericho stated, the ship stopped in Iran. I'd put my money on the hypothesis that Sayyaf and the other two containers got off there—then one of the commander's analysts… his name is…" Fields shuffled through his papers. "I can't find it," he said.

"Glen Sorenson," said Jericho proudly.

"Whatever," said Rushworth. "Go on, Richard."

The admiral saw Jericho's face go red.

"So this analyst, *Sorenson*, sees a body hanging off the stern of this handy-size freighter as it's turning into the Baba Channel. British sources confirm a Mayday—three men overboard. We get a search-and-rescue thing, but no bodies show up. All we do know is that the captain is missing, along with another crewman, and someone who we've just learned boarded in Houston."

Jericho glanced at Cottrell Herndon. His eyes spoke clearly.
Behind the camera.

"That's just great," moaned Rushworth. "Do we have this *someone's* name?"

"No," replied Fields. "Not yet, at least."

"Border and Customs?" The harassing began. "You know this?"

"No, but we'll look into it."

Rushworth searched for another victim through glasses that magnified her wrinkled eyelids.

"Transportation?"

The TSA representative said nothing.

"Coast Guard, aren't you supposed to monitor boat traffic?"

"Madame Chair, we get hundreds of freighters—"

"Save it. HSA?" The chair then answered the question herself. "Never mind."

Rushworth's voice trumpeted out her nose. "Look…We are the Nuclear Committee of the United States of America, so I shouldn't have to ask these questions. Is this *someone* a domestic asymmetric threat from a sleeper cell whose work was done—and if so—what was he up to, and what the frick happened to him?"

It was clear to Jericho that grace and patience were not Rushworth's strong suits.

"We've got an opportunity to assess our thirty-billion-dollar intelligence overhaul."

Nobody in the room moved.

"I want to know who he is or was—and what happened to those boxes." Her raised fingers closed to a clench. "That's two simple requests."

Rushworth waited only a second. "CIA, don't feel like you're being left out. Get Islamabad to hold that ship right where it is—now!" Her glare waned little. "Every additional second, the puzzle loses pieces. We need manifests, crew rosters, passports—before Karachi intelligence scours the ship and ruins what forensics might be there."

"Working it." The officer left the room.

"Thank you, CIA." A gratified smile appeared. "So…anybody… why Houston?"

"That port serves eastbound traffic," the ICE representative answered.

"So does Jacksonville. Try again."

Drumming two fingers on the table, he thought for a moment. "If he was an alien, maybe his visa expired and was waiting for his ride."

"So until then he stayed out of sight and behaved himself," she added.

The man rubbed the bridge of his nose "Still...even if he got picked up, remember they couldn't hold him. Houston's a sanctuary city."

Rushworth slouched deep in her chair, spreading her palms open toward the ceiling. Her neck muscles contorted. "Whose frigging side are those morons on?" she whined.

THIRTY

Chicago October 3, 2003

"**H**ampshire hog," said Horowitz.

"What the hell is that?" Cotsworth asked.

"You know, P-I-G. Bacon, sausage, ham—all that shit gentiles eat."

"Horowitz, take pity. Are you sure? Why a pig?" Cotsworth felt a stratospheric rise in his blood pressure.

"You're asking me? You told me the source was reliable."

"Why would anybody keep a pig in an apartment?"

Cotsworth envisioned the snout sucking water from the toilet then nuzzling Morgan at night.

"Maybe the guy was planning to roast it."

"You're not helping. Anything else to tell me…that's useful?"

"It came from a litter born in August 2002."

"I said *useful*, not *useless.*"

"Sorry, Cotsworth, that's it."

———

The FBI agent thought about pigs all weekend. Monday morning it was the first call he made.

"Horowtiz, this is Paul Cotsworth."

"Hey, need mustard?"

Instead of saying *fuck you*, Cotsworth asked, "How did you know when that pig was born?"

"They analyzed that crap you gave me, then a program linked me to the National Swine Registry."

"The what?"

"Registers pedigrees. Began in July 2002. All sires have their DNA cataloged. Protects breed purity, whatever that means. I guess that keeps the price of bacon up for those—"

"Give it up, man! Can you just give me a name and a number there at Purdue? Somebody I can talk to myself?"

"Give me a sec…" He gave him the information.

"Thanks," said Cotsworth.

"Hey, let me know."

Not likely…

———

"Better Scurry Farms, good morning," the Slavic voice rumbled.

Cotsworth identified himself as an FBI agent then gave the man the necessary disclosures. "Sir, I'm calling from Chicago."

"Yes?"

"Are you the owner?"

"Yes."

"And your name is?"

"Mister Demetri Kubiak."

"I understand, sir, that you owned a hog…a sire…" Cotsworth looked at his notes again. "*Aingeni Black*. Is that correct?"

Kubiak answered proudly, "My pig!"

Cotsworth looked at the time. However long the call took, it beat a trip to a pig farm in Texas.

"Big pig…much fat. Make many good pigs before slaughtered. You want to buy sperm? Much left!"

"Thank you, but no." Cotsworth was already scribbling on the next page of paper. "Sir, did you have anybody working for you when Aingeni was alive?"

"Let me ask wife."

Cotsworth heard some indecipherable back-and-forth yelling in the background.

"Only one man here for a while. Say he owned land in I-o-way and want to learn about sheep and goat."

"Do you recall his name?"

"Wife very good with names," said the farmer. There was more yelling. "Here. She talk to you."

A deep female voice said, "Le Mon...Jaylo. Le-mon-jay-lo."

Cotsworth asked the first name for grins. He already knew what it would be.

"Jimmy," she replied.

Jimmy Laymonjaylo—Give me Lemon Jell-O...

"Here, my husband now talk," she said.

There was crackling as the phone was handed back.

"Mr. Kubiak," asked the agent, "did you pay Jimmy to work for you?"

"No pay him. He want to learn...so he pay me." A pause was followed by a panicked voice. "I pay taxes."

"I believe you." The FBI agent scratched his head. "Did Jimmy use a check or credit card to pay?"

"No check. Money. Give much money."

"Did Jimmy spend time with Aingeni?"

"Jimmy spends time with all animals. Learned to cut them open... and Jimmy very good with knife."

The agent wrote everything the man said.

"Wife says fingers like dancer when he cuts."

Cotsworth had found what he was searching for. "So he cuts them up like he knows what's inside?"

"Yes."

That fits...

"What did Jimmy look like?"

"Wife think much sexy. Dark hair, beard...but talk little."

"What else did Jimmy do when he wasn't with the animals?"

"Never sleep. Running in dark. Read. Listening to iPod."

"Very good," said Cotsworth. His efforts were rewarded. "I know you're busy, Mr. Kubiak, so I don't want to keep you."

"Is Jimmy okay?"

"We are all worried." Cotsworth couldn't say much else. "Do you think that you and your wife could help me draw a picture of Jimmy?"

"Yes."

Cotsworth would have a composite artist there in forty-eight hours.

"Sir, I won't keep you any longer. I know you have work to do. All I request is that if Jimmy comes back, please let me know." Cotsworth gave the man his personal phone number. "Thank you and good-bye."

He disconnected before bursting out in laughter. "You couldn't make that up!" His lips quickly pressed together, and the seasoned FBI agent frowned.

A Hampshire hog was about to have its DNA entered into the National Missing Person Database under the alias of *Jimmy Laymonjaylo*. To the best of Cotsworth's knowledge, it would be the first time an animal achieved such status. The absurdity, however, would bring him no closer to the answer someone with a friend in Washington wanted him to discover.

Wesley Randall Morgan, MD, was still missing. From everything that Cotsworth had learned, he surmised the man would stay that way.

THIRTY-ONE

October 14, 2003

The United States Government will "meeting" you to death…and nothing is ever solved, Jericho felt like announcing to those in the room. Defying the desire to fidget, yawn, or slouch as others around her occasionally did, she sat upright in her chair, viewing the presentation on the screen. Her heels were off, but no one would see that. Working with her analysts was sheer pleasure compared to the tedium she was presently enduring.

Yet even Jericho's ego wasn't immune to the rungs of the career ladder. She fought such aspirations intensely, grateful that her time at sea with women and men who protected the country were the best years of her life. Long forgotten was the drudgery, replaced only by fond memories and awe as the massive powered steel maiden sliced through the water, directed by the veins of human energy coursing within the superstructure.

When her mission as the Chief Security Officer for the Naval Security Group ended, so did the wanderlust. At first she denied the hormonal clock inside, then she grudgingly conceded to its tinnient reality. Fear gripped her at the thought of coming home. She had her parents and a brother, but no real roots or friends except for those in the navy. Uncomfortable with the notion of a desk job, she considered continuing her graduate studies at the Naval Academy.

Jericho tried dating both civilian men and officers. Of the handful she had known intimately—she was deceptively charitable as to the number—none was willing to compete with her devotion to duty. One night she spoke about her patriotism to an F/A 18 Hornet pilot on their communal pillow.

"*I fight for forty percent of Americans,*" he said unabashedly, "*the rest of them I'd just as soon strafe.*"

Resigned to her frustration when she found out he was married, she stopped trying altogether and closed the gates.

Cottrell Herndon first learned of Jericho when she became a midshipman at Annapolis. Leaving the University of Wisconsin after her freshman year, she started again, excelling to the head of her class. Impressed by her leadership style and critical thinking, he requested the new ensign be under his command. After Herndon moved on, she stayed for another tour. Jericho called him when she got back to the States.

"*How 'bout lunch with the old man?*" he asked right away.

Out of uniform, they met at an Annapolis restaurant overlooking the Severn River. They laughed and told tales, sharing a bottle of wine—her first in many months.

"*Lainey,*" the admiral said, "*there's a good position for you available at the Annex.*"

"*A land job?*"

He leaned forward so no one would hear.

"*The Office of Naval Research needs someone to get its projects running with the Directorate of Science and Technology. You'll drive things at the DST that'll keep you out front...and it suits your stubborn need for independence.*"

The opportunity would move her career forward, plus she could live in Alexandria with its views of Washington across the Potomac. That excited her too.

"*I appreciate your confidence, Admiral.*"

With a grin, he said, "*You'll love it...and you can—*"

"*Let me guess...spend time with clean-shaven marines?*"

"*Never would-a thought it,*" he grinned again.

"*Admiral, I can take care of myself, you know.*"

"Cottrell, please, when we're away from the shop. Cotty would be even better."

"Oh, I couldn't!" To Jericho, respect of rank was imperative.

"Yes, you can..."

Afraid he might take her refusal as a personal insult, she conceded.

"Okay... Cotty... I accept."

The deal was validated with a handshake and a toast. Jericho got a mortgage on a townhouse and commuted to work near the Pentagon.

The charitable, breezy lunch was a world apart from what happened two years later on a bright September Tuesday.

The admiral called her the next morning. The conversation became encrypted after the first hello.

"As you can guess... all those sons of bitches want to go nuclear, and not for electricity." His resigned anger echoed in her ear. *"We need to redirect our tactical understanding toward the Middle East, not Russia. Elaine... I know you're doing good things with DST, but now, as the new director of the NGA, I need your expertise and am putting you in for a transfer."*

Jericho changed jobs in one day—leaving behind whatever morsels remained in a life she couldn't build. Her only mission was clear: protect the country. Nothing else mattered.

Unaccustomed to daydreaming, Jericho hadn't heard Richard Fields's opening remarks. Crossing her legs, she took a sip of cooling tea and unwrapped one of the small hard candies from the glass dish waiting a slight reach beyond her briefing papers.

"We've learned from interviewing the ship's cook named *Nidal,* that three men—Jamil Sayyaf, we talked about him last time; *Hamid,* a Somali; and Nidal—came into our country apparently hunting for some male R and R. The port gate security logs confirm their entrance." He scratched his head. "We've learned from Nidal about the additional man who boarded in Houston."

Everyone in the room was still, wanting to hear more.

"His name is *Barif Ali*," said Richard. "Middle Eastern. Claimed to grow up here. Immigrant parents, blah, blah. Spoke Arabic. Hung out with Sayyaf."

"Scrub more information on him?" asked Rushworth.

"No threat signature," Richard said. "A clean skin."

Another one with no background... Jericho knew such invisible recruits were an ever-present concern.

"Continue," said Rushworth.

"According to Nidal, the shore party connected with Ali, who claimed to be waiting for a crewman they'd never heard of, but miraculously they all hooked up."

"Never in a million years will I believe that was a chance encounter," said the FBI liaison.

"Me, neither," said Cottrell Herndon.

"Especially when," added Fields, "according to crew interviews, it turns out that Ali and Sayyaf were pals aboard—"

"So it was a ploy to fool the other two." Rushworth cut him off.

"While ashore"—Fields inaugurated his next comment with a smile—"Ali took them to a nearby strip club called *Puss 'n Boots*. We're going to check it out. There's a neon-breasted cowgirl in front dancing around a—"

"Don't endow us with any more details, Richard," said Rushworth amid the snickers. Her pencil clinked them to silence. "Just find out what you can."

"We could be on that as soon as this weekend, Madame Chair."

There were more snickers.

"Ahem..." Rushworth took a sip of water.

"Ali was quiet and reserved, almost gentle, but also a determined fellow. Might be enough for a forensic psychological evaluation ..."

Fields looked at his notes.

"A strong deckhand—did more than his fair share of heavy lifting. Also spent time exercising, *while* reading the Koran." His smile grew. "An unusual approach to piety. What else can I tell you?"

He squinted. "Ali could bone a chicken incredibly fast. *That's* a useful skill to impress one of your future wives..."

Rushworth cleared her throat again.

"Ha! Here…" His controlled smile stayed intact. "Should mention… Ali came aboard with a Pakistani passport, don't know whether it was stolen or maybe counterfeit, but the first mate said he got a new one in Trinidad, issued…Lebanese. Don't have anything more on that yet."

This is no incidental tourist taking a junket. Jericho's curiosity blended with irritation.

Rushworth said, "So let me understand this: Houston Port Security never checked his old passport? Abrams, you have an answer?"

The ICE representative appeared tentative. "Normally…we don't pay attention to departing freighter crews."

"I didn't know that." Her words chilled the room. "That's idiotic," she said. "Is it the Nuclear Committee's task to show every deficiency in national security?"

ICE continued. "We've mined *Barif Ali.* There's nothing."

Jericho knew the problem. None of the hundreds of databases was linked. Each needed to be queried individually, but low-level security clearances prevented many analysts from data sharing. Ninety-five percent of all intelligence was never correlated.

"Did you include the modifiers *hardworking* and *religious?*" someone asked.

There was laughter. Even Rushworth smiled—an aberration from her usual phlegmatic self.

"No editorializing." Her severity returned. "Continue, Richard."

"His bunk and storage drawers were searched. No fingerprints, which I guess isn't surprising. The few items of clothing—blue jeans, T-shirts—had been recently laundered. A hair specimen found in the jean's pocket is currently undergoing DNA analysis."

"I'm trying to expedite that," interrupted the FBI officer. "Working on his biometrics with the crew. Had to get authorization to send a team over, but they're there now."

"Keep me informed on that," said Fields, looking at Rushworth as if they were ready to reveal a shared secret. "So our agents walked the deck. They said there was no way anybody, let alone three men, even drunk, could go overboard, based on meteorological and oceanographic data."

On the screen Fields projected the image of the torso hanging from the stern. "We've enhanced this." The red laser pointer jiggled on the silhouette. "Look."

Jericho had seen it before.

"This is a backpack. In Houston the security guard did remember a man who fit the description of Ali was carrying one." Jericho was still. "Madame Chair, it's known that Ali and the captain didn't get along, and somehow, without the crew noticing, he must have figured out a way to throw the captain overboard. The Somali too."

"So the working hypothesis is this had something to do with Sayyaf and the cargo?" asked Rushworth.

"That's my estimate." Fields pointed to the backpack again. "And this...is Ali trying to get off the ship."

Jericho's expression never changed, but she recalled Sorenson's words weeks earlier when he saw the same image for the first time.

Holy shit!

THIRTY-TWO

Karachi October 24, 2003

"**N**o." Morgan added a smile for good measure.

The market vendor brought the mango shake closer to his mouth, insisting he taste it, but Morgan firmly declined the offer. The mango shake he drank on his first day left a poignant impression that had begun with a gurgle in stomach, reaching the other orifice by afternoon. When he wasn't crumpled on the grubby sheet covering the sagging mattress, he was spewing diarrhea into a toilet that barely flushed. Hobbling back to bed, the salmonella toxin would peak again, reviving the nightmare of Caroline suspended in space, her hand never able to grab his in time. Even as he sat on the porcelain spewing slime, the vision remained, smothering him with dread.

The next morning, after the desk clerk bought him some antibiotics, bismuth, and tea, Morgan felt well enough to stand under the corroded nozzle in the shower, worshiping the feel of tepid water.

The weeks since had been uneventful for Morgan's stomach as the ounce of opium-laced bismuth plugged him every morning before he headed out to explore Karachi. Taking tea in cafes throughout the city, he eavesdropped on conversations, enjoying the distinctive gliding tones as the Karachiites pronounced vowels. He listened to the khutbahs (sermons) at the mosques, bartered with the street vendors, and argued local politics with everyone. Much of what he heard and said was in English, some in Arabic, and he even began to decipher and use bits of Pashto.

Wherever he went, the smell of wood smoke and fires cooking lamb, fish, or offal parts greeted him from the crisscrossed alleys and markets. He'd stop to taste the cuisine and enjoy the company of men sitting near piles of rugs, spice jars, and mountains of shoes. Returning to the hostel often late in the evening, he'd smell his armpits and his stool in the commode. He reeked of curry, onions, and coriander. That was his intent. He no longer smelled like a foreigner.

———

As his understanding of the cultural archeology expanded, Morgan ventured closer to the crowded ghettos where the peons, craftsmen, and servants lived in tenements, and gangs of unskilled men from the tribal territories would leave to work day and night. Those who remained watched for trespassers, guarding neighborhoods where the police did not come—and the law was Sharia justice.

One morning Morgan looked in the mirror at his mangy hair. His beard overflowed his cupped hand—improper by custom.

"Time for a haircut and trim," he said. "Perfect. It's Friday."

A visit to a ghetto barbershop would give Morgan a measure of how he was adapting in his character. The experience could be dangerous, possibly treacherous—all the better.

On the drooping bed, Morgan placed the satchel in his lap and gently ran his fingers along the gray rope woven in a serpentine pattern over a sturdy fabric shell. The bag contained everything he owned. When he slept, he put his leg through the strap. When he was out, it was always over a shoulder.

A man tried to yank the satchel away once as Morgan stood on a busy sidewalk. He looked into the thief's eyes, and asked in terse English if he wished to be castrated. The man stepped back into the crowd and was gone.

Morgan unzipped the satchel and placed the revolver, bullets, clothes, passport, and Koran beside him. A fingernail picked at a thread inside. Created by a tailor in Berwyn, the secure thick lining was quilted and had numerous sealed little pouches. One split open. Acquired months earlier from numerous Chicago banks, a pleat of well-aged rupees went into Morgan's pocket. The satchel contained enough cash to get him wherever he needed to go, buy what he needed to buy, or bribe whomever he needed to bribe. There was plenty.

He put everything back inside the satchel and left the hostel.

———

Morgan got out of the tonga and stepped over a crack in the pavement, knowing the minuscule boundary marked the demarcation of two distinct worlds. He briefly looked around. He was already being scrutinized, his every movement suspect.

A distant woman standing on a crumbling curb drew her headscarf higher across her face. Her act of modesty was an ominous warning that visitors were not welcome.

In respect, Morgan lowered his gaze and kept walking, counting his heartbeats.

Normal—almost slow. Then he smiled.

ممنوع الخط على الحائط
No graffiti on the wall

The neighborly request scrawled on the cracked masonry was to the point. He heard young voices and looked toward the source of the gleeful sounds.

With magnetic curiosity, children gathered in an expanding circle around him. A small boy raced with his friends, trying to keep up. Suddenly blue in the face, he stopped to crouch and pant. Morgan knew immediately. The child had Tetralogy of Fallot—the same heart problem that killed his sister. Without surgery Morgan knew the child would be dead in a year. The image was a stark reminder of his distant past but no longer his concern.

Morgan kept walking deeper into the ghetto.

"Najis! Their entire being lives in the cesspool!"

From a radio distorted oratory of the khutbah and cyclic cheers of the crowd echoed from buildings across the street, the mullah's sermon blasted from Morgan's destination.

"Unclean! Every pore! All liquids in the filthy bodies! If they live among us, they have no solace! No hope! Shave their heads! Make them identifiable to the pure!"

Morgan entered the shop, greeting the sole barber. Enjoying their morning caucus, several men seated in scattered chairs nearby nodded with collapsed smiles. Morgan nodded back and sat down. The barber gave him green mint tea served in white china and stoked the incense thurible.

"Unless they live under these conditions..."

The exhortation from the radio continued.

"The vilest of creatures...upon which the serpent crawls...have no protection from the sword!" The sermon flowed like an indulgent river as the revilement amplified. "Those who do not believe...will burst in flames! And his wife...laden with maggots...will have a rope stretch her neck!"

The crowd's enthusiasm climaxed.

"No leniency! Banish them to Hell!"

The barber shut off the radio.

"What is your name, friend?" asked the barber.

"Ali. Barif Ali."

"Where do you come from?" asked one of the men.

"Beirut," Morgan answered.

After he got the passport, Morgan found a travel guide about Lebanon aboard the *Sagar* and studied it intensely. He could comment about the neighborhoods, culture and history, but hoped their questioning wouldn't get more specific. The book was a decade old.

"Why are you here?" asked a customer.

"I wish to travel this beautiful country for a time, Inshallah."

The barber flapped a towel across the chair to scatter any hair while his other hand offered the seat to his new customer.

"Barif...please."

Morgan sat down with the satchel resting on his feet. The man wrapped him in a herringbone gown, folded a tissue-paper collar around his neck and then pulled a comb through his hair.

The barber stepped back to study the shape of Morgan's head and his beard. With a learned nod to what he needed to do, he picked up a pair of scissors.

"Did you read the damn British defeated us in cricket?" the barber asked.

"Hyenas," Morgan said.

Their communal irritation with the outcome became intense. Suddenly the barber shifted the conversation. His beads of sweat concentrated the emotion brought earlier by the speaker on the radio.

"Dhimmis! Jews and Christians...all guilty!" the barber said.

Morgan agreed heartily.

"They spread mischief in the land...the satellite MTV!"

The sharp scissors chattered with increasing speed. Morgan sensed the barber's animated passion as the metal blades gnashed together.

"Pour molten lead into the ears of those listening to the music of whores! Execute the Zionists who sell the filth!" the barber said as he held up a chipped mirror to show off his handiwork.

Morgan nodded his approval. "You should work in Beirut! God has blessed you with the gift of supernatural hands."

Manual hair clippers appeared.

"My electric shears blew up."

The man showed him the metal remnants with frazzled wires.

"The electricity is deadly and it goes on and off...mostly off," he said. "The government is a puppet of Satan." He paused to ignite the incense again. "Their CIA trained Mujahedeen to fight the Russians. Now Satan wants us dead too. So they cut off the electricity, and the water makes us sick!"

From the sidelines, a man said, "But God is on our side."

The clippers mowed through Morgan's sideburns then shaped his beard. Soon he was lathered and tilted flat on his back. The straight razor removed the stray stubble from his cheeks and neck. Occasionally the barber would slap the blade across a leather strop clipped to the old cast-iron chair. Without pause the barber continued his railing—his now raspy voice unremitting in conviction.

"We want Sharia law...and free markets." The razor was moving across the taught skin above Morgan's carotid artery. "We will smite the necks of the foreign meddlers!"

"Spill their blood in the gutters for the dogs to lick," said another voice.

"I, my brother, my cousins, our clans, our tribes against the world," responded Morgan.

"Muntaz!" exclaimed one of the patrons. *Wonderful!*

The saying was often spoken to their children from an early age: Unity above all.

The barber held up the mirror a final time. Morgan admired his salt-and-pepper beard.

"Tell us, Barif..." The questions resumed from the cohort of men. "How long have you been here?"

Morgan squinted, looking confused. "Two weeks perhaps."

"Did you arrive on a ship?"

Morgan had to quickly manage the accelerating interrogation.

"I traveled overland," he answered. "So many honorable people... and beautiful places! I wish I could see everything!"

"Men who work at the ports speak of the disappearance of an American aboard a freighter." The man cleared his throat.

What went wrong? His pronunciation perhaps...

"I have not heard such," said Morgan. "My journey was long, and through the countryside!"

The situation was deteriorating rapidly.

"We would love to see the places. Show us your passport."

Morgan's body remained relaxed. There were five other people in the room. Shooting them would be too loud, but the scissors and razor were close by on a pedestal. They would make a bloody mess but if necessary provide a means for escape.

"They hold it where I stay," Morgan said calmly.

"Ah," the barber laughed, breaking the subtle animus. "You are smart to keep it there. Many thieves on the street."

"Friends," Morgan rose, slinging the satchel over his shoulder. "I must be on my way."

"Brother, we invite you to prayers and fellowship," one of them said. The request was cordial but sinister in its delivery.

"Your generosity is more abundant than the stars, my brother," said Morgan. Such a gathering would not bode well for his neck. "Perhaps another time…Inshallah."

The man nodded in silence.

Morgan paid the barber, shaking his hand before looking a final time at both sides of his head in the mirror. He rubbed his beard. "What fine work! My friend, I will give your name to all who ask!"

The barber nodded in thanks.

"Peace be with you," Morgan said to the group, raising his hand to bid the men goodbye.

"Allahu Akbar!—*God is great!*—" he said with a broad smile and walked out of the shop.

———

Lying on the mattress, drenched in sticky air, Morgan was awake. It was mercifully quiet. The couple in the next room had finally stopped fucking.

He heard the grinding squeal: bad brakes.

That wasn't unusual in Karachi.

The sound came again but lasted longer as the automobile was too quick taking a turn. Morgan's ears reached out to listen more intently.

Another squeal—closer. He estimated the distance.

Sounds like that blue Toyota…

He had seen it twice on his way back to his room.

The squealing was closer.

The grinding ceased at the front of the hostel. In the darkness he slipped toward the window and looked out, using a small mirror.

A police car pulled up immediately behind the Toyota. All the automobiles' doors opened at once. Machine-pistol bolts cycled.

No coincidence.

They would find his room empty.

Morgan hung the unzipped satchel over his shoulder so his hand could drop inside to fire the loaded .357.

He stepped into the hallway, threw a leg over a back window's threshold, and scaled down. Receding deep into the garbage-filled alley, he paused in the opacity to look back.

A flashlight beam lit the corridor then shined out the window, painting the alley with light.

"Ali!" a man shouted.

Morgan recognized the voice. It belonged to the man at the barbershop who had invited him to prayers. He had to have been the one who notified the police.

Morgan heard a woman's shriek.

They had entered the adjacent room.

"Charmouta!" one of the men shouted. *Whore!*

Morgan had seen her at the hostel with several men. She was likely an outcast, earning a living the only way she could.

Her screams pulsed to sobs as they beat her.

Morgan knew the punishment wouldn't end until she was dead. There was nothing he could do to help. His haircut had cost her life.

"You do *not* want to meet me again," Morgan uttered, slipping deeper into the darkness.

He emerged onto the next street, zipped the satchel, and walked toward the intersection. He was near Korangi Road and the Towers of Silence. On the ancient mounds inside, the Zoroastrians placed the corpses of their dead for the buzzards.

Morgan vaulted the wrought-iron fence around the towers, dropped to the ground, and crawled. Hungry vultures would provide cover until morning, when a train ticket would carry him north.

THIRTY-THREE

Alexandria, Virginia October 28, 2003

Jericho went for a run when she got home. She needed the athletic escape from the tedium that began in the morning with the exhausting committee meeting.

Disappointed, she cut her jog short and came home to a hot shower. Wrapped in a warm terrycloth robe, she poured a glass of chardonnay and let the armchair devour her wilted body. After a few sips, she was snoring gently. When she shifted a little, some of the briefings on her lap fell to the carpet.

The phone rang. Both eyes snapped open.

"Good evening, Elaine."

"Cottrell?"

The two hadn't spoken for two weeks. He'd been in California with his grandchildren on a vacation.

"I suppose you're dusting your townhouse," he laughed.

She was still drowsy, making his deep voice sound like winter wind blowing over the Wisconsin cornfields—a faraway remembrance.

"No, just...reading," she lied.

"Girl, you need to get out more."

"God love you, Cottrell...you never stop trying."

"We need to talk privately," the admiral said.

"Okay, going secure."

It was rare for a senior analyst to have a STU phone at home, but during her time working at the Annex, one was installed so she could take calls from distant time zones. When she went to the NGA, Herndon made certain it stayed.

While waiting for the connection, she took another sip of the wine. The sweetness stuck in her mouth.

"So, Elaine, you didn't get raked over the coals too badly, did you?"

"I assume, Cotty, you're not speaking in the abstract. Is that the reason we went secure?"

"Just snooping about the meeting. Wanted to hear your thoughts on how it went...plus I've got something to tell you."

"I'm confident I represented your office with proper—"

"In other words," Herndon said, "you loved it."

"Not really, sir," Jericho said, but he was right.

In his absence he had asked her to represent the NGA at the Nuclear Committee meeting. Jericho appreciated the admiral's confidence, but taking his seat at the conference table put her next to Rushworth. With the presence of another woman so close, Rushworth seemed to be more empowered beyond her normal Machiavellian self.

"Welcome, Elaine," she'd said, oozing charm. *"I know the gentlemen will take pleasure with the company of an additional woman."* With flourish she filled Jericho's water glass, wiping the lost drops with a napkin. *"Girls seem to do the housekeeping."*

"Commander Jericho," the admiral laughed, "I know you're fibbing. Priscilla is a condescending ego-saturated nutcase."

"I hope the NSA isn't listening," she said.

"Let them," he countered. "She's your typical political appointee. Darlin', better get used to it. 'Cause I bet you might be sitting there again."

"I appreciate your faith, sir."

An air-conditioned chill descended over her. A small blanket on her legs covered all but the Minnie Mouse bedroom slippers, a young niece's Christmas gift and a private side no one would ever see.

"Anyway, Lainey, I've got a bit more info on your sweet little ol' freighter that wasn't mentioned at the meeting, got it from one of my sources."

"Do tell." Jericho yawned. "I'm finally awake."

"Ah!" he said, "I knew it! You were sleeping!"

"Because I'm overworked and underpaid."

"Of course!" The admiral chuckled. "I'll tell you, they're dumber than stumps over there! Using open frequencies, forgetting we're listening. Karachi port authority attempted to move our favorite freighter to a more isolated area. Seems she was taking up space from paying customers. When the port pilot tried to power up the starboard bow thrusters, breaker alarms go screaming."

She could hear his pen clicking.

"And guess the ol' problem."

"Cotty, it's too late for more theater."

"It's so darn good!" he exclaimed. "The wiring harness in the forward bulkhead shorted! So what do the nuggets do? Open the hatch! Pew! Putrid gas blows right into the engineer's face! Flattens the guy! They had to call an ambulance."

"Let me guess," Jericho said. "Dead bodies."

"Yup, Lainey. Two of them! See…isn't this fun?" The admiral didn't balk at describing the details. "Their drippings basted the wires!"

"Yuck."

"The coroner reports—"

"So they weren't Muslims," Jericho injected.

Pakistani murder investigations required autopsies, but Islamic law wasn't so accommodating.

"Correcto! One sounds like that big Somali who came ashore in Houston—had a single wound through an ear, deep in his brain. The captain had his heart torn open from the inside."

"How?" she asked.

"Looks like the pick of a fire ax."

"Nasty," Jericho said.

"Ever swing one of those things?" Herndon asked.

"No."

"Dad had one on the farm," he said. "Heavy! The guy was darn strong to swing it that accurately. Can you imagine?"

Jericho wasn't thinking about how someone could kill that way, only the reason. It had to be Ali. He was dirty—for certain.

"Got more, Commander. The captain's..." Herndon searched for the right words. "His penis was cut in half...by teeth."

"That's almost...too much information." Jericho sighed. "So you think it was a gang rape gone badly?"

Herndon replied, "The crew mentioned the captain, the Somali and onboard extracurricular activities, if you know what I mean."

"I'm afraid so," she acknowledged. "Maybe Ali was involved in a jealous quarrel?"

"Probably not. He hung around with Sayyaf. Neither of their profiles as supplied by the crew suggests such dalliances. Maybe Ali was just an unknowing guest at a party he didn't want to attend."

"Hmm." Jericho pondered. "So there's still no confirmation if Ali's alive or dead?"

"Nope. CIA isn't sharing any of those questions with the Pakistani Inter-Service Intelligence Directorate."

"I'd expect that," she said.

The ISI was renowned for its duplicitous behavior. It was impossible to know who the inside moles were. Better not to disclose information unless necessary.

"If he's the one we saw on the stern...suppose he did jump," Jericho suggested. "It's a nasty swim to shore. Sewage and sea snakes, if I recall."

"Locals actually use that beach," Herndon added.

"I have to wonder if Ali was planning to get off anyway or suddenly had to," said Jericho. "I can't fit all the pieces together."

"Time tells all. Eventually we'll learn more," said the admiral. "Made for a good bedtime story, though."

"More like nightmares, Cottrell."

His tone softened. "Hey, darlin'..." He knew she was tired. "Get some sleep."

"Aye, sir. Goodnight."

Click.

Untouched since their call began, the chardonnay was warm. Jericho drank it anyway. Releasing a frustrated sigh, she chewed on her lip, trying to understand.

"Why did you get on that ship?" she asked herself, and aimed to learn the answer.

THIRTY-FOUR

Chicago October 30, 2003

Jon Pruitt called Cotsworth, who scrambled for Morgan's file and his yellow notepad. Research had been dormant and that hadn't set well with the FBI director. Then yesterday a deluge of new information began to arrive.

"I received a call from Cay's alma mater," Pruitt told the agent.

"That's the University of Virginia, right?"

"Yes," replied Pruitt. "Actually, three calls, the same day. One after the other."

"Interesting…"

"To say the least," replied Pruitt. "First, it was the president of the University Foundation, then the dean of the Graduate School of Architecture, then the president of the whole darn place."

"What made you so popular?" Cotsworth asked.

"A letter arrived, sent from Wes's attorney."

The father sounded glum.

"Go on, sir."

"Wes made a substantial donation to the school in Cay's name. The letter said it was a birthday present for her."

"How much?"

"It's bequeathed in two parts," Pruitt replied. "The first, a check for nine hundred thousand dollars."

Cotsworth exhaled audibly. "That's substantial. And the second part?"

"Life insurance."

"The amount?" asked Cotsworth, knowing Morgan's term policy had been increased eighteen months earlier.

"Four million," Pruitt said. "My wife and I were rather awed with that."

"I can imagine, sir," agreed Cotsworth, his pen tapping the pad for a moment before continuing. "I will share...that similar amounts were donated to his hospital. Dr. Merrimac called me yesterday."

"That's a hell of a lot of money," said Pruitt.

"Then there's the half million donation to his mother's nursing home," commented Cotsworth, summing the numbers. The total amount of cash in discussion was less than the sale price of the townhouse. Adding the other assets, the FBI agent calculated that from the beginning Morgan had retained at least $400,000 in untraceable currency.

What the hell is he doing? he doodled on his yellow pad.

Cotsworth waited before speaking again. The father became overwrought when talking for too long about his daughter.

"Mr. Pruitt...did Wes ever mention a desire to travel?"

"Cay wanted them to go to the Italian countryside. Because Wes worked a lot, he put off getting a passport, but he reassured her he'd get one."

"He never applied," replied Cotsworth.

The FBI agent couldn't understand the reason Morgan would procrastinate.

"So, Mr. Pruitt, let me ask you again...When you two last spoke, can you think of anything else that he said?"

"Just how Connie and I were holding up, that's all."

Pruitt offered nothing more, and Cotsworth realized he probably wouldn't. Try as he might, the agent had uncovered nothing that might offer some understanding about what Morgan might be doing. Pruitt's own relationship with Morgan was a dead end. A black hole seemed to consume any information about Pruitt's background. That usually meant only one thing: spycraft. That hunch implied the father could be the impetus behind the directive from Washington. If true, Cotsworth didn't expect to ever learn any more.

"As you know," the agent said, hoping a little goodwill might yield more insight in the future, "there was a box in the trunk."

"We were told."

"Our people have gone through it thoroughly, and I have the authority to now release it to you, if you'd like."

"That would be appreciated."

"I'll send it right away," said Cotsworth. "If you hear of anything—"

"I know," answered Pruitt.

Their call ended.

Cotsworth whistled after cradling the receiver. "So you upped your life insurance, dished out a pile of cash, but kept a piece for yourself."

The money was not enough for a thirty-six-year-old man to live on forever.

Why did Morgan make the insurance bequests? Did he think he was going to die?

He stared at the artist's composite of Jimmy Laymonjaylo, then at the picture on the driver's license. They were the same face.

The agent opened his door and yelled across the noisy office. "Does anybody have a road atlas?"

One waved above a distant desk. He took it, went back to his office, and closed the door. Creasing the binding open to the page of eastern Texas, he stared at the greater Houston area.

"Okay…No hotels, no gas receipts…no money trail for two years…"

Except the millions that showed up as donations in the last forty-eight hours…

"You abandon your car by hiding it in a public place…and quietly slip away."

Cotsworth had reviewed days of airline passenger manifests.

"You didn't fly anywhere."

He expected as much.

"So why Houston? You must have checked it out before. Would explain some of that mileage."

Using a drafting compass, Cotsworth drew a circle around the airport to a radius of twenty-five miles.

His index finger traced the interstates west and north from the airport.

"Hitchhike to San Antonio? Dallas?" There was a smile. "No...I think not, not with that face—locals would grind you into fertilizer."

That meant Morgan took a different mode of transportation... somewhere.

He drew another circle at fifty miles.

"Clear Lake? No, probably not Johnson."

He laughed at his own joke. NASA didn't take walk-ins.

"How about Central America?"

If Morgan was carrying a lot of cash, that could make sense. His money would last a long time in any of those countries—and even without a passport he could still move around easily.

"Belize would be way up on *my* list..."

The compass drew an even wider circle. Cotsworth paper clipped the pages open, leaned the map against the bulletin board at the back of the desk, and stood up. He stepped away and stared at the thirty thousand square miles contained within, including Beaumont and Port Arthur.

One thing was immediately obvious. The blue color grew larger with every ring the agent had added.

"Did you get on a boat?"

From the beginning Cotsworth's conviction hadn't changed.

Each move was planned, he just didn't understand why.

THIRTY-FIVE

Lahore, Pakistan

abr...

S The word defined the enigma surrounding Morgan as he sat another day, inhaling dust, swatting flies, and studying the huge market's pandemonium oozing beyond the sidewalks and into the streets.

A grotesquely painted bus rattled through the filthy shroud of late-October air. A young man emerged as it pulled away, shepherding three goats along the bricked median dividing the road. The animals stopped to munch on the remnants of green plant husks dumped from a passing pull cart.

Morgan used the satchel's handle to clean his teeth, leaving his mouth tasting fouler than before. He tried to wash it away with a gulp from his bottle. With tea, rice, honey, and sesame seeds available in every market, the slur was quick to make. What had kept him alive during his run in the desert provided a nutritious snack anytime he needed one—but it still swallowed like glue.

Shifting slightly on the bench, he struggled with his subsiding desire to wait much longer, so he spoke the word under his breath.

Sabr...

Patience—when God wills it.

He resumed his expressionless audit of the zigzagged electrical wires cobwebbing the space above the awnings and draperies. They repeated their graceless pattern everywhere he looked. His eyes drifted back to the expansive balcony with its filigreed tiles, peeling mismatched paint, and chipped plaster before lowering his gaze to scrutinize again the numbers carved in a wooden placard on the padlocked Gothic doors. Despite their peeling varnish, Morgan remained confident the address given by Jamil was correct.

The afternoon breeze peppered his face with grit, providing a slight chill that came as a welcome relief after muggy Karachi. He draped a light wool overcoat bought the day before through the satchel's strap and noticed the shopkeepers were shuttering their windows. The pause in retailing meant they were getting ready for prayers.

He looked at the locked doors again. Omar might not even exist. *Sabr...*

An amputee sat down next to him. With a fierce stare, he held his hand out until Morgan gave the beggar a few rupees. He watched as the pathetic skeleton hobbled away before suddenly stopping in the middle of the street. The beggar leaped up and down on his sole leg, waving his crutch over his head, pointing at the opening balcony doors.

A quick snare drum roll-off directed Morgan's eyes the same way as bagpipe reeds struck in at the next downbeat. Four pipers dressed in green and white plaid kilts marched forward in step and fanned out along the railing, letting the harmonized bass and tenor whines pour the Glen Miller melody on those below.

"The Beauty!" the beggar shouted over the noise while hopping closer into the thicket of men. "The Beauty has arrived!" he shouted again.

As the pipers parted in the middle, a diminutive figure covered in a red burka emerged.

Whoa, Morgan was curious. Was that color permitted?

In one hand the cloaked person held a large woven basket. The other hand wafted upward to beckon the crowd with enticing waves until finally reaching deep into the basket and sowing them with flowers.

———

Morgan returned to the bench that evening. The few remaining pink and red petals spun up from the sidewalk in the occasional gust of air. A gold frame was hanging on the door. The handbill announcement within said simply:

Seating Begins at Seven P.M.

As the hour grew closer, men gathered, milling near the entrance. From loudspeakers the street filled with Glen Miller music played by bagpipes. The wooden doors opened. Morgan bought a ticket, elbowed in with the rest of the men, and took an aisle seat in the century-old theater. Every row filled quickly, forcing stragglers to lean against the walls. Morgan did some quick multiplication—business was good.

The house lights darkened and the male odors condensed. With another drum roll, a collective howl from the spectators swelled to the rafters as the bagpipers started to play behind the black curtain.

It opened. To loud cheers the pipers marched off to the wings, surrendering the stage to a troupe of performers who made the cabaret equivalent to any nocturnal theater Morgan had ever seen in Chicago. For two hours the audience jumped and applauded, shook raised fists, and shouted while vigorous dancers in lurid costumes gyrated to the segued racket of disco and rock.

The show's finale came to its climax when a raven-haired beauty with large forlorn eyes appeared through a dense snowfall of white rose petals, wearing a sheer wedding gown.

A woman? Morgan questioned. *Ah...the red burka...*

She sang a mournful ballad about her martyred lover while stroking his explosive vest returned from Paradise. Batting long eyelashes, she crooned into the mic'd muzzle of an AK-47 rifle pretending fellatio that concluded with her delicate cheek pressing against the barrel and her head slumped in everlasting sorrow.

The audience went berserk.

Morgan joined the bravos as the assembly applauded for an encore. Dressed in black, the cast and crew returned to the stage, joined hands, and started singing.

"Everybody loves somebody sometime…everybody needs someone somehow…"

When the spectacle ended and the lights came up, the satiated male gathering slowly dispersed. Morgan stayed seated. In time he was alone, waiting and thinking.

It was a eunuch—*a hijra*—acting as female.

In a culture that hid women and openly deplored pornography, men could still revel in living fantasies. Revered and trusted in harems for centuries, feared for the curses the "third gender" could conjure at a whim, hijras exploited their nature by entertaining at public events such as weddings and parades. Those more mysterious and exotic performed privately or were kept as personal attendants.

A stagehand wearing a bathrobe approached Morgan.

"Peace be with you," he said.

"With you also," Morgan said. "My name is Barif. I seek Omar."

The man left as quietly as he had come.

The shimmer of a gold watch announced a tall man who came down the stairs to the side of the stage. A rakish white ponytail fell over a black silk tunic. The cuffs of his sapphire slacks broke exactly over satin-red opera slippers. When he came close, he smelled of pipe tobacco and offered his hand without concern. Morgan knew he had to be sighted in the crosshairs of a gun.

"Masa'a Alkheir," the man said in a baritone voice. "Ana Omar." *Good evening. I am Omar.*

Morgan stood up submissively, aware every movement he made would be evaluated. Any error meant death.

"As-salaamu 'alay-kom. Esmi Barif Ali," Morgan said. "Ana Sadeeq Jamil. Howa Beysallem A'leik." *Peace be with you. My name is Barif Ali, friend of Jamil. He sends his greetings.*

"Ha!" Omar took his hand as if he were going to keep it. "Akhoya Qualli A'n wosollak." *My brother apprised me of your arrival.*

Morgan gave an eyes-down bow.

"Loghatak El'Arabeya Tayebah," Omar complimented. *Your Arabic is good.*

"Akhouk Modarress Mawhoub." *Your brother is a gifted teacher.*

"English?" asked Omar.

"Ezza Tehebb," Morgan answered. *If you like.* Pleased by his performance, he was still glad to get a break.

"Tonight..." Omar said, "did you enjoy it?

He nodded.

"The bagpipes...Sheer genius, you'll agree. The English colonialists used the cries of dying witches to scare us, but now the noise is fun. I designed the kilts myself to match our flag. The show is worthy of San Francisco, don't you think, Barif?"

"I have never been," said Morgan.

"Such a decadent and beautiful city." Omar beamed. "America has many immoral impulses but displays them with such fervor, it's difficult not to admire their deceit." His long teeth exaggerated the dim light from the chandeliers. "My brother spoke about Houston... the women that danced naked."

"Jamil asked for his friends. Neither of us enjoyed it."

"My brother is priggish," he said with amusement. "The experience was good for him. Just what he will enjoy in Paradise!"

Morgan sensed Omar's brotherly bond of affection.

"Chaste maidens, voluptuous breasts, and lustrous eyes..." Omar's arms swept through the air. "This place also inspires such dreams."

He quieted and called to a stagehand to bring tea.

"Brother, where are you staying?"

Morgan mentioned a Lahore hostel.

Omar grimaced. "For prostitutes and thieves. No good will come to you there." He took Morgan's hand. "You stay with me."

"Your kindness is beyond measure." Morgan bowed again. Jamil had made good on his promise.

The tea arrived.

"Do you need to gather your possessions?"

Morgan showed him the satchel.

"Ah, yes." Omar lifted it in admiration and nodded in approval. "Of this I was also told. I'd like to travel with one small bag. When one dismisses worldly bondage...Paradise is obtained without second thoughts."

The men drank tea, then Omar said, "You have a coat."

Morgan showed him. Omar's fingers snapped, and the same stagehand appeared.

"Have Nadia come," he commanded.

"Of course," whispered the man, who turned and left.

The sultry balladeer who had licked the rifle barrel sashayed toward Omar. With tilted hips, Nadia stood close to him, stroking his ponytail, looking up into his eyes.

Omar said to Morgan, "Barif, you will never come here again."

Morgan nodded with understanding.

"The ISI came several days ago. They asked about you."

Morgan knew the police would interview the *Sagar*'s crew. Because he and Jamil had been close, they would follow a lead to Omar to determine if he knew anything about Barif Ali.

"Do not worry," Omar continued, "I spoke the truth to them. 'I've never met the man...'" He looked at Nadia. "Bring me a large burka."

She returned carrying the black fabric.

"Barif, your coat could be recognized by the police," he said, taking it from him and handing it to Nadia.

"Get rid of this," he said, exchanging it for the burka, "and we will go home."

Morgan watched the hirja fade into the darkness, as though floating away on invisible water.

"Put this burka on," Omar instructed him.

Morgan fumbled with it "Didn't you ever cover a woman?" he asked, laughing. "Let me do it."

The black bag dropped over Morgan's head. Through the rectangular opening, Omar spoke at his eyes.

"You will wear this to my home...a few minutes' walk. Because women are forbidden here, you and Nadia will leave from a separate door in the adjacent building I own. Perhaps you remember seeing it when you sat on the bench." Omar laughed again. "I pay spies to watch. That amputee you gave money to…one of many."

He pointed to a hallway. "When you step to the street, wait there until I bolt the front door…then follow me."

"I understand."

"Remember: a woman does not strike her feet firmly on the ground to make known what is hidden. Stay at six paces behind and watch closely. Under no circumstance should you speak or look at anyone, including me—even if I talk to you."

"I understand."

The final lights clicked off after Morgan entered a corridor that ended at a door. He went outside and waited. After Omar locked the theater doors, he walked away. Morgan and Nadia followed in silence.

———

Candle flames danced and incense smoldered as they sat on soft cushions surrounding the remains of a tray of lamb. Morgan's toes rubbed the exquisite wool rug that warmed the floor.

Omar's wit sparkled between draws on his pipe. A quiet lingered until Morgan complimented his host again.

"Dal ghosht," said Omar, "with ginger and garlic. The cardamom blends perfectly with the garam masala, do you think?"

It was obvious that he was much pleased to show off his sophistication to subservient guests.

"The split peas…are one of my favorites as the winter approaches. Your mother…she cooked well?"

"No. We ate humbly. Condemned to a life without a father."

Morgan kept his storyline fixed, without adding embellishment. Omar would listen for inconsistencies, for which Morgan would give no opportunity.

Nadia brought a basket of warm bread brushed with oil. With a coarse file, she ground salt from a brick. The grains sparkled as they rained down.

"Himalayan, from the bazaar in Namka Mandi," Omar bragged. "I have my own supplier."

When they finished, Nadia returned with a dessert of sugared carrots, pistachios, and almonds in a warm cream stew. Omar saw Morgan covertly glance at Nadia ladling desert into bowls.

"Nadia...Handsome, isn't she?"

Morgan nodded slightly.

"She was first runner-up in the Pan-Asian Contest for Beauty. They wanted her for Lollywood because she has an angel's voice... as you heard," adding proudly, "and she is also a wonderful cook."

He murmured some pet name. Morgan saw the pale eyes shine as she poured tea. "She's better than a wife," Omar bragged again, "of which I have four."

As Morgan expected, their voices were never overheard.

"When one of my wives makes me an unsatisfactory meal...I am obliged to beat her." He laughed harshly. "Better with a guest that Nadia cook. And Pashtuns make better company...loyal and devoted." Omar smiled. "Even my brother agrees their souls are special."

Morgan nodded, but now he understood. Because he and Jamil spent so much time together, Arwan must have believed there was more to the relationship that he wasn't seeing.

"Women..." Morgan contrived a sigh. "Nothing but trouble. It is a privilege for them to wipe their faces on our shoes."

Omar nodded. "So true. Men should use them as they wish." He looked directly at him. "Barif, did you ever intercourse an American woman?"

"Once."

"I am envious! Was it gratifying?"

"She moaned like a cow." Morgan swallowed hard to cover his enmity. "A mount of the devil."

"An impressive quote!" Omar released a pleased exhale. "Abu Nuwas is one of our great poets."

"I read as much as I can."

Omar took a sip of tea. "Give me your passport," he instructed.

Turning several pages, he looked at Morgan's picture and admired the stamps from various countries.

"Quite well done. The man does good work." He chuckled. "For a handsome price, no doubt."

"Expensive only if one cares for things of the world," Morgan replied.

Omar reached for the gift wrapped in linen that had been presented to him by Morgan after arriving at his home. Omar held the checkered wood grip and rolled the nickel-plated cylinder.

"A John Wayne…six-shooter?"

"As in the movies…"

"Where did you get it?"

"From a cowboy in Texas the night I met your brother." Morgan told the story.

Omar studied the metal engraving before squinting down the barrel.

"Alas, I am afraid of guns…but am grateful for your generosity. That you have given this to me honors your friendship with my brother and respects my trust."

Nadia headed toward Omar. "Leave us alone," he ordered.

She returned to the kitchen.

Omar loaded three bullets and spun the cylinder before locking it in place. Stooping over Morgan, he cocked the revolver in his right hand. "I apologize for my clumsiness." He picked up a candle. "You see…I'm left handed. Open your mouth."

Morgan did as instructed.

Using the votive to illuminate Morgan's mouth, Omar tapped his teeth with the muzzle, his index finger resting on the trigger. If the chamber had a bullet and Morgan flinched, the remnants of his brain would ruin anything behind him. Morgan would at least go to his grave knowing that his host would be deaf.

Omar's scrutiny continued. In Chicago, after refusals from every dentist he asked, Morgan finally offered a large enough sum of cash and succeeded in getting his silver fillings drilled out and glass ionomer placed over the dentin and other teeth. The coating eliminated nerve sensitivity, and in time it had stained, making all his teeth look rotten.

Morgan sat still, waiting for the examination to end—one way or another.

Omar released the gun's hammer and stood quietly, using the candle to look at Morgan's pupils, then brought an ear close to Morgan's nose to evaluate his breathing. It was slow and controlled.

"Forgive my concern," Omar said, placing the candle on the table before removing the bullets from the gun. "Your trust *is* strong."

He wiped the revolver with the linen cloth then folded it around the pistol.

Apathetic to what he had just done, Omar said, "Your teeth are bad! I have a friend here who is a fine dentist."

The ruse worked.

"You are very kind, but I will not need them much longer, Inshallah!" replied Morgan, knowing Omar didn't give a shit about his teeth.

Omar took the passport from the table and placed it in his tunic pocket.

"Jamil has brought you to me. I will do as my brother requests." He touched the pocket. "You no longer need this."

Barif Ali had become another human body living among the countless billions. Whatever time remained in his life was dwindling. All Morgan needed was enough of it.

"More tea perhaps?" Omar asked.

"No…thank you."

"Tomorrow we pray at the Badshahi Mosque. You will be impressed. Sixty thousand people under the red sandstone minarets. But now, we rest."

Morgan nodded as Omar spoke.

"When the time comes, we will journey. Inshallah."

THIRTY-SIX

Pruitt Farm Early November 2003

The doorbell rang. Connie Pruitt returned to the kitchen with a package. The return address had Cotsworth's name at the top.

"The wheels of government at work," she said.

"This may be a first," countered Jon. "Amazing. Cotsworth kept his promise. Maybe there's hope for the country."

He flicked open his pocket knife and stuck the blade under the sealing tape.

"Please be careful," said his wife.

"Are we ready for this?" he asked.

Seeing and touching the contents would be more disheartening than just hearing about them over the phone. Reality set in. Jon paused and removed the knife. The couple silently contemplated what was inside with homage reserved for a funeral urn.

Protected by Styrofoam peanuts, each item was wrapped in white tissue paper. After all the bundles were spread on the granite countertop, Jon reached in a drawer. Removing a plastic trash bag, he pulled open its mouth.

"I think Cotsworth mentioned envelopes. We don't want to risk missing them," he said.

"That would be a tragedy," replied Connie, who slowly poured the packing material into the bag.

The two envelopes joined the bundles and the CD.

The Macallan bottle had been taped shut with a note stuck to the label.

> Mr. and Mrs. Pruitt,
> I hope someday you find solace, perhaps these will help.
> P. Cotsworth
> PS: It's illegal to mail alcohol, but I did it anyway.

"I can still see Cay's face when she first tried this. She thought I was trying to poison her! Ha!" There came a satisfied look. "We gave that girl some seriously expensive tastes. I guess that's what life's about. Learn what you love and enjoy it often...because..."

The tears came.

Connie stroked his hair. "Stop, Jon," she said. "Cay and Wes wouldn't want it. These are gifts...presents. Please...Let's treasure this moment for what it is."

He kissed her gently on the forehead. "You've been the strong one," he said. "That...*you* gave to Cay."

"She got her wit from you," said Connie, tugging his hand toward another bundle of white. "Now come on, Blue. Christmas came early. Open another."

The two brandy snifters sparkled in the light.

"Look at that pattern," she said. "Cay told me she spent days looking for just the right ones." She smiled knowingly. "Remember what you told her?"

"You mean that crap about good crystal enhancing the taste of Scotch?"

"You used that line on me...and Cay was the result." Her fingers tickled his neck. "I learned *my* lesson."

"I suspect she tried it on Wes."

"Mothers don't imagine such things," replied Connie.

"When Wes first visited," Jon began, "he acted like a deer in headlights around us. But I knew he couldn't keep his hands off her." A shrewd smile delivered more mirth than his wife had seen for a long time. "I've kept it a secret from you. Remember that time when he surprised Cay with the bridle for Goethe? That afternoon when I went down to feed the horses, I heard what sounded like a saddle hit the tack room floor, and I thought, *That's odd...*So I went to investigate and, um, they were in there—"

"I imagine, getting into mischief." Connie covered her face to mimic embarrassment.

"Damn! You'd think kids their age would realize they might get caught."

"That's why *I* suggested they stay in the cottage," said Connie.

"Mothers understand such things more than they let on, I've learned," Jon said with an obliging nod.

"That's right," she replied.

For a long time they admired the photograph and the painting.

"We'll hang both together," said Jon.

"Yes, we will," his wife agreed.

He opened the box from Tiffany's and brought the diamond engagement ring close to his eyes.

"These stones set him back a little, I hazard." Jon handed the ring to his wife. "I remember, after her first engagement, Cay told me she didn't care about diamonds anymore...just wanted somebody who'd love her. The girl probably rankled up a storm when he bought this."

"Cay told me they'd gone looking, but I don't believe she knew," said Connie, "I suspect Wes was going to...New York...to give..."

"Oh, boy...I didn't know that," he sighed. Pruitt hugged his wife. "I just can't imagine..."

"Nor can I," she said in his arms.

Still embracing, Jon picked up the CD in one hand. "I don't think I can stand to listen to whatever's on this...at least not today."

As Connie's head rested against his chest, he opened an envelope.

It contained Morgan's social security card.

Jon Pruitt grimaced before he opened the other envelope. Together they read the note from Morgan.

He looked hard at his wife.

"We have no family left," he said.

"We have each other...and memories. Let's keep them happy."

She wiped his cheek.

The father looked at every item again.

"Do you see anything more in this?" he asked.

"They were in love," said Connie.

"That's obvious. But I worked with spies too long not to look beyond the first blush." Pruitt grew quiet for a moment while he thought.

"Wes took care of kids. That takes a kind heart. Probably one reason Cay loved him so much."

His closed fists drummed weakly on the counter.

"I hope this fellow Cotsworth figures it out…"

"What are you suggesting?" asked Connie.

"Hell. Maybe my optics are too fuzzy and I'm just projecting my feelings…"

"Jon…What is it?"

"Wes wouldn't have left these things just to be found." His crow's feet compressed. "He could've easily buried this box or just thrown it away."

"I can't see him doing that," countered his wife. "His sentiment was too great."

"It's more than that." Jon Pruitt could finally articulate his reckoning. "Wes is covering all contingencies. Whatever he's doing, wherever he's gone…he still has some small hope he'll come back."

THIRTY-SEVEN

Alexandria, Virginia Early November 2003

The twilight licked the top of the Washington Monument—the winking obelisk serene and confident. In uniform, Commander Elaine Jericho stood on her balcony with her gaze locked north of the Potomac River. She saluted and offered the silent supplication she spoke every night to the Almighty:

Please forward this to my friends…
I will remember.

Discarding the uniform on the bed, Jericho pulled on an emerald silk turtleneck and tucked it precisely into the waistband of her black wool slacks. After seating the zipper pull, she made certain the pleats hung straight and slipped on a pair of black leather flats. She wiggled her toes.

"These are so comfortable," she said.

The clasp on the string of her grandmother's pearls latched then Jericho removed the pins from her bun grazing her fingers through it to relax the coil. After shaking her head several times she back-brushed her hair to tease in volume and stepped over to risk a stare in the full-length mirror. With a liberated smile, she put on her waist-length coat, picked up the designer tote, and pranced out the front door.

———

"Evening, Ms. Jericho."

"Good evening, Andrius," she said as the maître d' took her coat.

"The same quiet table, if you'd like," he said, picking up a menu. "Anyone joining you tonight?"

She shook her head and smiled, hiding her disappointment. "No. Just me…"

"Good special tonight," he said. "I think you'll like it."

Only a few blocks from her home, she frequented the place whenever she could. The eclectic cuisine stimulated lost memories of distant seaports and clearer times, while the wait staff, brotherly to a fault, provided personalized attention to the redhead, as well as counsel when they thought she looked sad.

"What does a pretty woman like you do?" they often asked.

"I push papers," was always her reply.

They'd shake their heads as if to say: What a waste!

Flattering and consoling as they were, Commander Elaine Jericho preferred to be tucked away in a far corner and dine alone, getting lost in thought.

They brought her a glass of wine before Jericho looked at the menu. Never once disappointed with what was poured, she took a taste. With the glass stem held in her fingers and her elbow resting on the table, she leaned her forehead forward into her wrist and closed her eyes. The memory never left.

The Navy Annex where she had once worked was only a mile west of the Pentagon. She could still hear the compressing screams of the 757's engines on its murderous final approach—then the concussions—then the plume.

Fire.

Sirens.

Chaos.

Death.

"What would you like for dinner, Miss Jericho?"

Her thoughts broken off, Jericho pointed to a Moroccan chicken dish flavored with harisa sauce.

"With a glass of that Tempranillo I like, please," she requested.

Her unwound hair grazed ever so slightly across her shoulders as she took notice of an attractive man several tables away. He smiled at her and raised his glass.

Jericho felt for the tote bag hanging on the back of her chair. Concealed inside was her real world. In recent years, she was authorized to carry a handgun. The titanium hammerless .38 Special had no safety and held five hollow-point rounds. An FBI agent trained her until she could rapidly empty all the chambers into a plate-sized target at twenty feet.

You look like a great guy, she wanted to say, but instead she shook her head in discouragement. In another life she might have been flattered, and interested—but not now. The secrets she carried made her suspect of anyone without a formal introduction. Distrust had to be paramount.

The man went back to his meal. Jericho thought about her day as she had more wine.

"This image was run through FBI, Interpol, Mossad…essentially every database," Fields had said. *"The software applies a Wilcoxin Ranks Test. The significance level between this picture and any others on file is 0.0005."*

"Whatever," said Rushworth.

Meet your new ghost, Jericho wanted to say.

"The hair fiber in the jeans pocket is nothing more than contaminant… Sus Scrofa," said Fields. When he saw their confused faces, he added a smile. *"Wild Eurasian boar."*

"A closet ham eater," somebody joked.

Jericho's dinner arrived. A few bites offered a brief reprieve before her rehash of the meeting continued.

"Local FBI in Houston dispatched an agent to Puss 'n Boots," said Fields.

Rushworth glared when he used the name.

"None of the dancers remembered anybody that night, until I think one girl recalled a bald black man who ponied up a galling one-dollar tip."

Rushworth listened unamused but Jericho agreed silently the amount was scandalous.

"Then there's the report of a security guard at the port discovering a worker who was passed out in his diesel pickup truck that night. The cowboy couldn't remember much. With beer soaking everything in the cab, he didn't even know how he got back to the port. He had run into these fellows earlier at the port and again at the club. He tried to describe them, but his recollection became a hodgepodge of confusion as he tried to recall what happened next."

Fields quoted part of the transcript verbatim with the impromptu editing of the profanity.

"'Man! When I woke up, my side hurt worse than when my mama paddled my butt. A hangover never hurt so bad. Lost my damn Colt Python that night. That gun cost me a lot of money!'"

Fields looked at the group. *"Took him a week to realize the pistol was missing...along with fifty rounds. Cowboy did say it was registered."*

Months later the ATF still hadn't found the paperwork.

Rushworth couldn't dignify a response.

"I know who has it," said Jericho beneath her breath while she reached for her wine.

The absurdity would be humorous if it weren't so serious. The whole government seemed to exist in a state of restrained confusion—except for the military when it was finally given the order to attack.

Jericho rolled the wine around her mouth, examining the lingering flavors before her thoughts returned to the meeting.

"Does anybody have an inkling who this Ali person is?" asked Rushworth.

Fields spoke. *"All sources are quiet."*

"Even our guests at Gitmo?"

Fields shook his head demonstratively.

"We've spent an inordinate amount of committee time discussing this man," said Rushworth. *"Nothing presented so far suggests he's a credible risk for right now, so finding out more is the job for the FBI."* Her facial expression gave the order before the gavel hit the block. *"I'm putting this item in Old Business."*

Heads nodded.

Rushworth looked hard at Jericho. *"Commander, anything new about those cargo containers?"*

"Still looking for them, Madame Chair," the officer said crisply.

"Let us know—only—if you get new intel," Rushworth said. *"While you're at it, keep looking for Sayyaf's cane,"* she commanded.

Jericho's cell phone vibrated and hummed on the tablecloth. She was glad to get Rushworth's temperament out of her brain. A headache was already on the way.

"Hey, Lainey! How are you tonight?"

On an unencrypted line, she knew any specifics would be talked around. Jericho waved over the waiter.

"The bill please," she whispered, then said, "Good evening, Cotty."

"Great party today, don't you think?" he asked.

Jericho wasn't impressed he felt that way during the meeting. Every time their eyes met, his aggravation worsened hers.

"The best ever," she said.

Maybe it was the wine, but Jericho was too tired to play along.

"Glad you had a good time!" By the gusto in his voice, he was enjoying the exchange. "I'm going out of town again," he said. "Are you willing to play with my friends in the sandbox?"

"Oh sure," Jericho had to say yes, with regret.

"I'll have the guest list updated for the next luncheon."

By now she'd had enough chatting. It was time to wind it up. "Say, Cotty?"

"Yeah, darlin'."

"Do you think it's all right if I keep the library book checked out a while longer?"

"I don't think the school would mind for now," he answered. "Don't go overboard," he laughed at the inside joke, "or neglect your other studies."

"Okay." Jericho said. "Good night, Grandpa."

"Give my love to your husband and kiss the little ones for me," he replied.

The connection ended.

In her dreams…

———

Wine was the lousiest sleep aid in the world. Jericho woke with a headache from a mistake she rarely made. Her misery compounded when she recalled that before even getting the admiral's okay to dabble a bit more in her research, she had asked Glen Sorenson for help. The request probably bordered on illegal, but she needed his data-mining expertise.

"*This is all I want you to do, Glen,*" she had said, withholding more details, while hoping his efforts would never be uncovered.

When Jericho arrived at the NGA, Sorenson was snoring facedown at his workstation, his glasses resting on the keyboard. Zamani saw her approach the young analyst.

"Pulled an all-nighter, Elaine," Z said, never using her first name unless he was certain he wouldn't be overheard. "Working the keys, smoking data for you. I offered to help, but he wanted to do it himself. Kid's got pride."

"Pardon me?" she asked. "He was here *all night?*"

"Began right after his shift. Wanted it done before this morning."

"Seriously?" she asked.

"Sure enough," he said.

Zamani was about to nudge Sorenson, but Elaine's hand stopped him.

"Let him be. You go home."

Jericho gave a motherly smile to the man whose wavy long brown hair looked like a tangled mop. He also needed to get a life outside of work. She found him some coffee, placed the cup near his nose, and she went to her office.

Soon there was a knock.

"Morning, Commander Jericho!" Sorenson greeted her with the steaming cup in hand. Even with the wrinkled shirt and vestiges of a beard, he acted better than she felt.

"Why didn't you go home?" she asked.

"Was mining your data. It was fun. Great challenge! I learned a lot!"

Jericho felt even worse. Now, however, it was her stomach and not her head.

"It wasn't an emergency," she reiterated, knowing Glen had either missed that point or, more likely, didn't care. She couldn't help but admire his dedication while at the same time pray his after-hours foray would never be appreciated for what it was.

"No worries, ma'am. Like to see it?"

"Of course."

"Come back to my cube when you've got time."

Jericho followed. He got her a chair, which she pulled close then crossed her legs—a brief but pleasing diversion.

"There were a trillion data points, but man...the server is fast!"

Keys clicked, the mouse moved. The caffeine had found his brain. He grinned his playful smile.

"I had backpacks from everywhere," he exclaimed, displaying the entries. "So I added all the adjectives I could think to describe its functions and did what geeks do: surfed the web to find wilderness outfitting equipment. Check this out! The bag!"

He grinned again.

"Ballistic nylon...an inside volume of a carry-on suitcase—and... doesn't sink!"

He turned toward her.

"Why this one, you ask? Because it has an inner bladder and double zipper! Completely waterproof!"

"Glen..." She tried to contain what little enthusiasm she had. There wasn't much to the discovery. "Any ardent hiker could have that."

"True. But this one fits the exact profile of the bag on your guy's back. So I worked my sources..." He bit his lip. "Err..."

"Skip the details."

"Thanks. Let's just say I chewed through some serious electrons, looking at newspapers, news programs...boatload of bananas." His fingers never stopped moving on the keys. "I boiled the hits to less than a hundred and sieved through each manually."

Sorenson enlarged the grayscale picture showing the backside of a man with a baseball cap, short hair, and a backpack.

"This one fits the parameters, and...*this* dude's boarding a bus on a route that goes to the port...in the correct time window."

She shrugged and started to stand.

"I have more," he added, holding her wrist. Immediately looking contrite, he pulled his hand back. "Sorry for touching you, ma'am."

"Glen, lighten up." A warm smile. "Tell me."

"I reconstructed the image...more 3-D-like." Triumphantly, Sorenson leaned back in his chair. "That backpack and the one on the freighter stern are identical." He hadn't quit until the job was done. "This bag was also photographed at a Bush airport bus stop with the same guy, shades and all."

She put her hand on his shoulder. "How was this taken?"

"From an uncovered parking lot security cam."

Date, time, and a device number were displayed in the upper right corner as he beamed.

"Let me know whether you need anything else. Day's young."

Amazed, she said, "Glen, you do good work." His efforts were faultless. "Very good work." She stepped back to salute. "Thank you, Mr. Sorenson!"

"Here." He handed her a jump drive.

"Glen..."

"Ma'am?"

"Don't keep any files."

"Already taken care of."

Sorenson's passion for a challenge was impressive—his devotion to her equally so.

Jericho left his cubicle feeling ill. This surreptitious research had gone way past the purview of what she was entitled to request or do. Using domestic surveillance data to scrutinize the activities of people on American soil—gathered by an analyst under her tutelage—brought her close to a court-martial and prison. Sorenson could end up there too. That anxiety made her headache worse.

THIRTY-EIGHT

Aboard the *Khyber Mail Express* Mid-November 2003

The sudden pitch jarred Morgan awake, jerking his body back and forth. Wedged between the end of the upholstered bench and Omar, the last thing he remembered was the clickety-clack of the rails luring him to unconsciousness. Moments earlier, it seemed, the horizontal sunlight was streaming through the dirty window, illuminating a scene of upside-down automobiles, pale billboards, and long shadows. The blackness of the glass window reflected Nadia's face gazing outward in her usual trance. Seductive Lahore belonged to his past, and now there was only countryside. Seconds passed before Morgan was oriented. He felt for the satchel.

The strap was still over his shoulder.

A prickle crawled up his back from the cold air. At Omar's insistence Morgan was with them in first class, being ferried to Peshawar. Controlled by his host, who was really his custodian, the journey was Omar's final gesture of largesse before Morgan was taken to the frontier as another fresh offering destined for martyrdom.

He looked at Omar in his black salwar kameez. His expensive watch and shoes were left at his home in Lahore.

"Best to be like a chameleon and not invite disapproving eyes of clerics," he'd said at the train station.

His muted attire clashed with Nadia, who stood beside him like a bright flower. The courtesan's canary yellow sarong and red dupatta couldn't temper the brilliance of her gold and diamond necklace, nor could it eclipse the tasseled saffron purse and Louis Vuitton suitcase.

Over the weeks Morgan's fondness for the oddball human had grown, in contrast to her vain keeper, who, as the genial tour guide, had dragged him by day throughout Lahore to look at monuments and mosques, only to abandon him in the sitting room of his home to wait until his return from the theater, when they would indulge in another caloric meal and dessert. Morgan knew after his first evening that the red carpet would eventually be yanked away.

Seeing him stir on the bench, Omar leaned toward him with narrow eyes.

"Barif, you whisper the name *Cay* when you sleep."

Morgan held a stone face as Omar's cheeks inflated with his smile.

"To dream of lying with virgins in Paradise…"

With drawn eyelids Omar took a deep breath. Pretending to be enthralled by the scent of perfume, his chest and head slowly rose together and he said, "You will have a full stomach too. The champli kabobs in Peshawar are world renowned. We will have them this evening—"

Bang! Bang! Bang!

Their heads shot forward as the air brakes crushed against the wheels. A piercing screech enveloped them as metal ground to metal.

Just as suddenly, their bodies pushed back into the upholstery. The train shuddered, slid, and stopped.

Blasting caps, Morgan knew. *Three in a row…*

It was the universal railroad warning. A problem lay ahead—unusual for a well-traveled rail line, even at night.

Morgan listened, trying to hear through the porters' clamor as they leaned out the open platform doors to look.

The hammering volley swept from the engine to the last car. Part of their glass window shattered, showering glass throughout the compartment. When the spew of bullets paused so the users could load new magazines, anguished screams came from the porters dying on the ground. Shrieks swelled from every car.

Fresh clatter silenced the engineers in the front.

"Dacoits," Omar whispered.

Morgan knew bandits robbed even the *Khyber Mail*. They'd start in first class with the wealthy passengers, move toward the rear, then escape. Anyone resisting along the way would be shot without hesitation. The entire affair would last only minutes.

Morgan heard radio chatter outside and tried to count the number of voices.

Four?

From a different angle a machine gun shattered another window.

No. Maybe six.

Omar reached above and removed Nadia's suitcase from the rack. He handed it to Morgan.

"Open it," he said, "quickly."

Wrapped in the linen napkin, it felt familiar. Morgan loaded the revolver just as the lights went out. Rough voices entered the front of the train car.

Morgan dropped the suitcase next to the floor and pushed it closer to Omar with his foot. Neither Omar nor Nadia saw Morgan's left arm, hand, and gun retract inside his kameez. The sleeve hung limp, like an amputee. Sucking saliva, he let it drool out his mouth and started to spastically convulse his torso.

Omar reached down for the suitcase.

A violent kick pushed open the compartment door. Two masked men dressed in black crowded inside, both gripping Russian Makarovs. The reliable nine-millimeter pistols were cocked. The second man used a flashlight to study Morgan's contorting wet face then looked at Nadia. Omar remained bent over.

With the gun pressed into Omar's neck the first dacoit said into a radio, "Almost done in this car."

A coarse voice responded. "We're moving back."

The second dacoit barked at Nadia. "Get up."

Trembling with fear, she stood up. The necklace sparkled.

"Give it to me," he ordered.

She raised a hand to curse him.

The side of the flashlight smashed her face. She collapsed, coughing weakly. The clasp broke as she fell away.

"Nadia!" cried Omar, moving toward her.

Bang!

The Makarov fired, splattering most of Omar's neck to the floor. With his head dangling by a few remnants of muscle, the caged blast startled both robbers. They stared at the spurting blood as the body tumbled over.

Morgan trained the barrel of the cocked .357 at an upward angle and pulled the trigger.

The high-velocity bullet entered the flank of the closer dacoit. Still accelerating, the jacketed mass of energy exited unabated and tore through the heart of the other man. The lead-and-copper fragment finally stopped in the wood panel near the window.

Both men crumpled onto Omar, making the floor a heap of bloody bodies.

A hail of bullets pulverized what remained of the window. Morgan covered Nadia from the flying glass shards, grabbed one of the Makarovs, and dropped the revolver into the satchel.

Over the radio the same voice asked, "Are you okay, Shabir?"

Morgan shouted with a garbled voice, "Found much money!"

He shoved the bodies aside to get the suitcase, opened it quickly, and felt around inside. There was clothing but not his passport.

Waving the flashlight for an instant outside the smashed window, Morgan shouted, "Come! Get the case! I'll throw it to you."

Morgan peeked out the frame at the approaching man.

"Here!" Morgan shouted, heaving the suitcase toward him. As the man bent to pick it up, two rounds from Morgan's Makarov found their target.

Morgan took the radio then padded down the dead dacoits. Each man carried a grenade and a second magazine. After checking the pins, Morgan put the grenades in his satchel. He swapped the used magazine for a fresh one and crammed the other full one in his waistband.

Morgan rifled through Omar's pockets, searching again for his passport. Unsuccessful, he handed Omar's wallet to Nadia. The lack of identification on the body might slow the search for Nadia and, in turn, him.

A flash caught his attention. He grabbed the necklace.

"Come," he ordered in Pashto.

She tried dragging Omar by his ponytail, unable to comprehend he was dead.

"Nadia! Come!"

Morgan pulled her away while she grabbed her purse.

He glanced both ways down the corridor then led her by the hand to the next coupling platform.

"Going to car four," said the radio.

"Meet at car five," answered Morgan.

Morgan and Nadia jumped to the rail bed and ran along the train until she tripped on her dress hem. He reached into the satchel and handed her his kameez.

The tunic top ended above her ankles, exposing only her painted toenails and sandals. Using her teeth, she tore a strip of cloth from the bloodied yellow dress and tied back her hair. Morgan balled up the remainder of the fabric and threw it deep into the brush.

The radio crepitated. "Hurry!"

Morgan turned it off. Moving from wheel to wheel, they crept toward the back. Multiple footsteps pounded above them. Nadia pulled the revolver from his satchel. There was no time to argue.

He pointed for her to climb to the front platform of the fifth car. Nadia scaled the metal steps, vanishing in the shadows. Morgan removed the pin from one of the grenades and squeezed the lever to ignite the fuse.

Hiss...

He side-handed the globe under the train so it would roll down the opposing embankment.

Four one thousand...

He plugged his thumbs into his ears while covering his closed eyes with his fingers.

Six...seven...Exhale!

The explosion turned the world white-orange as angry echoes bounced over the countryside. Morgan lobbed the second grenade under the train as he vaulted up to the rear platform. Two figures were looking out windows at the glowing mushroom cloud as a third man rushed to the forward door. Morgan heard Nadia's gunshot but didn't see the man's head rip apart.

He covered his ears and eyes again and exhaled.

The car shook as the fireball ascended both sides.

Morgan opened the door, dropped to one knee, and took aim.

The closer man fell onto his flashlight. A moment later, the other man hit the floorboards—the beam illuminating the both faces. The sheen of death was descending.

With smoke pouring out the muzzle, Morgan moved closer.

"Mercy," pleaded one in a fading whisper.

Morgan would offer none.

He picked up the flashlight. To temporarily blind the passengers, he shined it in their faces while he moved to the rear platform. On the gangway he turned it off and called for others on the radio.

No response.

They had killed all of them.

He scaled down to the ground. Nadia reappeared, purse in hand.

The clamor above grew louder as the passengers peered through the windows. The authorities would arrive soon. They had to get away quickly.

The couple ran along the rail ties until coming to an overpass. Morgan released his pistol's safety and cocked the hammer. The barrel followed his eyes as he scanned the darkness.

Animals and distant trucks were all he heard.

They slid down the embankment, and in the darkness saw what looked like starved ponies.

Motorcycles.

Morgan shoved the Makarov into his waist band, pried off one of the bike's ignition caps, and hot-wired a twin-cylinder Honda. It chugged to life. Nadia stood nearby, her eyes transfixed on the train.

"Nadia!" he shouted over the clanking growl.

She mounted behind him, sliding the revolver into the satchel. The tasseled purse drooped over her shoulder as her arms went around his waist.

The throttle edged higher and the wheels spun and caught. After driving several hundred feet through the brush to cover the tire marks, the Honda returned to the road. The Grand Trunk Highway was no more than a mile or two distant.

As the motorcycle accelerated, Nadia pressed her wounded face into his back to shield it from the wind—but mostly the dust.

THIRTY-NINE

Dodging debris and animals, they wove through the dried ruts on the frontage road that clung alongside the highway. The throttle was open most of the time on the straights, until a curve strained their balance and forced Morgan to slow down. While the headlight rattled on its mounting, gravel from the washboard road pinged in the fender wells and sprayed their legs.

Nadia jabbed him in the ribs and pointed to a sign. Morgan drove them west toward Chakwal, the province capital. The road became hilly and full of switchbacks as they got closer. A mile outside, they got off the motorcycle. Morgan wiped the handlebars with his shirt and pushed it off a ledge into a deep ravine. Satisfied when he heard the metal smash on rocks, they walked to the outskirts of the town. At sunrise, they heard the muezzin in the distance.

The couple sat down in a cluster of large bushes, and Morgan used the growing sunlight to examine Nadia's face.

He smiled.

"Not bad," he lied when he saw the welt on her cheek from the gun and the red ring around her neck where the gold chain left its mark as it was yanked off.

In his former life, Morgan could have easily treated her injuries with common items found in every operating room. That wasn't going to be possible today. For now, Nadia's wounds would have to be treated by the medicines and creams he found in the first souk.

He rubbed dirt on his bloodstained pants and shirt to hide the dark red color.

"Wait here out of sight," he said and walked to town with his satchel.

———

An hour later Morgan returned wearing new clothes. He handed Nadia a fresh sarong and hajib. She went deeper into the bushes to change then came out and sat down next to him. He used eyewash containing a drop of tea to reduce the redness then removed a small towel from a plastic bag and dabbed her face and neck with the diluted saltwater mixed with lemon juice. At first she grimaced, but then she looked stoically at the distant mountains. After it dried, he applied camphor paste to the wounds. A cold compress would have helped reduce the swelling, but no ice was available.

It was the festival of Ramadan, but they were so thirsty and hungry they ate bread, yogurt, and honey, and took tea. Removing his rope circulet, he pulled off his keffiyeh and let frequent smiles obscure any indication of deeper concentration. Fatigue was accumulating, but Morgan had meticulously trained to ignore it. They had to keep moving and get through Chakwal. The longer the pair lingered, risk compounded. The city recruited more soldiers to the Pakistani army than any place else in the country. When the news spread about the attack on the *Mail*, those loyalists and the local tribes would thoroughly apprize any visitors. A petite eunuch with a purple face would draw attention.

Nadia's presence put Morgan in danger, yet abandoning her might be worse. Besides, she might know of Omar's intent. Morgan would keep Nadia with him.

His sweaty hair dried, and Morgan scratched his head. He put the white and black checkered keffiyeh back on and handed Nadia the necklace. She glowed with sad appreciation as she examined the broken clasp, and then she leaned over and softly kissed his cheek.

They walked several more miles until Nadia motioned to a beautiful park wrapped around a Hindu monument. A cluster of trees made pleasant shade in the pastoral respite, and there was even a delicious cool breeze. They sat down together on a bench.

Nadia unsnapped the clasp of her purse and pulled out a flip cell phone.

Seeing Morgan's unsure expression, she said, "Dost." *A friend.*

He nodded—a real one, he hoped.

Her suffered smile told him a double cross was improbable. Pashtun culture assured protection of one's personal guests—a code of honor instilled from birth. If the sojourner maligned that respect, however, the host's vengeance would be guaranteed, ruthless, and served cold.

While Nadia talked, Morgan walked to the street, reached into his waistband, and discreetly dumped the Makarov and extra magazine through a sewer grate.

FORTY

Houston Mid-November 2003

Puss 'n Boots was not a good place for unaccompanied women, especially attractive women. The noise, music, and raunchy dancing made it difficult to think, the constant interruptions made it impossible.

Zamani might have kept the gadflies away, Jericho thought.

That terrible idea had crossed her mind briefly, but appreciating the clientele at the club, she realized even a marine with a Middle Eastern face would be hassled. Then there was Z's wife. Jericho felt sick thinking about how a rumor of impropriety could hurt their marriage.

But Jericho knew better than to go alone. Years before, while the fleet was laying over in Cape Town, she naively accepted an invitation from some of the male officers to join them at a club for some world-renowned entertainment. Jericho ended up so disgusted she left on her own, promising never to step foot in such a place again.

Jericho remembered her former chief petty officer worked in Houston for the FBI. Thorill Carstens agreed to help her friend.

So they sat with painted smiles while the drinks and beer accumulated and the men buzzed over them, hoping for more than conversation. Her hair pulled back with an alligator clip and wearing only the rank of single female, Jericho realized too late her ill-conceived jeans and boots were the wrong uniform, made worse by a white blouse that in the smoky humidity was clinging to her chest. At least Carstens had a gun on her—somewhere.

"All too predictable," Thorill yelled. "Guys never grow up. What is it with them?"

"There have to be men out there better than these," Jericho yelled back.

"Don't count on it, Elaine. They're only in those stupid books of yours. What they really want…" Carstens pushed her index finger against Jericho's hip. "Is what you keep in *there*, baby. Nothing more."

Shots of tequila came next, the waitress pointing to the ingratiating provocateur under a cream Stetson. Jericho gave him an officer's smile and turned away. When he tried to rise to come over, she shook her head.

Jericho nudged Carstens and pointed to a young woman in spiked heels and little else, slinking on all fours across the stage. She faced the audience to accept money in her garter then sat down with her legs open and shook her curly head of hair. Her fingers rubbed the G-string.

"Is that her?" Carstens asked.

Both had reviewed the roster at the front door, displaying the night's performers.

"She's the one they interviewed," Jericho said.

"Good asset management," said Carstens.

"We should all be so lucky," shouted Jericho.

After many requests to their waitress, the floor manager finally came to the table. His ostrich boots spoke to the largesse of his position—when the price was right.

"This isn't a raid," shouted Carstens, presenting her badge. "All my friend wants is a few minutes with that dancer," she said.

With a smarmy smile, he ushered Jericho backstage to a private room.

The young woman entered smoking a cigarette. Wearing a polyester robe, she sat down close to Jericho and spread her legs slightly.

"Honey," the officer said, "I'm not here for that."

"You ain't here to take my baby, are you? Please don't!"

"No," Jericho said gently. "I'm not going to take your baby."

"Then can I have some money?" the young woman whimpered pathetically.

Jericho put a hundred-dollar bill in her garter.

"You don't want nothin'?" she asked, her tired eyes revealed only despondency.

"If it's all right…" Jericho said, "I just want to show you a picture."

She handed the woman the sketch of Ali.

"Did you ever see this man?" asked Jericho.

"Yeah…dragged a bald black guy away from me. What a skank! Gave me a dollar."

"What color was this man's skin?" Jericho pointed to Ali's face.

"Shit-tan-like."

"Did he say anything to you?"

"I can't, like, hear nothing with that fuckin' music."

"What else do you remember about him?"

"He looked like an asshole."

"I'd agree with that." Jericho tried for more. "Anything else, maybe about the other men he was with?"

"No."

Jericho stood to leave.

"Hey, lady…" The dancer flicked the bill with a finger. "Thanks for this. You're a really good person…like my mama. When my boss, like, hears I got a hundred from you…he'll let me dance more in private." She gave a broad smile, mashing the cigarette butt in an overflowing ashtray. "Help feed me and my baby…and I can, like, finish school."

"You take care of yourself and your family, you understand?"

Jericho felt sorry for her, but there was nothing she could do to help. She didn't even want to speculate what really might happen to the money.

When Jericho returned to the table, she gave Carstens a disappointed nod, and the women headed for the door. As they stepped outside, the manager chased after them.

"Hey!" he hollered at Jericho. "You and your girlfriend want to party together with her?"

"Wrong!" shouted Jericho. Both women vice-gripped his forearms, dragging him until his back was pinned to the wall. Passing patrons watched in amusement.

"Bad manners don't fit those spiffy boots of yours," Carstens said. "Now, my *girlfriend* here is going to ask you some questions. I'd advise you to be polite when answering."

"About a year ago last summer, do you remember this man?" said Jericho, thrusting the picture in his face. "Had three others with him."

"No! I swear to Christ, I remember everybody. Maybe I was off that night."

"Are you certain?" Jericho brought the picture closer. "Because we can find out if that's true."

"I swear to God! No! I don't remember him! I don't want any trouble with you!"

"Dirtbag doesn't know him, Elaine."

"Okay. Then there's just one more thing," Jericho said to her friend.

Jericho's boot heels clicked together as her lips elevated to his ears. She wanted to rip out his diamond earring. She didn't like what the woman was doing with her life, but that was her choice. Men who extracted a living or fulfilled their fantasies from such behavior, however, she detested.

"Listen carefully," her authoritative voice hummed. "That princess I was talking to—That's none of your business!" Jericho squeezed harder, making his face contort. "So if she loses her job... or you start pimping her...or, God forbid, she finds an accident and leaves her child an orphan, I'm holding your greasy behind responsible. Remember my friend here..."

Jericho's face directed his eyes to Carstens.

"I guarantee she'll be back to check." Jericho let her heels descend back to the ground. "Any questions, Mister?"

"N...n...no...ma'am," he stuttered.

"Good boy," Jericho said, releasing her grasp. Her attention shifted to Carstens. "Come on. Let's get out of here."

The women walked to the agent's car.

"The FBI could use your sweet disposition for our failed interrogations," Carstens smirked.

"Don't encourage me to use bad language in my reply," Jericho retorted.

Both women laughed.

The next morning they went to the wharf. The security guard who was on duty that night was waiting for them in the office. Jericho showed him the sketch.

"Can't say," he said. "Like I told those other agents last month, lot's a people go through here, in and out by the dozens, like rats."

He looked into Jericho's discouraged face.

"Besides, if he came past me, think he'd show his mug to me or the camera, seeing as how you're so interested in him now? Don't you think he'd know that back then?"

"Man's got a valid point there, Elaine," said Carstens. "I reviewed the file from before. Nothing's changed since."

"Okay," said Jericho to the guard. "Sorry to get you in here so early for this."

"Ain't a problem," he answered. "Glad to help. If he ever passes through again, do you want us to tie him up? Or just kill him?"

They laughed as Carstens shook her head and gave him her card, but to Jericho his sentiment was refreshingly appealing.

The cowboy came in next.

Reeking of beer, he nervously admitted he couldn't remember the man's face.

"That Arab bastard kicked my kidney. Pissed blood for a week... the fucker." He grimaced. "Sorry, ma'am."

"Don't worry about it," said Jericho. "Anything else you remember?"

"Sum bitch spoke 'Merican."

"What do you mean by that?" inquired Jericho.

"Ain't no drawl, you know? Ain't no redneck...or Texas cracker neither."

"I don't understand," Jericho said.

"Speaking Yankee, but not like 'em high-collar shits in New York City," the man said. "Just plain 'Merican, like on the TV news."

Jericho's puzzled look remained.

"If his ass," the Texan said, "comes around me again—"

"No," interrupted Carstens, "you can't shoot him. Besides…" She showed him her card then tucked it into the band of his hat. "Have to find your gun first. Right, cowboy?"

"Shit, if that ain't true."

"Be smart." Carstens pointed to his hat. "Call me."

The women left for the airport.

"Thorill," Jericho said as the car approached the departure gates, "what does it mean, 'speaking American'?"

"When your bad guy speaks English, he has no accent," responded Carstens.

"Why?"

"That cowboy you talked to had a sharp ear," Carstens began. "TV networks don't want their key anchors to sound like snobs or Southerners, so they hire them out of the Midwest."

"I didn't know that," said Jericho.

As the car pulled alongside the curb, Carstens looked at her friend. "He's a Midwesterner, Elaine…and probably a US citizen."

"A homegrown beast," Jericho stated.

Carstens popped the trunk release and both women got out of the car. With Jericho's suitcase next to her on the ground, Thorill spoke bluntly. "Elaine, listen very carefully to what I'm going to say, because I can't warn you enough."

"Okay." Jericho felt her friend's concern spill across the small space between them and smother her.

"If this Ali turns out to be an American citizen, your infatuation with him is over, understand?"

Jericho nodded.

"You chase this guy too far and it won't just be the end of your career, it'll put you in jail. Federal time is no fun."

"I assure you, Thorill, it's crossed my mind."

Carstens took both her hands and held them warmly.

"This weekend will be just us having stupid fun." She gave Jericho a hug. "Protect that attractive backside of yours. If need be, destroy whatever goods you got, despite your dogged desire to the contrary. Be smart! Keep what you've done so far to yourself."

Smiling, Carstens saluted. "Never given orders to an officer before. Glad we're friends!"

———

The flight home to Washington provided Jericho time to think. Managing satellite imagery was predictable; playing detective without precise images was disorganized and frustrating, a canvas that needed many more brushstrokes than she first realized. Interpretation of that data—she was learning—was much more difficult.

One thing was clear: her detective days were over. What she was doing was illegal. Her duties were limited to nuclear geopolitics; snooping around well beyond that scope was a major breech of her jurisdiction. Ali was a matter for the FBI, and not her affair. She'd never know any more than she did right now.

Fatigued, she returned to her book. The worn blue leather cover revealed habitual use and masked a world of rare but pleasant diversion. She affectionately thanked her mother for instilling the habit as a teenager. Romance novels were a simple way to escape life. Whenever at sea, she brought a boxful, but there was never time to finish them.

After a few pages, she sensed a warm rush and tried to rationalize her present life with what she really wanted.

The dancer got sex—but nothing more.

She looked at the pages opened in her hands.

An ice cube clinked in her empty plastic cup. Her life was hopeless. Washington was filled with young women and far fewer men. The males who played the game of government used those favorable odds to encourage the next conquest to lie on her back.

Pigs at the trough, she conceded.

Jericho sat upright.

Her mind flooded with questions expecting instant answers—responses that would frustratingly have to wait until the next morning when she got to work. The first question plagued her the most.

Why would Ali want to be around pigs?

FORTY-ONE

Washington, DC Monday, November 17, 2003

"**R**ichard, don't play games with me," Jericho warned. "Ms. Rushworth told me to find Sayyaf. I'd like the DNA sequence."

"She made a joke," he replied sarcastically. "Didn't you get it?"

Jericho's face was almost the color of her hair.

"Besides," Fields continued, "what's a pig got to do with nuclear terrorism?" A yawn followed. "The forensic report was clear. Don't you have better things to do? Like, you know, there is a war going on in Afghanistan…in case you forgot…and—"

"I haven't forgotten." Her voice controlled, she put down the cup of tea. "That specimen may suggest a country visited or place of origin…and help find both Ali and Sayyaf."

"You're serious? A pig?" His tone was insulting. "How about satellites? We redirected two platforms so your analysts could look for those containers. I'm sure you'll agree that verifiable data takes precedence. The Chair turfed Ali. If they find out anything, I'll call you. He's not on *your* priority list. Now…if Priscilla's decision isn't good enough for you…"

Her face matched her hair again.

More times than she preferred to acknowledge, Jericho had witnessed the same thing in bureaucrats. It was never about their sworn duties; it was all about their own self-interests—climbing to the top by any means available and avoiding pitfalls that might detour the ascent. What was even more disgusting was when open zippers helped leverage the way.

Jericho dismissed the inconceivable thought, certain it was the result of her casual reading. Her singular desire was to get the DNA footprint. Fields's rebuff would eventually flounder.

"You think that, as CIA, you control the agenda," Jericho said, "You'll remember—as *Priscilla* likes to say—we're in this together. I have clearance to review any concerns of the Nuclear Committee's activities or details in reports." She paused. "You can make this easy on both of us or hard on you. And if need be...I'll speak with my director."

Carstens's words bounced in her head when Jericho threatened to bring the admiral into the fray. Maybe now it was she who was overinflating her station. She softened her voice.

"So, Richard...what's it going to be?"

"Have it your way."

"Thank you." She added syrup to her words. "I do appreciate your time with this. If *I* discover anything, and that is a big *if*, you'll know."

The DNA signature arrived by e-mail two days later. As expected, Fields copied Rushworth just to bait Jericho, but she didn't care. She'd gotten what she wanted and went to Glen Sorenson, who beamed when she approached.

"Do you have any clue how one cross-matches DNA?" she asked,

"Well, no...but let's see." The keystrokes began. "Here we are, Commander, you compare what you have with a repository for such information...like CODIS."

"Suppose it isn't human."

"Like alien? From the agency's Roswell floor?"

He looked too eager.

"Perhaps closer to Earth...like farm animals...pigs, specifically."

A series of clicks.

"Amazing!" Sorenson said. "This thing almost answers the question before the query's finished." He showed her the screen. "Several databanks in the world do it...biggest one is located at Purdue."

"Can you access the system?"

"Give me a second." More clicks. "Here we are...ready and waiting."

Jericho handed him a jump drive. It contained one small file.

"Ask their library about that sequence...please."

Sorenson clicked and pasted. "Done."

"Really?"

She, too, was amazed at the speed.

"Yes, ma'am." His disarming grin seemed incompatible with his intellect. "Their firewall was trivial. I cut through it like a knife in soft butter."

His enthusiasm made her heart pound more as she drew Glen deeper into her obsession.

"Check it out," he said proudly. Jericho leaned forward, a hand pressing on his shoulder for support.

Sorenson tried to keep his mind focused, but his boss seemed less intransigent in recent weeks. She also appeared more ruffled, for reasons impossible to contemplate.

"Any idea what this gibberish means?" she asked.

"Not yet," he said, his fingers fluttering again. "The specimen is from a..." Sorenson paused, scrutinizing the screen. "What's called a Hampshire male...which we already know is a pig."

He took a swallow of water from a plastic bottle and gave a frustrated head shake.

"There's not enough DNA to verify identity or lineage."

Regrettably, Jericho began to realize, Fields was probably right. The organic material meant nothing—another dead end.

Sorenson watched her tongue hover over her clear lipstick and knew she was thinking intently. "Why are you looking at this, Commander, if you don't mind me asking?"

"It has to do with the backpack, Glen," she replied. Her stomach started churning again.

"Well, I'll admit, some men are pigs," he offered, trying to subordinate any worry she might have about his curiosity.

"Yes, they are." Caught by her casual response, she amended her words. "Not all men, Glen, just a few." She pointed at the screen. "Whoever this pig person is, well...he could be dirty."

"I would be too, hanging around with pigs."

She laughed, glad for his adroit joke.

"Can I help you find out more?" he asked.

"Thanks, but no." Jericho downplayed his eagerness. "Call it…" Muting her words, she shook her head forcing a sincere smile. "There's nothing here, Glen, and we've more important work to do. Great effort, though. It's a waste of everybody's time."

She'd say no more to him.

FORTY-TWO

Monday Afternoon

"**T**hem Hampshire hogs are ugly mothers!" Cottrell Herndon remembered too well. "When Pa cut 'em...they squealed fierce!"

As the pen clicked, Jericho sensed a memory swelling from his youth.

"And, darlin'?"

She held a blank expression.

"When those boars escape to the wild, they get big...rooting around at night, digging up crops! Then they get hairy...and grow tusks! Once that happens, they are mean. I mean *real* mean. Don't want to mess with them or they'll charge you. Had a three hundred pounder chase our truck once."

"What happened?"

"The old man blasted it with his 30-30. Good barbecuing that night." He flipped the photograph back. "So what do you think about Priscilla moving up to deputy director?"

The rumor had circulated for several days.

"I hadn't given it much thought," she said. "I learned long ago not to listen to gossip."

"Will you ever give me a frank opinion?"

"Sir...About intelligence, yes. In matters of people, especially her...let's just say, I don't want to be quoted."

"Circumspect as usual," he said with a chuckle. "Plus, I expect you don't want her to misunderstand your infatuation with pig DNA."

"That's not my concern." Jericho shook her head. "Ali got on that freighter one way but off very differently, and it has to be those containers, particularly with Sayyaf in the picture. Why Rushworth punted the thing just like that"—Jericho snapped her fingers—"to the FBI confounds me."

"She sees forests, never trees." He laughed. "You're a lot smarter than she is...and more astute. She knows she's a political appointee. Maybe she's jealous."

"Of what?" Jericho asked.

"Your intellect...and, of course, your red hair."

"Stand down, Admiral." Jericho winced. "I thought we were having a serious discussion." An affectionate smile followed.

"I read you, Commander." His pen started clicking again. "Look, Lainey...ever stay at a Ritz-Carlton?"

The memory of her only midshipman indiscretion came back.

"Not for a while," was the muted reply.

"Mention something as insignificant as a room-service tray left too long in the hallway to the concierge, housekeeper, whoever—that employee owns the issue and makes sure it's taken care of. Call it what you will—job security, pride of employment." The admiral smiled. "That obsession is part of your job too. The same with your staff! They're devoted because you are. Your crew evaluations were the same! Why do you think I picked you?" The pen clicking never ceased. "All those working research in the cubicles are just like you and me. We aren't the problem. We're the fixers."

Herndon sat back in the wooden captain's chair. The glued joints creaked as he crossed his legs.

"By 'n' by, truth is truth. Few in government take ownership of anything, and never after four o'clock. Superb benefits, though."

He paused, enjoying the rare opportunity for candid conversation.

"I wouldn't sweat over this Ali fellow, Elaine. Time will tell. Don't let him distract you much.

All she said was, "You're right."

"Hmm, I sense your confidence on this whole episode remains subpar."

"Cottrell, the scenario is still troubling whether or not Ali's in it. During multiple passes over Yemen, we traced the truck treads east for miles, until we found those containers at the bottom of a cliff." Jericho rocked her head back and forth. "Along the way we saw no evidence of any change in tread depth—always shallow—so maybe those never had anything in them from the get-go."

"Even if the ship's log doesn't reflect another stop, the at-sea timeline is too protracted," the admiral said. "Unless, of course, they just went sunbathing for a few days in the Gulf of Aden." He added his usual chuckle.

"They *had* to have made port somewhere during that window," Jericho replied. She had learned over time to ignore his sidebar comments. "If the remaining two containers had maraging metal as NSA reported, it would make sense for the *Sagar* to stop in Iran, then the material was probably taken underground at Qom—frustrating we didn't see any of it…all intentional."

"Yes, Yemen was a grand illusion." He was clicking his pen as his jowls wagged. "Our enemies are smarter than we are sometimes."

"They knew from the beginning there was a good chance we'd be looking, and for the most part their scheme went well." She sighed. "We did chase the bait, but what they didn't anticipate was that Ali—"

"That smart guy—Sorenson's his name—did a great job," interrupted Herndon wishing to move on to a topic that he hoped would delight her.

"Thank you, Cotty. I'll tell him you said that."

"Lots of unexplained elements in play, Elaine." He added, "So now this whole thing will get passed on to somebody else."

"Let me just add this thought," Jericho said, not yet willing to take the hint. "I've no doubt that Ali was getting off in Karachi. If he did kill the others—and I suspect that was the case—it just hastened his plans. I'm convinced Sayyaf and Ali will meet again—on purpose, but finding either of them will not be easy."

"I agree...but we'll see," said the admiral shifting forward in his chair. "On a lighter note..."

"There is one?"

"Would you like to be *shiny brass* again?"

Her green eyes fluttered when she heard the words. A promotion in rank was coming, but with good came bad.

"I've been offered a seat with the Joints," Herndon said. "So there's a new billet for you! Yours for the taking..."

Jericho swallowed hard.

"I'm recommending you for Assistant Director of Global Operations, starting next year...*Captain*." He belly-laughed. "That means, of course, that immediately your workload will pour on you like a manure truck at an organic farm."

"I don't believe you."

"It's true, Lainey. You'll be at the epicenter, as they say, of intelligence. We're going have to win this war in little steps." He beamed with pride. "Who's better than you? You'll fight to cut through the crap."

"While dying in bureaucratic hell..."

The current meetings she attended made that concern very real.

"Commander, your devotion to this country is the finest example of American patriotism."

She blushed. "Sir, I don't deserve it."

"You don't wear allegiance on a lapel, you live it. I can't think of anybody better than you to find the sons of bitches before they spoil tailgating with a dirty bomb after the Tide crush Auburn." He clenched his jaw shut. "Ah! I just hate it!"

A moment passed for his repartee to return.

"Mostly I know you'll take the job...because you enjoy Priscilla's company so much. Watching you annoy her these last weeks has been a pleasure."

"I hope you're kidding, Cottrell."

"Can't stand her."

"I meant about the promotion, Admiral," she replied. "You honor me, sir."

"You honor our country, Elaine Jericho."

"You know I don't care about anything but the security of the United States of America."

"Because," he laughed again, "you think the safety of her citizens lies in understanding the life story of a hairy pig? I'm still working on that one."

"Yes, I do, and that's my final Jeopardy answer." She shook her head in frustration. "I'm not a libertine. I'm an officer with a sworn duty."

"Lainey, you're already learning the art of bullshit."

"I'll live with my frustrations," she said. "We lost so many that day—so many *good* people! My God!"

The admiral saw her eyes grow moist as her voice became subdued.

"You invest your entire career protecting a great country...and every election cycle we go backward, dealing with new self-righteous appointees."

She sniffled, clearing her nose while her hands opened in frustration. "Then we've got the politicians...They're the worst. It's bad enough they're snide to you in private while you're trying to do your job, but then...they feel empowered to do the same thing in public."

"Good feeling, huh?" replied Herndon. "Try dealing with a House Subcommittee on Intelligence. There's a misnomer if I ever heard one."

"Maybe I am playing my cards now," said Jericho. "I'm tired and hoping you were just kidding me about the appointment."

"Lainey, we're all tired." He reached over and affectionately placed his hand on her shoulder. "Just so you know...Bill Platter will be moving up, taking over for me."

"Admiral Platter's a good man," she agreed. "Fair too. Just not as sweet as you."

"Aw...You can call me anytime just to say that."

Herndon reflected silently about his decision. Starting out, she'd be the youngest associate director the NGA ever had. In every capacity he knew Jericho was the right person for the job, but her relentless intensity still gave him pause. Her professional life had matured richly, even though she approached every project with the same enthusiasm as cooking on a stove with only front burners. Jericho's private life, despite Herndon's promotion to the contrary, remained in neutral. He'd try to help one more time.

"Before your coronation," he said, "I'm also recommending you for a little vacation. You're due. Last time I checked, you hadn't taken a day off in two years."

"Impossible. Not now."

"I could make it an order."

"No."

"Would two weeks be long enough?"

"Admiral Herndon, I respectfully decline your offer…sir!"

"Look at me, Commander." He had his big, sly grin. "Let down that red hair, get rid of those damn shoes you complain about, and *get away*. Maybe to some place with sand, water, and boys. The world isn't going to end tomorrow. And if it does, at least you'll leave it with a drink in your hand. Just make sure it's got one of those pink umbrellas."

"I can't now, sir," she said, "not with what you just offered me. I owe too much to my colleagues. They're part of me, and I'm part of them."

"They'll understand. They do understand. Deputize Zamani in your absence."

"I will take your recommendation under advisement!"

He knew he lost. "You're so stubborn."

"Redheads are. You should know by now." She let her voice relax, remembering his rank. "I trust my position is clear, sir."

"Okay, you win." He would argue no more. "I'm assuming, then, you'll accept the Assistant DGO position?"

Her common sense told her to say no, but her ego overruled. "Yes, Admiral."

He rose, she followed. They stood face to face and firmly joined their right hands. Herndon stepped back and saluted her.

———

Extracting the composite sketch from the folder, she stared at Ali, squeezing her eyelids to distort the edges, hoping the fuzziness would concede a secret.

The face was devoid of expression.

She looked at the picture of a man with a backpack at a bus stop.

The enemy wasn't only overseas. They were cloaked in applause at school plays, standing on freshly mowed grass, grilling cheeseburgers, and waving to neighbors. Ali was one of them, and there were so many more.

"Oh, well…" she said, slipping the picture back inside the crevasse of the folder. Ali became another piece of randomness in a universe of terrorist entropy.

She stood up and pushed her feet into her heels. After smoothing out the wrinkles in her skirt, the officer's cap went smartly over her exhausted brain.

As Elaine Jericho shut the office door, she saluted the men and women around her. The responsibility they carried was remarkable. Maybe it would be better with her closer to the helm, until she recalled what Herndon had said to her in the past.

"You call me obsessive? Stubborn?" she confided to the walls of the empty elevator after the doors shut. "I'm more like *insane*."

FORTY-THREE

Western Punjab Province Late November 2003

Bitterness...
A warm rush...

She was impetuous, this mistress, standing on her tiptoes, licking his neck, her diaphanous skirt crumpled between them, her crotch rubbing hard against his firm penis, making him want to fuck her, fuck her just as much as she wanted to bathe in his blood.

She was back inside him again, the heroin swarming deep in his brain. Morgan craved her visits—and the pain would go away.

Pain...

He had hurt for so long, but then, for a while, nothing would hurt. The pain would be hidden far, far away. He knew it would come back. It always came back—but right now it was gone. Sweat seasoned his tears with salt, and he was again drifting on a warm, sybaritic sea, ready to ejaculate...

Then he slept.

———

A fly landed on his leg.

Swoosh....

The sound swept from behind as a small sprig chased after the insect, shooing it away. A slight wisp of cool air followed. As the puff passed, Morgan shivered then writhed, the mat's coarse fibers pricking his wounds.

He vomited, stunned by the tiny hot pokers of agony.

The blessed unconsciousness was gone.

Nadia, where are you?

His swollen eyelids cracked open. A brigade of ants paraded past his nose, carrying dried spit for their monarch. He tried to focus on a crocheted topi that bobbed and rocked. Beneath the knitted skull cap was the face of a boy, maybe seven.

Swoosh...

The tiny bough never touched his skin, but the waft brought the tang of ripe goat shit. He tried to vomit again, but nothing came up.

Dying awake! That's how he felt. A cold steel knife edge was again slicing its precise line through his skin, while operating-room lights cooked the guts spilling out of his belly.

No anesthesia.

Swoosh...

Nadia was late.

———

The bangles clinked as her henna-tattooed hand shooed the ants. Suddenly he smelled bitter vinegar, then the horniest woman on Earth was fucking him again and again, their bodies shuddering, then exploding each time they came.

Bliss...

His heart raced. Through his pinpoint pupils, Morgan watched the eunuch return the vial of powder to her purse. She sat down, crossed her legs and cradled Morgan's head in her lap. As sweet tea poured in his mouth, he heard the dissonant muezzin's call to prayer—the last of the day. The loudspeakers were far away. Chewing rice and bean stew with lamb meat, he tried to think. Through the haze he began to remember, the first time he was able to recall anything.

The driver...He was so fucking hopped up on neswar...

———

The Toyota had screeched to a halt when Nadia waved it down at the park. When they got in, the wiry driver with hot eyes squeezed the black gum of tobacco, hashish, and heroin between his teeth and pressed his foot hard on the pedal. Slobbering ceaselessly and never once touching the brake, he accelerated toward every obstacle in front. Morgan sat quietly, awaiting the tragedy to reach its final act, while Nadia said nothing as the ends of her hajib flapped in the wind's slipstream through the shot-out rear window.

Morgan saw the mountains looming beyond the forest of burkas that walked with children in tow. In linked succession, men with fixed gazes alongside the road monitored every unknown car, wary of imprudent outsiders who dared to tread into their world.

From the few words Morgan heard Nadia say on the phone, he knew a five-star resort was not his destination. When he saw a small store, he requested the driver stop, ostensibly so he could buy them some food and tea.

What he really hoped to find were antibiotics.

The column-shift jalopy skated diagonally for a dozen feet, stalling in a cloud of gravel dust and oily exhaust. The driver killed the motor and, with baleful-looking sewage leaking from both corners of his mouth, vaulted out and leapt to open Morgan's door. No sooner had Morgan gotten out but he saw the man light his next of a seemingly endless chain of cigarettes, while taking a leak on the rear tire.

Morgan placed meat, cheese, and bottled tea in front of the shopkeeper and peered over the man's head to a shelf with a row of glass jars. Morgan looked at the labels.

"Ten of those," he said, pointing to the antibiotic ciprofloxacin, hoping the logo meant it was real and not rat poison.

The man counted out the tablets and poured them into a paper cup. He presented his open hand for payment.

Morgan gave the shopkeeper the revolver and bullets. It was best to get rid of them. Wherever he was being taken, the more naked he was when he arrived, the more likely he'd live to see the next day.

There was the added consolation that if his new handlers decided to use him for target practice, at least it wouldn't be with his gun.

The shopkeeper nodded his approval, placed the piece in his lap, and reached farther beneath the green checkered table cloth. Grasping Morgan's wrist, he pressed an egg-sized chunk of black Pakistani hashish in his palm and closed Morgan's fingers. With a knowing smile, he pointed at Morgan's groin, then pumped his hand up and down briefly over the table.

"Enjoy, with or without your wives," he laughed.

When he returned to the car, Morgan gave the ball of dope to the driver, who pinched off a wad and wedged it behind what few back teeth he had, for safe keeping.

The solitary road race began again.

———

The next day Nadia bathed him. After watching her stoke an oil drum fireplace with a chip of dung, she motioned for Morgan to stand.

He sat up and studied his crusting leg scars through the dim light of the kerosene lantern then looked at his arms. He flexed his muscles. None of the long bones were broken. A deep breath without splinting pain told him his lungs and ribs were okay.

He stood, keeping his bare feet on the rug.

Unsteady at first, his balance soon returned. His limb and core strength was diminished, but his reflexes and proprioception remained intact.

His body worked, but would take effort to rebuild it.

Nadia washed him from forehead to feet with a sponge, repeatedly soaking it in warm lemon water while Morgan looked around the small room.

He saw the bucket he used for urine and stool, which Nadia dutifully emptied every time she came. He assessed the simple plywood walls, supporting a flat-beamed ceiling. The irregular-shaped opening where the stove pipe stuck out was sealed with mud. The poorly hung door was locked from the outside. The only window had an inner smoke film and bars on the outside.

He shivered.

The air was cooler, so he had to be at a higher altitude, perhaps in the foothills of mountains. He squinted through the window and thought he saw snowy peaks.

West of Chakwal?

The sun's low angle made it impossible to tell. He'd have to wait until morning.

How long have I been in this shed?

He looked at his legs wounds. The inflammation and swelling were almost gone.

Nadia's face was healing. The faded henna tattoo covering her hand told him Ramadan was over.

Two weeks?

He looked at his legs again. New pink tissue surrounded red.

These injuries are more like three or four weeks old...

The bath continued.

Morgan remembered the Toyota sliding to a stop and four armed men walking toward them on a gravel path. While opening her car door, Nadia had greeted them like old friends. When their conversation melded with sinister laughs, he presumed his body would soon be in danger and crammed a handful of the antibiotics into his mouth.

An AK-47 barrel had bored into his ear. When he got out of the car they put a sack over his head before dragging him over small stones to some trees. Bound spread eagle between the low branches—they took turns with a braided rope slapping his back while they asked questions, hunting for lies or a forgotten verse. They examined his foreskin to see if he was circumcised—searching for any excuse to slit his throat.

They had asked about *Cay-hay*—baptizing his wounds with gasoline for sleeping with a slut.

With each lash he screamed but never yielded.

Morgan looked down at Nadia gently toweling him dry. He didn't know how his limp body had gotten into the shack except that the Pashtun creed always protected a friend. Maybe she had dragged him herself...

Morgan watched her dab a finger in a pot of honey to seal each scar with the ancient bandage. When she saw his face, she smiled. He smiled back, masking his deeper thoughts.

She's the only one alive who heard me say Cay's name while I slept on the train.

His gut muscles tensed. The high from the heroin was fading again.

Nadia continued painting his wounds.

When she finished, she looked at him with a satisfied smile.

"Leave it...please," he said weakly.

Nadia pressed the vial in his clammy palm and grinned as Morgan fondled it between his fingers.

She had addicted him, perhaps a consequence of a good intention—perhaps not.

Morgan gave an appreciative stroke down Nadia's long hair all the while contemplating wringing her neck.

His stomach wrenched and he tightened his throat, hiding his misery behind a persistent smile implying gratitude for her kindness, but Morgan was thanking her for a very different reason.

The intent of the beatings was submission, not to kill him. He had passed their bona fides and would become a terrorist-in-training.

FORTY-FOUR

Fairfax, Virginia December 2, 2003

Halogen lights illuminated the polished table covered with laptops, coffee cups, and wrapped, inexpensive hard candies. Before the chairs were filled with her congregation, the pencil tapping began.

"Good morning," said Priscilla Rushworth. "Let me begin by confirming the rumor," she said through a restrained gloat, "that I have accepted the position to serve as a Deputy Director of CIA."

Polite applause bred a monarch smile on her face.

"You can't imagine the honor." The woman was insufferable. "I transition to my new role by year's end. The person who will sit here..."

As they looked at one another, the thumping in Jericho's head intensified.

"Let's just say the list is short."

Rushworth's concluding remarks grew wearisome.

"We must understand our enemies and...know their world. This rule goes back to the earliest days of espionage."

She told the story of the Trojan Horse—for ten minutes.

"So remember: Source all evidence. Acknowledge ambiguity. Don't assume. Provide other analysis. Strive for accuracy. Work closely with your colleagues."

Avoid interagency jealousy, the press, and sanctimonious elected officials, Jericho wanted to say. *And above all else...keep your pants zipped.*

Rushworth concluded with the drummed mantra of the government. "We're all in this together."

The CIA's report came first.

"Madame Chair, I know I speak for everyone here... Congratulations!"

Murmurs of approval lapped through the room. Perhaps they were just thrilled to be rid of her.

CIA continued. "We published yet another attack on the *Khyber Mail*. Nothing new there...but it's disconcerting that a country with nuclear weapons can't even protect its trains. A Gambit satellite took a look. Thought you'd enjoy seeing the handiwork of the bad guys."

A fourteen-car train was surrounded by emergency vehicles. Passengers in line for buses were sequestered from at least two dozen body bags.

"Elaine..." Rushworth whispered to get her attention as if she was preparing to share secrets about a party the night before. She slid into the CIA's empty chair and cupped the microphone. "Cottrell gave you a very strong recommendation."

She moved back to her seat before the penetrating smile disappeared.

"Any questions?" asked Rushworth. "No? Good. Fine. Let's move on, then, to Middle Eastern Nuclear..." The composed smile returned. "Commander, go ahead...please."

With no additional evidence about the cargo containers, Jericho reviewed a series of other images and their correlated intelligence from other agencies, and concluded, "We caught this panorama in western Waziristan. An interesting place, even without a nuclear reactor." She used a laser pointer. "Here's a cluster of vehicles with weapons under the tarps—undoubtedly another terrorist camp. We've published this."

"Can we recommend that a drone strike?" said an air force officer.

Rushworth interrupted. "We leave those decisions to State, CIA, and the Department of Defense." Muffled blowing from the ventilation system could be heard over the silence. "Anything else, Commander?"

"Still hunting for a black and white stick...and Ali." Jericho smiled professionally. "I'm confident they'll show up."

"Keep looking." Her response was tinged with irritation.

"That concludes my report, Madame Chair."

"Thank you." Rushworth's lips barely moved.

After the other members presented their reports, Rushworth said, "This committee will adjourn for ten minutes."

In the corridor Admiral Herndon caught the arm of his favorite officer.

"Elaine, watch yourself. Priscilla can nix your appointment."

"I'm not playing a game, Admiral. Rushworth asked a month ago and I'm reporting as instructed. We can't destroy any camp we see. We dismiss a suspected terrorist in this country, but I'm told to hunt for a cane. Fine! Tell me my job and how to do it, and I'll collect all the information nobody will use!"

"That's what I like about you, Lainey. You take no prisoners. Priscilla doesn't have much recourse anyway...and the friction's mostly fun."

He motioned with a hand and the two officers stepped farther down the hallway.

"There's a bit more about the train that wasn't shared in there."

The admiral turned so his words were not overheard.

"Nasty thing. AKs hosed down the porters, conductors, engineers. Then two of the robbers get popped in a first-class compartment by a single shot from a .357. A few minutes later, another's head gets split, soft-boiled-egg-like."

"I was going to eat some yogurt in a moment, if you don't mind," said Jericho, trying to cover her curiosity.

"There's amazing stopping power in those guns," he added.

Her face maintained a detached look.

"They used grenades too. Passengers thought the world exploded!"

"Some robbery," said Jericho.

"That's what's strange," the admiral admitted. "In just a couple of minutes, a bunch of bad guys are dead and two others are racing back along the tracks...a tall man and short, thin woman. **Guess** there were a whole pile of motorcycles waiting' for the thieves, **and** they took off on one." He pulled out a pen and started clicking it. "Strangest yet...they didn't steal anything."

"Nothing which happens in that country makes any sense," said Jericho.

Herndon dug in his coat pocket and handed her a picture.

"From a cell phone on the train. Facial recognition studies comparing it to your Mr. Ali are below threshold for a matter of confirmation."

"Why are you telling me this?"

"To make the point Priscilla just did, even though it was painful to listen to...bless her little heart." Herndon offered his familiar chuckle.

Jericho studied the picture. "I appreciate a similarity."

"That dog's not going to hunt," he laughed. "There isn't."

Her head tip challenged him. "Admiral, I don't care if the algorithm's degree of improbability was one hundred percent, the eyes are the same."

"Elaine...I'm telling this for a reason." He laughed again, sensing her tension.

"No one believes this could be Ali?" she asked.

He motioned her into a room.

"CIA says no."

Her arms folded in growing frustration.

"What about the gun?" she asked.

"The man fired the Makarov, and the woman used the revolver. Colt's made more than one in my lifetime."

"What about the bullet fragments? Who's the manufacturer?" she asked, checking the growing pitch in her voice.

"Getting good detective work over there ain't happening. Elaine, even in one of those blue moons, there isn't enough there."

"Let me see that again," she said, refusing to stand down.

"I'm bringing this to you to reiterate a point." Herndon's tone became sterner. "I thought the pig DNA thing was, well...you deserved your day with it. Hell…everybody gets bored without a little change-up."

"Are you reprimanding me, Admiral?"

"No! No! Just don't act all huffy to Rushworth, or even Fields. Heck, we all know that kid's her boy. Ignore them both, or that promotion will go speeding away like quail from buckshot." He patted her shoulder. "Your team does fantastic work. Your leadership proves I'm right in recommending you. The NGA needs your experience…and you deserve the job, but you need to stay objective. Remember—time tells all."

"You're right, Admiral." Jericho manufactured a sweet smile. "I'll put this in my scrapbook," she said in a coy voice over her shoulder on the way to the washroom.

———

The blue convertible Thunderbird sped down the parkway, the November air sweeping over her face. Her officer's cap tumbled to her feet.

"Stay there," she barked. "He laughed at me!" Her voice carried above the radio. "Twice! Then…that *pat!*"

The more she relived their conversation, the more insulting it became.

Aye, sir—she wanted to say to drive the point deeper into him.

"Crap! I should have taken the vacation!" Her foot jammed the accelerator. "Damn it, Herndon, you're wrong! You're all wrong!"

FORTY-FIVE

Morgan sensed Nadia was in the shack. She came closer, standing over him as he lay curled in a fetal position. He whimpered in pain. When she placed a pinch of heroin in each nostril, he rolled away so she couldn't see. A noisy inhale through his mouth became a quiet exhale out his nose that blew most of the powder to the mat. She placed the new small vial in his hand before he rolled back wearing a faraway smirk. Hiding the pain of withdrawal, even with slow weaning, was difficult. Stopping cold was impossible.

He had tried.

The heroin was too powerful, whispering seductively at first in his ear, letting him yawn in defiance. Within a day, tears and slime from his nose grew worse. The day after that came diarrhea, then his muscles grew stiff, like rigor mortis. He couldn't hide from her, yet Morgan fought back. He didn't want the poison back inside, but his body insisted it did. So he let her visit, only a little at a time. He had to control it.

He would, somehow.

"Hurry," Nadia said, nudging him.

Morgan looked at his Koran on a folded white cotton cloth. A fresh salwar kameez and raglan sweater lay near his boots and satchel. He was going somewhere today, a colder place.

As he dressed, he stretched to relax the muscles of his legs and arms, but the door banged open and two men with Kalashnikovs burst in. They bound his wrists and slipped a burlap sack over his head, sealing the bottom with twine. The gun barrels rudely ushered him down the path into the backseat of a waiting automobile.

Another man crammed beside him was praying on each panted breath. His resonance foreboding, the hurried words spoke of forgiveness and faith. Morgan sat in silence, the air inside his sack becoming stale, making him feel like shit. He slowed his breathing, trying to subordinate his body to his mind.

After an hour, the potholed ride ended.

He heard a heavy metal gate move. His car door opened.

"Barra!" a chilly tongue commanded. *Get out!* Through the bag a Kalashnikov muzzle bore into his scalp, persuading him to move.

The guns prodded him up a rocky road where Morgan counted two voices greeting his escorts. They were stationary and elevated. He kicked pebbles as he walked and heard them clang on a vehicle.

"Kollo Tamam," said a man above him. *All okay.*

After a brief silence, a radio emitted a pair of electronic clicks. Moments later, Morgan heard the same words again from the radio. The clicks repeated.

Ahead, unified male voices were celebrating midday prayers. A wave of nausea came over Morgan while he tried to assess their numbers. Silence descended as they approached.

Morgan sensed men on either side shifting to form a gap, which immediately resealed once he was inside the congregation. He and his backseat companion were shoved to the ground. The binds on their wrists were cut and they were commanded to remove their boots.

The prayers continued.

Morgan yawned inside the hood, praying the worsening symptoms of withdrawal would pass him by. He hadn't had a hit in hours.

At the end of the prayers, both men were ordered to stand, and Morgan's hood was yanked off. They stood inside a semicircle of rugged men and older boys dressed in desert fatigues, their weapons close by like adoring children.

A bayonet pressed in Morgan's side, while its owner yelled, "Pay attention!"

Every noise jangled his nerves more, but Morgan knew any suggestion of disinterest would mean his death. He bit his tongue hard.

A sturdy man with a stronger face stepped forward—his leather belt holstering an automatic pistol and radio. His thick handlebar mustache and beard couldn't hide the scars. He had to be the camp leader.

"One of you betrays us," he said.

With his thick black-rimmed glasses, Morgan knew the man was severely nearsighted. As his words clung in the air, his finger panned between the two of them with penetrating malice. He pushed his glasses back up his nose.

A rifle butt thudded into the stomach of the man next to Morgan. He collapsed as a wet spot expanded from his crotch down both pant legs. Six men dragged him to a thick log, shackled his wrists with rope, and yanked his arms wide so his head and neck jutted forward. He screamed, pleading for his life.

Morgan saw a talwar flash. The long metal saber mirrored the noon sun as the executioner stepped out of the background. Twirling it in broad arcs to loosen his shoulder, his deep-set eyes appeared bolted on his arctic face.

"The unrighteous has been tried and found guilty of conspiring with infidels!" the leader shouted. "His prayers counted as sins!" The crowd cheered. "There is no substitute for obedience!"

He pulled off the condemned man's hood, so his eyes faced Mecca. As a camera shuttered, the swordsman lopped off his head with a single stroke. To avoid spurting blood from the stump, he jumped back and joined in the cheers of *ALLAHU AKBAR!*

The head was still rocking in front of a crooked red trail as the mustached leader grabbed its hair, lifting it high. A fine trickle of blood streamed to the ground.

The cheers grew louder.

"He atones for his betrayal! We slay him before our people forget his lies!"

Men placed the body and head on a wood plank. Both would be delivered to the family as a warning to others. The men applauded as it disappeared, then the assembly began to break up.

A young man who was barely out of his teenage years approached him. "My name is Khalil," he said.

"I am Barif," said Morgan. "Peace be with you."

They shook hands and embraced.

"Exciting, wasn't it?" asked Khalil.

"Na'am!" answered Morgan. *Exciting* was not how he truly felt. His stomach was cramping. The full-blown craving for heroin was imminent, but he had to eke out what enthusiasm he could.

"My first one!"

Khalil's zest for such horror reassured Morgan he had been invited to the right place.

"Do not worry…There will be others!" said Khalil. "Come." He took Morgan's hand. "I will show where you stay."

They entered a wood-frame cabin with an uneven floor lined with carpets. On each were folded clothes and a Koran on white cotton. Khalil pointed to a rug.

"This is yours. It slept a great martyr," he said.

"I am not worthy."

"We all become worthy," Khalil said. "I'll get you tea. Tawfik will see you after you rest."

"As he wishes…"

When Khalil left, Morgan stepped outside to some bushes. He urinated then vomited. He found the small vial deep in his pocket and a small pinch went into his nose.

———

Khalil guided him down a jagged trail leading to a small home. A side entrance opened to an office. The hinges creaked as he opened the door.

"When Tawfik comes, I will leave," he said.

They waited. Morgan absorbed what he could with a quick scan of the room. The sword that had beheaded the man two hours earlier was in its sheath, hanging on a wall.

Handwritten notes were tacked on bulletin boards; travel guides for American and European cities and piles of maps and newspapers lay on tables and a desk. A hand-crank sharpener screwed on the leading edge was neighbor to tray of pointed pencils. A radio was in a charging cradle, its status light a steady green. On a bookshelf were several English novels, the top one with a bookmark. Whoever Tawfik was, he was well educated.

Morgan saw a computer. He stepped forward slightly, bumping Khalil enough so his thigh hit the desk. The screen came on, requesting a password. That was a problem.

Through the wall Morgan heard a female voice that quieted before the connecting door handle twisted.

The man with the mustache and beard entered. He used a finger to push his glasses higher on his nose.

"Tawfik…" Khalil bowed then said to Morgan, "I will come back for you later."

There was a blood chit stitched to his sleeve. The piece of silk offered a reward to anyone who helped the bearer get to safety. The American soldier who had worn this one probably didn't make it home alive.

"Ekhla'a Qameesak," Tawfik ordered, pushing his glasses up again. *Remove your shirt.*

He studied Morgan's back wounds, nodding his approval at the contusions, some of which still oozed.

"You are resilient," said Tawfik. "Someday your wounds will smell sweet."

"I am a servant of God," said Morgan.

"You have proven such by taking care of Nadia." Tawfik suddenly offered his hand. They shook warmly. "Nadia…She is becoming beautiful again, but misses Omar much." His eyes looked up. "May God have mercy on him."

Morgan was intrigued. The more he pondered the coincidences, he was confidant she wasn't just a plaything.

"So she has taken care of your needs, yes?"

"Yes." It was clear Tawfik knew about the heroin.

Morgan had accumulated two vials in his satchel, hoping the amount would be all he needed to wean himself off. The charade between pretending and wanting would be difficult to hide. He had to convince Tawfik he was hooked—that if the drug was taken away, he'd be willing to blow himself to bits just to end the misery, martyrdom be damned. But Morgan had no true interest in that graphic endpoint.

"Will there be more?" he asked in a childlike voice, planting the impression he would be obedient without flaw.

"Of course," Tawfik said.

A deep laugh ensued, the long tufts of hair flapping from his ears. He stuck his little finger deep inside one, vigorously working it up and down to scratch an itch.

"You are here and not dead because you spoke the truth." His stained teeth showed through the generous smile. "The other man today did not and was not so…*lucky*, as you might say."

"Kollo Tamam," crackled the two-way radio.

Tawfik clicked the transmit button twice. Moments later he responded again the same way.

"Nadia brought me this."

Tawfik removed the satchel from under the desk, reached in, and removed Morgan's Koran. He fanned the pages as though he was skimming a magazine.

"You've treated this with respect."

He dropped the book back in the satchel, which he handed to Morgan.

"You will learn many things here. "You told Jamil you wish to bring fear to Chicago—and you will."

His demeanor became more congenial.

"Before then, sometime"—he pretended to shoot a Tommy gun—"you will tell me about gangsters!"

The meeting was over.

Khalil was waiting outside for him.

"Everyone knows that as a boy in Swat he killed Taliban," he said with admiration. "Five in one morning after prayers. A single shot to the head…like dogs."

Morgan nodded.

"Now we kill infidels together!"

The pernicious narrative was thankfully short, but Khalil's admiration was understandable. No doubt Tawfik earned his reputation, and shedding blood was necessary to impress weak-hearted devotees that he was in control of their lives. The bold act of picking up a severed head was to the point, and one he had likely perfected after many performances.

As they walked Morgan saw trucks resting on bald tires with shattered windows, others were loaded with tarpaulin-covered crates. A steel-walled dump truck sported a large-caliber Russian machine gun aimed down the road over the gate.

There was no sign but the message was clear: Uninvited guests not welcome.

Amidst empty ammunition and fuel cans, and thousands of soda bottles, dust-coated vehicles on tire rims provided cover for boys playing hide-and-seek with baying goats wearing tins bells. As a billy raced past, Morgan saw its likely objective: the fenced pen, several hundred feet away, would provide refuge from the chase.

The rest of the camp was lost to the boredom of the Friday afternoon. In the quiet Morgan heard the sound of soft thunder and looked into the clear sky. Contrails from American fighter jets billowed north to south.

Khalil pointed at them and said, "Afghanistan."

———

After the prayers at sunset, the men lined up to eat. Morgan stood at the back waiting his turn. He scooped smelly cheese from an urn using hunks of coarse bread. A ladle soon poured dark broth with turnips in his bowl. White sheep eyes floated on top.

He ate everything.

With dusk a generator roared to life and a color television was lifted onto shipping crates. A DVD movie showed the Towers collapsing and the Pentagon in flames. The images energized the men. Morgan cheered with them.

Tawfik rose, adjusted his holster with a virile tug shoring up his crotch, and began to speak.

"We bring the infidels jihad...without fear. We kill Americans alone or with their families. They are not as dangerous as they think."

The droning liturgy had to have been repeated every time there were new members in the audience.

"The day of wrath is near. Distress! Anguish! Ruin! Destruction! Thick Darkness! God has created you!" His finger swept over them. "You are a sacrifice."

During a pause Morgan heard the radio's crackling liturgy. The lookouts were reporting in.

"They will walk like the blind. Their blood will pour like dust when their flesh rots, and fire will consume them!"

The men cheered again, unified by the moment, then parted for their shelters. Morgan found Tawfik and offered his hand to thank him for his hospitality. He was able to steal a glance at Tawfik's wristwatch.

Unhurried, Morgan walked slowly to a rise in an open space and stood in the darkness admiring the speckled sky. He was slightly out of breath. That had to mean the altitude was around seven thousand feet.

He found Polaris and slowly raised both arms, pretending to stretch. The angle to the star was greater, indicating he was more north than expected.

He looked for Andromeda and calculated its position based on Universal time.

He was farther west, too.

The place where he stood was close to the Durand line along the Afghanistan border.

"They think he's hiding there," Jon had told him months earlier.

Morgan was in Waziristan. It was an ideal starting place.

He yawned.

The seductive voice of the heroin began whispering again from his pocket.

God, he hated that shit!

But...he wanted it!

He became paranoid. Every tree had eyes. They were staring at his perspiration, counting each drop as the whisper amplified again to screams.

"Fuck...y..."

He retched hard, the violent gagging tearing at his insides. Before he could control it, he dropped to all fours, vomiting. The sheep's eyeball landed beneath his nose in a slush of goo. He felt diarrhea dripping.

"Oh...Cay...Help me..." he prayed.

He clawed the ground, waiting for the nausea to pass. Finally able to stand, he grabbed an oily rag from the top of a truck motor and wiped his mouth, his ass, then threw the cloth behind him.

Walking to the cabin, he inhaled a tiny amount of the white drug. Morgan knew it wasn't going to be enough.

"Going to have to kill me to stop me...you assholes," he uttered while his stomach churned.

FORTY-SIX

Alexandria February 11, 2004

Exhausted by another day in her new role as Assistant Director, Jericho was lost in a hypnagogic dream—standing on her destroyer's bridge, the purifying breeze washing her face as she scoured the ocean's horizon, joining in the game with the sailors on watch, trying to discern the first distant object on the surface at nautical dawn.

The mouse ears on her slippers wiggled. The remaining papers, resting on the blanket draped over her thighs, plunged to the floor, waking her with their irate rustle. Her tired eyes opened into the glare of the table lamp, and she took a deep breath. As her breasts rose and fell beneath the soft cotton tank top, she squinted at the digital faceplate on the stereo. It was dark. She didn't remember the timer turning off the sound and focused on her desk clock.

"Three a.m.?"

Again the evening had blended into night, only to become early morning.

"Geez..."

She reached for the lamp and switched the three-way bulb to low, tempering her eyes until she woke up more.

When Jericho began her new role at the first of the year, her life was managed to the second and her late-night research on Ali stopped. She was just too busy. The vigil was constant and her analysts at the NGA were the obstinate custodians, searching for fresh dangers on many fronts. When she had run the Middle Eastern division, Jericho enjoyed working with her staff as they speculated and formulated. That pleasure was gone as her time was swallowed into coordinating information and directing further intelligence gathering on the expanding war in Afghanistan and the assault in Iraq. Any data now came to her in monotonous summary briefs eschewing imagination. She had become what she loathed the most—a bureaucrat, and she hated it.

Swirling the cold tea in the cup's bowl, she got up to make fresh.

In a few leftover minutes the weekend before, she had again begun sleuthing the pig mystery. The single snip of DNA and sixty-five thousand pig farms dotting the nation's landscape created a vexing improbability that one incomplete piece had ended up in a terrorist's abandoned pants pocket. There was no sense to it, making clear why Fields and the others had dismissed its discovery as fallacious.

Jericho's unwavering belief held contrary. For whatever motivation, the specimen's livery had been around pigs and had carried the contaminant along for the ride. It was a classic needle in a haystack, and no different in principle than anything else the NGA hunted for. With enough effort, data revealed answers—if one had enough time—and that was Jericho's consistent obstacle. Yet when she could, she kept coming back to Ali. The deeper she delved, any residual doubt about her quest being irrational vanished. The admiral had warned her about consuming obsessions, yet the only logical solution was to pursue the information to its conclusion. Settling in as assistant director, her public persona hadn't changed, but while at home, sleep could wait.

"Where was I?"

She scooped the papers off the floor and placed them on her desk.

Her initial attempts had produced nothing useful. The major producers in the swine industry thought she was a front for ICE and refused to reveal any employee information without a court order. That wasn't going to happen so Jericho tried another approach.

A call to Purdue University gave her a quick education on the glories of pig breeding. Animal size...quantity of back fat...more money per pound...The selling of donor sperm before the profligate beasts were themselves ground or sliced, fried, or baked for breakfast tables made clear the reasons to categorize the hog strains.

The hog specialist was so flattered he invited her to Lafayette to attend a lecture he was preparing. She wanted to thank him by sharing the true importance of the information.

Of course, she couldn't do that.

He would never have believed it!

Yet after her gracious regrets, the geneticist still sent her the library of swine DNA from the last two years.

Jericho had no idea what to do with it—but Glen would.

Bringing his expertise into her fixation at this point was the consummate bad idea. Such an indiscretion would definitely end his career.

"So...Glen," she said, pretending he was sitting in her kitchen while she went for more tea. "How would *you* figure out where the DNA came from?"

Jericho knew what he'd say: "Give me even the rawest data and I will find the answer."

The rules never varied.

She found the stereo remote. With soothing classical jazz filling the room, she hurried to her computer. As the keyboard chattered, Jericho said to the screen, "Pigs with a tendency toward fatness...."

She downloaded a file about Hampshire inheritability estimates that predicted how often a suckling would express the desired traits.

"Tag the unlabeled gene loci..."

She was humming as she munged data—gluing together whatever information there was.

"Stir in a million or so Purdue hogs...Just like making brownies!"

The network program waited for the command.

"Hit *Enter!*"

The software made predictions based on evolving probabilities. The satellite computers applied the principle as they examined patterns in the Afghan roads, evaluating changes that could indicate the Taliban had dug a fresh hole to hide a bomb. Searching for a subgroup of pigs with the same small gene sequence was no different than studying dirt. The information obtained might be sufficient for Jericho to trace the pig's family tree to a sperm supplier, the farm, and the breeder—who might know Ali.

That was her hope anyway.

The icon kept spinning. Her networked computer was working on it. Covered by a blanket, Jericho lay on the sofa and fell back to sleep.

———

The soft light of the winter morning woke her. While more tea steeped, Jericho went back to her computer, instructing it to translate the newly refined data into a more recognizable form. When she returned from showering, she'd have the answer—maybe.

With water dripping beneath her robe, the cursor flashed the results.

There were a dozen swine farms in Texas that matched pieces of the DNA. On the floor were her two pictures of Ali. She winked at both.

"I'm going to find you," she sang sweetly.

The redhead shook her damp tresses. The day would be notable: For the first time in her career, Captain Elaine Jericho would be late for work.

FORTY-SEVEN

Waziristan February 18, 2004

With the beast's head toward Mecca and the bound back hooves kicking him in the groin, Morgan slammed the goat to the ground, slitting its neck with one pull of his knife. To uproarious laughter he lifted the writhing carcass by its hind legs as blood poured out. When it stopped, his blade found the highest gap in the neck bones and pushed through. Cramming the head into a leather bag, he bound the opening and heaved the sack toward the cheers. Six excited horses stomped and tugged, restrained by men struggling to hold their bridles. Morgan waved to the crowd with a big smile.

It was time for polo.

He had become their butcher, amazing them with the dexterity and speed he could slaughter and field strip anything on four hooves. The sheep and goats knew they were fair game every day and scattered when his lasso appeared. Providing the much-desired buttermilk and curd, the red-colored Sahiwal cows were always spared, so were the horses that served for sport and to ferry the lookouts to and from their posts.

In a cloud of flies, Morgan filleted and diced the goat meat, tossing pieces into a huge stewpot. When he finished, he left the entrails in a pile for the vultures and carried the pot to the outdoor kitchen, placed it on the propane-fueled stove, and added root vegetables, salt, and curry.

He scratched his crotch vigorously annoying the fleas.

Morgan looked around. All the men were in the pasture watching the game. He did two-dozen squats and push-ups, rinsed his hands in a bucket of water, and reached into his pocket.

"Goodbye, bitch," he said to the vial, throwing it into the woods. Breaking the stranglehold of heroin had taunted his will more than his run in the desert. She would never have the pleasure of his company again. Tawfik still believed otherwise, as Morgan frequently came for refills. The deception was important; the concern of being cut off had to appear very real.

———

For almost three months Morgan lived and trained as an al Qaeda and Taliban disciple. Each morning, after the tired and cold hilltop sentries were exchanged for fresh, prayers at sunrise would conclude with a cross-country run in the crisp dawn on empty stomachs and a dip in a mountain stream.

They would dress in fatigues and balaclavas and line up lunging with bayoneted rifles while a video camera recorded their chants of "Butcher the Jews" and "Death to American Satan."

Some days included assault drills and live weapons fire with an inexhaustible supply of bullets. Morgan became so familiar with the AK-47 he could fire several hundred rounds, take it apart for cleaning, and reassemble it in less that a minute.

Other days included bomb making and test detonations. Within the thirty-five-hundred-square-mile picturesque hills was an abundance of detonators with Cyrillic stamps, oxygen cylinders, TNT, acetylene canisters, grenades, and mines. Children, often one-armed amputee victims of Russian butterfly mines, would stand on the rises in the ground and cheer in excitement as the men competed for the bragging rights of hitting the remains of a truck with a rocket launched from a speeding motorcycle.

Within the nest of pit toilets, rebar-supported clay and wood cabins, explosions, and zinging bullets, the men would drop on their knees and pray next to the weapons while the hot steel barrels crackled and cooled amid the desert flowers.

From a smorgasbord of options, techniques designed to maim and kill humans were tested and refined. Imaginations ran rampant, looking for continuous improvements in mode of delivery and destructive power.

Self-detonation had never been Morgan's desire. As much as he could, he tried to avoid participating, yet he still joined them when they took the latest designs into the forest, pacing off the distance between denuded trees after detonation. He watched the men seal coats with ball-bearings and wire the charges to batteries. The misguided paradox was impossible to imagine, yet every activity in the camp bred a similar malevolent purpose. The beheading on Morgan's first day made that point crystal clear. Tawfik was unambiguous about what he expected of his recruits, and he would apply any means to ensure compliance.

Sequestered out of sight from their overt ambitions, Tawfik also trafficked heroin. Poppies thrived in western Afghanistan, harvested by people who ignored their pledges to substitute corn and wheat, which suffered in the dry cold and arid heat. Morgan would see men on horseback towing mules into camp, or diesel trucks would roll through the gates. Booted footsteps would compress the rock path to Tawfik's office. Complaining that he had to urinate again, Morgan would step outside and listen to the voices and rude laughter while Tawfik's and his trusted collaborators exchanged crates and boxes.

Week after week Morgan eavesdropped on conversations that began to divulge trace clues about a meeting. The location was never mentioned, and names were never used. Radio traffic diminished to the point of silence protecting the information from *SIGNIT*—signals intelligence gathering technology. Smaller arms and shoulder-fired rockets accumulated, all of which were tested, cleaned and placed in the cabins. Bulk food and water arrived. Stacked alongside the weapons, space inside the cabins shrank. Trucks were repaired and tires replaced.

Morgan had to get into Tawfik's office.

———

Shrouded in the shadows during dinner, Morgan first saw Nadia in the distance covered with a sheer burka that shimmered in the moon's flush. Every man saw her. Their conversations became shortened until in collective anticipation they grew quiet and hurriedly finished the evening meal.

The generator came to life to power black lights and strobes. The music accelerated to arouse their senses, and she stepped into the single spotlight. The burka slipped away to reveal an iridescent blouse and open neckline with Omar's necklace. In skin-tight jeans, her hips began an ecstatic sway to the music that was met with a unified gasp.

As the music grew louder, her hips gyrated more, until they began thrusting forward with each exotic beat. Above her head fluorescent fingernails fluttered like leaves in a wind, until they drifted down her chest. Appearing unable to catch her breath, with her head tipped upward in ecstasy, she bent slightly at the waist and stroked the inside of her thighs repeatedly, until the pumping of her buttocks grew so intense her eyelids fluttered and her mouth opened to orgasm. Drawing from their collective arousal, she poured back their lust.

Morgan fought his intense desire to succumb to her intoxication. Nadia glided over to Khalil and ran her fingers through his hair. Mesmerized, his gaze locked on her face as her fingers tickled his neck. Morgan knew Khalil had to be close to ejaculating, but before he could she drifted away, abandoning the young terrorist to resolve his frustration later. His hand rose to try to stop her, but she pulled out of reach.

The performance repeated with another man called Bashra, who tried to touch her chest, but his desire met a similar retraction as she left him and came to Morgan.

He admired her face. It had healed well, likely from the assistance of a plastic surgeon. She touched Omar's necklace, then the back of her fingers combed through Morgan's tangled hair, walked down his cheeks, and came to rest on his shoulders. They mirrored a smile. The music quieted and the lights went dark.

She moved to stand alone beneath the moon. With a carnal shudder, her open palms reached high to present her climax as an offering to the heavens, and then she sang the soulful melody he'd heard in Lahore. When it ended, she stepped into the shadows and was gone.

Whatever was about to happen, Morgan knew he was going to be part of it.

FORTY-EIGHT

Ringed by male snores and grunts, Morgan lay on his mat thinking. Why had Nadia come to the camp? He hadn't seen her since she nursed his wounds months earlier, then during her performance last night she had touched Khalil and Bashra. Perhaps at that moment she just being kind—but then applying the same seductive moves on him? From what Morgan had observed, virtue without motive wasn't consistent with Nadia's nature. Later, his concern grew as he stood outside the cabin, watching the men come in to sleep. Bashra and Khalil didn't return.

He was in danger, he concluded. Escaping the camp was imperative—but he still had to steal into Tawfik's office. There had to be information inside that would help him.

Before the first light of dawn, he rose quietly and dressed. As he reached for his satchel, a trio of footsteps paused briefly outside the door before it flew open violently waking the other men. A bright flashlight blinded Morgan.

"Ali!" The command came from behind the beam. "Tawfik wants you! Move!"

One of the camp leaders brought his AK-47 barrel to Morgan's neck, reinforcing the order then another picked up the satchel. Their gun barrels directed Morgan out the door toward the office. Once in the office, he was instructed to stand with his back against a wall. One man pressed a pistol muzzle in his temple. Several feet away, the other two pointed their rifles at Morgan's chest.

Tawfik entered through the inner door of his house.

"I have learned more about you," he said, zipping his fatigues. He dumped the contents of the satchel on his desk, picked up Morgan's Koran, and looked at several random pages. "Jamil sent a message to me, delivered by Nadia. He was told about the men you killed aboard the ship after he left, and…that you got off before it made port."

The Koran went back in the satchel. Tawfik placed the bag on a shelf.

"I cannot believe what you say you are because you did not tell me these things! I must know everything about my men. I trust them! They are principled!" His voice rose in anger. "To send you back to America for jihad—what you say you desire—is not possible!" His mustache never moved. "You have not submitted! Your pride betrays you—and me!"

If Tawfik felt deceived, he would believe Morgan had also misled others in the camp and that could put Tawfik's authority at risk. Commanding men to opt for personal annihilation required unconditional control. Tawfik could never tolerate the presence of someone he didn't fully trust.

He drew the saber from its sheath on the wall and pressed the flat side against Morgan's neck.

"You saw what this did!" He turned the sword on edge pressing the blade edge into Morgan's skin. "It cured an unrighteous man's sins!"

Tawfik stepped back and laid it on the desk. After he caught his breath, he said, "But because of what you did for Nadia,"—it was clear Tawfik had a premeditated intention—"I won't whack off your head."

He paused to let Morgan behold his magnanimity then smiled wickedly, bringing his nose close to Morgan's. "So I will give you what you do *not* want. Incineration here in Pakistan—without preparation, except to let the instant fire ready you for Hell!"

Tawfik went to his desk, opened a drawer and removed a butterfly coil of thick twine. He sat on the edge of his desk then held out the coil for the men.

"Bind him from behind," commanded Tawfik.

The guard with the pistol pushed Morgan's shoulder. He turned with his face to the wall. As the twine wrapped in a figure-of-eight weave around his wrists, Morgan kept wedging them slightly apart trying to maintain a millimeter or two of give in the knot. He squeezed his eyes shut.

"Look at me!" Tawfik barked.

Morgan turned around, his eyelids almost closed.

"Damn you! Look at *me*!" Tawfik shouted.

With a downcast gaze that barely met Tawfik's glare, Morgan released an actor's tear.

Tawfik saw it and slapped Morgan's face hard. As more tears came, he slapped him again.

"A man cries blood! Women cry water!" he said with a cold laugh. "As I thought, the poppies have made you weak."

Morgan's sniffed hard and audibly gulped the snot from his nose.

"As you will see," Tawfik said, "Khalil and Bashra *are* prepared. Today—their wounds *will* smell sweet! Blessing their families with honor...Models for others to follow!" Tawfik came close again. "But you," his finger pressed between Morgan's ribs, "You, as the infidel Americans say...are just going along for the ride."

He pushed his glasses back up then held up a large bag of heroin. "When the sun is high today, you will beg to throw the switch yourself!"

Turning away, as he opened the door to the house he laughed and said, "When I see your charred bones on the TV...I will rejoice!"

The men pushed Morgan to the meeting area where the entire camp had already gathered around Khalil and Bashra. Their heads were shaved clean and their beards were gone. They wore embroidered green headbands, white shirts and pants. The men chanted their names.

Morgan saw a jagged piece of glass on the ground and he inched forward until a butt stock slammed in his gut. Collapsing to the ground, he writhed on his back while the men standing nearby spit on him. As Morgan tried to catch his breath his fingers searched and found the glass. Before the guards forced him to his feet it disappeared between his wrists.

They took Morgan to a van with tinted windows, pushed him in and lashed his legs to the metal struts supporting the middle back seat.

Morgan strained his neck to look in the back of the van and saw a lumpy rug. He had no doubt what was hidden beneath. Slowly the piece of glass began to work its way from between his wrists to his fingers.

Khalil sat to the left of Morgan, Bashra to his right. Both wore unbuttoned oversized shirts covering vests. They mocked him.

"What's it like to die for nothing, Barif?" asked Khalil.

The front door opened. The pit-faced driver brandished his Makarov, touched it to Morgan's forehead then with a smile added a quick look down its sights toward the other men. He winked and holstered it. If necessary, everyone's participation would be involuntary.

Nadia climbed in the front seat, turned, and gave each of them a callous smile. Holding her eyes on Morgan, she showed him a vial of heroin.

She saw him yawn, then gave an unsympathetic head cock as he advertised a pleading look. She raised her bag so he could watch her drop it inside. By delivering him to his destiny, her Pashtun duty had been fulfilled. She turned and faced front. She would not look his way again.

The motor coughed, and the van began to roll through the gate and down the road. The driver turned on the fan and rolled up his window. They were soon soaked in sweat, but Morgan could see that the driver wasn't just clammy from the warm blowing air. His face expressed worry-laced intent as the van shifted one way then back while passing another rock pile.

His intense concern meant only one thing: Mines.

The stuffiness condensed the humidity, making Morgan's skin slick. As the glass edge gnawed the fibers of the twine, he soon felt some release. His surreptitious work continued until they could slip freely out of the knot, then he stopped.

The van staggered along the road. Behind his seat, amid the serenade of rattles and creaks, Morgan heard metal cylinders banging against each other. As they bounded along, Khalil and Bashra engaged in an occasional animated conversation trying to express their excitement, but mostly they sat in silence, staring out the windows.

After passing several hamlets, the driver stopped and Nadia got out. As she walked away, she showed the back of her hand once to bid them good-bye, turned onto a side path, and was gone.

The widening roads grew thicker with traffic and the signs grew specific. The van followed an arrow. They were going to Peshawar.

"Where?" asked Khalil.

"Qissa Khawani," said the driver. "On Fridays the market is filled with immodest women and men holding hands."

Morgan noticed both men were perspiring more heavily as reality approached.

"I need to piddle," said Khalil.

Morgan knew even the most resolute martyr lost bladder control at the end—a telltale giveaway to anyone who noticed.

The van exited the roadway, stopping deep in an overgrown lane. The Makarov came in view before Khalil and Bashra were allowed to steal into the bushes.

"Ana kaman?" asked Morgan. *Me too?*

The driver shook his head, until Morgan released a fart. The driver knew smelly flatulence inside closed windows might cause nausea, weakening the young martyrs resolve.

With the pistol pointed at Morgan's head, the driver untied his legs and motioned him toward some trees. With his loosely bound hands behind his back, Morgan wiggled his waist while pulling his pants and underwear just below his hips, freeing his right hand from the knot at the same time. Morgan farted again, smiled at the driver and squatted.

The man turned his back.

Pulling up his pants, Morgan jumped noiselessly and buried the jagged glass deep in the man's neck until blood gurgled in the windpipe. The body gaged, coughed, and fell to the ground.

Wiping his hands on the driver's shirt, Morgan picked up the Makarov and dropped the magazine to count the bullets. He racked it back in place and confirmed a round was chambered.

In the distance, Morgan heard Khalil and Bashra talking so he patted down the driver's pockets removing a small transmitter and a bulging wallet. Morgan opened it and quickly looked at the number of large bills.

"Blood money," he chided the dead man. "Won't get you to Disney World anymore"

Sliding both items in his pockets, Morgan clicked the pistol's safety off, put his hands behind his back and walked to the van.

Khalil and Bashra smiled at Morgan until they noticed he approached them alone.

"Take those vests off and drop them," he said.

"No," said Bashra.

"Sorry," Morgan replied. The Makarov came forward. The bullet ripped through Bashra's pelvis knocking him to the ground. He screamed in pain.

When Morgan saw Khalil reaching for his detonator, he put a round through the man's wrist. Khalil buckled over.

"Bad luck," Morgan said. "Should have done as asked."

Morgan walked to Khalil, lifted up his shirt, and yanked a wire off the battery then he walked over to Bashra. He'd be dead shortly. Morgan bent down and disconnected the same wire and motioned to Khalil. "Now, take your vest off and go get the gorilla."

Trembling, Khalil loaded the driver in the front seat.

Morgan looked at Bashra. He'd let him exsanguinate for a few more minutes before moving him.

"Khalil," Morgan said, "Open the back and pull off the rug."

Pairs of propane cylinders were wrapped with duct tape and nestled in cardboard boxes filled with nails. Wired to a radio receiver and car battery, plastic explosives lined the inside walls.

"Nice." Morgan grimaced when he saw it.

The planned horror would be sequenced. The vests would detonate at specific points on the street. As terrified shoppers fled, many would run in the direction of the parked van. An instant after the C-4 blew out the sidewalls, waves of nails and propane fireballs would kill anyone within fifty yards. In a crowded market, scores would die.

"Take that shit out," Morgan ordered.

Khalil pretended to reach in but spun around and lunged. Morgan kicked his neck, rupturing his airway. When the gasping ceased, his body would join Bashra in the back seat.

Morgan tossed everything in the thicket except for a screwdriver and a small amount of C-4. He wired it to the receiver and battery and placed the charge under the passenger's seat.

After starting the engine, he looked at the gas gauge.

"Too much." Morgan got out to siphon several gallons to the ground.

With the bodies loaded, he draped the hand-knotted rug over the driver then looked at the two bodies in the back seat.

"Fear not, my friends." He started the motor. "I'll make your wishes come true today."

———

Some women carried bags on their covered heads, while others walked with braided hair and bright lipstick. Everywhere men sat in cafés drinking tea and arguing after the noon prayers. A crowd of giggling schoolgirls skipped past, their heads decorated in white hajibs. A watchful teacher strode behind, mindful of her children as they wove through the shoppers. Morgan smiled and waved at them, then resumed his evaluation of the pedestrian flow while automobiles wove the bustle together.

Morgan's stomach churned. The market had been well chosen for terror, so he drove slowly through the surrounding streets, searching for a less busy parking space. He put up his window so no one could see in. The drying blood grew more pungent.

On an overpass above a wadi, he found a spot on a one-way street. Hopefully, the debris would blow toward the dry creek bed, minimizing the danger at street level. Morgan prayed he could time the explosion to prevent innocent deaths. The news reports only had to mention that three bodies were discovered in the wreckage—the number needed to convince Tawfik and the other planners that Barif Ali was dead and the driver had escaped as planned.

As people passed without curiosity, Morgan studied the parked cars across the street, and then shut off the motor. Reaching down to the floor of the backseat, he turned on the receiver and took another look in the side mirror. He opened the door and walked diagonally against traffic down the street to the opposite curb to a small sedan and got in. He put the screwdriver in the ignition and turned it.

The motor started.

Ripping a pocket out of his shirt, he gloved his hand with it, turned the wheel sharply toward the street and engaged the parking brake. He shifted the car into gear, rolled down the window and got out.

He waited for an opening in the traffic, quickly glanced around, reached his hand in the car then released the brake.

The car forced itself into middle of the street, blocking everything that moved. People stopped walking to study the driverless vehicle.

Morgan looked at the scene over his shoulder while he walked away.

No one was too close to the van.

He toggled the switch and ran away from the frenzied swarm.

FORTY-NINE

Morgan bought some new clothes and shoes from a street vendor. He changed in a café washroom then drank tea and watched the TV news reports.

"In synchrony throughout Pakistan today, several car bombs blew up...yet another attempt to terrorize our citizens. This explosion outside the Qissa Khawani market"—the TV showed the mangled van lying lopsided on the street—"left shoppers in shock, but miraculously there were only a few minor injuries. The three vehicle occupants are the only confirmed dead. Although the perpetrators of these horrible acts remain unknown, sources confirm that a passport found in the debris of this attack suggests one of the terrorists was a Lebanese national, possibly with ties to Hezbollah. His name is being withheld by the ISI while their investigation..."

Morgan smiled. It had been a pain-in-the-ass day until he heard that.

Either Nadia or Tawfik had placed his passport in the van. That might have helped their cause, but it sure as hell benefited his. He was dead, and truly—a phantom.

Morgan stole a motorcycle. By dusk he stood at the mouth of the road that led to the camp. Watching bats whizz around, gobbling insects, he took a swig of his pabulum from the water bottle. In the fading sunlight, he looked across the meadow at the craggy cliffs, then at the ridgeline to his side.

Sneaking back into the camp was not a task he relished, but with the events of the last twenty-four hours his confidence grew that Tawfik had information that would be helpful. Nadia's arrival last evening and his subsequent rude sendoff that morning had thwarted his original plan but he was trained to adapt. Still, Morgan hated to come back to the zealot purgatory, but would have anyway.

He wanted his satchel.

The road, with its hidden mines and machine gun at the top end, would be an impossible approach. Rubbing his beard with a dirty hand, Morgan assessed the cliff area where Tawfik had his home. Crossing the carpeted meadow to climb the rocks would take until after sunrise. The lookout on the ridge would see him. Before that he had to get through the bushes lining the road. They were unquestionably decorated with stick mines; Morgan had seen them crated in the camp. Strung together by wire, any step could set off a chain reaction that would shred flesh for yards.

Morgan blew deeply into his cupped hands for warmth and looked to his right side at the steep, rock-studded hills rising where only mountain sheep grazed. No human visitor would come from there. The spine of the ridge was well above the lookout. He pulled the driver's Makarov from his pocket. The six remaining bullets would provide little protection. Stealth would be his bodyguard.

He walked back down the road several hundred yards, dropped into a slight ravine, and began climbing.

The clear starlight guided his feet while the rocks hid him. Protected by the isolation, he relaxed in the constant breeze. For a time his mind drifted, and he imagined Caroline was with him, walking by his side under the stars.

Ahead in the distance at the ridgeline, a horse whinnied.

Morgan dropped to the ground and listened. Slowly he lifted his head.

With his rifle shouldered, the lookout shuffled to the top. Never even glancing Morgan's direction, he soon returned to his chair and blanket, assuming that whatever had startled the horse was probably just a sheep.

When Morgan heard the lookout checking in, he knew he had two hours. After using Jupiter's position to mark the time, he rolled several feet over the ridge and slowly stood up.

The man was already snoring.

Morgan estimated the number of paces to get around the lookout and began his skulk below the ridge.

He crawled over the top to look at the camp gate. The second lookout was slouching on the truck's tailgate under the machine gun.

"Stay right there and you'll be fine," Morgan pretended to warn him. Masked by his black clothing, Morgan vanished amidst the trees trunks.

There was one more group of sentries, and they would be the noisiest: he would stay far away from the goat pen.

Morgan got to the office door and licked his fingertips to lubricate the door hinges; the morning before, they had squeaked.

Using a little flashlight, he recovered his satchel and Koran, then looked at a calendar with a newly drawn circle on a Friday twenty-eight days hence. The wall map had pencil marks where two roads converged in a tribal area of Swat. There was a pinhole mark several miles away.

If correct, the site was well chosen. In that district there was no such thing as a casual tourist. The locals could quickly identify any outsider. Morgan's death writ was simple housecleaning: the elimination of anyone not related by blood before the men in the camp made the journey.

He heard footsteps.

Morgan's flashlight went dark while he stepped out of Tawfik's first line of sight. The latch jiggled, and he entered, closing the door behind. He went immediately to his computer, where his hand found the mouse. When the screen lit up, his eyes saw a reflection, but it was too late.

Morgan's blow to the stomach knocked the wind out of him and he bent over. Loosing his glasses, he tried to find air. Morgan's fist slammed into Tawfik's nose. Before he dropped to the floor, Morgan grabbed him to quiet his descent.

He raised Tawfik's bleeding face and bridled the satchel's handle into his mouth to prevent him from crying out.

Tawfik's eyes narrowed.

"You're dead," came a wet grunt.

"I'm haunting you," Morgan whispered, tightly gripping the man's balls. Pressing his face close, he whispered, "I saw the map. The meeting..."

"Go to hell," Tawfik uttered.

"Let's try again." Morgan squeezed his testicles harder then smashed his forehead into Tawfik's bleeding nose. "Will bin Laden be there?"

"Fuck you, American," Tawfik spluttered.

"We're not communicating," Morgan said in his ear, exchanging the rope handle for a rag.

Tawfik tried to punch him but missed. Morgan reached into the box of sharpened pencils and jammed one through Tawfik's cheek. The point came out on the other side.

"You need fresh air," Morgan whispered again, yanking the pencil. "Up! Now!"

Morgan raised the man's arm high behind his back and forced him out the door. When Tawfik resisted, Morgan broke his arm.

He pushed Tawfik to the cliff and pulled the rag out. As Morgan held him off balance by his belt, he leaned Tawfik over the edge and said, "Will *he* be there?"

A goat bayed. Men would soon be up and moving.

"No escape, whoever the fuck you are," Tawfik growled around the pencil. "They'll cut you up slowly."

Morgan pulled him back, watching his face flush with relief.

"Afraid of heights?" Morgan asked. "Cay wasn't."

Morgan punched his gut again. When Tawfik's jaw dropped, Morgan crammed in a clump of fibers.

"Pig," he said, "a souvenir from America."

The man couldn't spit them out.

"Only the...righteous...who submit..." Tawfik tried to say.

"You *really* believe God wants to annihilate innocent men and women?" asked Morgan.

Flashlight beams slashed the darkness. Men were moving everywhere, calling Tawfik's name. Morgan had less than a minute to get away.

"Fuck you…"

Morgan turned him again into the void.

"Weak delivery," Morgan said calmly, "but tell me, and I'll spare you."

The flashlights were coming through the forest.

"He'll be there," his voice rasped, still trying to spit out the hairs glued in his mouth.

"Thank you," said Morgan. "And—for future reference, I've deceived you again. Here's how."

He released Tawfik over the edge, his scream ending with the thud.

Crouching, Morgan raced along the cliff until he dove into some bushes. He removed his shoes and put them in his satchel, hooking it over his shoulder. Footsteps approached as he sank below the rim, his toes and fingers searching for cracks.

A deep voice yelled for silence then shouted, "Tawfik?"

There was no answer.

He called to the lookout on his radio.

"Fire flares!"

Dark trails streaked up from the ridge and popped. Hissing magnesium lit the world.

"There!" someone yelled.

Before the flares burned out, several more ignited. Ivory-white lightning sprayed from the floating meteors.

"Tawfik?" they shouted together.

"A rope!" a voice yelled.

Morgan kept descending, invisible in the sputtering light. Nearly vertical, his fingers throbbed until his toes found a ledge. He paused to catch his breath.

A rope dropped near him, then pebbles splattered as it began to sway. Someone was rappelling down. Morgan could tell his boots were desperate for contact. More stones tumbled as the rope whipped against the cliff.

The night sky remained alive with flares.

Morgan saw legs, and he closed his eyes. When heavy breathing came near, Morgan reopened them. The whites glowed.

"Shabah alkhair!"—*Good Morning!*—Morgan said cheerfully, punching him in the face.

The man's grip slipped. Before he could cry out, his face shrank and the sound of a cracking coconut ascended. Taking hold of the rope, Morgan repelled to the meadow.

FIFTY

Santa Fe, New Mexico February 17, 2004

Cottrell Herndon congratulated Jericho when she told him about the week off.

"Good to go west for rest," he said, trying to lead the next question without actually asking.

"And...No, Cotty," she said, answering his inferred curiosity. "I'm going alone."

———

For three days she let her stress dissolve as her skin was kneaded in oils and cleansed in salt rubs while the entrancing fragrance of sage calmed her mind. Each evening she ate in another distinct bistro then strolled to an obscure bar. Enjoying a glass or two of wine she let well-groomed men make conversation, and became one of the pampered women from her novels. Jericho enjoyed each fantasy, but as she lay alone in bed the last night, the weight of conscience returned. She knew the trip was a deception to everyone, especially herself, but hoped maybe someday it would be real.

Jericho drove east into the bleak Texas Panhandle. Her methodical sifting through the handful of hog breeders and litters with the correct DNA sequence finally led her to the seller of the sperm. Despite the gloom of the overcast plains, she was glad to be away from Washington and the tedious briefings and the meetings.

First she had to endure the smell of the pens while ignoring the yelps of jubilant pigs as the Demetri Kubiak pumped putrid sludge into their troughs. The proud farmer had insisted on a tour.

"They like," he gleamed. "Leftover prison food. They like after Thanksgiving best. Stuffing, potatoes, pumpkin pie." He saw the remaining color leave her face. "You no like this."

No, she didn't.

"We go to house. Wife making coffee," he said. "Feel warm and better."

Kubiak directed her to a dilapidated armchair, where she sat recovering, safe for a time from more banter. The coffee arrived.

"Mr. Kubiak, as I explained on the phone, I've learned about your hog farm because of a sire named Aingeni Black."

"Aingeni," he replied like a proud parent. "My best pig ever. Much money for sperm. Here to buy some?"

The vision returned of a pig humping an artificial vagina, and she paused before answering.

"As I mentioned," her lie began, "I work for a private agency, and a man has listed being at your farm in his résumé. I know you've probably had a number of workers in your employment over the years…"

"Not illegal," Kubiak interjected.

"Oh, no! I'm sure of that, sir," replied Jericho, reaching for her briefcase. "I just thought if you saw his picture, you might remember him. I know how busy you are, and I don't want to take up much of your time."

Jericho handed him the composite sketch.

Kubiak's wife sat down with them. The couple's eyes met in a surreptitious exchange. They were quiet for a time, then the husband handed the picture back to Jericho.

"Jimmy Laymonjaylo," he said.

"Yes, it is," said Jericho, rubbing her dry tongue over what remained of her lipstick. "He worked around Aingeni?"

"Maybe two times only," he said. "Work more with sheep and goats."

"Was he a hard worker?" Jericho had to sound convincing for only a little longer.

"Yes."

"How long did he work for you?" she asked, grateful the conversation was almost over.

"Only…" Trying to remember, he squinted at the ancient chandelier. "Two weeks?"

"Really!" Jericho said. "What a great impression he made on you for such a short time."

"Yes," said Kubiak.

"I must be off," Jericho said, gathering her briefcase. "Your words are helpful."

"Why is working on my farm with Aingeni so important?" the farmer wanted to know.

"As you said yourself, Mr. Kubiak," Jericho began, amazed by her ability to improvise while this nervous, "Aingeni improved the quality of Hampshire hog back-fat for the breed…in general," she added.

Kubiak smiled proudly.

"That Mr. Laymonjaylo was familiar with Aingeni underscores what we already know." Her deodorant wasn't working anymore. "That's why I showed you his picture before I confirmed his name. We needed to be sure that he was who he said he was."

Jericho stood up, hoping her overcoat was close. "So again, thank you. I must be off."

"If you have more questions, Mees Jericho—"

"I'll be sure to call," she answered, while shaking his hand.

———

Jericho stopped for gas in Tucumcari, New Mexico. The February wind was dry and tinged with red dust as she filled the tank.

Once she had learned the name *Laymonjaylo*, she had to get away from the Scurry Farms. Despite their salt-of-the-earth personas— friendly and never suspicious—Jericho's conscience was pushing her heart so high in her throat she felt they knew she was lying. She wasn't sure if anything they said had been worth her invested risk. None of it made sense. Why would Ali only have pig hair in his pocket, and not from other livestock? At least she now had a name she could cross-reference.

Jericho got back in her car. It had taken an hour of driving before her trembling subsided, but with Scurry Farms now in the past, she finally relaxed again. She had a few vacation days remaining and thought about visiting a former colleague who was doing postdoctoral studies at Los Alamos. She glanced at her watch. Too late in the day to make the drive, she decided to get a hotel room in Santa Fe. When she reached for her phone, there was a missed call from an unrecognized number.

It wasn't the NGA. Jericho's senior aide would have left a message. Cottrell Herndon would have too, and he would never bug her short of an emergency—not after his years of ribbing about vacations. Unless the call was a misdial, the person would have to try again.

The Ford sedan merged back onto the interstate. She turned on the satellite radio and listened to jazz to pass the monotonous time during the drive back to Santa Fe.

Her cell phone rang.

The call came from the same number.

Jericho answered it.

"Hello…" she said.

"Elaine Jericho?" asked a male voice.

"Who's calling?" she asked.

"Agent Paul Cotsworth of the FBI, Chicago office."

"I'm driving," she said over the music. "Hold on…"

The phone dropped to her lap. She put on the turn signal, decelerated to the shoulder, and returned the phone to her ear.

"What is your name and title again?" she asked.

"Paul Cotsworth, Special Agent, FBI, Chicago office," he repeated.

"Why are you calling?" Jericho asked.

"Seems we have a mutual acquaintance," said Cotsworth.

"Pardon me?" she replied. "Is this official?"

"I realize this is not a secure line, but I'd like to talk to you. I believe you might have information about a case I'm working on."

"I'm not able to speak freely with you," she countered.

"Sure you are," he replied. "Let me be clear: you can...and will."

"What makes you think that?" she asked. These types of spontaneous calls were very dangerous.

"Seems you and I both have mutual friends—Mr. Kubiak and *James Laymonjaylo*," said Cotsworth.

Jericho caught her breath. *Did Kubiak just call the FBI?* She wanted to kick herself. She should have used a pay phone and not her cell to call him. *But why the Chicago office?*

Then she remembered Thorill Carstens's words: He's a Midwesterner.

"Ms. Jericho?" Cotsworth asked. "You there?"

"Yes...I'm listening," she said.

"Do you think we could get together for an off-the-record conversation? Casual, you know, maybe in a neutral place?"

"I'm on vacation right now," she answered.

"Near Texas," he said with a slight chuckle. "How about lunch Friday in Chicago? Would that give you enough time to get here? I admit, February weather might be less appealing than where you are, but my accent will be easier to decipher."

"I'm not liking this," Jericho said.

"Captain Jericho..." said Cotsworth.

When she heard him use her title, she had no option.

"Yes, Agent Cotsworth?"

"I give you my word," he said again. "Our lunch will be private. Shall we say Friday, twelve thirty, at the Berghoff? It's on Adams."

"A restaurant? Isn't that too unsecure?"

"Naw," he replied. "The place will be noisy as hell at lunch time."

"Guess that works then," answered Jericho. "How will I recognize you?"

"Don't worry," Cotsworth replied, "I'll see your hair."

The FBI agent tipped back in his chair and read the officer's biography. A lot of the specifics were redacted, but there was enough of her career there to impress him.

It was damn fortunate that Demetri Kubiak thought to call him. Why the NGA was interested in a missing pediatric surgeon was most intriguing—particularly because an assistant director of a major government agency had visited the same pig farmer with a different drawing of Morgan.

Until that afternoon Morgan's file contained too many nothings for Cotsworth to further investigate his disappearance. Given enough time however, the FBI agent knew every narrative filled. What he hadn't imagined was the answers might come with the help from a Wisconsin-born naval officer who worked with spy satellites.

FIFTY-ONE

Swat District, Pakistan February 19, 2004

The bus stopped near a crumbling roadside bridge. While Morgan waited for the noisy diesel hulk to disappear in its dust cloud, he glanced around to make sure he was alone. With the early-morning sun stretching his shadow, he climbed down the weedy embankment and stepped into the stream fed by the snowfields thousands of feet above him to the east. His boots startled a trout.

"Damn...water's cold."

Morgan walked several yards until he was hidden under a canopy of tree branches. He removed a belted holster from his satchel and buckled it so the Makarov hung within easy reach under his coat. His finger checked the silencer. Bought several days before from a purveyor in a side-street shop in Kohat, Morgan went out of the city that afternoon and fired a number of practice rounds at a can. Quiet as promised, he cleaned and oiled the pistol, reloaded the magazine, and slipped the piece in his bag.

He looked around again. Nursed by the cool water, wild crocuses prepared to bloom under budding skeletons of peach trees while falcons suspended themselves in the updrafts. The serene surroundings tempted him to relax, but he knew better. Death remained imminent. He'd already been upright and motionless for too long, offering an invitation for a sniper to practice.

Morgan's walk upstream began. The soaking trek had purpose. He'd leave no footprints, and moving water was less likely to have mines.

Turning around, he scanned the receding valley floor for movement.

A pair of wild sheep grazed along the bank, munching tender spring grasses, ignoring him. He moved his satchel to the other shoulder and continued his ascent.

The pine forest thickened, and the creek's mouth ended in a rippling pool fed by a waterfall. Beyond was a high mountain pasture filled with sheep tended by an older man and two boys. Tethered by a leash to the smaller boy's wrist were two hoggets straining to run off.

Morgan waved and shouted, "Allahu Akbar!"

The man beckoned for him to come close. They shook hands.

"I am Abdullah." He introduced his sons. "Essam and Mohammed." The father's words were thick, making him difficult to understand. "Where do you come from?" he asked, offering Morgan fresh sheep's milk.

"Kohat," Morgan replied.

"A place very hospitable to strangers!" the father said. "I remember from when I was younger."

"Be assured, my friend, Kohat has not changed." Morgan smiled, gently squeezed the shoulders of the boys and handed each of them each a small chocolate bar.

"I commend you, Abdullah!" Morgan said. "Your sons are sturdy. Your blood is strong!" He offered his hand again. "I must continue. I have many miles to go before dark, Inshallah!"

"Where are you going?" asked the shepherd.

Morgan tapped his chest, pointing in the distance.

The father's eyebrows lowered while he shook his head in disapproval.

"Dangerous. Taliban patrol," he said. "You should camp here tonight. We would be honored." His concern was clear.

"You are most kind," Morgan replied but pointed again and started walking. "But, I must go. May God bless you and your sons."

"May He make your path safe," the father called. "Inshallah!" Morgan turned, put his hand over his heart then waved.

The sons stood close to their father, his arms resting across both boys' shoulders. They answered the wave and continued to tend their flock.

The trail continued for miles until it squeezed to a narrow ridge leading to an overhang and rock pillar. Morgan knelt, rolled on his back, and shimmied until he could see around the vertical outcropping.

The trail zigzagged higher. With his binoculars he studied the marred cliffs dotted with caves and stone porches, inventorying several and their heights above the ground. He briefly admired the colors splashing the soaring peaks, then before slithering to look over the edge, he placed shades on the lenses so the binoculars wouldn't reflect the sun.

On a promontory half a mile away was a three-story building. Morgan saw no movement and the doors were shut. The chimney was cold.

He lowered the binoculars, laid his head flat, and waited motionless for several minutes. Then he began a more detailed appraisal.

The highest terrace of the building commanded a view of the entire valley. A camouflage tarp covered a large irregular contour. He adjusted the focus to study more carefully the angular outlines under the other tarps.

"I bet that's a fifty caliber gun and extra ammo."

On the second level, a door led to a deck with a table and several chairs facing the steep, protective bluffs. The ground-floor patio had cracked tiles and a gravel path that led to a small nearby building.

A resolute smile came across Morgan's dirty face.

It had to be an outhouse.

A metal gate barricaded the entrance while the decaying masonry wall surrounding the compound held coils of barbed wire strung along the top through twisted rebar except for a small space in back.

There were three directional spotlights. One was mounted on the high deck and two more on the wall.

He continued his survey west across the amorphous rocks, grass and sagebrush now covered in the twilight's haze that blended with twirling sand. A long serpentine road ascended from the flatlands to the compound's front gate—the sole entrance.

While drinking some of his sticky porridge, Morgan estimated the distances from his location to various places around the building and grounds. When he was finished, he crawled into a deep rill and fell asleep.

———

Two frustrated voices woke him. The men were loud and had walked the entire night without finding the stranger who had stepped off the bus at the trailhead wearing hiking boots and carrying a shoulder bag. When the hiker wasn't waiting to board the bus on its return trip, the driver called it in.

The men discussed what the sheep herder had told them: that the hiker had left the meadow on the path that led to the cliffs even after warning him not to go that way. One of the men said the father should have killed him, and come into town to report it.

"The fool!" said the other.

Morgan removed the Makarov from its holster and held it ready.

They stopped outside the crevasse where he lay. Laughing, one of them urinated into the dank hole near Morgan's face while the other man used a radio to report their lack of success so far in their search.

Breathless, Morgan waited to move until he could no longer hear their tromping footsteps. He wiggled out of the crack into the sunlight and peeked at the cliffs. Struggling up the path, their guns swung behind their backs, he saw the men talking with animated hand gestures, expressing gladness their uphill search would end soon. Morgan knew they'd have to return the way they came.

Keeping off the trail and in the woods wherever possible, Morgan started back. From time to time, he hid behind trees listening through the insects and birds for sounds that didn't belong. When he was confident he remained alone, he resumed his quick pace.

A young ram howled from some bushes. The pasture was close. Suspecting the animal lost, Morgan hoisted him over his shoulders and continued on his way. He soon heard loud bays and saw the flock scattered. A kettle of vultures soared above the green space.

A sheep must have died.

He released the ram and continued on the trail, looking for the father and his sons. Ahead, buzzards floated down through the trees toward whatever was dead below. As Morgan approached, one bird seemed to be perched in the air, gobbling a piece of skin. Unruffled, it stared at him.

Morgan glared back.

The huge bird's talons gripped deeper in the father's scalp while its beak tore away another piece of flesh. His sons hung from the same limb, the unwrapped chocolate bars in their mouths. The hovering stench grew repulsive.

"Barbarians..." he said shaking his head in disgust.

There was no time to bury them. The men were on the trail behind him. They would see that the bodies were gone and call for more assistance. A search would concentrate in the lowlands where they would leave guards, possibly trapping him.

Morgan continued down the trail. It began to taper into a narrow chute with bedrock steps. He suddenly stopped, instantly tense. The small pile of stones hadn't been there yesterday.

He stooped to see drops of dew clinging to a trip wire. His eyes followed one end to a sapling at the overhang where it was tied to a branch. He traced the other end into the grasses.

Morgan backed up, pulling several yards of thread off his belt. He tied it to a tree on the opposite side of the path then weaved the line to the sapling. After another surgeon's knot, the trap was reset and he resumed his descent.

Flushed by movement ahead on the trail, a startled bird squawked and took flight.

Someone was ahead of him.

Morgan dropped from the trail into a ravine and followed it to an overlook. A Russian Uaz truck was parked at the trailhead where he'd started yesterday. He jumped to a lower clearing, rolled into the forest to another ledge, and climbed down to the valley floor, where he raced through the underbrush. At a sharp bend near the truck, he sat off to one side with the Makarov in hand.

Two men shuffled along the path, breaking the boredom by kicking stones. A voice blurted over their radio. "We could not find him. Heading back to the truck."

One man responded, "We are almost there."

Morgan took off the safety when he heard their boots crunching stones.

"Hola, amigos!" he said.

Their AKs slung uselessly, the confused men looked at him, then at each other.

"I need your wheels…"

Puff.

Puff.

Morgan added an additional bullet into each of their heads before dragging the bodies deep into the brush.

He sat in the truck with their guns, thirty-round magazines, and two grenades lying on the shredded seat next to him. Morgan drank from some bottled water he found in the back, took his boots off and stuck his feet out the driver's window to air his socks.

He opened the glove box. There was an open pack of cigarettes.

"Tsk…tsk," Morgan said. "How disobedient…"

He lit one, hoping the tobacco would blunt the memory of rotting flesh.

It didn't.

He continued to wait.

When sounds of thunder tumbled down the hillside, Morgan flicked the second butt to the ground and pursed his lips, slowly exhaling a long cloud of smoke.

"Enjoy Hell," he said.

FIFTY-TWO

Chicago February 20, 2004

Arriving downtown after a cab ride from Midway airport, Jericho left her bags with the Palmer House Hotel concierge and sat in the lobby sipping tea, trying to read the newspaper. Restless, she put on her raincoat and walked along State Street in the drizzle, looking in store windows until it was time to go the restaurant.

She stood inside the corridor away from the revolving door, studying each man who came through. Eventually he'd appear.

"Elaine?"

Jericho turned when she heard her name.

"Hello," she said.

"Paul Cotsworth," the white-haired man said, secretly showing her his badge then offering his hand.

"Where did you come from?" Jericho asked, shaking it.

"Through the bar entrance." He smiled immediately. "Wanted to give the place the once over before we met."

"And..."

"Everyone's seen your hair."

"A lifelong problem," she replied.

Cotsworth seemed trustworthy, but despite his disarming humor, Jericho's edginess remained.

They walked to the host station.

"You're holding a table for *Smith*," said Cotsworth. "The one in the far corner."

"Yes, sir," the man said. "Follow me please."

They hung their coats on the wall hooks and sat down.

"Calling you *Elaine* okay?" Cotsworth asked. "My last rank was master sergeant."

She laughed cautiously. "Of course. I'm still on vacation…I hope."

"Reality will return soon enough," he said. "I'm convinced sometimes it's best not to leave town."

"Been my modus operandi for years, and look what happened. It got me diverted from New Mexico to Chicago in February."

"Sorry about the crummy weather," he apologized.

As Jericho unfolded her napkin, he glanced at her manicured nails. His first impression was consistent with her résumé: She was a perfectionist. The naval officer had excelled in what had been until recently a male-dominated world, and her rank and position spoke clearly of a tenacious spirit. She was certainly an elastic thinker. That trait gave her a dynamic advantage in the spy world. Why she had parlayed that into research on Morgan baffled him. Cotsworth decided to let small talk rule until they finished eating.

While their waiter cleared the plates, Cotsworth said, "I guess we need to get started."

Jericho placed the tea bag in the stainless server. While it steeped, he watched as she measured a teaspoon of milk into her cup.

"Do I have a choice?" she asked with a sideways tip of her head.

"Probably not…but I hope that's neither here nor there." Cotsworth sipped some coffee. "I said our words would be private. I'm not secretly recording us or planning to take notes."

"Thank you," she said.

"Tell me," Cotsworth learned forward and said quietly, "what you do at the NGA."

Her pupils grew huge at his bluntness.

"That's some opener," Jericho replied. "What I do is classified."

Cotsworth leaned forward more. "Let's do this right, okay? I'll help." His voice lowered. "You're a United States Navy Captain, who, before becoming an assistant director of the National Geospatial Agency, was in charge of its Middle Eastern nuclear division."

He smiled, but not gently. "Maybe with your spiritual awakening in New Mexico you've forgotten the NGA does global satellite intelligence procurement?"

"I just can't say anything."

His beating fingers quickened in ire.

"Let's start over." He had more coffee. "Pretend this is a first date, let's try that." He added a more cordial smile. "So tell me, Elaine, what do you do for a living?"

"Let me answer you this way." She could not tell at what point his bravado met frankness but at least it was now clear that he knew enough about her to ease any lingering concern about security breeches. "Jimmy Laymonjaylo is an alias for someone the agency was interested in."

He heard her use the past tense.

"An alias," he said. "Do you know his real name?"

She nodded. "Barif Ali."

Cotsworth responded quietly, "Barif Ali…"

She nodded and stirred her tea.

"Let's just refer to him as *Jimmy* for right now," he suggested.

"Agreed."

"Why is your employer interested in Jimmy?"

"Several companies are… *Were* might be more accurate."

"Were…" The past tense troubled him. "Okay. Keep going."

"Jimmy boarded a tramp freighter in Houston, carrying a fraudulent Pakistani passport with the name *Ali*…later he started using a Lebanese one."

Cotsworth scratched his head. She was handing him puzzle pieces, but none were fitting together, so he simply said, "And…"

"His entrée to the freighter and confidant while aboard was a known"—Jericho whispered, her voice barely audible—"nuclear terrorist." Her napkin shielded her lips so no one could read them. "Close to…bin Laden. Inner circle." She sat back and looked around the restaurant.

"That's interesting," Cotsworth said.

It sure as hell was! The information confirmed his belief that Morgan left Houston by boat, but with a terrorist?

"When I was in my earlier position," Jericho began to whisper again, "we knew while Jimmy was aboard that ship, it was transporting a high-grade type of steel used in centrifuges—from Africa to, we believe, Iran. The other player on board, who I'll leave nameless, coordinated the materials passage start to finish."

"Do you think Jimmy's presence could be incidental?" None of this was making sense. "Maybe he wasn't dirty?"

"Not likely."

"Why?" Cotsworth asked. His curiosity increased more.

"Jimmy appeared out of nowhere and contacted one ship from dozens of possibilities. None of this is coincidence."

Looking out the windows, she drank some tea and grew silent as if she was finished talking.

"Please, it's too early for intermission," Cotsworth said.

She smiled. "Inbound to the Port of Karachi," Jericho continued, "we found the freighter by satellite. An IR image showed a body hanging off the stern."

"M..." Cotsworth almost said Morgan's name but caught himself. "Jimmy?"

The current story was still too incredible to associate it with the name he knew.

"Yes," she said. "There's more."

"I'm hoping so."

"That was after he probably killed two men, including the captain."

"Whoa." Cotsworth held up his hand. "Thinking about that one..."

Recalling the pictures from the Midway that Brosinski had given him, Cotsworth knew Morgan was capable of killing. If true, there had to be a damn good reason.

"Why would he do that?"

"Not certain," answered Jericho. "A friend of mine thinks there may have been an assault on him or maybe an attempted rape—"

"I'd kill them too," he commented. "So...what happened to Jimmy after that? Crew throw him overboard?"

"Nobody knows," Jericho said. "But *I* think a satellite picture taken right after that suggests he intentionally jumped ship."

"Jumped ship...You're making this up 'cause it's crappy weather outside, and you're bored."

"I wish," she replied.

"Anybody know if he survived?" Cotsworth asked.

"Weeks later there was a robbery aboard a Pakistani train. Some bullet fragments came from a .357."

"Now I know you're making this up," laughed Cotsworth. "But please continue. I don't have anything else to do."

"Jimmy stole one in Houston," she said. "I think those are his bullets, but the rest of my coworkers don't."

"I'd have to agree with them without ballistics." The agent shook his head. "Even so, why would he rob a train?"

She shrugged.

"Where he is now?" he asked.

"No inkling." Her voice trailed off. "Alive or dead, I just don't know."

"This is fun." Cotsworth looked at his watch. "More tea, or perhaps a drink?"

"Just tea please."

Amused, he watched her again measure the milk as the tea bag hung in a fresh pot of hot water.

"So how do you come to know Demetri Kubiak?" he asked.

Jericho stirred her tea, deciding how to answer. "Shipboard evidence discovered in Karachi by a field team."

"What evidence?" he asked.

"Found it in his clothing," she answered. "A pig DNA fragment."

The fucking pig! Cotsworth wanted to yell.

"The Purdue swine database provided the possible cross matches. Took a while because the sample was corrupted. I applied some software and eventually found Scurry Farms."

"*You* found Scurry Farms?" he asked.

She nodded.

His head was propped on his curled palm to hide astonishment. "The picture you showed the Kubiaks?"

"Composite made by the detained freighter crew in Karachi."

"Solid detective work," he complimented. "How the hell did this research get appropriated to you...in your position?"

She was chewing on her lip. "The particle was dismissed by others as contaminate."

The woman was smart—and stupid!

"Everyone ignored Jimmy because he was a 'clean skin' here and left the country without consequence. I thought they were too quick."

"So when the august minds discounted it, you took it on yourself..." The woman was foolhardy as well as obsessive-compulsive. "Does anybody know you're doing this?"

"No comment," said Jericho.

"Elaine, you're way outside your jurisdiction...wandering in a place you shouldn't be."

She nodded meekly.

"You did this because..." He couldn't imagine why the woman would be so fool-hearty.

"Paul, you're never going to believe this," Jericho said.

"Oh, I might."

"Satellites alone can't protect the country. I thought we skirted the issue without integrating the facts."

"Jesus..." he said, shaking his head in disbelief. "From what I learned about you, your career is well launched. You're screwing it up with possibly...jail."

"I know."

His head rocked back and forth.

"If you promise me," he began, "that you'll go home and not visit this again, we'll talk some more."

"I'm game," she replied, with gloom in her voice.

Cotsworth wanted to brighten her mood. "Sure you don't want a drink?"

"Yes, I'm sure." No, she wasn't. "Okay. Maybe some white wine?"

Cotsworth flagged their waiter. A glass of wine and a beer arrived soon after.

"To sharing information and interlinked databases," he toasted.

"Don't use that at a wedding," Jericho laughed.

She was feeling better.

"Anyway, I'm investigating Jimmy too," Cotsworth said.

"Why?" she asked.

"First off, do you know what *Jimmy Laymonjaylo* means?" he asked.

Jericho shook her head.

"'I'm hungry for *lemon Jell-O, give me some.*'"

"Oh damn!" Jericho blushed.

It was an old joke about how a less-literate mother named her baby from the daily menu at the hospital. The name fooled a pig farmer and, worse, an intelligence officer.

"It's okay, Elaine. Remember, we all get hoodwinked."

Her face remained red.

"We found a bigger piece of the same DNA that came from an apartment in Chicago."

"What?"

Jericho put her glass down and squinted at him.

"Forensics traced it months ago to Scurry Farms, so I talked to Kubiak—by phone. Saved me from going there. Maybe your Wisconsin upbringing made you immune to those sorts of smells."

"It didn't."

"He called me right after you left to tell me," Cotsworth said, "that another person wanted to know about *Lemon Jell-O.*" He smiled. "Said he hoped he was doing the right thing."

"A decent man," Jericho commented.

"So here's my quid pro quo. You should know that *Barif Ali* is also an alias," the agent said. "*Lemon Jell-O* and *Ali* are really someone named Wesley Morgan...Dr. Wesley Morgan, a heart surgeon here in Chicago."

"What?" Jericho exclaimed.

"Operates on babies...at least used to...and was good at it... and a decent guy... I gather that's unusual for surgeons. I assumed they're mostly assholes."

Jericho was too shocked to laugh with him.

"Then, almost two years ago, his life...poof...gone."

Jericho didn't believe they were discussing the same individual.

"Morgan's been the focus of a Missing Person investigation," Cotsworth said, "my personal project for months now."

"A missing person?" she said with surprise.

Cotsworth pulled a thick file from his briefcase, slipped his finger behind a tab, and folded it open. He turned it around to show her a picture.

"That's Ali," Jericho replied. "The pictures I have are different, but it's him, no doubt."

"Right." Cotsworth was looking at the image upside down. "Good-looking guy, isn't he?"

"Yes," she showed no more than passing curiosity.

The agent handed her the picture of Caroline from the brochure.

"What a pretty girl!" Jericho exclaimed.

"They were in a serious relationship," he replied.

The agent's finger lifted another tab.

"Her old man owned a Beltway company designing spy equipment. Made buckets of dough, cashed out, and retired in central Virginia as a gentleman farmer. Name's Jon Pruitt."

Jericho studied the white-haired man, glancing only briefly at a phone number and address written beside it.

"Don't recognize him or the name," she said, shaking her head.

He closed the folder.

"Airport security in Houston found Morgan's car abandoned and searched it," said Cotsworth. "A box in the trunk was addressed to Pruitt...so, naturally, they called him. Then, the next day, I get pulled from every active case and I'm assigned to work just on Morgan. All I can imagine is that Pruitt must have known somebody way up the tree and asked for help. I won the hand... lucky, I guess."

"Or that good." The man deserved a compliment. "So...what was in the box?"

"A few items belonging to Morgan and the girl...plus a letter asking the father to take care of them. The final remnants of Morgan's life."

"That's grim," Jericho said.

"The rest of his story is wrapped in shadows." The FBI agent smiled. "I was getting ready to close the file, then...Who would have thought a pig would bring you and me to lunch?"

"Why would Morgan go to Scurry Farms?" Jericho asked.

"And play with barnyard animals? That's a million-dollar question..." Cotsworth shrugged. "Morgan's generated more than one of those. He's left a trail of bread crumbs that don't lead anywhere—that is, until I now find out he's vacationing with a nuclear terrorist. Until an hour ago, that would have been too preposterous to invent."

"I echo *that* sentiment," Jericho said.

"I have whatever access I need to follow up on this thing, so I'll dig around a little more." He wet his throat with some beer. "You've given me another colorful thread to tie onto this fraying ball of yarn. Who knows how many more of those there are. I will say, a stop in Pakistan might not have even been on his itinerary, if he has one. That place sure isn't safe for Americans."

Cotsworth sucked in his cheeks, shifting his jaw back and forth. "Anyway, assuming he's alive, until he's picked up by Interpol or tries to come home, there's probably little else I'll be able to discover."

He leaned forward again. "Elaine, you're on a limb ready to snap." Cotsworth's tone grew serious. "Leave this thing alone."

Jericho's cell phone rang.

"Excuse me." She saw the number. "Work."

The brief conversation was vague. After disconnecting, Jericho gave Cotsworth a perturbed look. "Duty calls. They need me for a meeting tomorrow."

"The ball and chain," he said. "Got mine too."

She rose to leave but sat again. "Paul, what happened to his fiancée?"

"Her name was Caroline." His voice softened. "She was at a breakfast meeting at Windows of the World."

"Oh my God…"

The thumbs of both hands rubbed little circles against her temples as she became absorbed in impassioned contemplation, her eyes motionless behind the caged space her fingers created in front of her face. Everything Morgan was doing was now clear.

Shaking her head so Cotsworth wouldn't suspect she was thinking too much, Jericho contemplated the reality a moment longer, then said, "That's just awful! Her poor family…and Morgan!" She released an audible exhale. "I understand their pain completely. I lost friends that day too."

"We all did," Cotsworth said.

She took the last of her wine and sighed. "Could I just…see those pictures again? It's just unbelievable. She was so beautiful."

"Yes, she was," said Cotsworth, reopening the file. He handed it to her.

Jericho looked at Caroline's picture then held her eyes on Jon Pruitt to memorize his phone number and address.

FIFTY-THREE

Washington, DC February 21, 2004

The Saturday-morning meeting surprised many. Ski trips to West Virginia were canceled and pancake breakfasts at home with the kids were missed. Despite a midnight arrival in Washington, Jericho was awake before her alarm clock.

She didn't really get any sleep. The revelations shared by Cotsworth melded her apprehensions into perplexity. It was easy to swap Ali's name for Morgan's, but if he was attempting to do what she believed, there was no way to validate it with only anecdotal evidence. No one would believe her anyway. Besides, with Cotsworth giving her the same stern warning as Carstens, it was best to let her exploits remain concealed.

In low heels, she walked as quickly as she could to the Metro, then five blocks to the White House, her long legs getting her there a few minutes early. At the security gate, she paused to catch her breath, her intrigue growing by the sudden need to meet in the Basement.

Several other ranking officers cleared security with her. After salutes they walked briskly together to the front portico door.

Inside, her raincoat vanished in the hands of a marine corporal. In the washroom she adjusted her cap and tugged her uniform jacket taut. When she emerged, she was escorted to the briefing room. Crammed with gray and black suits and uniforms, Secret Service agents appraised every nuance. At the far end of the room, the current and former NGA directors, Bill Platter and Cottrell Herndon, were talking to President Reeves. When the admiral saw his favorite officer, he beckoned her over. She saluted the trio and Herndon introduced her. Handshakes followed.

"Captain Jericho returns from her first vacation ever, Mr. President," Herndon kidded, "just to join us today."

Reeves laughed. "Refreshed, I hope, Captain," he said. "How was your time off?"

"Marvelous, Mr. President," she lied.

"You're lucky you got away," Platter said. "We're going to be busy."

"Please take your seats." A pleasant but authoritative voice called to the uniformed and suited assembly.

"That's our cue, officers...duty calls," said Reeves. "A pleasure meeting you, Captain."

"My honor, Mr. President."

"Gentlemen..." Reeves nodded to the admirals.

"Sit behind me, Elaine," Platter whispered.

"I've been told," she whispered back.

Reeves approached the center seat.

"Good morning, all." Known for his relaxed charm, the man seemed embarrassed by the encircled formality. "Please...sit."

Chairs moved.

"Thanks for coming on short notice...and on a Saturday. I know it's time away from your families or...maybe a vacation." The president found Jericho, acknowledging her with a concise smile. "However, you're also cognizant of your responsibilities...such is *their* burden in *our* call to duty. I thank you and *them*."

He paused, his face filled with determination. "Time to get to the crux of this. Our Director of National Intelligence, Mr. Tomlinson, will discuss the reason. With that, I give him the floor."

Jericho recognized all the faces. The intelligence directors, the joint chiefs, and secretary of state were present; behind them were their immediate coadjutors. She saw Rushworth. Their eyes connected for the briefest instant.

"CIA's in charge," Jericho said to Platter, who acknowledged with a single nod.

"Good morning," said the DNI. "I echo the president's sentiment. Thank you for coming on short notice. My remarks will be thorough but brief.

"Over the past few months we've been evaluating a rhythm change in our electronic and spectral surveillance, corroborated by recent human intel. We confirm with ninety-eight percent reliability actionable intelligence that our number one target, Osama bin Laden, plus al Qaeda and Taliban representatives and a liaison from Iran—the list is specific—will meet in Swat three weeks from yesterday. We have the location."

The DNI adjusted his reading glasses and took a sip of water. "This face-to-face meeting will finalize plans necessary to collapse the Pakistani government, with the ultimate goal, as you can suspect, of acquiring their nuclear arsenal. Some in ISI believe that much of the military will rally to that cause."

Even those who already knew sat in rapt contemplation.

"Jamil Sayyaf, the limping nuclear weapons expert who worked on Pakistani bombs, is invited...if that tells you anything. He's been unusually busy. We know he delivered centrifuges and reactor steel last fall through Bandar Abbas, and more recently has been coming and going through Pakistani border checkpoints—*bypassing* might be a better term—and has now taken residence close by in Mingora."

The DNI sneezed then blew his nose. "Sorry. It's the February dampness. To accelerate fear in Pakistani citizens, a coordinated escalation of terrorist bombings has started in their cities. It's a distraction...to terrify and rile the populace."

Tomlinson concluded, "We believe we have an opportunity to create a major interruption in al Qaeda's plans, acquire and exploit site-sensitive information, and...without adding any unneeded emphasis, extract our friend Osama." His face held a determined expression. "Mr. President..."

"Thank you." Reeves stood. "This will be an American operation only. In part for secrecy, but more so, the responsibility to interdict shall belong solely to the Unites States. I will notify the president of Pakistan before we enter their airspace, preventing any ISI mole from thwarting the plan. I will inform our NATO allies immediately after that."

He stopped to canvass their looks. "We want Mr. bin Laden. He's going to be ours, and he will be brought to justice as the world watches." He motioned to the DNI before sitting down. "Mr. Tomlinson, please continue."

"Thank you, sir. Admiral James Llewellyn, in charge of Joint Special Operations Command and Operational Security, will now give a summary of the National Command Authority plan. The items relevant to each agency will be distributed following this meeting, so your offices will be your next destination. Advise those on your staff they'll be working today, tomorrow, tomorrow night, and so on. Tell them to bring a toothbrush and a change of clothes, but tell them nothing else until it appears in the timeline."

His lips became straight. "I'll say it anyway: don't plan to sleep until it's over."

———

"Captain Lainey Jericho, lovely to see you," said Herndon, emerging from his private office, grinning his familiar disarming smile.

Her hand trembled when it met his. Swamped with work, the appointment was delayed until late in the week, and that only worsened her anxiety.

"Aren't you supposed to be working on the world peace initiative?" She looked thinner beyond her usual slender self.

"Admiral, we need to speak in private."

Her familiar kinetic tendency wasn't there. In fact, she seemed on the brink of panic.

"Of course." He guided her to his inner office. "No calls," he said to the officer at the closest desk, "and please bring the captain some tea and milk."

Herndon shut the door.

"Sit down, Elaine," he said gently.

She sank in the armchair. There was a polite knock, and a steward presented the tea to her. When the door closed again, Herndon said, "You haven't been sleeping…"

"No." Her conscience hadn't let her.

"To be expected…we're all under stress now."

Jericho grimaced. "That's not it, sir."

"Drinking?"

She shook her head. "No…sir."

The admiral pulled his wingback chair closer, condensing the space to make the conversation feel more private.

"Okay. I'm no longer your superior officer…just your friend… which I am, by the way." He put his hand over hers. "What's going on, Lainey?"

The years of discipline returned. She sat erect.

"Cottrell, I have to report my exploits to you and ask your advice, even…even if it means disciplinary action. I also…do not request any special favors or leniency."

"Jesus, Elaine, spill it."

"I've been over and over it," she said.

She detailed her activities surrounding Ali, the farm, and Cotsworth. At one point she thought Herndon was enjoying the tale.

"You discovered this yourself?"

"Yes. Well, no…not in the beginning, at least. Glen Sorenson helped, but I didn't know what I was looking for." She cast a wary look. "Please keep him out of this. He was acting under my direct authority."

"No problem." He sat for a time. "So what do you think Morgan's doing?" he asked.

Jericho said, "I believe he's hunting for the same person we are."

"How could he do that?"

"He's certainly smart and shrewd enough to try. A man who believes he is going to die is dangerous…worse than a tiger stalking prey."

"Do you really think he could survive in the tribal frontier?" Herndon's lips formed a half frown. "I'll bet he's been dog food for months."

"Suppose not...and he's found out about the meeting? It could devastate the operation."

"That isn't going to happen, Elaine." He shook his head with conviction. "One man can't get in. CIA's tried to get in time and again. When they out you, it's your head. Impossible to get close."

Jericho didn't even hear the pen clicking.

"As to your extracurricular activities...I'm impressed...but you did go way overboard in your research. I warned you." He grinned slyly. "I think I can say with confidence I doubt anything will come of it. I'll discuss it off the record with Platter. It'll go away...I reckon."

"Thank you, Admiral." Jericho sighed. "Back to work, I guess."

"I think so," he said.

"Thank you again, sir." She rose to salute.

"Captain Jericho, our country needs you."

FIFTY-FOUR

Pruitt Farm March 2, 2004

"E dward Gordon, Assistant Director of the FBI, calling for Mr. Jon Pruitt, please."

The number was blocked.

"Yes, sir," Gordon said. "I'll be happy to have you call me back."

Connie was by his side as Pruitt wrote down the exchange.

"FBI..." Pruitt said to her after hanging up. "Senior enough."

His expression grew worried. Connie's followed in empathy as Pruitt dialed the number.

"Edward Gordon." It was the same voice.

"Jon Pruitt returning your call," he said.

"Sir," Gordon began, "I know you're aware the FBI has been investigating the disappearance of Dr. Wesley Morgan, who, I understand, was in a relationship with your daughter." He paused, cleared his throat and said, "And let me say this before I go any farther...I'm sorry for your tragic loss."

"Thank you," said Pruitt.

Reality began to sap his longstanding denial.

"Regarding Dr. Morgan..." he said, "and I don't know how to say this easily..."

"None of it's been easy," replied Pruitt. "Please...speak freely."

"Sir..." Gordon sighed and continued. "Dr. Morgan liquidated his assets and left the country last fall. His movements after that were completely unknown until recently. Although details are sketchy, we believe he was traveling under a false passport—"

"That's odd," interrupted Pruitt. "Why so?"

"Unknown. There are gaps in our information," Gordon answered.

"I'll say…"

"Unfortunately, sir, I have bad news."

"Please."

"Earlier this year there was a car bombing in Peshawar…that's in Pakistan, sir…"

"Just tell me," said Pruitt.

His eyes began to well with tears. Connie sensed the worst.

"According to sources in another of our agencies that I won't identify, Dr. Morgan's passport…at least the one he was traveling under…the false one…"

"Get on with it, man!" Pruitt raised his voice in frustration. "I can already guess what you're going to say!"

"Well, sir…We can neither confirm nor deny the circumstances with certainty, but we think that Dr. Morgan was an occupant in the vehicle…and lost his life."

"Was his body recovered?" asked Pruitt.

"That's a problem, sir," said Gordon. "The specifics of the tragedy were only recently clarified to us by the Pakistani government. There were…multiple parts of several bodies…burned beyond recognition in the wreckage. They were cremated together."

"Christ on the cross," Pruitt said. "Is that all you can give me and my wife?"

"I'm sorry, sir," he said, remorse pouring from each word. "There's nothing else to share."

FIFTY-FIVE

Darra Adam Khel Arms Bazaar March 4, 2004

It was a time for Morgan to be audacious. Serene and disinterested, he stepped around the notorious guides hustling safe passage and walked past the wind-tanned faces guarding the bazaar's gated checkpoint.

For barter, he sauntered in with the two AK-47s from the truck; he had rupees to pay the balance and buy whatever else he needed. A hidden grenade would provide a final gesture if warranted. But it wouldn't likely come to that. The huge arms market was a neutral zone where sworn adversaries and centuries-old tribal feuds were placed in check at the entrance. Business was business. Trading in guns and other lethal gadgets of human ingenuity possessed rituals that were both historical and absolute.

Make your best deal and get out.

From the beginning Morgan knew he was being watched—at least until the eyes found another fresh subject. Then he felt released to wander and converse, no longer suspected of being a rogue. His scraggly looks and body odor offered more than enough evidence.

For a time he drank tea and talked to men with blown-off hands and fingers while inventorying what lay displayed proudly in the stalls under corrugated tin roofs. Behind a distant razor wire fence lay pallets stacked with large wooden crates—many with Russian or Chinese lettering. Guarded by heavily armed men whose foreheads were wrapped in keffiyehs, the tarantula eyebrows, long eyelashes, and almond-eyed gazes told nothing of the menace hidden behind.

"Enfield."

A gray-haired bearded man elevated the rifle near Morgan's face as though he was offering his firstborn grandchild for inspection.

Morgan leaned the AKs against the table and took the piece. With deference he ran his fingers over each square inch of the stock and faded blue metal. He opened the breech, looked down the barrel, then placed his ear close to the action and opened and closed the bolt several times.

"Smooth," he said.

"Like baby's skin," replied the man.

With the buttstock blocking his face, Morgan glanced past the cartons of American cigarettes, fake antiques, and stacked flasks of brandy to evaluate a rifle with a synthetic folding stock, short barrel, and scope.

Continuing to keep the owner's attention on the Enfield, Morgan asked, "Have you had this beauty a long time?"

"My great-grandfather killed a British soldier and took it as a prize."

It was honest pride, total bullshit, or a little of both.

Morgan shouldered the rifle and peered down its sights. A bullet from an Enfield was powerful and flew true, making the rifle a Taliban favorite for long-range sniping. Through the corner of his eye, he continued studying the other rifle with its integrated silencer, night-vision scope, and large magazine.

It was time to turn the deal.

"You cannot sell this treasure," Morgan said, pulling out a piece of cloth from a pocket. As a sign of respect, he thoroughly wiped the Enfield's metal surfaces removing any oil left by his fingerprints before handing it back. "I sense your grandfather's spirit."

The man looked disappointed.

"Besides..." Morgan laughed, "it is too heavy for my hunting journey far into the mountains with my son."

To distract anyone who might be watching, Morgan gripped the barrels of both AKs.

"These hunks of metal," he said, "are too inaccurate for the sport." He made sure the man saw him glance at the scoped gun to the side.

The old man discreetly surveyed the crowd before touching the lightweight sniper rifle.

"I killed a Russian for this." He smiled and nodded his head at the memory. "Very accurate...deadly for many, many meters...easy to carry...and cannot wake the family. It will hunt in the dark, if you desire."

Both men laughed.

"Can I examine it?" asked Morgan, also concerned that interest might raise suspicion of the wandering guards.

"No." The man added a vigorous headshake.

"I understand." Morgan nodded. He reached into his satchel. His fingers flashed a large wad of bills.

The man whispered, "I'll sell it to you if you wish, but we cannot trade here. You should buy my Enfield now even though the price will be high."

"I would be honored to have it," replied Morgan.

"It is yours," the man answered. During a prolonged handshake, money, the AKs and a piece of paper exchanged palms. "We will meet later at my home for prayers and tea. Inshallah."

FIFTY-SIX

NGA March 5, 2004

With feet parallel, knees aligned and back erect, Elaine Jericho sat outside Admiral Platter's office trying to control her apprehension.

"Tea, Captain?" the second lieutenant and admiral's personal assistant asked. He knew she always took some if the wait grew long.

"No...thank you," she replied quietly.

Occasionally Jericho had daydreamed about the implausible chance she and the good-looking man might have dinner together. Because of protocol, she knew it would never happen. After Herndon had briefed her yesterday about the morning meeting with Platter, the fantasy was gone.

The inner office door opened and Herndon walked out. She snapped to attention and saluted.

"At ease," he said, his familiar grin absent. "Lieutenant, if you'll excuse us for a minute."

"Certainly, Admiral." He rose, gave a quick salute and went into the corridor.

"Elaine, one more thing you should know...and I just found out about it within the last hour...Rushworth insisted she be present to represent the CIA."

Jericho winced when he said that.

"Platter and I balked at first, but then decided it was best to let her speak her piece here, in private."

There was an indisputable change in Herndon's tenor. "I'll stand by your side…the best I can…but for God's sake—just let the woman talk."

"What do you mean?" Jericho asked. Worry spread over her face.

"It's got to be this way, Elaine," Herndon said. "Sorry."

Saying no more, they went into Platter's office. Jericho immediately snapped to attention. Herndon shut the door and stood with Platter as he came away from his desk. Rushworth put her coffee cup on a side table and uncrossed her legs. Choosing to stand away from the pair, she folded her arms, not letting the uniforms to one side alter the scowl she aimed at Jericho.

"Stand at ease, Captain Jericho," Platter said. "You understand the reason you're here, Captain?"

"Admiral Herndon briefed me, sir," she answered.

"Then I won't labor through those details," Platter said. "But I need to say this: Captain Jericho, I'm well aware of your desire to stand firm for your country…but your recent activities are highly irregular."

"To say the least," Rushworth fumed.

"Madame Director…if you don't mind, I'll have the first words," he retorted. "As you know, Captain Jericho, you've been working outside your position and responsibilities, investigating a US citizen without proper authorization."

Rushworth charged immediately. "And Captain…this is what gives the government, *my* agency, and the PATRIOT Act a bad name! And, gets us smeared by the press—all of which makes it impossible to do our jobs…properly!"

"As I was saying—" Platter continued.

"What about your oath, Captain Jericho?" Rushworth gulped for more air. "Along with being insolent, you've violated the public trust! You could undermine future intelligence efforts! And right now, you may have risked our plans to capture bin Laden! What the hell were you thinking?"

She came within an arm's reach of Jericho.

"Ma'am—" Jericho began.

"Don't call me *ma'am*! I'm not military!" the woman corrected her. With a whine, she said, "I worked a long time for my title. It's *Madame Deputy Director.*"

"I apologize, Madame Deputy Director."

"Okay, let's settle down," said Herndon.

"Cottrell, I'm not finished!" Rushworth almost shouted. "Jericho, if you had information, you should have informed CIA instead of chasing around...talking to pig farmers...the FBI!"

Rushworth gave her a chilling stare. "And how did Cotsworth get involved? Somebody pulled his strings, I'm certain! I'd just love to know who!"

She pushed her glasses up her nose, stepped back and snarled. "By the way, he submitted his report—and will keep his job. He thanks you very much!"

Her lips rolled inward while her cheeks puckered. After a hard sniff through her nostrils she continued. "I've been instrumental in finding that bastard bin Laden...and now, two damn weeks before the most major, important covert operation since the Manhattan project, and I have to worry about this?"

Both admirals looked shocked by her presumptive audacity.

"But God help you, Jericho," one corner of Rushworth's mouth drew in and up to form a unilateral smile, "if your antics cause the President to violate Pakistani airspace to assault a family picnic!"

Herndon chuckled out loud.

"You get what I mean, Admiral," said Rushworth.

"Response, Captain?" asked Platter.

"Madame Deputy Director," Jericho began, "you quashed the Ali investigation. If it weren't for me, this information would have never been discovered."

"What!" Rushworth shouted. "How dare you? Of all the unmitigated gall!"

"Captain Jericho," Platter said, trying to regain control, "what do you believe Morgan is doing?"

"You value her opinion why?" asked Rushworth, her voice snippy. Jericho looked at Platter. "I don't know any longer, sir."

"You sure did until recently!" injected Rushworth.

"Go ahead, Elaine," Herndon said.

"What? You address a subordinate by her first name?" Rushworth interjected. "I'll make sure this doesn't just end with her."

Herndon looked severely at Rushworth. "Be careful with your threats, *Priscilla*." By using her name maybe she would smolder long enough for Jericho to answer. "At present we are discussing intelligence information. Do you understand?"

Rushworth's jaw stayed firm.

"Captain…if you please," Platter said.

"Sir, Agent Cotsworth searched for Morgan and discovered nothing." Her voice trailed off. Regaining focus, Jericho continued. "Now we learned that he left a trail of death…which is very different from saving babies. Everything he's done appears calculated, so even if his passport showed up in a car bombing…he might not be dead. What's he doing? I really believe he's over there trying to kill bin Laden."

"Compelling fantasy, Jericho, a doctor turned vigilante," spewed Rushworth. "Over the death of a woman? Not a chance! Men get over women when they see the next skirt! Doctors are the worst."

Herndon's eyes rolled.

"Here's a far more plausible scenario." Rushworth again moved close to Jericho. "We know that freighter was dirty, and by happenstance one of the crew was a nuclear terrorist, whose brother mules him toward a terrorist camp. So what *I* think is going on is that after the woman's death your Dr. Morgan went crazy…developed Stockholm Syndrome, and headed to Pakistan thinking he'd polish his jihadi skills, then come back to America with an armful of doll-shaped WMDs for his patients."

Jericho winced. "I can't believe—"

"It's no wackier than what you suggested, Captain, that is unless you think Morgan's movements are just the result of a series of coincidences," impugned Rushworth. "But if for some far-fetched chance he is still alive and attempting to do what you say—"

"Priscilla," Herndon said, intentionally using her first name again, "I'd wager big money Morgan's long dead, either in that car bombing or beheaded somewhere along the way. I can't imagine any of this is going to affect bin Laden's extraction."

"Unless the ISI has picked him up!" Rushworth's anger flared again. "They'll think he's CIA and pry any information out of him they can use, then they'll backchannel a warning to the Taliban... and..." Rushworth snapped her fingers. "That's that!"

"Collaborative sources tell us the meeting's still on," Herndon replied in a controlled tone.

The hush lasted a moment.

Rushworth smacked her fist on the top of the closest wingback chair. "It *really* would have been helpful to know this crap, oh—shall we say—in *January*, so we could have factored it in!"

"Madame Deputy Director," Jericho began, "I informed Admiral Herndon as soon—"

"The road to hell is lined with lame excuses!" Rushworth scoffed. The corners of her lips curled slightly. "And actually, Cottrell, I agree. This idiot is dead, or our sources would have told us otherwise."

After the intensity of her harangue, neither admiral could believe Rushworth agreed with Herndon's conclusion without argument. There was something more she was waiting for.

The lioness seemed to salivate. "So let's move on to a more pressing problem. Gentlemen, what are we going to do with"—she thumbed toward Jericho—"her?"

"Madame Deputy Director...Admiral Herndon and I have discussed Captain Jericho's misconduct," said Platter. "Captain?"

"Sir." Jericho came to attention again.

"The Navy and the Department of Defense want you to go away... and there are only two ways that will happen," Platter said. "Neither is negotiable. Admiral Herndon, continue, please."

Jericho felt like she was about to tumble down a crater opening beneath her feet. She had no idea if her friend was going to help push.

"Captain Jericho," Herndon began, "you may request a trial in military court. That is choice one."

He paused so she could consider her chances for success in that venue.

"Here's choice two. Your service records indicate you have three years and change until your twenty-year mark. You may take a one-month leave of absence effective immediately, be given two hours under guard to clear out any personal effects from your office, surrender clearances and badges, and vacate the NGA. You will be demoted immediately, and in thirty days' time report to the commanding officer at the navy base in Kingsville, Texas for your new assignment. There you will serve your country as instructed until discharge."

Jericho knew Herndon had fought hard for her. His career was probably ruined as well.

"Number two is what I recommend," he suggested.

"But—" Rushworth began, but Herndon held up his hand to silence her.

"This situation is a military matter, Madame Deputy Director, not civilian," Herndon said. "These options were approved by DOD legal affairs and signed off by the Chief of Staff."

He looked at her. "Lieutenant Commander Jericho, do you have anything more you'd like to say?"

Addressed in the lower rank, she knew her fate was sealed—the final act by her friend to save what was left of a shattered career.

"No, Admiral Herndon, thank you, sir!"

"Then...you are dismissed."

She saluted. Neither officer acknowledged the gesture.

FIFTY-SEVEN

Virginia March 6, 2004

Jericho called Jon Pruitt from a pay phone.
He called back.
"Who are you?" he asked.
"A friend."
The woman sounded nervous.
"Do you perhaps have a name?"
"Wesley—"
"Hmm..." Pruitt cut her off. "You don't sound like a *Wesley*."
"May I come to your home for a visit?"
Pruitt thought about it for a minute.
"Do you know where it is?" he asked.
"Sort of," she answered.
"Our place is on the left one half mile after the last church, just before the highway ends."
"Is tomorrow afternoon okay...maybe fourteen—er...two?"
"That would be fine."

———

The Thunderbird's top folded down. Jericho wrapped the scarf around her neck, turned the radio up, and headed for the interstate.

"Arrest me for speeding!" she screamed to the wind.

No longer having to dress formally, blue jeans and a leather jacket were her chosen uniform. An hour later, after she exited the highway, she felt like she was flying above the country road, passing cars whenever she could. The freedom was irresistible!

"Crap!"

Jericho missed the fluttering American flag topped with long white ribbons. She pulled into the next driveway and turned around. Slowing the car to look longer, she held back tears as she entered the lane.

Stopping on the circular driveway near the broad porch steps, she used the rearview mirror to help her fingers tame the red hair.

Jon Pruitt came out the front door; Connie followed several steps behind.

"Hi," she called, smiling. "I'm Elaine Jericho."

"Hello." Pruitt walked down the steps with a hand in his coat pocket. "Could you please tell me more?"

"Sir, I am..." Her hands stayed visible on the wheel. "Well...I was a shipboard intelligence officer for the navy." There was a grimace. "Then I worked at the NGA...in charge of Middle Eastern Nuclear Recon...then became an assistant director...and...now...Now...I'm former everything...Exiled in four weeks to a navy base in Texas."

"Good fishing lakes there," Pruitt said.

"I'll have to learn."

Motioning toward the house, he said, "Come in. It's warmer."

"Thank you, sir."

They climbed the steps, stopping on the porch.

"My wife, Cornelia."

"Ma'am."

"*Connie*, not *Cornelia* or *ma'am*," his wife corrected them both.

They entered the house.

"Ms. Jericho..." Connie said.

"*Elaine*...please."

Connie began again. "Would you like some coffee or tea?"

"Elaine," said Pruitt, "you look like you could use Scotch."

"No, sir, but thank you, sir…and thank you, Ms. Pruitt. Tea would be wonderful…if it's not too much trouble."

"Not at all. Let me put your jacket on a hanger." Connie sensed the woman needed a moment. "I believe you'd like to freshen up. Come. I'll show you the washroom."

After the women left, Pruitt chuckled. She was typical military, but much more attractive than most.

Jericho returned.

"Come on into my study, Elaine," said Pruitt, opening the door and motioning her to an upholstered chair with a footstool. Jericho watched as Pruitt pulled a Glock from his tweed coat pocket, opened a desk drawer, and laid it inside.

"Please, take your shoes off and relax." He led the way by sitting in an adjoining chair and letting his loafers drop to the rug.

The tea arrived a few minutes later.

"Elaine, I didn't know if you took anything in yours, so I brought some milk and sugar." Connie served them both and said, "Let me know if there's anything else you need…and, if he gets talking about orchids, I'll rescue you."

Jericho smiled.

"Thanks, sweetie," Pruitt said to her.

Connie shut the office door.

Noticing her unsteady teacup, Pruitt stayed silent, letting Jericho settle down and relax.

"Blue's an unusual color for orchids," she said, looking at a tall terrarium full of them.

"*Cattleya minervas*," he said, his face showing no emotion. "Wes gave them to my daughter because they matched her eyes."

"Beautiful," she said.

"Elaine, I don't understand yet why you sought me out, but you're with a friend," he said. "I assure you, you can speak openly about whatever is on your mind. Once I had all the clearances you've had. My respect for their intent has never changed."

"Yes, sir."

"Please...*Jon.*" It was wonderful having a young woman in the house. "Washington's a hundred miles from here...and you drove out for a reason."

"Okay." She was calming down. "Sorry I was obtuse when I called. For so long, I've worried about being overheard."

"I know that feeling," Pruitt said with a smile. "Our home gets electronically swept every couple of days, and this room in particular was designed to be safe. So...what would you like to tell me?"

"I know people think Wesley Morgan's dead..."

Pruitt looked at her but made no reply.

"I think he's alive."

His face continued to show no emotion.

"What leads you to believe that?" he asked.

"There's information confirming his presence in Pakistan."

"Interesting vacation spot." A droll smile formed.

"I'm sorry, Jon. Forgive me. I've been very upset. Normally I don't think haphazardly. Now that I'm sitting here, I'm beginning to get my composure back."

"Take your time."

"Let me start from the beginning," she said.

The tale required a second pot of tea, sandwiches, small cookies, and another bathroom break. When Jericho returned, she concluded the story.

"You see...it wasn't until I spoke with Mr. Cotsworth that I put it together. When Caroline...died...Morgan threw in the towel. I don't believe he's dead, despite the car bombing. My intuition says he's too cunning."

"Intuition?" mused Pruitt. "Is that allowed in the satellite business?"

"Conjecture leads to more research, just not for me anymore, I guess."

"As you've discovered, your employer takes a dim view of such things."

Pruitt looked at his watch. It was late afternoon.

Jericho saw him. "I'm sorry sir, I should go."

"Not at all. I was thinking Scotch would taste good right about now. Care to join me?"

"I have to drive back."

"Perhaps a little?"

"Okay, a little."

When he headed for the bottles, Jericho looked again at the picture of Morgan and Caroline. Her blue eyes twinkled above a regal smile.

"Caroline is stunning," she said. Jericho could tell the father imagined his daughter in the present, so she phrased her words that way.

"Takes after her mother, fortunately."

"I'm not so sure."

"Wesley's good looking, too."

"*Wes...*" said Pruitt. "He insists on that name. Thinks *Wesley* is stiff."

Pruitt handed her a snifter and sat down before raising his glass to toast.

"To your success...which again buttresses the American credo that *no good deed goes unpunished,*" he said. "Ought to be stitched in the flag."

"Feels that way sometimes," she agreed.

"Sounds like you've had a hectic but interesting few months."

"I guess," Jericho said. Unsure, she asked anyway. "What did you do, sir, if I may?"

"Things related to OTDR."

Optical time domain reflexometry. The process analyzed fiber-optic cable integrity, but Jericho heard what he didn't say. If Jon Pruitt had devised a process to tap into fiber-optic transmissions without noticeable interruptions, he was wealthy, more likely rich. She knew he'd give away every cent to have his daughter back.

"Timely," she said, flattered he would share such secret information.

"Yes, it was." He saw her ring and changed the direction of the conversation. "So you went to Annapolis."

"Transferred after a rough first year at Madison. Nobody there liked an unabashed patriot."

"Those lairs can be unwelcoming sometimes," he agreed.

As the Scotch relaxed her, Pruitt sensed a protected personality revealing itself. Her ankles crossed the other way on the footstool while she unconsciously reached back and took out the clip holding her hair. After a gentle shake, she ran her fingers through it and began to pet some strands.

"Pardon me for asking, but...are you married?" he asked.

"Only to the navy. A poor substitute...That's obvious now."

"Another splash?" he asked after a moment.

Jericho agreed, without even thinking.

"My life's been good, I guess, maybe not as much fun as others. But, Jon, if I may...I have to say, today, it's just nice to be in your home...with you and Connie, just talking...The way life should be."

The Scotch continued to work its magic.

"Families are important," she added. "I visit mine too infrequently, I'm afraid."

"Elaine, don't be too hard on yourself," said Pruitt. "Life offers many paths...and not all are chosen."

"So true," she agreed, knowing he was probably thinking about his daughter.

"There are things in this world that we can't anticipate. Look at Wes. He's willing to pay the ultimate price because he believes it's more important than his life. By your behavior, I suspect you're much the same."

"How do you mean?"

"Wes is doing what he thinks is right...and...if he survives, I hope he'll learn to live again."

"Jon, forgive me...I'm not following you. I said I *believed* Wes was alive, but I have no proof."

Pruitt stood up, walked to his desk, and placed his glass down on a coaster.

"I'm going to show you something, Elaine...then we're going to have dinner together and Connie will drive you home. She doesn't drink much. That's safer for both of us."

"Oh, I can't impose..." Jericho's protest was weak at best.

"No arguments. Besides, we have a place in the city. Connie will spend the night there and I'll come to get her in the morning.

There's someone I need to see in the District anyway."

Pruitt removed a manila file folder from a drawer.

"I received a call from the FBI in Washington maybe ten days ago. They told me Wes had been dead for months...in the car bombing. After Cay's death, the stress of being told *that* was almost too much for Connie and me to bear. Then"—he handed Jericho a piece of paper from the folder—"this came from Wes's lawyer last week."

He smiled doggedly. "Attorney-client privilege is a wonderful failsafe. I was able to get help tracing its point of origin to Mingora." His grin continued. "I guess I still have some friends."

Jericho gasped, her fingers trembling as she read the e-mail.

Jon and Connie,
Destiny overcomes darkness. The loss of Cay sealed my fate.
I will succeed or be with her.
With love, your son

She looked at Jon with tears in her eyes.

"Wes really *is* still alive..." Her words were barely audible.

"I've never doubted that, Elaine," said Pruitt.

"He's going to try to kill him."

"Yes," Pruitt said. "I've believed that for a while too." A kind smile carried his next words. "But all I had to rely on was my...intuition."

"The meeting is Friday near Swat," she confided.

"Switzerland of the Middle East," he said.

Jericho's countenance grew dubious. "And *we're* going to try to capture the bastard."

"Interesting quandary for all parties involved, wouldn't you say?" said Pruitt.

FIFTY-EIGHT

Mingora, Pakistan March 15, 2004

The wooden spoon shoveled another bite of ice cream into Morgan's mouth. While he ate, he surveyed the people walking along the streets. Men stopped to greet friends and take tea while children played marbles on the sidewalk in front of stores that boasted pre-colonial flags flapping alongside hand-woven rugs. Drivers squeezed between the narrow canyons of two-story hovels, their heads stuck out of the windows like dogs sucking air.

There was nothing visibly female anywhere, save for the occasional black cloud that silently drifted past or sat on the open tailgate of a passing van, clinging tightly to elderly relatives or the stalk of a horizontal floor fan with its incidentally spinning blade. Morgan knew it was impossible to decide who the bad guys were. The Taliban dressed like everybody.

He wandered back to the young vendor, smiled, and bought a second cup of faluda.

With his feet propped up on a newly purchased backpack and his satchel by his side, he slouched in a tattered folding chair borrowed from a shopkeeper and used the fresh wooden paddle to dig out a bite. The candied bean strings strewn on the top of the dense dessert were a pleasant oddity. The conglomeration never seemed to melt. Each cold dollop rolling on his tongue tasted better than the one before.

He'd probably get a third serving. It was that good.

The scope of the Vintorez sniper rifle poked his leg through the backpack.

Damn, that's one powerful gun...

The subsonic muzzle velocity and noise suppressor kept the rifle silent, yet the Teflon-coated nine-millimeter bullet could still burrow into steel at one hundred yards. Morgan had spent the final week in the nearby hills, applying what Tony taught him—aligning the sights, then correcting for drift, wind, target elevation, and practicing with the night-vision scope.

When he got back to his room at the hostel, Morgan would take the gun apart cleaning it with surgical precision. Every item of equipment was checked and rechecked to make certain it functioned without fault. When he was satisfied, he organized the components in the backpack so each could be accessed in sequence.

A pearl of ice cream fell on his tightly trimmed beard, and his sleeve wiped it away. A nearby barber that morning had also shampooed and cut his mangy hair. His body felt born again from the indulgences.

"I'm ready, Jon," he said behind his lips, hoping the e-mail he had sent from the Internet café had gotten to him. Anyone who had seen him huddled over the computer keyboard would have paid no attention to the trivial act, but its content would be monumental to the man he'd grown to love, the father-in-law he'd never have. It would be Morgan's only message.

Between bites Morgan scanned a newspaper, pretending to be blind to movement around him and deaf to the incessant noise of buses, autos, and music that dumped out of every open store window. When rain fell, he lifted the paper over his head and looked at the bustling crossroads. Located in the heart of Mingora, all traffic moving through the Swat Valley passed that way.

Brakes screeched and everything with wheels stopped. A policeman in Raj uniform carved a path for three SUVs. Unhurried, the black beasts came through the intersection, turned a corner, and stopped in the bowels of a narrow side street. Several men got out.

As the gray brigade of salwar kameez, white shirts, and black pants walked into a rug shop across from where Morgan sat, Morgan held a conceited smile. One man had a limp—and used a dervish walking stick with white streaks in it.

Coincidences don't happen.

Morgan bought his third and final custard. He had to savor its sweetness again. The cardamom and vanilla were the subtle essence of the exotic perfume he sensed behind Caroline's ears the first time they danced. Each taste loitered on his lips, the flavors reminiscent of the Scotch she loved to drink.

He finished his third helping. It would never be enough, but it would be his last.

FIFTY-NINE

Noon, Tuesday, March 16

"**D**amn it's hot out here," Morgan's whisper was barely more than a breathed thought.

He used his teeth to squeeze the valve open on the rubber tube. He sucked in some water from the hydration pack and kept listening through the buzzing insects and occasional bird chirps for man-made noises. It was dangerous to raise his head, so he stayed buried with his backpack in the furrow he'd dug just before dawn, hidden under the dirt wearing tactical clothing and a balaclava that matched the plains surrounding him. Since getting off the bus the evening before, he had crawled nearly a mile, but before the first hint of light, his journey paused, and he had remained motionless since then, his hand holding the silenced Makarov by his side.

In six hours the darkness would return and he could move. In one more day and two nights, he would be at the base of the cliff.

He urinated through his pants into the ground. His groin grew warm, then cooled. He didn't care how crusty it got from the repeated soakings. With the fullness in his bladder gone, he relaxed and nodded off.

Afternoon, Wednesday, March 17

Morgan shrank his body deeper in the dirt. The voices were closer than others had been. His presence wouldn't be discovered unless one of them happened to step on him. That wasn't going to happen. His route was well outside the land-mine boundary being established. That assurance came earlier in the day when somebody tripped a wire. After an abbreviated scream, the permanent mistake distracted other men long enough for Morgan to look up, mark the perimeter and disappear back into the ground.

As the heat softened with sunset, Morgan began to snake through the brush and past rocks inches at a time. Smoke from distant crackling fires occasionally drifted his way, carrying the smells of roasting lamb and goat. He had no desire for either. He was ingesting all the calories and water he needed; anything more refined was irrelevant.

His crawl ended when he got to the cliff. He used the night-vision scope to scan his surroundings, noted the time on his watch and dug his final trench. He didn't want to stop or sleep. All he wanted to do was climb the hundred-foot wall, but that desire would have to wait. Twelve hours needed to pass, so he sat with his knees bent and stretched his back, then lay flat and looked at the stars.

She was up there.

"I love you, Cay," he said.

He knew he would join her soon.

When the golden orb finally set, Morgan settled into the hole and closed his eyes.

Nightfall, Thursday, March 18

With the darkness cloaking him, Morgan buried the gear he no longer needed and scaled the rock wall to the ledge. After resting, he used his binoculars to count the fires. There were dozens. Encircling every flame were vehicles, countless human silhouettes moving in every direction between.

He looked at the building below. Only one truck was present outside the front wall near the gate. A kerosene lamp glow emanated from several windows. An occasional shadow suggested someone was inside, but nothing more.

Morgan switched on his night vision scope and turned to scan the cliffs.

As of yet, no lookouts were in position.

He put the rifle away, removed the satchel from the backpack, and used it as a pillow. Beneath the overhanging stone roof, he waited for the sun to rise.

———

For weeks satellites had mapped the terrain and examined the passing trucks as they spewed exhaust. Deeper inspection revealed only normal sorts of cargo and boxes—and none of the trucks moving along the route ever turned from the road toward the building.

As the week progressed, motorized activity in the area increased. The machines in space watched men and vehicles collect in the meadows, and the embers from their fires streak toward the night sky. Every time a tarp was off the flat bed of a truck, a camera saw weapons. The NGA published the reports to a classified list of customers, who in turn integrated the information for their own needs.

Friday afternoon reconnaissance drones departed. Replaced by Predator Reapers with missiles on their bellies, they waited thousands of feet above the target while their engines spooled silently.

———

Concealed in the morning's shadows, Morgan was invisible on the guano-splattered perch. Blending in with the rocks, he watched the jamboree grow larger as more vehicles bounced into the meadows.

He removed his Koran and leafed through the pages as he had so many times before. His eyes stopped on feminine handwriting he immediately recognized.

ßÇÝÑ

Infidel.

"Nadia..."

His suspicion had been right all along. He wrapped the book in the white cloth and zipped it back inside his tactical pants pocket.

"That's thanks for saving your ass..."

SIXTY

Friday, March 19

A catering truck arrived in the morning. Morgan watched as it turned from the highway, staggered up the uneven road, and went through the open gate. It stopped on the side of the building. Two men got out with pistols on their hips. They opened the rear door and removed some power cables.

As they fed the male plugs under the barbed wire to the outside of the wall, one of the men cut his wrist on a prong. Morgan heard him swear.

"What a pussy…"

They fed the female ends into the building over a window sill, went back into the truck, and emerged with a generator and fuel can, which they rolled on dollies out the gate to where the cables hung. After they carried in large ice chests, tables, chairs, lamps and floor fans, one of the men parked the truck down the hill and walked back to the generator. He flipped a switch and went inside.

Morgan could hear the engine hum.

Behind him inside the cliff walls, Morgan heard radio chatter. He put on his headset and located the active frequency. The exchange included comments about exploded mines a month earlier on the trail.

"Sorry your buddies didn't leave me a few more for you," Morgan said. After confirming their positions through the binoculars, he hid back under the rock roof.

———

In the afternoon a van arrived. Men in desert fatigues got out with machine pistols strapped to their thighs. They opened the rear hatch, removed AKs, rocket launchers and surface-to-air missiles. Picking up their weapons each moved to an assigned position. Two of them appeared on the top deck of the building. After leaning the rocket-propelled grenade and surface-to-air launchers in corners, they removed the tarps.

Morgan's prior speculation was spot on. It was a fifty-caliber Russian NSV machine gun with lots of extra ammunition.

———

"Command, *Reaper One* here," said Predator pilot Mike Powers, as he controlled the drone's high-resolution camera from Creech Air Force Base in Nevada, nine thousand miles away.

"Go ahead, *One,*" said Sergeant-Major Coretta Graham.

"*One* reporting eleven men on site now. Two remain in structure. Three snipers in cliffs, one RPG, one SAM. Two men on the roof with NSV, RPGs, SAMs. Men on station at the outside corners. RPGs near northwest wall. *Unfriendlies* carrying sidearms, AKs, radios, extra munitions. Images and targeting data on the way."

"Command, *Reaper Two* radio check," said Brian Larsen who was maneuvering the second drone south of the target area.

"Five by five," Graham answered. "Go ahead."

"Command, there are fifty or more vehicles now—mostly pickups and cars—scattered through the fields west of the cliffs, almost a forest of AKs down there. Estimating several hundred men at a minimum, no evidence of children. You should be seeing this."

"Confirm," Graham replied. "We're getting them."

The team in the operations room at Central Command in Tampa, Florida, would manage the mission timeline and coordinate every offensive and defense procedure.

A few minutes before, commanding the Joint Special Operation, Admiral James Llewellyn had sat down behind Graham in his raised chair and plugged in his headset, listening to the conversation. For the moment the communication loops were busy but not overflowing. As the mission progressed, however, every exchange channeled through the Pentagon, the Combined Air Operations Center in Kuwait, CIA, NSA, and Central Command would constrict to cryptic acronyms.

On the giant video screen beyond the trenches of individual computer stations, Llewellyn looked at the processed images taken from the drone seventeen thousand feet above the target area. He knew reality for that place would change soon after dark.

"Admiral." Graham turned to speak off-mike with him. "I'll open the link to the White House shortly."

He nodded and looked at his watch. His world would get busy soon.

As sunset approached, the electric generator's hum became more distinct. Minutes later several cars and SUVs stopped at the gate. Morgan removed his balaclava a final time and smeared black camouflage paint on his face, neck and hands before inching close to the edge. With his finger resting on the Vintorez trigger guard, he watched through the scope, evaluating the profiles of the passengers as they got out. With weapons by their sides, figures in dark clothing assisted arthritic men with long beards and flowing white robes into the building. From the SUVs, bodyguards escorted several men in suits.

"Wants everyone there first," he said to himself.

The vehicles left the gate and went down the hill to park.

Morgan revised the tally.

"Nineteen guards…"

He rolled to his back. The night-vision scope on his Vintorez sniper rifle scoured the cliffs.

The glowing diode on a lookout's scope betrayed him.

One.

Another slight illumination came across a chasm.

Two.

A match that flared against black rocks was shielded too late. Three.

They hadn't moved.

Morgan shut off the scope and sat with his back against the rock wall. With the rifle across his chest and the headphone covering an ear, his eyelids drooped to avoid fatigue as he waited for the guest of honor.

Morgan's headphones crackled, jarring him. Through the binoculars he studied a procession of headlights passing the turnoff and continuing along the highway for several miles, then the beams went dark. At the extreme edge of the haze, the caravan seemed to be turning around.

"That's damn curious," he whispered.

Looking over the edge, Morgan saw the guards outside the wall step farther away. Their guns were no longer behind their backs but hanging from their shoulders horizontally by the slings, with the muzzles facing the directions they looked.

———

"Command, *Reaper One*...five new vehicles returning to target. Big SUVs."

"Copy," said Graham. "Admiral, the teams report ready."

"Okay," he said. "Tell everyone to stand by."

He pressed a button and had a private exchange through his headset.

"Thank you, Mr. President." Llewellyn nodded grimly to the men and women at the consoles.

"Ladies and gentlemen..." he said in a serene voice. "POTUS authorizes *Hell-bound Chorus*. I repeat: Operation *Hell-bound Chorus* is approved."

In the expected momentary hush, the admiral prayed silently. *Lord, protect us...and please forgive me...*

"Commence," he ordered.

The master command was relayed.

"*Chorus* initiated, sir," said Graham.

In Afghanistan the rotor blades of the Kiowa Warrior helicopters began twisting, then the SEAL teams aboard four Blackhawks heard the rush of air compress out their idling engines. As they throttled up, whimpers of the turbine blades blended into accelerating howls. The pilots adjusted the pitch levers, and the aircraft lifted away from the ground.

To provide close air support, a duo of heavily armed four-engine Specter Gunships released their brakes and the Spookys, as they were called, began lumbering down the tarmac. Miles away a pair of Thunderbolts climbed out of Bargram Airfield. The fearsome jets would clear heavier weapons in the surrounding area and soften up the target.

All the planes headed to an invisible rendezvous box in the sky close to the Pakistani border. In planned sequence they would cross into that country's airspace.

"Aircraft airborne, sir," Graham informed Llewellyn. "All are in the green."

The timeline instantly began to compress.

The five SUVs turned from the highway. The first two vehicles came through the gate, stopping close to the building's front entrance. With their motors running, the others idled at separate locations on the rock-strewn road.

Morgan turned on the scope and watched heavily armed men with body armor emerge from the close SUVs. He released the safety on the Vintorez. A silhouette limped from one SUV and shuffled inside. Hearty voices greeted him and called his name.

It was Jamil.

Morgan's attention immediately focused on the other SUV and the men clustering at the front passenger door. He had only a brief glimpse of a tall man who got out and immediately stooped, immersing himself in his guards while he walked. Morgan reset the safety.

No shot.

"Aircraft approaching the box," said Graham. "F-15s at station. All refueled."

Only one issue remained.

"Confirm *Composer* present," Llewellyn said.

Graham already had the answer. "NSA and CIA concur. Bin Laden is present."

Llewellyn pressed the button again. "Mr. President, the party has begun down there. *Composer* on site."

The pause while he listened was momentary, then he said, "Yes, sir."

The admiral nodded at Graham, hiding his tension. No matter the amount of planning, practice, or mayhem delivered, there could be no assurance anything would go right.

"Let's go get him," he said.

Argumentative conversations ignited with hilarity. The expansion of their voices told Morgan they had finished eating and were breaking into groups. Several men walked out the building's rear door to the small building. Morgan looked through the scope.

A tall profile flashed past the doorway and was gone.

Bin Laden disappeared inside again.

SIXTY-ONE

Morgan looked down at the building. His opportunity was rapidly fleeting. Killing him was all that mattered. There was nothing more.

His knife picked at the satchel's stitching. With a few sharp tugs, Caroline's two-hundred foot climbing rope peeled away from the bag's inner sack. He cut off a ten-foot piece and secured it around his waist. With the length that remained, he tied a running bowline slip knot, snared the loop over a stone arm, and cinched it tight.

Morgan rechecked his ammunition belt, felt for the holster and grenades, and let the rope's tail drop to the ground. He turned toward the cliffs and looked through the night-vision scope. He switched off the Vintorez's safety.

There was no breeze. The bullet would have no drift.

"For you, Cay."

He exhaled and squeezed the trigger. The first lookout's body writhed momentarily and became still. His companions died seconds later. Morgan swung the barrel toward the roof and took aim.

Pink mist sneezed from the first gunner's nose. As his companion turned in surprise, his open mouth swallowed a bullet.

The guards on the back corners died next.

Morgan threw the long rope down the cliff face then plunged from the ledge. Using the rope to control his fall he met the ground running.

"That's odd…" said Mike Powers.

"What's odd?" Larsen said back.

"Just caught an infrared blip, maybe a second one from Target Four."

"Maybe the dude's firing up a smoke," said Larsen.

"I don't know." He scratched his head. "Neither flared like a match."

Powers surveyed the cliffs for the other heat signatures then panned back to the flash site.

"Hmm…Can't see him anymore."

"Probably got bored and went back under his rock," said Larsen.

"Zooming out to three hundred feet. Getting an overview," said Powers. "Yeah…they're still grooving to the music down…"

He paused midsentence and focused on the roof. "Shit…Where are those guys up top? Brian, can you see them?"

"Trying…This far out is making it hard," Larson answered, directing his system that way. "No visual," he said a few moments later.

"Calling in." Powers flipped a switch. "Command, *Reaper One.*"

"Go ahead, *One*," said a flat voice.

"Had two quick blips from Target Four…now quiet," reported Powers. "Other three targets remain in cliffs. Roof and rear sentries not visible. I'm blind from this angle."

"Stand by," said Graham. "Reworking vectors."

Running low and fast, Morgan reached the gap in the barbed wire, looped the rope over the rebar, and hauled himself up until he straddled the edge. He pressed flat, searching for movement.

A man came around the south corner of the building, his machine pistol resting inaccessibly on his hip.

The Vintorez clicked.

The round punctured the man's vest—its energy shredding his heart and lungs.

Morgan jumped down and went to the body.

It was one of the guards who protected bin Laden when he got out of the SUV.

While grabbing the man's Heckler Koch submachine gun and extra magazines, Morgan heard water splashing on the ground. Someone ahead was taking a leak.

The guard stepped closer to see what was lying on the ground.

The Vintorez action clicked and another silent bullet found its mark.

Morgan took another HK and more magazines. The Vintorez could soon be empty, and, when needed, the HKs would deliver either a three-round burst or go automatic and carve a ferocious channel.

His search would begin from above. Jamming fingers between gaps in the mortar, he pulled himself up the bricks, each hand digging higher and higher. When his boots caught an empty joint, he pushed himself a few inches higher.

There were three men on the middle deck.

Click...click...click.

Eight rounds remained in the magazine.

Morgan catapulted over.

A Black Guard stepped out the door, preparing to fire.

Click.

Stealth remained Morgan's only ally—and not for long.

Pinning his back against the wall, Morgan hid in the shadows. Focused and calm, he listened. A booming voice in his headset was calling names. The radios of the dead could only echo back.

A flashlight beam swept the stairs. Its holder took several steps up and moved to him. With the same gentle tug Morgan used to tie suture, he pulled the trigger.

Click.

The body landed with a dusty thud.

Morgan stepped into the second-floor hallway. A lantern glow slipped around the edges of a cracked door. He pushed the door open with his foot.

Several men near the table looked bewildered by the interloper. "Who are you?" one asked.

"Looking for a friend," Morgan said.

The Vintorez ended the conversation.

An arm grabbed him from the side, knocking the rifle out of his hands. Morgan spun around in the air, belting a foot into the man's stomach, burying his knife up through the attacker's chin.

Hurried footsteps were coming up the stairs. Morgan pulled out the Makarov and crouched along the wall of the room.

An HK muzzle came first around the threshold, then a head appeared. The lantern light drew his eyes to the tumble of bodies.

His Makarov puffed.

The dying man corkscrewed backward. His arm hit the wall, depressing his trigger finger. The drumming salvo showered stone and splintered wood until the magazine was empty. With the final tinkle of brass, Morgan's radio erupted with a voice screaming for the SUVs.

He retraced his steps and vaulted to the patio roof.

Lights in the fields pierced the night. Vehicles from the meadow were moving toward the building.

Morgan dropped a grenade on each of the two SUVs parked at the front door. Whatever ordinance was hidden inside was detonated when they exploded. He sighted the machine gun on an approaching SUV. The tracer bullets created a red rope, making it easy to hit. The vehicle rolled over in flames.

The second SUV tried to pass it by driving off the road but it ran over a mine. Rockets inside launched multiple directions and exploded in the air over several dozen trucks and cars.

———

"What the hell's going on?"

Powers's monitor screen began to recover from the bleaching white light.

"That was at target!" Larsen shouted.

"Command, *One* here! Explosions!" Powers said quickly. "Phosphorus with secondary explosions...SUVs at compound destroyed."

Llewellyn stared at the screen, listening to the accelerating chaos in the loops. The Thunderbolts were still twenty minutes out from the target. What was happening?

"Oh, fuck me! Good hit!" shouted Powers while he watched multiple RPGs launch in random directions.

Over two hundred people, including Zachary Reeves, heard him. Nobody cared. The dead air hung a second longer.

"Command, rooftop NSV fired tracers at one of the approaching SUVs! Don't ask me why!"

Llewellyn spoke into his headset, "NSA?"

"Pickup in chatter shortly before, Admiral. Asking for help at the building. Confusion."

"No shit. Welcome to the club," Llewellyn said.

"Admiral," Graham interrupted, "Predator Two reports increasing human and vehicle movement."

"Any more, NSA?" Llewellyn asked.

"Sounds like a sniper inside."

"Sir," Graham interrupted again. "Pakistani airspace breeched... all green."

"Bring the Predators closer," Llewellyn said.

———

Morgan scaled down the outside of the building into thick smoke. Moving toward the door where the men had carried in the food, Morgan saw men approaching from two sides. He leveled his HKs toward each group. When the fusillade ended, he heard chairs crashing inside. He stuck a reloaded HK through the door, fired, and stepped in. Bodies lay scattered like discarded mops.

Inching through the smoke, he ripped an arc of bullets around the room, the staccato flash illuminating more men dropping where they stood. He stepped farther. A flare-up from a burning SUV blinded him.

He heard an accelerated exhale and turned toward the sound. Wood scratched across the floor, then stars in his head dissolved to nothing.

SIXTY-TWO

"**N**SA, Llewellyn here." He would ask directly, knowing the final decision to abort would be his and that window was closing fast. "Update me."

"Intercepts indicate gunman subdued. A number of guards and several guests are dead. Environment is quieting. Activity occurring inside the building."

"Sergeant. Predators report."

"Many vehicles moved toward compound and are blocking the road. No additional ordinance. Cliff lookouts, rear and roof sentries, other bodies on grounds not moving, in fact, appear to be cooling."

"CIA," Llewellyn mused, "*Composer* still there?"

"Affirmative. Impossible to ascertain more."

"Graham, time to target?"

"Twelve minutes until assault team contact, sir, all green." Her face wore the strain for them both.

Chewing his tongue, Llewellyn looked at the screen, thinking.

"Sergeant...is Captain Sherpao aware of the current events?"

In charge of the SEAL teams, Travis Sherpao was a Pashtun whose family immigrated to the United States three generations before. He was fearless and possessed an unforgiving temperament for those who chose to fight against the American flag. Strapped into the lead Blackhawk, he had been listening to the loops.

"Yes, sir," she replied. "He says *go.*"

Llewellyn furrowed his eyebrows.

"Continue," he said.

———

Morgan didn't want to move.

He couldn't move.

He heard a command in Saudi Arabic.

"Da'ouni Arah." *Let me see him.*

Strong arms righted him. Blood ran down his face. Above a steel-wool beard, Morgan saw a smile widen beneath a hooked nose.

"Good evening." The black eyes didn't move. "Tea perhaps?"

Osama bin Laden uttered to a man who pulled a kukri knife from a chest sheath. He came behind Morgan, cut the rope binding his wrists, next poking the blade tip repeatedly in Morgan's neck.

Pouring the tea himself, bin Laden handed it to Morgan. When he refused it, the knife nicked deeper in his skin.

"Jamil says you are CIA," bin Laden said. "Clever. They have never gotten so close."

When Morgan said nothing, the blade slashed his skin. He let the tea wet his lips. It had no taste.

"Not CIA," he said. As he spoke, the blood adhered to his lips felt like tape holding his mouth shut.

Bin Laden looked at Sayyaf. An eyebrow rose and the pretentious smile became a frown. "Did he fool you so much? Is he a Zionist?"

Jamil shrugged. "I do not know."

"Who are you, then?" bin Laden asked Morgan.

"My fiancée died in New York."

"Ah! You blame me?" Bin Laden clapped his hands together with the revelation. "I'm so sorry," he said. His mock remorse was soon annulled by an arrogant laugh.

A fly began feeding on Morgan's forehead.

"What puzzling virtue you Americans have!" He shook his head in persistent amusement. The room filled with laughter.

"You are immoral...and denigrate God. You elevate homosexuals... and worship naked women." His words lingered. "So many perversions!"

Bin Laden looked smugly at the men. "Too many to list..."

They laughed again.

———

"Eagle One calling in, Admiral," Graham said. "Getting painted."

Four F-15E fighter-bombers and their tanker were intentionally visible to Pakistani radar.

"Tell them to stay cool," he said. "Wolfpack status?"

Wolfpack—a quartet of F-15C Fighter Interceptors—was northeast below the mountains, hiding from Pakistani radar.

"Full bellies," said Graham. She held up her hand to delay him briefly from speaking. "Sir, NSA reports F-16s warming up at Peshawar."

"Time to Thunderbolt target contact?"

"Five minutes."

Llewellyn spoke into his headset. "CIA, confirm again *Composer*."

"Command, confidence level unchanged."

"Mr. President..." Llewellyn said into his headset.

"Finish it, James," said President Reeves.

The admiral looked directly at Graham.

"Sergeant...all sorties standby."

———

"Jamil tells me how you met." Morgan could see Sayyaf leaning against a wall. "A tale of folly our great-grandchildren will enjoy."

Sitting forward in his chair, bin Laden grinned while he stroked his beard and sipped tea for a moment.

"New York and Washington are the beginning. In America's zeal to use the atomic bomb, it conceded any indignation."

Bin Laden's nostrils snorted a breath, carrying hatred that radiated past his unchanging smile.

"America talks and talks. It talks so well. But Pakistan will come to join with *us*."

With confident stature, he tipped his head back and looked at the fractured ceiling. "*Their* weapons of mass destruction"—his smile grew wider—"Iran's, too, will belong to the true believers."

There was no doubt he was enjoying his monologue.

"My friend, you should know by now that the American Satan is lazy and won't fight, even if we scorch it to glass. That shall be only the beginning. Europe will follow, despite their appeasing pleas."

The vindictive smile waxed. "When the *Kuffars…all* the nonbelievers… are in hell, obedience will be upon those who remain, and the lands will unite in the Caliphate."

He placed his tea cup on a small table and picked up Morgan's knife, drawing his finger across the serrated edge.

"Death does not scare us. Our children do not fear it." Bin Laden handed the knife to Jamil. "Let us help you understand."

Hands vice-gripped Morgan, ramming his chest to the floor.

Morgan's thoughts became free, distilling to a singular focus. He could smell her hair and feel her back arch, her blue eyes dancing as they made love.

Guttural laughter, the same that Morgan had heard once in the cafeteria, spread contagiously through the men.

"Allahu Akbar!" The men shouted the supplication.

Morgan prayed he'd join her today.

The sole of a dirty shoe crushed his head in the floor.

To be with her again…

———

"Captain Strafford has acquisition," said Graham.

The A10 Thunderbolt's targeting image magnified on the screen.

"Command, *American 11*," called Strafford. "Master-Arm on."

"Attack execute," declared Llewellyn.

Graham relayed the order.

"Roger." Strafford said.

The A-10 pitched down from one thousand feet.

Don't hit the damn building, Llewellyn reminded him telepathically.

"He's firing," reported Graham. Her atonal voice never changed.

———

Like a feather, the knife blade floated past Morgan's eyes, coming to rest on his neck. Its gracious mercy would soon cleanse the horror born from the finality of her haunting words.

"Hi. This is Caroline Pruitt. I am unavailable. Please leave a message."

———

"All true to target," Graham reported.

Streaming concussion missiles exploded at the base of the wall.

SIXTY-THREE

White.
Brighter than the sun...
No breath...
His muscles contorted violently.
I'm dead.

——◆——

The huge vacuum imploded, ripping apart any flesh outside the wall. Inside the building, the concussions knocked everyone to the floor.

"Pulling up...looking." Strafford banked forty-five degrees. "Building remains intact. You're up next, *United 175.*"

——◆——

The men fell away from Morgan, the knife lost in the dust. His fingers struggled with the ankle knots until someone jumped him, wrapping an arm around his face. Morgan tasted sweat and bit hard, jamming his elbow into the attacker's ribs.

——◆——

The second Thunderbolt fired.

"Command, *United 175*..." The pilot relayed as he turned. "Bottom of the hill clear."

The flashes illuminated Jamil trying to crawl away. Morgan grabbed a hunk of masonry and raised it over his head.

"Eat this," he shouted, crushing Jamil's skull to mush.

Morgan pulled apart the knots, threw the rope over his shoulder, and started his hunt again.

"Coming back around," Strafford radioed.

He fired the Gatling cannon.

"NSV destroyed. Checking again…American 11 outbound."

"Getting plinked," the pilot of United 175 reported. A heavy-caliber gun was firing through the sunroof of the remaining SUV. "Bugger getting a visit."

The SUV became a fireball.

"That's it for us," the pilot called. "United 175 leaving."

"American 77 copies," the Spector AC130 command pilot said. "Coming in."

"United 93 staggered on the flank," Graham told Llewellyn. "Sir, there are Pakistani F-16s heading northeast on burner. AWAC has acquired," she said.

He nodded.

Aboard the first Spooky gunship, the captain placed his finger on the master-fire trigger.

"Preparing to fire," he said.

"Weapons ready," replied the fire control officer. He put his hand on the dual trigger. "Confirm target."

"FCO, terrain confirmed." A slight bank left. "Going into pylon turn…plowing the field."

Alternating groups of twenty-five-millimeter Gatling guns gimbaled up and down, raking the ground at eighteen hundred rounds a minute. Whatever was left alive in the three square miles wouldn't last much longer.

"Firing cannon."

Dozens of rounds peppered the ground with explosions. The second Specter hit the meadow's outer flank.

Their jobs finished, they powered up and began to climb.

"Sergeant, tell Wolfpack to acquire those Pakistani fighters. Contact Air Chief Marshall Anwar Raza."

The AWAC uploaded the intercept coordinates.

"Wolfpack One vectoring," said the wing commander. There was brief radio crackle. "Flight, Push, Attack frequency."

The three other fighters confirmed the radio change.

There was a strange quiet. Llewellyn could almost feel the twenty-nine thousand pounds of thrust pour from their afterburners.

"All wolves hot. Mach 2.4. ETA...two plus ten," said Graham. Raza's on line."

"Fifteen-second reminders."

Llewellyn watched the Wolfpack's progress.

"One minute gone, sir."

The admiral pressed a button. "Anwar...James Llewellyn."

"Llewellyn, what the fuck are you arrogant assholes doing? Starting World War Three?"

His English was faultless, as was his use of it.

"Air Marshall Raza, we've been friends a long time." Llewellyn was stalling, waiting for the F-15s to arrive. "The United States is conducting an operation to extract a bad person from Swat. It will be over in sixteen minutes."

"You've violated Pakistani sovereignty. Our fighters..."

"Wolves have acquired," Graham whispered in the loop.

"Anwar, my F-15s are on top of you." Llewellyn could hear yelling in the background, confirming what he just told his friend. "I will clear them to fire if our aircraft are attacked. Do you copy?"

Jesus Christ! President Reeves tried to check his shock, praying to God that Llewellyn was bluffing. The interdiction was on the verge of drawing both countries into a full-scale war.

"Kiowa One coming on station," reported Graham. "Ball going up."

The helicopter's sensor platform rose above the propeller to guide in the Blackhawks.

Morgan didn't understand or care what was happening outside. Amid the rubble he found an HK and sprayed a circle of bullets through the room. His search resumed.

"James, my F-16s will break off." There was momentary static. "I give you fifteen minutes before my hornets swarm. Understand?"

"Yes, thank you."

"Bastard Americans..."

"Couldn't agree more." Someday Llewellyn would laugh, but not now.

He cut the connection. Intolerable seconds passed as he waited for Graham's confirmation.

"AWAC confirms Pakistani fighters turning."

"Tell Wolfpack to unlock in ten seconds."

"Yes, sir," said Graham. "Kiowa Two now ringside."

The second Kiowa took station high above the compound to keep all the helicopter blades apart—and watch for other trouble.

"Command..." The Blackhawks were calling in. "North Tower and South Tower teams on final approach."

The four Blackhawks were twenty seconds out.

"Reaper Two here, acknowledge now!" The quick words drew Llewellyn's immediate attention. "Large flatbed vehicle approaching from the west. Signature suggests SAMs aboard. Permission to Hellfire."

"Standby," said Graham. "CIA, can you corroborate?"

"Images suggest burkas. Confidence level not acceptable."

"What! Say again?" questioned the sergeant.

A new voice jumped in. It was Rushworth. "Vehicle may be carrying women, understand?"

"This is Reaper Two! Burkas leaving vehicle! Permission to Hellfire!"

"CIA!" Llewellyn yelled.

A missile hit on a Blackhawk would be catastrophic.

"Launcher going erect! Request permission to fire! They're energizing!"

"*Reaper Two*, this is James Llewellyn—fire! Fire! Fire!"

Larsen had the laser already locked. The drone shuddered with each launch.

"One, two, three missiles true at Mach one point three." The race would only last seconds. "Too fucking close!" His microphone was keyed. "Go you fuckin' rockets!"

The truck, launcher, and burkas evaporated.

"Jesus Christ!" shouted Larsen. "That was just stupid! Did they hire a new girl at CIA just for this?"

"Um, Reaper Two," Graham called, "you're live."

"Copy, Command! Opinion here remains unchanged! Whoever that woman is, she's an idiot! When this is over, send her ass out here for some face time with me. Reaper Two out."

The other Predator descended to eight thousand feet. Llewellyn saw the eerie static electric glow of the helicopter blades as the rotors hit dust particles in the air.

"North Tower Alpha firing." A pair of concussion missiles from the Blackhawk collapsed the roof, another rude dose to anyone below.

The helicopters hovered over the smoldering compound, their doors open.

"Standby to insert!" Travis Sherpao instructed his SEAL teams.

They prepared to fast rope down.

"Remember...possible friendly on ground," Sherpao said through his radio.

A private communiqué from Llewellyn regarding that prospect jogged Sherpao's memory. He recalled a conversation with a former SEAL named Tony months earlier at a tribute celebration for fallen colleagues.

"*This doctor's fiancée died on 9/11!*" he'd said, adding with only a half laugh, "*The guy insisted he would kill Osama himself.*"

While quarantined with the assault teams after their final mission briefing, Sherpao mentioned the possibility of a lone wolf. Every SEAL team member agreed to press for mission completion. Failure wouldn't be theirs.

As Sherpao listened to what was happening on the ground, damn if it wasn't perhaps a reality.

"Make sure your air is on!" he reminded his colleagues.

Their faces were sealed inside shatterproof masks with integrated night-vision.

Graham and Llewellyn exchanged glances.

"Admiral," she said, "we are dead on timeline."

"Advise the teams this is now a *kill* mission. With what's gone on down there, I've no stomach for more risk."

He didn't give a damn if they blew bin Laden to bits.

From each side of the helicopters, tear gas canisters fired through the holes in the roof. More canisters spewed white clouds outside.

"Insert now!' said Sherpao.

Connected to the outrigger, he dropped to the ground first. He saw a man emerge from behind the wall, preparing to fire an RPG. Sherpao's gun stopped him with a two-round burst.

Twelve black apparitions fluttered to the ground and formed into trios. Their patterned search began.

"Twelve-minute mark," came into their helmets.

———

Morgan's brain felt thick—full of mud. The building shook again. A wood beam dropped on his shoulder, dislocating it. He fell, inhaling dust and choking. Illuminated by the fire, he saw bin Laden scrambling away.

"Not this time!"

Morgan tackled him, ignoring the pain in his shoulder. Wrapping the rope around bin Laden's neck, he shoved a clump of pig hair in the terrorist's mouth.

"Pig...from America!" he screamed in his ear. "Suck on it to Hell!"

The noose tightened.

"For my Caroline!"

The man struggled more.

A wave of tear gas overwhelmed Morgan. His grip slackened. Bin Laden rammed a fist to his testicles. Morgan grunted but held firm.

The SEALs were probing the inside spaces, entering a room of tangled chairs and tables. Stepping on broken plates and splattered food, they passed multiple bodies.

"Four down near back wall," Sherpao heard. "Not our work. Moving."

He heard gunfire outside until a slash of white streaked from Warrior Two.

"SAM neutralized," said a voice.

"Nothing upstairs but dead bodies," radioed another SEAL.

Sherpao's trio stopped outside a door with a hole in it. There was an active struggle on the other side.

———

"Admiral," said Graham, "more Pakistani fighters scrambling."

"Call the Eagle Fighters in," Llewellyn said. The situation was deteriorating. "Get Wolfpack refueled," then he spoke directly to the White House situation room, "we may need your help shortly."

He looked at Graham again then reflexively at his watch. "Tell them only five minutes. We either get that SOB this time or we try again."

———

Morgan's universe constricted as he tightened the rope noose more. He gave it slack and pulled again.

He felt ecstatic.

"Wes..."

His grip held firm.

"Wes...no..."

The man was struggling less.

"Flash-bang," said Sherpao.

The grenade went through the hole.

The blast stunned Morgan, knocking him flat. His grasp on the rope softened.

"No more killing, Wes."

The bedlam around him dissolved to silence. He became transfixed.

"Not for me..."

That music! He had heard it before! His memory reached back then came forward.

"Dante...go scout!"

One of Sherpao's men released the dog. The Belgian Malinois jumped over the door blown from its hinges.

Eddies of red spun inside Morgan's eyelids. Consumed by the acrid smoke, he coughed hard. When he opened his eyes, Dante's intense stare was body-checking him.

Morgan breathed in and coarsely whispered, "A...friendly face."

A light blinded him. New men were in the room.

"My name," Morgan shouted, "is Dr. Wesley...Randall...Morgan." He was panting. "From...Chicago."

Sherpao heard the three-minute warning.

"Name the football team," he said, stepping closer.

Morgan had only seconds.

"The Bears..." Trying to breathe, he wanted to give him more. "Won the...'85...Super Bowl..."

"Command," Sherpao radioed, "we've got *Wildcard.*"

"Admiral! What crap!" Rushworth spoke in the loop. "We want Osama, remember?"

"Shut up, Priscilla!" President Reeves cut in on the line.

"He was here..." Morgan wheezed. "Couldn't kill him...passed out."

"Stay put," Sherpao said, looking at his bloody neck. "Just breathe." He spoke into his headset. "*Wildcard* wounded."

The steady voice from Washington said, "Outside teams to extraction perimeter."

Dante raced everywhere while the SEALs picked through the remaining rooms.

"Dad-gum-it! No contact," said Sherpao. "*Composer* went in a rathole. Must be in a tunnel below." He paused to control his irritation. "Damn!"

"Hunting season stays open." The resigned reply came through space into his ears.

"Withdrawing now. Taking' my hat off to Doc, though." Sherpao chuckled. "Got some big balls! Sign that boy up."

He came back to Morgan and saluted. "Sir, let's get you out of here."

SIXTY-FOUR

Morgan collapsed in the seat while a medic harnessed him. The young man shouted in his ear, "Want some water, sir?"

It took Morgan a moment to connect with the friendly Southern twang. Before he could answer, the man dug in a chest, twisted off the cap, and handed him a plastic bottle. Cold and sweet, the water was gone in seconds.

His gloved hands inspected Morgan's neck wounds. The antiseptic stung, but he was too numb to move.

The medic shouted, "Lucky these are superficial." He started an IV in Morgan's arm. "Gonna give you an antibiotic and clean you up good. Get that shoulder fixed up later. How 'bout some morphine?"

"No morphine," Morgan shouted with a strong head shake.

The medic cupped headphones over Morgan's ears. They instantly came alive. A penetrating voice demanded an immediate answer.

"Doc's aboard," the pilot radioed. "Tower One Alpha team recovered...Going airborne." Static. "Adios down there."

High above, a satellite relayed the words. Morgan couldn't smile but felt the same way through his throbbing brain.

The helicopter accelerated.

The SEALs had been on the ground only fourteen minutes.

"All teams, James Llewellyn here...good try, Americans! POTUS sends his thanks. We'll get *Conductor*. He can run, but can't hide forever. Sending friends along while you clear the airspace."

The F-15s screamed past, shuttering the Blackhawk airframes.

"Tower Teams, good evening! Eagles at your service!"

Through the cockpit window, Morgan saw the orange glow of their engines as the jets turned to assume their flanks. His headphones crackled again.

"Dr. Morgan, this is *Eagle One*...We're bringing you home."

SIXTY-FIVE

Alexandria Friday Morning March 19, Eastern Time

Elaine Jericho decided to take the morning for herself. She was sick of the parade of realtors and their clients who opened her closets and glimpsed inside the unsealed packing boxes, asking where she was moving.

She turned up the volume so the music blasted through her earbuds, hoping it would drown her indelible disappointment. After she went running on the Potomac trail, she planned to sit in a café and drink tea, immersing herself in one of her books, trying not to look at any clock.

If the strike had occurred, it was already over anyway. Someday she'd hear scuttlebutt or read the story in the newspapers, but she wasn't certain she even cared. All Jericho wanted to do was withdraw to the next place and get on with her life—whatever that meant.

When she finally returned home, she didn't hear the phone ring until there was a break in the music.

The blocked number made her stomach churn.

"Hello," she answered.

"Elaine, its Cottrell."

"Admiral..."

Their former rapport wasn't there.

"Sorry to bother you," he said. "Do you have a minute?"

"Of course, sir. How may I help you, sir?"

Her words held no emotion.

"I wanted you to know..." he said.

"Yes, sir."

He sensed false indifference.

"We didn't get him."

"Sorry."

"It wasn't your fault. He escaped through a tunnel, but his day will come. Got a trove of information the spooks are dissecting. State and POTUS are repairing the damage with the Pakistanis."

"I wish I cared."

"Well, this other bit might perhaps cheer you."

Her heart skipped.

"Someone you may be wondering about is coming home."

He heard the gasp as she grabbed the counter's edge.

"Elaine, are you okay?"

"Yes...sir." She added, "Thanks so much for calling, Admiral."

"Lainey, I'm sorry 'bout all this. If there's ever anything I can do for you..."

"You already have, Cotty...You already have."

———

The pay phone rang. Jericho answered it.

"How are you doing?" Jon Pruitt asked her.

"I'm packing and doing other mundane chores that compliment my new ordinary life," she replied.

"Not much fun," he said.

"Doing my duty." She sounded mournful. "Jon...I want to share good news with you."

Pruitt was certain what it was. The day after she visited the farm, Pruitt called on President Reeves at the White House to show his friend Morgan's email and mention the unfortunate circumstances that fell on a navy captain who, while attempting to protect her country, had corroborated Morgan's possible whereabouts. Reeves said he would do what he could for both Morgan and Jericho.

Early this morning Reeves had called and told him of Morgan's rescue, but Pruitt would give the moment to Jericho.

"Please, Elaine. My heart can't tolerate prolonged anticipation from an attractive woman."

"Jon...All I know..." Her eyes were misting. "Wes is coming home."

SIXTY-SIX

Pruitt Farm Four Months Later

When Morgan got back to the States, he needed an operation for his neck wound and another for his shoulder; he refused plastic surgery for the scars on his back. Those medals he would keep. Through it all he refused narcotics. Vowing to never enter that dark place again, he grimaced from time to time, but nothing more.

Every morning, he examined his incisions in the mirror while the nurse changed his dressings. They looked damned good and were healing well. His bruises inside, however, were not.

Jon Pruitt had made certain a psychiatrist monitored Morgan during the CIA debriefings. Through a one-way window, the physician watched him in the reclining chair as he perspired, repetitively flitted his gaze toward the door, then the doctor, then the ceiling.

As Morgan told his story, his interviewers would later marvel in private about his disciplined ability to learn and train for a task considered impossible. With each subsequent session however, the evidence of Morgan's torment compounded until the psychiatrist medicated him to reduce his stress. For a time the nightmares still broke through. Eventually Morgan's traumatic anxieties softened. Able to be managed as an outpatient, he was discharged. Jon brought him to the farm.

The Pruitts paid for everything.

Every dawn Morgan stretched with a yoga master on a hidden knoll away from the house. After breakfast, while he met with his therapist, Connie placed fresh flowers in his room and made his bed. Morgan would often sit on the porch rocker and read—sometimes it was the Bible or the Koran they discovered in his pant's pocket. He meditated often, and started running again. Slowly, his crippled mind began to heal. He was no longer feeling rudderless.

Then his therapist suggested he care for Caroline's horse, Goethe.

For a week Morgan struggled with the proposal. He finally asked Jon to take him to the stables.

His reunion with Goethe was bittersweet. As he stroked the horse's forehead, he whispered into an ear, "Sorry, buddy...just going be just me now."

His fingers ran along the bridle hanging nearby on the wall. The rich hand-stained leather with raised stitching and brass nameplate was a present he had given Caroline on Goethe's birthday.

Intentionally clearing his throat to emphasize an expanding grin, Jon said, "I remember what happened the day you gave that to her."

Morgan nodded with a much-needed smile.

One month later

Goethe had already trotted in from the pasture and was waiting along the corral's rail. He whinnied as Morgan climbed over the fence.

"What a mess!" Morgan said. "Goethe, what you been up to with that tail? Spanking the mare?"

He shook his head in mock annoyance.

Goethe swished his flaxen tail wide as the chestnut gelding snorted. A treat was coming.

Morgan opened his hand. "It's the peppermint you like."

A pair of red-and-white-striped sticks crunched and was gone. The horse bounced his head up and down, giving tentative thanks.

"Not to worry," Morgan said, using his fingers to untangle the horse's mane. "You won't get cavities. They're still sugar free, just as your mistress always insisted." He gave a slight thump on the horse's hip. "Come on. Let's get you cleaned up. Jon and I are riding later."

They walked together into the stables.

"Care for nail polish today?" Morgan asked.

Goethe snorted and clomped into his stall.

After Morgan picked through one of the front hooves, Goethe pushed his nose into Morgan's bent rear, signaling the time to switch. When he finished the last back hoof, Goethe's tail splashed his face in thanks.

"You're welcome," Morgan said with a gentle pat on his flank. The tail swished again. "Remind me tomorrow to trim that thing."

Goethe nickered. The best part was coming. The horse loved the currycomb.

With each circle of the short plastic teeth across the barrel hairs, little clouds of dirt and clay splashed the sunlight.

"You can only get this filthy if you're rolling around, scratching your back!"

Goethe's ears turned toward Morgan as he spoke. He stopped brushing and came to the horse's face.

"Don't think for a second I don't know that's what you're doing," he said sternly.

Their conversation weaving wherever it went, Morgan finished with the right side and started on the left. Goethe's ears turned away, but Morgan paid no attention. A front hoof stomped a few seconds later.

"Magnificent animal," said a voice.

Morgan didn't look and kept brushing. "Yes," he mumbled.

"Got a minute, Wes?"

Morgan's stomach muscles tightened as he glanced at the door, where a man stood dressed in a suit. A few feet behind, a bald head in a darker suit had a curly wire coming from the ear.

"Jon said you'd be down here with Goethe."

"Every day," Morgan replied.

The president moved closer.

"I remember when Cay first got him," Reeves said. "Her father wasn't sure about the name, but long before, Jon had learned never to argue with his daughter...so *Goethe* it was."

Each time the gelding heard his name, he whinnied.

"Frozen music," Morgan said.

"Pardon me?" asked Reeves.

"Architecture is frozen music," Morgan replied. "It was Cay's favorite saying. Johann Goethe coined it—she named him in his honor."

"I didn't know."

The president tipped his head toward the Secret Service agent who stepped back and left the barn. The sincerity in Reeves's face grew.

"Cay was my goddaughter," the president said. "I wanted to come by...to see how you're doing, but I know you needed time. I waited until Jon gave me the okay." Reeves lowered his voice even more. "So...how *are* you doing?"

"I'm improving," answered Morgan.

"I'm glad to hear that."

They stood an arm's length apart.

"Wes...I'm so sorry. You were both lucky to have each other, even if it was tragically too short. Jon and Connie were blessed too." His tone stayed somber. "They're still lucky...with a man like you."

Morgan said nothing.

"Cay would have been proud of you."

Morgan shrugged.

"What you did was impossible...to say the least."

"Had to do something," Morgan said.

Reeves gave a suppressed chuckle. "That's a hell of an understatement."

"I hope you get him someday," said Morgan.

"We will." Reeves paused. "Wes...there's more I came here to say."

The president held out his hand.

"Along with my personal gratitude...On behalf of the citizens of the United States, I thank you for your service to our country."

Morgan reached to shake the president's hand until he realized he was still holding the currycomb. When he stopped his arm, both men looked down and smiled as Morgan pulled it off. Reeves tried again—successfully.

"If there's ever anything I can do for you...Jon and I are old friends." Reeves produced a thoughtful smile. "I guess that's...very old friends. Just tell him."

"Thanks..."

"Going to go give Connie a hug and get out of here before I blow Jon's privacy. Had to sneak away. Press, you know." The president turned to leave and paused. "Anything, anytime, Wes."

And he was gone.

———

Jon Pruitt flew to Chicago to meet with the Merrimacs and Janie Bonwitt. Seated in the fourth-floor lounge of the Four Seasons Hotel overlooking Michigan Avenue, Janie teared before they even ordered cocktails. Shaking his head, Pruitt handed her his hand-kerchief. When the waiter came to take their drink orders, Ross Merrimac asked for a margarita instead of following his wife's lead of iced tea.

Shandra scowled.

"Queen," Ross said, "I don't drink much...but I'm going to have one today."

Janie blew her nose again.

"I wanted to ask you face to face," said Jon. "Wes told me he couldn't bear to come back to the city, at least not yet. It was too soon...Too many memories...We talked about it. Because you were so much a part of their lives, he hoped you would join us in New York."

They quickly agreed.

"Is anyone else joining us?" asked Janie.

"What do you mean?" Pruitt asked.

"Didn't you mention a woman was involved in his rescue?"

Pruitt reflected for a moment.

"Well...Yes...I told Wes a few weeks back, he had a guardian angel who helped him get home—that she had called to tell us he'd been rescued."

"Did you ever meet her?" Janie asked.

"Connie and I had her over for dinner to thank her."

Quick white lies were a skill he had perfected over the years.

Janie began to smile. "Is she pretty?"

Not understanding her curiosity, Jon scratched his head. Merrimac exploded in laughter, shocking his wife even more by taking a gulp of his margarita.

"Janie," Ross said, "there you go again!"

Another long sip followed.

"So, Jon..." Janie pestered. "This girl who helped him...She's pretty?"

"She's a very beautiful redhead...and equally as smart."

Ross Merrimac laughed again while Pruitt appeared only more confused.

"Jon! What are you waiting for?" Bonwitt's smile grew huge. "Introduce her to Wes! You've got her phone number, I hope!"

SIXTY-SEVEN

The North Tower site was busy. Dump trucks, cranes, and bulldozers never stopped moving debris. Morgan was at the bottom, below the street noise, walking, looking up and down at the four sides that rose around him. Ahead, a cement mixer and its operators waited. Wearing hardhats, the Pruitts, Merrimacs, and Bonwitt walked with Morgan, followed at a respectful distance by a swelling number of ground crew.

"Thank you for letting me do this," Morgan said when he reached the pit.

"Our honor, Dr. Morgan," replied the foreman.

Concrete poured in the hole as Morgan knelt on one knee and dropped in the engagement ring.

———

The next morning, before the September 11 anniversary ceremony, Morgan and Jon Pruitt stood at the small pool at Ground Zero and together raised the snifters filled with the remaining Macallan. After a taste they placed the crystal on the ledge and gently lowered blue orchids in the water. Red roses joined them. Pruitt put his hand lovingly but firmly on Morgan's shoulder.

"Wes, time to go."

Morgan gripped the railing as he stepped to the dais, unsure of the emotions he was about to face.

Caroline's name came last. The tears were impossible to hold back. His world changed the first time she kissed him, offering her love without condition, her blue eyes penetrating deep into his soul. Even in her final moment of life, she filled him with joy and hope. Yet Caroline would never succumb to the uninvited will of others and she chose to die on her terms—so she jumped.

It was now time for Morgan to say good-bye.

"Caroline Alora Pruitt," he said proudly. "My beautiful Cay…"

He looked beyond the collective sadness to the holy place where she was entombed, where the day before he finally gave her the ring.

"My darling Cay, I love you…and will forever."

Epilogue

The ceremony ended. Jon, Connie, Ross, Shandra, and Janie surrounded him with their hands linked together. Shandra offered a prayer. Arm in arm, they cried.

When their emotions settled, Jon said, "How 'bout we stretch our legs a bit?"

Bathed in muted glory, New York City was emerging from the paralysis of that morning. Strolling along, talking about things they'd never remember, they paused frequently while the women window-shopped. It was carefree and that was good. The last several hours had been a strain on them.

When they got to a stoplight, Janie said, "Ladies, I know some really great places uptown where we can shop!"

Merrimac shook his head and said, "No...I think I'd rather get some coffee and meet up with you girls later."

Jon agreed.

"Abandoning us! Ooo! You're no fun!" said Janie, looking at Jon and Ross. "Well, boys...then be dearies and get us cab, will you? Pretty please, with sugar?"

Jon Pruitt pointed across the street to a Starbucks. "Wes, go grab a table and we'll find you."

Morgan nodded.

With a mug of green tea, Morgan sat on a stool at the window and picked up an abandoned *New York Times*. Thinking he might read it, he put it in his lap and first looked out the window. The women were gone. Taking a sip of the hot liquid, he scanned the newspaper's headlines. His eyes returned to the date.

September 11, 2004.

Three years and a lifetime had passed.

Morgan looked around the room for Jon and Ross. They still hadn't arrived. He began reading the only story in the paper that was important.

"Is anyone sitting here?"

Her voice startled him.

"Not yet," he responded. Glancing her way, he offered the adjacent seat with an open hand.

"Thanks. I've been standing for hours in these heels. My feet have had it."

This time Morgan looked at her longer.

She was breathtaking and impeccably dressed. Invisible hose climbed into an olive gabardine skirt, its waistband sealed by a tailored jacket, while a brilliant gold and teal scarf looped over her crisp white blouse. Orbiting outside fresh lipstick, lush red hair cut in a long bob swirled about her face. There was no coffee cup in sight.

"A special day," she said.

He nodded, ill prepared for conversation.

"To some," was his reply.

"Were you there this morning?" she asked.

Morgan nodded again, his lips fixed.

The woman looked at his damp eyes. His hair was streaked salt and pepper, scattered by the morning's breeze. His suit coat drooped as though it had been stitched with elastic thread, the weight of one spirit plus thousands more pulling down his shoulders.

She wanted to hug him, caress his hair with her fingers, and whisper, "*It's okay...It will be okay.*"

"If you can imagine," she said gently, resting her handbag on the counter and sitting down facing him, "I heard a man on the subway say he couldn't remember what the Towers looked like."

"I'll never forget," said Morgan, shaking his head.

"Oh, forgive me!" The woman seemed to panic and stood hurriedly. "I'm being rude. I should introduce myself."

Extending her hand, her bracelet knocked over his tea. It ran like a quick river onto the newspaper and splattered to the floor.

Embarrassed, she said, "I'm so sorry," fumbling for his napkin, dabbing what she could.

"Don't worry about it." He gave a placid smile. "Gravity happens."

Her right hand and fingers were damp and sticky. She wiped them on her skirt.

Morgan glanced around the room. His friends were nowhere to be seen. A person long ago had taught him about coincidences.

"Can I start over?" she asked cautiously.

He chuckled. "Do I need to get more tea for that?" he inquired.

She blushed, bashfully offering her hand again. Their palms slipped together and held. Her grip was confident and firm, but she still seemed out of her element.

"Hi. I'm Elaine Jericho," she said, "but my friends call me *Lainey*."

He smelled perfume.

"Name's Wesley Morgan." He smiled. "But please…Call me *Wes*."

September 11, 2001
We will remember

AFFIRMATIONS

This novel would not have been possible without the encouragement, patience, and inestimable love of my wife, Diane. In addition, I will forever give credit to my wonderful family and friends, who inspired me with storyline ideas, editing and encouragement ad infinitum. I also thank my formal editors, Leigh and Julia. Finally, this loving brother gives special gratitude to his only sister who during a hike in Rocky Mountain National Park in 2007 told him that this would make a really good story.

Betsy, I have finished. May you rest in peace.

Author Biography

A physician himself, T.W. Ainsworth, like most Americans, couldn't get the horrific events of September 11, 2001 out of his mind. But rather than simply dwell on it, he chose to write about it. Using the cathartic expression of fiction, *The Architect of Revenge* grapples with the common feeling of the day—the desire for revenge—and follows one man's journey not only into the heart of al-Qaeda but also into his own. The author lives in both New Mexico and Florida and has learned much about faith, friendship and forgiveness from the writing of this story.

Contact: author.architectofrevenge@gmail.com
Facebook: TW Ainsworth
Twitter: @Ainsworth_TW

42287896R00273

Made in the USA
Lexington, KY
15 June 2015